The mistress of the hags surged forward, lashing out with her claws, and Rodrick lifted up Hrym to block. Her reach was astonishingly long, though, and she managed to scratch his side with one of her black talons, raking down from beneath his rib cage nearly to his hip. Just a scratch, but Rodrick stumbled back, hissing at the pain and dropping his guard.

"Steady on," Hrym said, and Rodrick struggled to raise the sword again. Actually *fighting* with a sword wasn't exactly his strong point; he seldom needed to do more than wave Hrym around and pose dramatically. Hrym was doing his best to make up for Rodrick's failings, sending a cone of icy wind toward the hag, who adroitly dodged. Rodrick gritted his teeth and swung Hrym in her direction, flinging a spear of ice at her and slashing her arm, which trickled a thick black substance in lieu of blood. He was dimly aware of Zaqen battling another hag, flashes of greenish light appearing off to his right as she lashed out with spells. The horses and even the camel had panicked, plunging off the ice and trying to swim for shore.

Hrym was humming by then, icy vapor billowing up and down the length of his blade, working up to one of his truly impressive magics. The sword's true capabilities were not fully known to Rodrick—perhaps not even to Hrym himself—but with enough time and effort Rodrick knew the sword could summon rains of hailstones the size of grapefruit, freeze enemies in solid blocks of magical ice, and perform other freezing wonders.

Someone struck Rodrick from behind—the unattended hag, presumably—and he stumbled forward. Then the hag leader was upon him, smashing his arm aside—and Hrym flew from his nerveless fingers . . .

The Pathfinder Tales Library

Liar's Blade

Tim Pratt

paizo

Cover art by Tyler Jacobson.
Cover design by Andrew Vallas.
Map by Robert Lazzaretti.

Paizo Publishing, LLC
7120 185th Ave NE, Ste 120
Redmond, WA 98052
paizo.com

ISBN 978-1-60125-515-0 (mass market paperback)
ISBN 978-1-60125-516-7 (ebook)

Publisher's Cataloging-In-Publication Data
(Prepared by The Donohue Group, Inc.)

Pratt, Tim, 1976-
  Liar's blade / Tim Pratt.

   p. : ill., map ; cm. -- (Pathfinder tales)

   Set in the world of the role-playing game, Pathfinder.
   Issued also as an ebook.
   ISBN: 978-1-60125-515-0 (mass market pbk.)

   1. Swordsmen--Fiction. 2. Thieves--Fiction. 3. Quests (Expeditions)--Fiction. 4. Magic--Fiction. 5. Imaginary places--Fiction. 6. Pathfinder (Game)--Fiction. 7. Fantasy fiction. 8. Adventure fiction. I. Title. II. Series: Pathfinder tales library.

PS3616.R385 L53 2013
813/.6

First printing February 2013.

Printed in the United States of America.

For D, my favorite swordsman

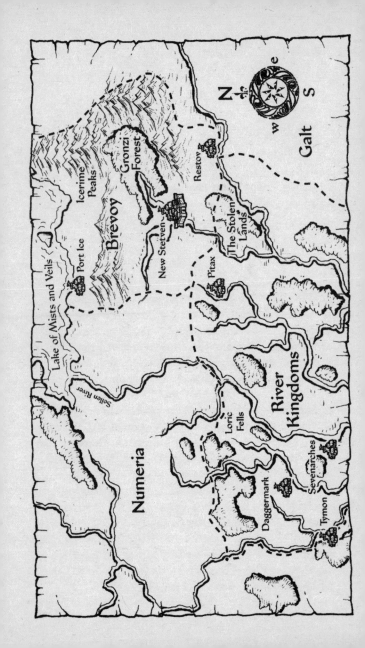

Chapter One
Two Sought Employment

"Why would anyone want to meet at a circle of standing stones?" Rodrick leaned against one of the mossy monoliths and gazed up at the darkening sky. "Who wants to talk business out in the woods? I prefer taverns for this sort of thing. Taverns are traditional. It's easy to get a drink in them. Also, I live above one. Very convenient."

"Our mysterious prospective employer obviously doesn't want to be seen in public with you," Hrym said from behind Rodrick, voice muffled. "I can't say I blame him."

"Possibly he doesn't want to be seen at all." Rodrick rubbed the faint scratches on his cheek where one of the tavern wenches had raked him with her fingernails yesterday. He'd only made a *suggestion*—and he'd even offered a fair price. How was he to know she was a newlywed who took her vows seriously? At least she was married to a milkwater shopkeeper and not one of Tymon's countless over-muscled gladiators, or Rodrick might have faced more serious injury. "Maybe he's a fugitive from justice or something. We do have some history of working with criminals."

"Besides one another, you mean?" Hrym said. "And anyway, what justice? We're in the River Kingdoms. In Tymon, no less, where most arguments are settled by the parties mutually agreeing to beat each other bloody. But suppose it is some rank villain. Would you turn down the job?"

"I might. I'm an honest man now, Hrym—at least on this side of the border. And at this point in time. As far as anyone knows. It's easier to make a profit off a dishonest man, true. But you have to admit, this is a suspicious way to organize things, luring me out here all alone. Present company excepted." Rodrick was relatively comfortable with his position, standing with his back against a great huge block of stone, with sightlines as clear as he could get in the forest. At least no one would be able to stab him in the kidneys. But there were still too many shadows gathering for his liking. "Picking the lock and leaving a note on my pillow. Telling me to come here at dusk if I'd like to make some money. And leaving me that little bag of gold as, what, an incentive? A deposit? A retainer?"

"Lovely gold," Hrym said dreamily. "Just pile it up and let me sleep on it, I'll be happy as happy can be."

"Yes, I know. You have such simple tastes. I still say we should have just taken the bag of coin and scampered off. I'm tired of Tymon. The only reason I stayed around after we lost all those bets at the arena was because we were too poor to travel in style. But we've got a bit of money now—"

"Yes, but if we leave, we'll miss out on making *more* gold," Hrym said, practical as always. "It's not like we have any other prospects for gainful or illicit employment at the moment, and that little purse won't last long. Not with the way *you* run through money. You spent the last of our savings on the second-prettiest wench in the tavern, you may recall."

"The first prettiest was unavailable," Rodrick said absently. "But, look, don't you think anyone stupid enough to give me a bag of money *in advance* is, by definition, too stupid to work for? Trusting my reliability doesn't say much for their judgment."

"Or they could be stupid enough for us to make a *lot* of money off them," Hrym said.

Rodrick pondered. "Fair point. "

A moment later, the underbrush rustled, and a figure stepped forward from the shadows. Not quite short enough to be a halfling or dwarf, but definitely on the small side for a human, draped in a bulky cloak that seemed to hint at some concealed deformity—a hump, perhaps, or an off-center surplus head. The cloak was made of good fabric, though, dark green and richly embroidered along the edges with peculiar spiral patterns in dark blue thread.

"I am Zaqen," the figure said, voice pitched high enough that Rodrick guessed the speaker was female, though it was hard to be sure. "You are Rodrick, of Andoran?"

"I'm from all over," Rodrick said. "And I'm pleased to meet you." He gave her one of his more roguish smiles, because it never hurts to be charming.

Zaqen giggled, and Rodrick's smile slipped a notch. People who giggled for no reason worried him.

"Is it true," she said, "that those who hire you also hire . . . your sword?"

"A warrior isn't much good without his sword." In truth, despite the rumors he'd caused to be spread throughout the region, Rodrick wasn't much of a fighter. He preferred to stab people from concealment if stabbing was called for—but one had to keep up appearances.

Zaqen sidled closer. "Yes, but . . . you have a *special* sword?"

"Special is a good word for me," Hrym said. "Also 'amazing' and 'wonderful' and 'amazingly wonderful'—"

"The sword talks!" Zaqen said. "How marvelous. I'd assumed that was an exaggeration." She craned her head, trying to get a glimpse of the magical weapon sheathed on Rodrick's back.

"I am no *it*," Hrym said. "'He' would be better, or any honorifics you choose."

"Apologies, O mighty blade," Zaqen said, her tone deeply amused.

Rodrick sighed. Of course she'd heard about the sword. The only people who wanted Rodrick for himself alone in recent years were magistrates, city guards, and the occasional irate spouse.

"May I see it—I mean, him?" Zaqen scuttled a few steps closer, almost obscenely eager.

"Yes, let me out of this sheath," Hrym demanded. "I can't see anything."

"Your senses are *magical*," Rodrick said. "It's not as if you have eyes. I don't understand how a leather scabbard can possibly impede your vision." But he stepped away from the standing stone, reached over his right shoulder, grasped the hilt of the longsword, and drew Hrym smoothly from his scabbard, holding him aloft to sparkle in the . . . well, twilight. Noonday sun would have been more dramatic.

Hrym *was* looking especially radiant tonight, though: a blade of living ice nearly four feet long, transparently crystalline at the impossibly sharp edges shading to milky white inward, and on through to a shimmering blue at the center, with steam rising in smoky tendrils from all along his length in the humid air.

"There," Rodrick said. "Meet Hrym, my partner. If this was all some elaborate ruse to lure me out here to steal my sword, you might wish to reconsider. The last person who picked up Hrym without permission lost half his arm to frostbite."

"Though if you offered me sufficient coin, say enough to fill the empty hollow of a medium-sized drained lake—" Hrym said.

"Hush, you," Rodrick said.

"No." Zaqen was suddenly businesslike. "I am not here to steal your blade. I am here to invite you to join me, and my patron, on a sacred quest."

"A quest!" Hrym said. For a sentient sword of living ice with no tongue, mouth, or even vocal cords, his voice was remarkably human. Hrym sounded like an old man who'd spent several decades running a shop that never offered credit, smoking a clay pipe on a porch and pontificating, and teaching his nephews dirty jokes. "I love quests. A sacred one, no less."

"A quest," Rodrick repeated, and sighed. "Well. It's not as if anyone's ever died horribly on one of *those*. Where is this patron of yours?"

"My master is busy with devotional matters. He is a very holy man."

"A holy man?" Now Rodrick did frown. "What variety of holy? The kind who disapproves of gambling and drinking, or the kind who likes sacrificing innocent virgins on altars of black stone, or . . . ?"

"The very wealthy kind of holy," Zaqen said. "And he has no interest in your morality, or lack thereof. As long as you can protect and aid us on our journey, he will be pleased, and you will be *generously* rewarded."

"And as for the other thing, you're hardly a virgin," Hrym said. "So let your mind rest easy on that point."

"Let's have a few details," Rodrick said. "Or even broad outlines. Where are we going, why are we going there, who's trying to kill us along the way, and what are you offering to pay?"

"We are going to Brevoy." Zaqen lifted her face to look at Hrym, still shining in the dusk. Her face was entirely human, though not particularly pretty: snub nose, thin lips, eyes of two different colors, one blue and one green—and the eyes looking in just *slightly* different directions, lending her gaze a fishlike quality. "To the very edge of any map *you're* likely to have seen. We seek a sacred artifact of great power, locked away for millennia. No one in particular is trying to kill us, but the River Kingdoms are dangerous places, and parts of Brevoy are little better. And, of course, where there are great treasures, there are often powerful guards, and other interested parties seeking the same prize . . . My master and I are not without resources, but neither of us is particularly skilled with weapons, and simply having a strong man with a long blade in our party will act as a deterrent against many common bandits—"

"He asked about payment," Hrym said. "That's the one part I actually care about, so don't forget to address it, please."

Zaqen cocked her head, doubtless wondering—as many had before—what a magical sword could possibly want with gold. "My master is traditional. We will pay all expenses, of course. If you help us reach our

goal, Rodrick, we offer your weight in gold as reward."
She paused. "Or an equivalent value in gems, treasure,
property, or a promissory note drawn on a leading bank
of Absalom."

"His *current* weight in gold, or his weight at the end
of the journey?" Hrym said sharply.

Zaqen blinked. "Excellent question. Astute. Forward-
thinking. Let's say . . . at the end of the journey?"

"Hmm," Hrym said. "I don't like it. Long overland
journeys tend to cause weight loss. But he's hardly
stout now, so I think we can do better. You'd better start
eating richer foods, Rodrick. I want you so fat you can't
sit on a horse by the time we reach Brevoy."

"Those terms are acceptable," Rodrick said calmly.
His *weight* in treasure? That would be enough to fill a
nice chest for Hrym to use as a bed, with plenty left over
for Rodrick to live in the manner to which he devoutly
hoped to become accustomed. And then there was the
artifact she'd mentioned—surely *that* would be worth
a bit of coin to the right buyer.

"What's the artifact?" Hrym asked. Rodrick
suppressed a wince. Hrym had a bad habit of tipping
their hand.

"It is a holy relic," Zaqen said. "Of no intrinsic value,
and worthless to anyone but my master's particular
sect."

Rodrick nodded. "I understand." Maybe what she
said was even true. But if this holy man's cult could pay
a man's weight in gold just for a chaperone, what would
they pay in ransom for the relic itself?

"When do we leave?" Hrym said.

"Meet us here tomorrow," Zaqen said. "Two hours
before twilight."

Rodrick frowned. "You want to travel by night?"

She shrugged, one shoulder dipping lower than the other. "My master sets the schedule. I gather there is a place to camp some two hours from here, where he wishes to spend the night."

"Who pays the coin calls the tune." Rodrick bowed. "I'll see you then."

Zaqen disappeared back into the underbrush, walking with a strange, hitching gait, but with surprising speed.

"Well then," Rodrick said. "I suppose that's settled. Let's head back to the Bloodied Flail and spend our advance money."

"You'd better keep enough gold to scatter over the bottom of a drawer in our rooms," Hrym said. "I don't intend to sleep on bare wood again."

"Sleep! As if you sleep." Rodrick slipped away from the standing stones, working his way along the old footpath in the direction of Tymon. The woods right around the city weren't especially dangerous— because of the gladiatorial arena, Tymon had the highest concentration of heavily armed warriors in the River Kingdoms, and they were all obliged to provide a certain amount of civil defense—but there were always bandits with no sense of self-preservation and skulking agents from the neighboring country of Razmiran, which coveted the wealth of Tymon. The value of caution was a lesson Rodrick had learned long ago. Though the exact lesson was more like, "Be cautious when no one is watching; if you want to impress someone, be ostentatiously bold, if the odds favor success."

Rodrick wasn't a coward, but he found that getting in too many fights tended to make his muscles hurt, which detracted from his enjoyment of sex, sleep, and other sensual pleasures.

They made it back to the main road without encountering thieves, thugs, spies, or mad wild beasts. Alive and walking with coins jingling in his pocket—what a pleasant sensation. Hrym was back in his sheath, keeping quiet. People tended to notice talking swords made of living ice. They gaped, or plotted to steal said magical sword, or just asked far too many tedious questions, so Hrym seldom spoke in public. There was also the element of surprise to consider. Discovering that your enemy was armed with *another enemy* had given many an opponent pause over the years.

Rodrick stopped by the gates to greet Chumley, the night guard he'd befriended on his first day in the city. That was one of Rodrick's little rules: if at all possible, get on friendly terms with the fellows capable of opening a gate and letting you slip out unnoticed in the middle of the night. The guard helped him tie Hrym's hilt to the scabbard with a bit of rough twine. In Tymon, ordinary people had to bind up their weapons or leave them with the guards while they were inside the walls, while full-fledged gladiators could use bare daggers for jewelry if they liked.

Rodrick strolled through the gate, nodding at the few familiar faces he saw, especially the heavily scarred ones. These were not people you wanted to have for enemies.

Most of the wooden and stone shops along the central thoroughfare were still open, though soon only the bars and betting parlors would be doing business. Off in the distance, the roughly palatial Champion's Fortress loomed above almost all the other buildings, overshadowed only by the Arena of Aroden, by far the largest structure in town. Rodrick had gone to a couple of the fights there—the ones he'd bet on most heavily— but his seats were so terrible he'd barely been able to see anything except the head of his "sure thing" rolling off across the sand at the match's conclusion. Blood sports weren't really his preferred game. Give him a nice bit of back-alley gambling instead, especially if he could provide the dice.

"Aroden." Rodrick paused to gaze at the arena. "Some god *he* turned out to be. Greatest scam ever perpetrated, don't you think? He claimed he was going to come back from the heavens and deliver us all from evil, and when the time came, he was a no-show. How many times have I pulled the same trick at an inn? 'Oh, I'll come back tonight and settle my bill.' Ha! Of course, they say Aroden died, which is a fairly good reason to miss an appointment, as these things go."

"I met Aroden once." Hrym voice was low and muffled.

Rodrick frowned. "What? *The* Aroden? Didn't he stroll away from our mortal plane ten thousand years ago?"

Hrym was silent for a moment. "Maybe I'm thinking of someone else," the sword mumbled. "You humans all start to look the same after a while."

Rodrick shook his head. "He was Azlanti—the *last* Azlanti. I doubt he looked much like the rest of us—"

"Bipedal. One head, with hair on it. Two arms. Close enough."

Rodrick snorted. It was often impossible to tell if Hrym was boasting, lying, deluded, or genuinely ancient. Even the sword himself often seemed unsure of his true history. But what mattered now was their future. If they were off on a long, harsh journey tomorrow, they'd better enjoy tonight.

Their current home was a room above the Bloodied Flail, close enough to the arena to hear the screams of the crowd if the wind was right. Despite the tavern's name, and the sign bearing an image of a multi-headed whip dripping crimson paint, the Flail wasn't a particularly violent or rough tavern. That was just the aesthetic in Tymon, the city of gladiators: blood, weapons, severed heads dangling by their hair, and so forth. For all that the place was founded on blood, it was one of the more *polite* places Rodrick had spent time. Something about the fact that every third person you met was a seasoned arena fighter bristling with weapons prompted people to mind their manners.

Rodrick kicked the mud off his boots before pushing through into the Flail's common room—the owner had given him the rough side of her tongue the first time he tracked in muck, and he believed in staying on good terms with one's landlady, at least until it came time to skip out on the final bill.

It was only just nightfall, so the place wasn't too full yet, and he got a spot next to the bar. The prettiest waitress, Sonya—the one he'd propositioned, getting a slap complete with fingernails for his trouble— narrowed her eyes at him and disappeared into the back, but Sweet Jill approached with a smile and poured him a mug of beer. He took a sip and smacked his lips. "Much obliged. Have I told you how your hair reminds me of the embers of—"

"Save it." She kept smiling, but he saw now that her eyes were serious. "Flirt with me tomorrow, if you're still alive."

Rodrick raised one eyebrow in what he knew to be a charming and suggestive way. "Unless you're planning to *ride* me to death—"

"It's Sonya," she said. "She didn't like the way you talked to her."

"I suppose I could apologize, though I can't imagine why her feelings should be hurt. I would hardly seek the company of a woman who wasn't beautiful and exceptional and amazing, present company most definitely included, so really it was a *compliment* when I asked—"

"You're from out of town." Jill sounded sad, which was worrisome. "You didn't know any better. I tried to tell her that, but she's still upset. Most of our patrons know better than to try and have it off with her."

"I didn't know she was married," Rodrick said. "Let alone *newly* married. I would have held my tongue if I'd realized." Not entirely true, but he would have approached things differently. "Why are we talking about such tedious things when I have a bag of gold and—"

"You should probably leave town." She tried to nudge him off his barstool with her hip.

"But *why*? Her husband is a fine man, I have no doubt, but he runs a shop, and it's not even something frightening like a weapon shop or a butcher shop. It's a general goods store. The man isn't likely going to challenge me to a—"

"No," said a voice from behind him, a deep bass rumble full of amusement. "But her brother might."

Chapter Two
Beast and the Beauties

Jill turned on her heel and walked away, and Rodrick regretted not heeding her warning. Now he had *complications*, when all he'd wanted was ale and company. He turned, not too quickly, leaning back against the bar to look up, and up, and up into the face of Sonya's brother.

"Forgive me," he said. "But you're related to Sonya? By *blood*? I mean no offense, it's just—"

"I was as pretty as her, before I took a maul to the nose, and a sword cut across my face." The towering figure bulged with an abundance of muscles, and wore a sort of leather chest harness with built-in sheaths that held a number of knives, hilts pointing up and down and off to every side. Rodrick really couldn't see any family resemblance at all, except that both had rather beautiful blue eyes. This man was deeply tanned by the sun, only his scar tissue as pale as the delectable Sonya's skin, and his face was like a mask of abused meat. "My name is Black Skell."

"Sonya and Black Skell. You were named by the same parents?" Rodrick picked up his mug of ale and brought it to his lips, only to have Skell dash it from his hands, spattering alcohol (and water—mostly water) across the bar, stools, and floor. Rodrick looked at the puddles. "The landlady is a stickler for cleanliness," he said. "She won't like that mess, and she can be ferocious in her displeasure. If you'd ever met *her* in the arena you'd look even worse than you do now."

"I am a bloodied gladiator of Tymon," Skell said. "I—"

"Oh, that's a tremendous relief!" Rodrick made a great show of wiping his forehead with the back of his hand. "I was afraid for a moment there."

Skell frowned, probably, though it was really just scar tissue shifting around. "You are new to Tymon. Perhaps you don't know, but gladiators who win ten fights in the arena are considered bloodied, and the bloodied here have special—"

"Special rights, yes, indeed, permission to carry bare steel, and being able to own property and so on—" Rodrick snapped his fingers. "You must own the shop Sonya's husband operates, yes? How nice, a family affair. But you bloodied also have special *responsibilities*, don't you? If you were just an ordinary, unbloodied sort, we could have a lovely bar fight here, and both be hauled before the magistrate, and both be duly punished. Why, you could even kill me, and flee to the woods one step ahead of grim justice. A bit of an overreaction for my supposed crime, but the option would be available to you." Rodrick ran his finger through a puddle of his ale on the bar and sucked a drop from his finger. "But you're *bloodied*. You can't kill me, because for a warrior of your stature to go around slaughtering nobodies like me would be an embarrassment to the Champion and the arena and other noble people and places and things. What's the punishment for a bloodied gladiator murdering a man at random in a bar? Being tossed naked into the arena with starving dire bears, isn't it?"

"You seem to know our customs, then," Skell said after a long moment.

"I make it a point to peruse the rules of any new city I visit," Rodrick said. "I find it saves difficulty later. Now, I have no intention of striking you, and I assure you I can't be goaded into a fight. If you attack me, it won't reflect well on you. You can't have me hauled in front of the magistrate, even if you are bloodied, because I *broke no law*. I never touched Sonya, and if she's so honorable that the very suggestion of impropriety causes her to unleash her brute of a brother on me, I can't imagine she'd lie to the law about the nature of my transgression."

"Perhaps not," Skell said. "But I can invoke the Law of Grievance."

Rodrick squinted, as if consulting a mental codex, though in reality, he knew very well what the man meant. "Ah. Yes. In the case of irreconcilable dispute, a bloodied warrior can challenge anyone, bloodied or not, to a duel in the arena."

"Don't worry," Skell said. "I won't insist on a duel to the death. I'll give you a good thumping, and then run you out of town."

"All this over a careless remark? Truly? I can't apologize to Sonya and buy you a drink and let bygones be themselves?"

Skell shrugged, his muscles rippling. "She's my baby sister. I've protected her my entire life. She takes honor seriously."

"Mmm," Rodrick sat back down on the bar stool. "I don't. Take honor seriously, I mean. I'm afraid I can't join you in the arena. I have to leave Tymon tomorrow afternoon."

The gladiator showed his teeth, many of which were filed to points. "I'm sure we can schedule something for tomorrow morning, then. Or even tonight. It's not as if our bout will take long—the fight manager can fit us in."

Rodrick sighed. "I don't fight for the amusement of others, Skell, any more than I dance like a monkey on a leash. I decline."

Skell put his hand on Rodrick's shoulder and squeezed. "You cannot decline. I am bloodied. I invoke the Law of Grievance."

"I hate that it's had to come to this," Rodrick said, truthfully. "Are you sure we can't settle this amicably?"

"I've made myself clear."

"Hmm. I see you're devoted to this path. Where I come from, if you challenge someone to a duel, the challenged party is generally given the choice of weapons. Do you think that's a fair practice in this case?"

Skell snorted. "You want to choose the weapons? Fine. I am a master at all forms of arms. I'm happy to bash you with a mace, or whip you with a flail, or lop off one of your feet with a battleaxe—"

"No, I'll fight with my own sword, if you don't mind. It's the weapon I'm most comfortable with. You can have a sword as well, of course, the best one you can lay your hands on."

Skell frowned, which meant he wasn't quite as stupid as Rodrick had assumed. He thought there was some trick here. "If you were an Aldori swordlord, I would have heard some rumor about it . . ."

"No, nothing so fine. I'm a good enough swordsman—I can hold my own—but nothing fancy, no."

"Very well, then. Swords it is. I'll schedule our bout—"

"If you must." Rodrick raised a finger. "But you should know. If you insist on meeting me in the arena, I will kill you."

Skell snorted laughter, and the rest of the crowd chuckled too. "You?" the gladiator said.

"Well, me, indirectly. More directly, my sword will kill you. Please reconsider, Skell. If you die, who will defend sweet Sonya's honor?"

"I have never been bested in the arena! I have won *fifty* bouts, fool. I have strength *and* speed. I weave a net of steel. I—"

"I have a magical talking sword named Hrym," Rodrick said, and turned back around on the barstool, beckoning the bartender, who just stared at him. "A drink would be nice," he said mildly. "I think we're just about finished here."

Skell grabbed his shoulder and spun him around. "A talking *sword*? That's your threat? Do you take me for—"

"Let's have the fight, Rodrick," came Hrym's voice, muffled by the sheath. "He talks too much. I'd like to taste his guts."

"That's disgusting," Rodrick said, over the general murmurs in the room. "Why would you want to taste anyone's guts?"

"I'm speaking metaphorically," Hrym grumbled. "I can't really *taste* anything—"

"It's a trick." Skell crossed his arms and frowned. "He's throwing his voice, like that bard we had here last winter."

Rodrick rolled his eyes.

"His sheath is steaming," the bartender said. "Look."

"Ah, yes," Rodrick said. "I didn't mention? Hrym is a sword of living ice. When he gets perturbed—that means 'annoyed,' Skell—he gets colder, and, yes, there can be a bit of steam. Nothing like the whoosh of white vapor when he pierces a man's guts, of course. Apparently all that ice hitting so much warmth—"

"I don't believe you," Skell said. "There are magic swords—we have some at the arena for special bouts. But swords that *talk*? They're the stuff of legend. Why would a smirking nothing of a man like you have a weapon of such power—"

"He rescued me from the hoard of a linnorm," Hrym said. "We've been together ever since."

"I don't like to boast." Rodrick caught Jill's eye and winked. "But, yes, it's true. I crawled into a linnorm's lair and came out with great treasure."

"Show me this blade, then," Skell demanded.

Rodrick shook his head. "That was almost clever, Skell, but I don't go around breaking rules for no reason. I'm not bloodied, so I can't carry open steel in Tymon. Or open ice, as it were. That's why poor Hrym is sheathed and bound up with twine so I can't draw him easily. Don't blame me—it's *your* law."

"I'm a magistrate," rumbled one of the men who'd gathered around. He was older, and had only one eye, and looked like a prosperous ex-pirate. "I'll give you a special dispensation to show us this sword of yours."

Rodrick glanced at Jill, who nodded and said, "It's true, he's an authority."

"Stand back, then," Rodrick said. "I'd hate for anyone to get frostbite." The circle of watchers obligingly shuffled back. After a moment's hesitation, Skell moved away too. Rodrick reached behind him and tugged free the knotted threads that bound the sword's hilt to the scabbard, then smoothly drew Hrym, who took advantage of the moment: steaming, shining, glittering like a scepter of diamonds.

"Oh, yes," Hrym said. "Look upon me. I am the icy death. I am the cold that freezes your heart. I am—"

"Yes, all that and more." Rodrick put the sword away. "Now, Skell, let us fight no more. We'll have a drink together and put all this business behind us—"

"Put that sword aside when we duel," Skell said. "Fight me as a man should—"

Rodrick snorted. "Oh, and will you put aside your fifty bouts' worth of experience? Your superior reach, and speed, and strength? Arming myself with a magical sword makes it *just about* fair. Besides, you agreed to let me choose the weapons. I choose magic swords at dawn. I'm sure you can get some sword that drips electricity or sweats poison or something—that would give you a sporting chance."

"Not really," Hrym said. "I'll freeze him where he stands, and then you can snap off his limbs like you're breaking icicles off a tree branch."

"That's true," Rodrick said, "but I was trying to make him feel better."

Skell looked at the magistrate. "The sword *talks*," he said. "Surely it counts as a combatant, not a weapon?"

This gladiator was *much* cleverer than Rodrick had assumed, though still too stupid to back down from a pointless fight. Rodrick could almost admire Skell's sheer bloody-mindedness. He could certainly relate to it. Nothing made Rodrick want to do something more than worrying that he *couldn't*. "Oh, talking swords are *people*, now? So if Hrym wins a few bouts he can buy property in the city?"

"Equal rights for sentient weapons is a dream that will never die," Hrym said solemnly.

The magistrate stroked his beard. "Hmm. Does the sword move? Fly, like? Can it fight of its own volition?"

"I wish," Hrym said. "Rodrick has terrible form. I'd do much better on my own."

Rodrick shook his head. "No, Hrym can't move. Speech and ice magics are more or less the limit of his capabilities. If he could move on his own, I imagine he wouldn't have chosen to lie unmoving underneath a linnorm's ass for all those decades before I rescued him."

The magistrate shrugged. "Magic weapons are allowed in the arena, Black Skell, and if the sword cannot move without its wielder, I see no reason to claim it as a combatant."

"Of course magic weapons are allowed," Rodrick said. "They make for a better show, don't they? Listen, I'll fight you if you insist, schedule permitting, but I'll feel terrible if I *kill* you, so—"

Skell snarled. "This isn't over, scum. Your sword can't save you from a knife in the back—"

"Magistrate, I realize I have very few legal rights here, but I'd just like to note that, if I show up with a knife in my *back*—not very sporting—then you might consider Skell a prime suspect, as all these witnesses can attest."

"Sporting!" Skell shouted. "You with a magical sword claim to be *sporting*—"

"I'd never claim such a thing!" Rodrick said. "I am a *pragmatist*, never a sportsman. But, you see, I am not a bloodied warrior of the Arena of Aroden. I am a mercenary. Honor is not a requirement for my chosen profession—but it *is* for yours. Now. Do we still have a date to duel?"

Skell hesitated. He was in a tough position, and Rodrick felt a whisper of sympathy for him. To back down now would be to show weakness, but being killed by an outsider's magical sword in the arena would hardly cover him in glory, either. The one advantage of showing weakness now was its basic survivability.

"He's offered to apologize," the magistrate said. "I think it's clear he didn't mean any harm. I'm as fond of Sonya as anyone, but people make drunken comments all the time. It's hardly worth fighting to the death over, is it? You've got a bright career ahead of you. Why waste it on this?"

Skell turned and stalked out of the barroom, and Sonya disappeared into the back again. The tension ran out of the room, though people kept stealing glances at Rodrick, and the sheath on his back. Rodrick cleared his throat. "Just so everyone knows, the last person who tried to steal Hrym got a handful of ice so cold it made his arm turn black and fall off."

"Not true," Hrym said. "The chirurgeon had to cut it off. After it turned black. It would have fallen off *eventually*, I'm sure, if he'd waited."

"That's true," Rodrick said. "I'd forgotten. Blocked it out. Gruesome stuff."

People stopped looking then, rather pointedly, and the bartender finally deigned to bring Rodrick another mug of beer. The mercenary—well, he *pretended* to be a mercenary, often enough—sipped it happily as the magistrate slid onto the stool next to him. "I don't suppose you'd like to fight in the arena? A sword that talks is a bit of a novelty. You could make some good money."

"No, thank you," Rodrick said. "I don't much like gladiatorial combat."

The magistrate grunted. "You said you're a mercenary. It's all fighting for money. What's the difference?"

"Why, when you're a mercenary," Rodrick said, "you get to see the world."

Chapter Three
The Priest, the Knave, the Sword

A ll clear," Jill said from the hallway, when Rodrick peeked his head out of his room the next morning to make sure Skell and his friends weren't loitering in the hall.

He grinned at her. "Want to come in here for a bit? I'm not entirely committed to this whole getting-out-of-bed plan. I could change my mind."

"I have more important things to do on my morning off," she said. "But I wanted to warn you again. Not that you listened last time."

"I'm a marvelous listener," Rodrick said. "Try me."

"Offending Sonya was bad enough—it's easy to do, but still bad. Now you've insulted Skell's honor, and made him look like a coward, which is very much worse."

"It's not cowardice to back down from a fight with a talking ice sword. That's just good sense. I made him look sensible."

"Skell doesn't see it that way. He won't attack you within the walls of Tymon, but once you get outside of town, if he thinks he can hurt you without being witnessed . . ." She shrugged.

Rodrick sighed. "Last night you told me to leave town, and today you tell me to *stay* in town. Are you sure you aren't just trying to keep me here for reasons of your own?"

"You aren't that pretty, Rodrick." She patted his cheek and sauntered away, putting a bit of extra sway into her walk, which he watched appreciatively. Tymon wasn't such a bad place, apart from the gambling losses, the ever-present smell of blood and sweat, and the scarred idiot who wanted to kill him. But all in all, it was good he'd found a job.

Rodrick dressed, strapped Hrym to his back, and went downstairs. He was almost to the door when the landlady, an iron-eyed woman from some frozen part of the north, glided into his way. "You'll settle your bill now," she said.

"I thought I might stay another—"

"I heard you say last night you intended to depart today." She crossed her arms.

"Ah, well, that was just something I said to discourage Skell from making trouble. Come, I'm trustworthy, you haven't made me pay in advance for—"

"You are welcome to return tonight." Her voice was as implacable as an advancing glacier. "I will even hold your room for you, if you like. But you will settle your outstanding debts now."

Rodrick grinned crookedly. "Of course. I'm delighted to set your mind at ease." He poured far too much of his advance from Zaqen into the woman's outstretched hand.

"I wanted to sleep on that gold," Hrym muttered as Rodrick stepped out of the tavern.

"I'd sooner tangle with one of these gladiators than deny that woman her payment," Rodrick said. "She's *formidable*."

He spent the morning putting his affairs in order: getting his daggers sharpened at the weapon shop—the big grinding wheel was faster and far less tedious than his own whetstone—and replenishing the contents of his traveling pack as best he could. A few healing tinctures from the alchemist's, salt pork and beef from the butcher's, and other odds and ends. He wanted to stop into the general store to pick up a few things, but he wasn't entirely sure he'd be welcome there after last night. He'd have to trust Zaqen and her mysterious master to provide any necessities he lacked.

Rodrick ambled toward the arena, not because he wanted to see the fights, but because cheap, tasty food was sold in the vicinity and he didn't know when he'd get another hot meal. Walking the circuit of the vast stone coliseum, awash in the bellows of the lunchtime crowd and the distant clash of metal, he sampled all the local delicacies for the last time. After gorging himself on grilled meats, roasted nuts, and a surprisingly spicy vegetable paste smeared on slices of fresh bread, he considered himself amply fortified for the journey ahead.

He stopped at the gate to take a few nips from Chumley's flask. The guard had just arrived for his afternoon shift at the gatehouse, and had heard about Rodrick's altercation with Skell. "He grew up around here," Chumley said. "He's always had a temper, and he always did dote on his sister."

"You could have warned me not to flirt with her," Rodrick said.

"Flirt!" Chumley's fat cheeks wobbled as he laughed. "I heard you asked her if she wanted to—"

"Now, now, I'd had a few drinks. I might have been a bit uncouth, but I meant no harm." He slapped the guard on the shoulder. "I really should be on my way."

"Fine, fine. Tomorrow, you bring the liquor."

Rodrick grinned. "Next time I see you, my friend, all the drinks are on me."

Chumley's face fell. "Oh. You're leaving, then?"

"It's true. I have been offered gainful employment, and must go where the coin calls. Tymon is wonderful at taking away a man's gold."

"Good luck to you, then," Chumley said seriously. "And watch your step until you're a few hours outside of town. The law isn't always so well enforced outside these walls, and if Skell kills you out there, well . . . it's not a murder if nobody finds your body, and there are plenty of rivers to toss you into."

"Sonya is a lucky woman," Rodrick said. "What family I claim wouldn't even blink if someone stabbed me in the neck, and they certainly wouldn't swear vengeance against someone who hurt my *feelings*."

"Well, you see, Skell and Sonya were orphans together, after their father was killed in the arena, and—"

Rodrick waved his hands. "No, please, spare me their heartwarming tale of hardship and survival and success, I can't bear it. I might have to cut his head off later, and I'd hate to hesitate because you told me a sweet story." He clapped Chumley on the back and strolled through the gate, then walked along the main road that led toward the standing stones.

"You stole his flask, didn't you?" Hrym said.

"It's more that I forgot to remember to give it back after my last drink," Rodrick said. "Besides, he's enjoyed nearly a month of conversations with me, a prize beyond compare. Surely I deserve some recompense?"

"It's amazing you have any human friends at all," Hrym said. "Oh, wait. You don't."

"At least I can move about under my own power, you great paperweight."

They continued into the woods, squabbling good-naturedly, as the sun sank lower behind them.

There were three horses at the standing stones, one loaded up with supplies, and a fourth animal tied up a short distance away, a sand-colored, long-necked thing with a large hump on its back.

"Is that . . . a camel?" Rodrick said. He'd never seen one in the flesh, only in pictures, and pictures didn't convey the smell. The beast stared at him with eyes far more intelligent and malicious than any horse's he'd ever seen.

"I don't like horses," Zaqen said, lurching around one of the stones, dressed in the same robes as before. Her hood was pushed down now, revealing her unlovely head, with tangles of greasy brown hair and those mismatched, slightly bulging eyes. "Or more properly, horses don't like me." Indeed, the conventional steeds shied away when she came too close. "Camels are more tolerant. Or, I suppose, they hate all riders equally."

"I wouldn't think a camel would do well this far north," Rodrick said, choosing not to inquire about how she'd come to possess such an animal in the first place. The mystery was more amusing.

"Eh, it's summertime now. And if the beast keels over dead from the cold later, I can just ride on your shoulders, hmm? We'll be ready to go soon."

"That's for the best," Rodrick said. "I've heard rumors of a rogue gladiator in the woods, turned to banditry and preying on travelers."

"I'm sure you can protect us from any such threats," Zaqen said. "Choose your horse. My master is indifferent to such things."

Rodrick looked the beasts over. He was a decent judge of horseflesh—it paid to know the value of things, especially when you might have the chance to steal one at any moment—and these were fine animals, and looked fresh. All were geldings, placid and biddable, obviously not warhorses or racers, but good strong steady plodders, suitable for a long journey. The black horse was the biggest and looked the strongest, so he went instead to the chestnut horse—show a little deference to the master now, and any future rapaciousness and thievery would come as more of a surprise.

Rodrick patted the chestnut's neck and looked over the saddle and other tack. Nothing ostentatious, but good quality, new or nearly new. This mystery master of Zaqen's had truly been blessed by his god financially. He began shifting some of the contents of his pack—the things he could live without if he had to take off on foot in a hurry—into the saddlebags. "Why hire me?" he asked. "Your master could afford a cohort of caravan guards for what he's paying me. Obviously I'm worth it, and more, but it does make me curious."

Zaqen fussed around with the bizarre tack on her camel. "My master prefers a small group, which can move more swiftly. Three people can live more easily than ten if foraging becomes necessary, too—we have money, but we're going places where there's nothing to spend money *on*. A man like you, armed with a weapon like Hrym, is the equal of several conventional guards. As for why he's paying you so much . . . it's no hardship for him. He has more gold than he could spend in a lifetime. Fish are not stingy with water, and the sun does not hoard its heat. If you serve him well, my master will reward you even further."

"What's his name? No offense, but I can't see myself going around calling him 'master'—"

"My name is Obed." A figure dressed in robes of blue so dark they were nearly black walked slowly into the circle of stones, his voice low and serious. "I thank you for joining our expedition." His features were entirely hidden beneath his hood, and even his hands were gloved.

"The pleasure is mine." Rodrick bowed low, though it was impossible to tell if such showy obsequiousness pleased the priest. "Zaqen tells me you are a holy man, though she hasn't mentioned which sect. Is there any special form of address I should use? Your holiness, or—"

"Obed is fine," Zaqen said. "But my master is eager to be introduced to the other member of our party, if you please?"

Obed didn't look eager about anything—he looked like a mannequin someone might use to display robes in a shop—but Rodrick shrugged and drew Hrym anyway, holding him up one-handed. The sword didn't sparkle and steam quite so gloriously now, since Hrym wasn't trying to show off, but the blade was still a marvel of crystalline clarity.

Obed stepped closer, head cocked. "Do you truly speak, sword?" Rodrick couldn't place the cleric's accent, with its mushy vowels and softened consonants, but there were plenty of places in the vicinity of the Inner Sea he'd never been.

"When I have something to say," Hrym replied.

"Ha!" Rodrick said. "And lots of other times, too. Hrym tends to be quiet around new people, but once he's grown comfortable with you, you'll grow very familiar with the sound of his voice. More familiar than you'd wish."

"Sword," Obed said solemnly. "How old are you?"

"Good question," Hrym said. "Hard to say. The years tend to run together when you're part of a dragon's hoard, and later a linnorm's hoard, just sitting in the dark, though the piles of lovely gold and jewels heaped on all sides help to pass the time. I've done a bit of adventuring here and there, of course—Rodrick's isn't the first hand to wield me—but . . . counting time has never been my strength."

That was an understatement. Rodrick had tried to ascertain some of Hrym's history when they first became acquainted, and the sword was maddeningly vague, either from reticence or simple forgetfulness. The sword was knowledgeable about a vast number of unlikely things, though, and occasionally came out with the most peculiar statements, like that comment yesterday about having met Aroden.

"You must be very old, though," Obed murmured. "Hundreds of years, yes? If not thousands?"

"They don't make them like me anymore," Hrym said proudly. "Craftsmanship, made to stand the test of time."

Obed inclined his head—or dipped his hood, anyway. "We are honored by your company, sword." He gestured to Zaqen, who brought over a mounting step and helped him onto his horse, which was quite the production, what with both of them wearing robes. By all appearances this might have been the first time Obed had ever sat on a horse. Once he was settled on the saddle, though, he sat with an erect and upright bearing, dignity personified. "I will lead the way," he said.

"Don't sheathe me," Hrym said. "I'll keep watch behind us."

"Suit yourself." Rodrick reached behind him with Hrym, but rather than slipping the sword into the scabbard, he just slid the blade along the outside of the sheath. Once Hrym was in the proper position, the sword generated a seal of ice, freezing himself to the scabbard's cracked and abused leather, sticking in place on Rodrick's back. If he needed Hrym in his hand, Rodrick could reach back and draw almost as swiftly as usual, with Hrym dissolving the icy glue in an instant. They didn't always travel this way because it made Hrym's magical nature evident, and because it was horribly damaging to the scabbards.

Obed jostled the reins, and his black horse began to pick its way through the trees, the supply horse tethered behind it, plodding along. Rodrick considered offering to tie the supply horse to his own mount, but decided he should wait a while for that. Such an arrangement *would* make riding off with the priest's possessions, presumably including a great deal of gold, easier, but he didn't intend to scamper off with a single horseload of loot just yet—not when there could be a greater prize waiting at the end of this journey. He'd have to learn more about this relic they were after.

Zaqen's camel knelt down to let her scramble up onto its back—why couldn't they teach horses to do that?—and then she set off after her master, the camel glaring around evilly at the trees, as if distrusting them. Rodrick nudged his horse toward the camel, intending to engage Zaqen in conversation, but his horse steadfastly refused to draw up companionably alongside, either because it didn't like the camel, or didn't like Zaqen, or both. He got as close as he could and said, "What is Obed a priest *of*, exactly?" He'd tried to ask that more circumspectly once or twice before, without success, so decided to hazard the direct approach. "I only ask because it would be useful to know if he's versed in healing magics, or the power to make a bandit's heart explode, or what."

"My master worships Gozreh," Zaqen said.

"Ah." Rodrick's knowledge of the deities was limited mostly to the curses he'd heard shouted while looting the occasional temple and the names called out in the throes of ecstasy by various devout women he'd bedded. "God of the sea and so forth, yes? Sailors and ports and such?"

"Goddess of the sea," Zaqen corrected. "And god of the wind. A dual deity, appearing male in one aspect, female in the other."

"Ah, that's right, I remember now. I always thought that sort of flexibility must be useful for finding companionship for an evening."

Zaqen giggled, and Rodrick smiled. Good. The odd little . . . whatever she was . . . had a sense of humor. He couldn't help but flirt, even with a specimen of femininity as decidedly unappealing as Zaqen. It was always good to keep one's skills honed. "Good money in worshiping Gozreh, then?" Rodrick said.

"The bounty of the sea can be very . . . bountiful," Zaqen said. "If the goddess wills it."

"Ha." Rodrick tried to move his horse closer to her, but it shied away again, making him sway in the saddle. "We're quite some way from the sea, though—" Rodrick began.

He stopped talking as an arrow struck one of his saddlebags, missing his leg by mere inches.

Chapter Four
Ill Met in Tymon

Arrow!" he shouted, and slid off his horse, using the animal as a shield. That wasn't very nice to the horse, especially since, if the beast hadn't shied away from Zaqen at just the right moment, the archer might have struck home with his arrow. Obed shouted a word, and a shimmering dome of twisting translucent colors appeared around him, dark rainbows swirling like the colors glimpsed in a soap bubble. Another pair of arrows struck the shield the priest had conjured and burst into splinters and fragments. Zaqen didn't get off her camel, but raised her hands and giggled.

Ten-foot-long black tentacles burst forth from the ground beyond the edge of the shimmering shield, like monstrous plant growths, writhing and waving and wriggling through the trees. Someone screamed, and one of the tentacles drew back toward the horses, dragging a man toward them as he struggled and hacked at the magical appendage with a dagger in each hand.

It was Black Skell, of course, trying to fulfill his promise to murder Rodrick.

"I sense no others in the woods," Obed intoned. "This bandit works alone, it seems." The shimmering shield around them vanished.

"I am no bandit!" Skell shouted. "I am a bloodied gladiator of Tymon—"

"You think you're bloodied *now*," Zaqen said, and giggled again. The other tentacles crept toward him, wrapping around his limbs, but to his credit, the gladiator kept gamely slashing away with his knives until both his arms were pinned down.

"Marvelous work protecting the group," Hrym said from behind Rodrick.

"Quiet, you. If swordplay had seemed appropriate, I would have fought with a will." He sighed. "So you're a wizard, then, Zaqen? Or were the tentacles Obed's doing too? I suppose they're a bit . . . oceanic."

The woman shook her head. "No, the tentacles are mine. I am a devotee of the mystic arts. They'll squeeze the life out of this thief in a moment."

"I know him," Rodrick said. "A gladiator from Tymon, as he says. A bit crap as a ⸻ ⸻er, but then, gladiators don't often have the chance to use ranged weapons. I suppose he's fallen on hard times, and turned to banditry."

"You . . . scum . . ." the bandit sputtered, but the tentacles tightened around his chest, squeezing the air out of him.

"I advised him against following this path," Rodrick said, which was true. "Skell, would you like me to kill you cleanly? I can strike off your head, if you like."

Skell's eyes bulged, though whether that was due to rage or because of the squeezing tentacles, Rodrick couldn't have said.

"No need," Zaqen said. "He's gone." The tentacles unwrapped from Skell's limp form and drew back down into the earth, leaving only a few scraped patches of dirt to mark their passing.

Obed was already continuing on his way, but Rodrick paused to look over Skell's body and make sure he was really dead. Such a stupid thing to die for, honor—and not even his *own* honor, but his sister's, which hadn't even truly been sullied! (Because Rodrick hadn't been given the chance.) What a waste. Rodrick helped himself to a few of the better knives from the man's harness and then hurried back to his horse.

"Looting the corpse," Zaqen said. "Good idea." She went to the dead man and leaned over him, obscuring his upper body from view. "Mmm," she said. "He has such pretty eyes."

Rodrick frowned as he mounted his horse, and a moment later Zaqen returned and climbed onto her camel. He glanced back at the dead man. Was that blood on his face? He wanted to ask Zaqen what she'd taken . . . but he was afraid she would answer.

As they set off after Obed, he said, "Your master hardly seems to need me along. The two of you seem quite capable on your own."

"I'm sure you'll be useful for lifting heavy things," Zaqen said. Was *she* flirting, now? Rodrick had been involved in his share of romances on the road, but he wasn't really open to the idea of such a dalliance with Zaqen. She was just too . . . odd, both in appearance and personality. Though after enough lonely nights on the trail . . .

No. Not even then. Probably.

"There are situations where magic is less useful than a mighty blow to the head," she went on. "For one thing, magic requires study or prayer, and once our spells are used up, we are but mere mortals, and not particularly adept with weapons. You can swing a sword all day long, though."

"True," Rodrick said. "Though I like to take a break from swinging my sword for lunch, and a light snack in the afternoon."

They continued riding vaguely eastward, setting a not terribly punishing pace. At this rate, it would take weeks to ride to Brevoy. "Just so I know what to expect," Rodrick said, "are we going to travel through Sevenarches?" Rodrick hadn't been to that kingdom yet, though he understood it was a pleasure for those who had an affection for nature—the sky was bluer, and the air was sweeter, among other things, because druids ran the place and valued such things.

"No, we'll veer north and go through Daggermark," Zaqen replied. "Then Loric Fells, Pitax, and the contested territory called the Stolen Lands, and then on to Brevoy proper." She shook her head. "That's assuming none of those kingdoms collapse and fracture into a dozen smaller countries while we're on the road, which is never a certainty in the River Kingdoms. Of course, Loric Fells is fairly stable, since it's nothing but a troll-infested wilderness."

"Daggermark doesn't have a nice reputation." Rodrick tried to be diplomatic. "A lot of paranoid poisoners, aren't they? But Sevenarches is the closest thing this area has to a safe country. If we went through there and swung north later, at least we wouldn't have to worry about being attacked by bandits again for a few days. Too many druids in Sevenarches for my taste, personally, but I'd think the priest of a nature deity like your man Obed would like the company, and it would certainly make the start of our journey more pleasant. And if we go that way we could probably avoid Loric Fells entirely and go through Gralton, which I'm told is safe enough if you don't talk about politics—"

"Too many fey in Sevenarches," Zaqen said. "I feel about fey the way horses feel about me. You don't need to worry about us being poisoned or assassinated in Daggermark. No one in this part of the world has any reason to want us dead. And the fact that everyone has a knife dipped in some sort of horrid venom makes the people of Daggermark polite, I've heard. As for Loric Fells, my master looks forward to the opportunity to revel in its natural splendor. You're not afraid of a few hags and trolls, are you?"

"Not afraid, as such, I merely prefer the company of druids to the company of such unpleasant creatures—"

"He just lusts after forest nymphs," Hrym said.

"That's not true. That is, I *have* lusted after nymphs, some particular nymphs, sometimes, but it's hardly as if my lust is limited *specifically* to nymphs—"

"If you're ever trying to figure out why Rodrick wants to do something," Hrym went on, undiscouraged, "just ask yourself: does it help him get money, or a woman? The answer will be one of the two."

"As if you're any better!" Rodrick said.

"I am better," Hrym said. "Women don't interest me at all. Only gold. That makes me much more focused and reliable than you are."

"The two of you enjoy talking," Zaqen said. "That's nice. My master tends to keep his own counsel, and things are often too quiet between us for my taste. Your talk will help to pass the time on the road, between people trying to rob and kill us."

At twilight, Obed called a halt near a rushing stream that fed a pool above a small waterfall. Rodrick wasn't fond of camping so close to running water—you couldn't hear people creeping into camp with knives in their hands with the rush of a creek in your ears all night—but Zaqen dismissed his concern. "My master will set up wards. Don't worry—if anyone tries to ambush us, we'll know. The sound of their bodies exploding should be quite audible. Though if you'd like, we can organize watches between us. I don't sleep much anyway. I could take half the night, and you—"

"I'll do the watching," Hrym said. "I don't sleep. Just jam me point-down in the center of camp. I can see in all directions."

Rodrick obliged, plunging the sword into the soft ground. Hrym emitted a bit of ice around his point to freeze himself more steadily upright in the soil, then declared himself satisfied. Rodrick helped Zaqen set up camp, which she did quickly and efficiently, gathering wood for a fire and filling a pot with water from the stream. "You've done this before," he said. "Do you do a lot of sleeping rough where you're from?"

The wizard snorted. "Rough? This isn't rough. Sleeping in a black cave full of giant albino spiders is rough, though I do love the sound of the lullabies they sing to their thousands of babies."

"You're an odd one, Zaqen."

"I have heard that before, ever since I was a child, often accompanied by an attempt to strike me, or a thrown boot. No one else seems to see the world quite the way I do. They find beauty in the ugliest things, and

ugliness in the most beautiful. It's you lot who are odd."
She squatted by the fire and began crumbling some
herbs from a pouch into the pot.

"Making stew?" he said. "Horribly impractical stuff,
stew. Takes forever."

"No. This is my . . . medicine, you could say. I'd offer
to share, but if you don't have the illness it treats, the
effects can be unpredictable, and seldom pleasant."

"Ah. Shall I see to my own dinner, then?"

"My master generally provides the evening meal,"
she said. "He enjoys it. But he has to tend to a certain
ritual first—"

"The priest is naked," Hrym said. "Not that I care—
you're all just blobby collections of limbs in varying
hues to me. But it seemed worth mentioning, from a
tactical standpoint."

Rodrick squinted in the gloom. Beyond the tethered
mounts, he caught a glimpse of pale flesh as Obed
slipped into the pool. "A ritual?" he said. "I've always
just heard them called 'baths.'"

"Cleansing is part of it," Zaqen said. "He is a devotee
of the sea, my master. This river flows down to the sea,
eventually, as do all rivers, and so he likes to submerge
himself in water every day, to renew his connection and
listen for distant whispers from the goddess."

"Distant whispers from the goddess flow upstream,
do they?" Rodrick said. "I'll be sure to remember that.
What is he *doing* in there, exactly."

"Meditation. Prayer. Centering his mind." Zaqen
shrugged, ladling up a measure of the pungent
medicinal water and pouring it into a wooden cup.
"Holy men." She inhaled the steam, then drank back
the contents of the cup, grimacing.

It was full dark by the time Obed emerged from the pool, rising from the water with stately dignity and dressing swiftly in his long robes before he approached the circle of firelight. He tossed a pair of fat salmon onto the ground at Zaqen's feet, startling Rodrick, who drew back. "Did you just catch those?"

"He's a priest of the sea goddess," Zaqen said. "Bounty of the waters, and all that."

"Clean them," Obed said. "I will eat the smaller. The two of you may split the larger."

"Very generous of you," Zaqen said, but Obed had already withdrawn to the far side of the fire, sitting on a flat stone just beyond the light. The wizard produced a thin-bladed knife from somewhere. "I'll clean his, you clean ours?"

"Fair enough."

"We generally eat our fish raw," Zaqen said. "It's better when it's actually alive when you start eating, but this will do. How about you?"

"Ah." Rodrick blinked. "I prefer it cooked, ideally with a bit of lemon, perhaps some roasted potatoes—"

"Please yourself." Zaqen shuddered, apparently disgusted at the thought of cooked fish. "We all have our own customs. It's not for me to judge." She set about gutting the fish with rather more gusto than precision, and Rodrick drew his own blade and found a flat stone to serve as a cutting board.

"All eating is repulsive," Hrym said. "Consuming other living things to survive? It's barbaric, really. It would make me sick, if I were capable of getting sick. Plants aren't so bad, I suppose, but meat—"

"You once told me one of your favorite sensations was being plunged to the hilt in the warm guts of a large animal," Rodrick said. "And now you scorn me for being carnivorous?"

"Plunging into the guts of a large animal isn't anything at *all* like eating," Hrym said. "It's about the *feeling*, you see, it's sensual—"

"So it's less like eating and more like sex," Zaqen said.

After a long pause, Rodrick said, "Remind me never to have sex with you, Zaqen."

The wizard tittered.

Rodrick had difficulty sleeping, even though his belly was full, the fire was warm, and his sword—probably the most dangerous thing for leagues—was keeping watch over him. He'd been part of a few adventuring parties over the years, and it always took a while to get used to sleeping with strangers. Rodrick wasn't above stealing everything and slipping away in the night, after all, so he was always keen to the possibility of similar betrayals.

Eventually he drifted into a thin and meager sleep, his unquiet dreams full of strange murmurings, and when he woke near dawn, Obed was crouched near the center of camp, speaking to Hrym in a low voice. When the priest noticed Rodrick stirring, he rose and went to the packhorse and began preparing for their departure.

Rodrick stretched, and after tending to his morning necessities, he drew Hrym from the dirt—the ice melting instantly to let Hrym slide free—and gave him a couple of swings through the air. "What were you and the holy man chatting about?"

"Dragons," Hrym said. "The man is interested in dragons, as many men are, and of course I am an authority on dragons—"

"A dragon used to sit on top of you for a while," Rodrick said. "Or so you claim. I'm not sure being underneath something a lot makes you an authority. By that logic, I'm an authority on ceilings."

"And poxy whores," Hrym said. "Oh, wait, you *are* an authority on those."

"I'm glad the man is talking to one of us, anyway." Rodrick let Hrym re-freeze himself to the scabbard on his back. "Actually, I'm not. I'd assumed he was just naturally taciturn, or too concerned with spiritual matters to engage in trivia like friendly conversation, but if he's willing to talk to you—"

"Can you blame him? I'm remarkable," Hrym said. "There aren't many intelligent swords of living ice, while mercenaries like you are common as mud."

"Not as common as that." Zaqen bustled around camp and efficiently stowed away their supplies. "He's unusually pretty, for one thing. Most mercenaries are a bit more battered about the face."

"Give him time," Hrym said. "The day is young."

Chapter Five
The Bleak Shores

They traveled the rest of that day at a fairly steady pace, using roads when they were handy, heading north and east through the damp forests. By noon, Rodrick's stomach was rumbling. "Any chance we could call a halt for something to eat?"

Zaqen shook her head. "The master wishes to reach a tributary of the river by nightfall. We'll be eating in our saddles today."

Rodrick groaned. "That's inhuman. All day in the saddle? I won't be much good in a fight if I can't feel my ass."

"Just wave your magical sword around, and I'm sure all the villains will run away." She fished in her saddlebags and brought out a wad of some kind of pale, mottled jerky. "Care for a bite?"

"What is it?"

"Meat."

"Yes, I'd gathered, but what *kind* of meat?"

"If you have to ask," Zaqen said, "you aren't hungry enough." She tore off a piece of the jerky, grinned at him around the mouthful, and then turned away.

"Listen, you have to at least *talk* to me," Rodrick said. "My mind will go as numb as my hindquarters without conversation."

Zaqen mumbled something, but her mouth was full, so Rodrick couldn't make it out. The tone hadn't been encouraging, though. Rodrick sighed and let his horse fall some distance back from the wizard and her strange mount, to his gelding's evident relief.

"You can talk to me," Hrym said. "I'm not good enough to talk to anymore?"

"All right, let's talk. Did you see what she did to Skell yesterday?"

"Of course I did. I see all. When I'm not crammed in that sheath, anyway."

"Do you care to *share* your observations, O all-seeing one?"

"She cut out Black Skell's eyes and put them in a little pouch," Hrym said.

Rodrick stared at Zaqen's back. Had her humped shoulder *switched sides*? He would have sworn it was on the left before. Was she truly misshapen, or did she just have particularly ruinous posture? "His eyes," Rodrick repeated. "Why would she do that?"

"She said they were pretty eyes. Perhaps she collects pretty things."

"I am aware that humans are not your area of expertise, as you've never spent a century sleeping underneath one of us, but cutting out someone's eyes and putting them in a little bag is not typical human behavior."

"She's a wizard," Hrym said. "They're a strange lot, aren't they? Maybe she needs the eyes to cast some spell. Maybe she can fling burning spectral eyeballs at people, if she has the right material to work with."

"Or they could be used for some kind of long-distance seeing spell," Rodrick said thoughtfully.

"Or that," Hrym conceded.

"Still, it's a grisly way to collect spell components."

"I'm sure she's just being practical. How likely are we to pass a shop devoted to supplying adepts of the arcane? She has to take her ingredients while she can. And, what, if she bought eyes pickled in brine from a shop, that would be better? They have to come from *somewhere*. Honestly, you're too suspicious."

Rodrick shook his head. "I can't get a handle on her. Most people are obvious. Her master is standoffish, but that's fine, I've known plenty of men who thought they were better than everyone else and didn't like mixing with the lower orders—"

"He talks to me. Recognizes quality when he sees it."

"—but Zaqen is just *peculiar*."

"Oh, I see your point," Hrym said. "Very good. Carry on."

"You see what point?"

"You're trying to understand their psychology so we can—"

"Shh," Rodrick said. "For all we know she steals ears off corpses so she can cast spells of long-distance hearing."

"You'll talk about how *peculiar* she is without worrying about being overheard, but you won't talk about our—"

"Quiet! Let's keep *some* secrets to ourselves, all right? Thinking someone's peculiar is just an opinion, and one I'm sure she's heard before. I daresay she *knows* she's peculiar—she's obviously not stupid."

Hrym didn't answer.

"I just think we should keep our own counsel regarding . . . more delicate matters, that's all."

Still no reply.

"It's going to be like this, then?" Rodrick said. "The silent treatment?"

"I'm just a sword," Hrym said. "Just a weapon for you to wield, your personal property, so when you tell me to be *quiet*, of course I obey, O great Rodrick, wielder of mighty Hrym the Frostblade, Bringer of Winter—"

"Never mind! I'll take the silent treatment."

They did stop eventually, to water and rest the horses—leading Zaqen to comment on the relative uselessness of horses as compared to her tireless camel—but then pressed on, never galloping, but proceeding as close to a trot as the landscape would allow. The River Kingdoms had a lot of trees, at least in Tymon, where the woodcutters weren't out in force, and it wasn't long before Rodrick was well and truly sick of trees. He almost wished for a bandit attack just to break the monotony.

They didn't reach the river that day, much to Obed's dismay, and Rodrick listened from their camp—an abandoned lean-to probably used by a hunter—as the priest complained in a low voice and Zaqen tried to soothe him. "Can you hear what they're saying?" Rodrick asked Hrym.

The sword said, "Oh, the general idea is that everything is too slow, this godsforsaken country is huge, and so forth. Zaqen is telling him that we'll be able to move faster once we reach Daggermark, where the roads are better. He doesn't seem mollified. Now he's asking her to . . . Ha. Watch this."

The priest moved a bit farther into the trees, and Zaqen followed him, carrying two huge waterskins from the supply horse. There was a flash of pale flesh between the tree trunks, and Rodrick realized the priest had disrobed again. Then came the sound of splashing water. "Is Zaqen dumping out those waterskins over him?" he asked, incredulous.

"Seems so," Hrym replied.

"But why? He went bathing last night. All right, Zaqen said it allowed him to connect through the stream's flow back to the great ocean of what-have-you. But what good does being doused in cold drinking water do?"

"Perhaps it's some sort of ritual cleansing?" Hrym said.

"It had better be. I hope it's not simple fastidiousness. We're going to be traveling for weeks—he'd better get accustomed to being dirty. And it's a waste of water."

"We're hardly in the desert, Rodrick," Hrym pointed out. "And even if we were, I'm a sword of magical *ice*, and ice is just frozen water. I can generate all the water we need. You just have to wait for it to melt first."

"You know I don't like drinking your meltwater. You *talk*. You're more or less alive. It's like drinking someone's tears. Or sweat."

"More like drinking someone's urine, I'd think," Hrym said.

"You are amazingly disgusting for something that doesn't even have a fleshy body, sword."

Zaqen returned after a while, cheerful and chattering, while Obed sulked or meditated or otherwise occupied himself among the trees. "No fish tonight, I'm afraid," she said. "But I thought I'd see if I could catch some fresh game. No reason to resort to our dried meat yet. Don't rabbits feed at twilight?"

"The feeding habits of rabbits are not one of my areas of expertise," Rodrick said, and Zaqen shrugged and slipped away. You wouldn't think she could move stealthily, given her awkward gait, but he didn't hear a rustle as she moved off into the bushes. Barely half an hour later she returned with the carcass of a rabbit dangling from each hand. One of the rabbits was missing its head, and the other was distinctly scorched. "You used magic to *hunt*?" Rodrick said.

"How else would I hunt? Do I look like a marksman to you?" She tossed the rabbits at his feet. "Care to prepare those for me, Rodrick dear?"

"I thought your master liked doing the cooking?"

Zaqen shrugged. "By 'cooking' I mean 'catching fish and eating them raw,' mostly, but we're all out of fish here."

"He's a priest, isn't he? Can't he just . . ." Rodrick waved his hands around vaguely. "Conjure food?"

"Of course he can. But have you ever eaten conjured food? It's always tasteless bread, or oatmeal, or some other bland stuff. Not the sort of thing anyone would choose to eat, especially with plump rabbits at hand. Besides, my master prefers to save such spells for emergencies. Go on, get out your knife—you didn't have to do even a token bit of fighting today, so the least you can do is butcher a bunny."

Rodrick dressed the carcasses while Zaqen brewed another pot of her medicine, then started to set up a spit over the fire. "Don't cook mine," Zaqen said, snatching up one of the rabbits.

"You're not going to eat that raw, too? The fish, all right, I've been in port cities where eating fish fresh and uncooked was the style, but raw rabbit?"

"Cooking ruins the flavor," she said.

"Aren't you worried about getting ill? I knew a fellow once who ate undercooked pork and died horribly—"

She pointed to her own chest. "Student of the mystic arts, Rodrick. I don't fall prey to things like ordinary *diseases*. I'm far more likely to die in a horrible magical mishap. Eaten by a spectral monster summoned inexpertly. Inadvertently transformed into a salamander. Things like that."

Rodrick set about roasting his rabbit, deliberately not looking at Zaqen as she tore the raw muscle from her own rabbit with her teeth. "No food for your master?"

"He's fasting," she said around a mouthful. "Just for tonight."

"Oh, good. I'm sure being hungry will improve his mood."

She swallowed and grinned. There was blood on her teeth.

"For a student of the mystic arts," Rodrick said, "I haven't seen you do much studying. I thought wizards had to pore over spellbooks at all hours of the day and night. Doesn't the magic fall out of your head on a regular basis, and need to be jammed back in by reading?"

"How do you know I don't read by firelight in the hours before dawn?" she said. "I don't sleep as much as you do."

"You didn't read last night," Hrym piped up. "You were awake, but not studying books."

She shrugged. "I have a very good memory. I don't need the books in front of me. I can see every page in my mind when I close my eyes. Much easier than lugging around a bunch of heavy volumes everywhere."

"I wasn't aware it worked that way," Rodrick began.

For the first time, Zaqen snapped at him. "I don't tell you how to swing a sword, so don't tell me how magic should work." She took her rabbit and stalked away to the other side of the fire.

"You've charmed another woman senseless," Hrym said.

"It's a gift." Rodrick roasted the rabbit over the flames and ate the hot, savory fragments with his fingers. Not quite the feast he would have chosen, but better than going hungry, and certainly better than eating raw anything that had once breathed and run.

He drove Hrym into the center of the campsite to keep watch again, then took a walk around the general vicinity of the shack just to move his muscles in a way that didn't involve being jostled all day on a horse. When he returned to camp, Obed was sitting with his back against a tree, eyes closed, either deep in meditation or asleep sitting up, and Zaqen was on her back, apparently watching the smoke from the fire drift up into the cloudy sky. Neither of them spoke to him, so Rodrick said goodnight to Hrym, gave in to his exhaustion, and curled up by the fire, too tired even to plot or scheme or fantasize about the pleasures he would enjoy as a wealthy man.

The next morning, after a breakfast eaten largely in silence, they finally reached the tributary of the Sellen that divided Tymon from Sevenarches to the east and Daggermark to the north. The water here was wide but relatively sluggish and not terribly deep—a nice surprise, as the River Kingdoms had a tendency to become the Marsh Kingdoms in places. Once the river was in sight, Obed drove his horse faster, and before Rodrick and Zaqen caught up, he was already in the water up to his neck, swimming far enough out that Rodrick still couldn't get a good look at his face.

Rodrick dismounted from his horse, then led the animal to the river to let it drink. After a glance at Zaqen, he sighed and led the other mounts to the water as well. The camel leaned its head down, sniffed at the water, then turned up its nose. Probably not the sweet oasis water it preferred, or else it was just being generally contrary.

"Your master must be half fish," Rodrick said, strolling over to join Zaqen, who was shading her eyes to gaze across the river.

"He gets his power from his connection to the sea," Zaqen said. There was no trace of annoyance in her voice—whatever he'd done to offend her the night before, she'd either forgotten or forgiven. "Not the path to power I'd choose, but it works for him. I hope there aren't any carnivorous monsters in this water."

Rodrick snorted. "Isn't there an entire settlement of horrifying carnivorous monsters not far away?"

"Outsea," she said. "Yes, a city of refugees from the waters of the Inner Sea, or so I'm told. Sea devils, merfolk, the occasional naga and sea hag and even a few ulat-kini and gillmen. I'd love to know how a bunch of creatures like that ended up stuck in a river settlement here. In the ocean most of them are at war with some subset of the others, but I suppose being so far from their ancestral homes, they have good reason to make common cause here."

"Will your man Obed be wanting to visit? Surely he's got friends among those races, and other worshipers of Gozreh?"

"I'm sure he'd love to pay his respects, but as you may have noticed, he's in a hurry. He wants to be out of the River Kingdoms and into Brevoy before the month is out."

Hrym laughed from Rodrick's back. "I hope he's packed a magic carpet, then. You feeble bipeds and your rideable quadrupeds will never cover the distance so quickly."

She sighed. "Yes, I tried to tell him his expectations were unreasonable. My master is a zealot, though." She glanced at him. "I don't mean that in a bad way. He has passion, and drive, and the impatience that comes with those qualities. It's admirable. But, I mean . . ." She shrugged, one shoulder dipping rather lower than the other. "The artifact we're going to recover has been waiting a long time. Another few weeks won't change anything. And it's not as if we're paying you by the hour."

"We would make better time if we went through Sevenarches," Rodrick said. "It's right there, just across the water. The grass is *actually* greener there, you can see it."

Zaqen shook her head. "Planning our route isn't one of your responsibilities. Get the horses ready—my master will want to push on soon."

Rodrick shrugged and busied himself with the mounts. "Ah, Rodrick, we have a problem," Hrym said from his back a moment later.

When Rodrick turned around, there was a short man wearing dirty leather armor behind Zaqen, holding a knife to her throat, and another man the size of a draft horse aiming an arrow at Obed, who bobbed in the water—not close to shore, but well within bowshot.

"Nice sword," the brigand holding Zaqen captive said. "I'll take it, along with everything else."

Chapter Six
Sword Against Banditry

Rodrick cocked his head at Zaqen. "No tentacles this time? Forgot to study your books this morning?"

"May I speak?" Zaqen said. The thief behind her frowned and mumbled something in her ear. It must have been assent, because she said, "My master instructed me to refrain from defending us if we were attacked again. He'd like to see if he's getting his money's worth out of you, I suppose."

Rodrick sighed. "Really? He's testing me? I'm offended."

"Just throw down your sword," the bandit said. "And move away from the horses. And the, ah—that animal that's not a horse. Whatever it is, I'm sure it's valuable. We're not *committed* to killing you—murder sometimes spooks the animals, and they're worth money—but we'll take the risk if you give us any trouble."

"If you insist," Rodrick said, and drew Hrym fast, whipping him down into guard position. Foot-long spears of bright ice—overgrown icicles, really, and ultimately about as aerodynamic as a bunch of fireplace pokers—flew from the length of Hrym's shaft, piercing the bigger bandit's leather armor and making him drop to his knees, gurgling. As soon as the bandit's aim wavered, Obed vanished from sight, head disappearing beneath the river's surface.

The bandit holding Zaqen's throat shouted, "I'll kill her!"

Rodrick shrugged. "The man in the river pays my wages. The one you've got there is just another employee. Do what you must."

"Oh, that's nice," Zaqen said, but she was grinning. "Good to know where I stand."

"Although, to keep the boss happy . . ." Rodrick approached the thief with Hrym's bright length in his hand. "I *will* kill you, after you've killed her. Just to show the local bandits that no one can harm a member of my party without dying, that sort of thing. And my sword here—which drinks souls, by the way—will taste your essence and consume your memories, and in my spare time in coming years I'll track down any friends and relatives of yours, and kill *them*, too. It seems excessive, I know, but I am a professional, after all, and I take my job seriously." Hrym then emitted a suitably eldritch modulating hum, which sounded a bit like a choir of angels having all their wings pulled out.

The bandit, altogether less cocky than before and stealing glances at his ice-speared compatriot, said, "Surely we can work something out?"

Rodrick smiled widely. "That depends. How much gold do you have on you?"

The thief sighed and let Zaqen go. "This is how *I* turned to banditry, you know," he said glumly, handing over his purse, and then his blades when prompted. "I was just a traveler passing through, and I was robbed, and I thought, 'Bugger working for a living, I'll just steal like these fellows do.' I joined up with Fat Belwas over there and we've made a decent living ever since. It's not even really against the law, depending on where you are in the River Kingdoms." His face took on a hopeful expression. "I don't suppose you lot are looking for any additions to your party?"

Rodrick, who thought that having *two* party members who planned to rob everyone else at the first opportunity was enough, said, "That would be up to the master, I suppose."

The thief squinted at the river. "He hasn't surfaced. Are you sure he didn't drown?"

Zaqen snorted. "He's fine."

The thief glanced at her. "Sorry about the knife to the throat, and all—"

She shrugged in her ungainly way. "It's not the first time I've been threatened with death. Or the first time someone in my group said, 'If you have to kill her, go ahead, we understand.' Story of my life."

"It was a bluff, Zaqen," Rodrick said.

"Now you tell me," the thief said. "And all that about your sword drinking souls and consuming my essence, that was a trick, too?"

"No, that was true," Rodrick lied.

There was a flash of movement by the river bank, and then Obed strode forward, dressed in his now-dripping robes. "I did not hire you to recruit people to our party," Obed said. "Or to show mercy to brigands. I hired you to kill those who threatened us. Kill him."

Rodrick raised an eyebrow. "This fellow is no threat to us now. He was never a threat to us to *begin* with. I won't murder an unarmed man. There's no point. I already have all his money."

Obed clenched his fists together. "Kill. Him."

"No," Rodrick said, not angrily or aggressively, but more in the tones of someone declining an offered cup of tea.

The two men stared at one another—or so Rodrick assumed. Obed's eyes were hidden in the depths of his hood, but he was literally shivering with rage.

"I'll just be on my way then," the bandit said, backing away rapidly. "Sorry to have inconvenienced you all—"

Zaqen gestured at him, almost casually, and a spray of hissing droplets flew from her fingers and spattered across the man's face and chest. He screamed and flailed his arms, dropping to the ground and rolling and writhing as thin tendrils of smoke rose from his body.

Rodrick raised his sword instinctively, but Zaqen just smirked at him and shrugged. "I kill whomever my master wills." Obed didn't overtly react to her action, but he was no longer clenching his fists or quivering.

After a moment the bandit went still, but kept whimpering. "What did you do to him?" Rodrick asked.

"Acid," Zaqen said. "Nasty stuff. Eats through leather, skin, muscle, bone. It'll even eat through steel, given time. I can spit the stuff out, too, so keep that in mind if you ever decide to steal a kiss." She winked. "Without asking permission first, that is."

Rodrick strode over to the bandit, who stared up at him with open, terribly conscious eyes. His face was ravaged, his skull showing through in places, and coin-sized spots of acid slowly burned all over his throat and chest. "Sorry," Rodrick said, and plunged Hrym into his heart.

"Ahh," Hrym said. "That's nice. Warm. Unfortunate circumstances, but still, feels good."

Rodrick withdrew Hrym, and blood geysered briefly from the bandit's wound, then subsided to a trickle. The man's eyes took on the glassy, empty quality of the newly dead, like the windows of an abandoned house.

"Mercy," Obed spat, and stalked away toward the horses. Rodrick started to walk after him, but stopped after a few steps, unsure about what he could possibly say—and about what he might *want* to say.

Zaqen, meanwhile, sidled over to the acid-spattered corpse, knelt down for a moment, and then rose. Rodrick didn't look, but he was fairly sure she'd scooped out the dead man's eyes for her grisly collection. The wizard came over and patted Rodrick on the shoulder, making him flinch. "Come along," she said cheerfully. "We've got miles to cover."

"Obed still wants me along on this little trip?"

"Until he tells me otherwise, I assume so. Do you still wish to accompany us?"

"Ah, well." Rodrick forced himself to brighten. "It's not as if the fellow wouldn't have killed us if we'd given him a chance."

"That's the spirit," Zaqen said. "No one forced him to take up the life of a bandit, and being spattered by acid occasionally is just the cost of doing business. Best hang back on your horse for a while, though. I'll try to talk to Obed. He listens to me, sometimes, when he feels like it."

They mounted and continued on their way, Zaqen drawing her camel as close to Obed's horse as she could. Rodrick brought up the rear, some distance away, for once not really interested in eavesdropping. From his back, Hrym said, "It's not as if you haven't murdered people before."

"Not *murder*, as such. I've generally killed just to save myself from *being* killed."

"Yes, but frequently you were saving yourself from being killed by people you'd recently robbed or cheated," Hrym pointed out. "It's not as if they didn't have legitimate grievances."

"I don't consider any grievance legitimate enough to stab me over. And killing for no reason at all? What's the point? I already *had* his purse."

"The master wanted to see if you could protect the party. Makes sense to me."

"'The master,'" Rodrick said. "Listen to yourself!"

"Hmm, good point. The way Zaqen talks, I'd forgotten that wasn't actually Obed's name."

"Perhaps he wanted me to die, so he could try to steal you, Hrym."

"If he wanted you to die, Zaqen would just shoot acid into your face."

"Ah, but then you wouldn't go with them, would you? If you saw them simply murder me, that is. I mean, they could try to pick you up, but you'd fight them. Wouldn't you?"

"If I had eyes, Rodrick, I would roll them at you now. Yes, I would fight them as best I could if they killed you. We're partners. I won't willingly serve one who slays you."

"So perhaps they're contriving to *have* me slain, so they can pretend they had no hand in my death, and convince you to work for them after that. What if *you're* the artifact they're after?"

"I suspect you're being paranoid," Hrym said. "I think I'd know if I were sacred to Gozreh, for one thing. But if you'd like to proceed with that as your working theory, I don't see any harm. A little paranoia is good for you."

The horse and camel halted, and Zaqen wheeled her beast around and clopped toward Rodrick. "You're forgiven," she said. "I pointed out how promptly you killed the bandit who was menacing him, thus demonstrating your skill. I also explained to the master that your refusal to murder defenseless strangers means you're less likely to attempt to murder *us* at some point—I told him a bit of conscience in a mercenary is a rare thing, to be treasured."

Rodrick let himself smile. "Do you believe that?"

"I believe we need you to get where we're going," Zaqen said. "And if the master hates you, we won't get far. I think soon he'll behave just as warmly toward you as he has previously."

"And you?" Rodrick said. "It really *was* a ruse. I would have killed the man if he hadn't backed down—"

"Ahem," Hrym said.

"I would have used *Hrym* to slay the man, yes," Rodrick said. "Or frozen his dagger so it shattered."

"Actually," Hrym said, "to be cold enough to shatter tempered steel, I'd have to make it so cold that his flesh would basically crystallize, so the dagger would be the least of his problems."

Zaqen laughed. "I wasn't worried for my life, Rodrick. My master told me to let you fight, but if you'd fallen to the ground and begged the thieves for mercy, I wouldn't have let myself die just to prove Obed's point. I am not without resources. Worry less about my hurt feelings and more about keeping us from being held at knifepoint in the first place."

They proceeded north along the riverbank, with Rodrick casting glances across the water to the green fields and forests of Sevenarches. They drew near a bridge, and Obed halted his horse to stare at it. The bridge arched high over the river, presumably to allow boats to pass beneath it, and it was the strangest construction Rodrick had ever seen. On the Tymon side of the river, the bridge was a practical object of timbers and lashed ropes, well made but far from beautiful. Halfway across its span, however, the bridge changed: the bare boards gave way to clearly living wood, growing branches in full green leaf and wrapped in vines and bobbing flowers, abuzz with bees and alive with the fluttering of small birds. It might as well have been a bridge into another world. One could hardly imagine a more perfect image for the transition from the blood-sport-fueled brutality of Tymon to the fey sensibility of Sevenarches.

"Can't convince you to cross that bridge, then?" Rodrick said.

"Far too many fey," Zaqen said. "Look at the far side! What kind of toll must they charge to keep up the magics on a bridge like that?"

Rodrick shook his head. "I haven't been in the River Kingdoms for long, but I know that's one of their fundamental commandments, one of their 'River Freedoms'—walk any road, float any river. No tolls, and no contested border crossings. Anyone can go anywhere. And anyone who tries to change that is swiftly taught the error of their ways."

"Freedom," Hrym said. "Freedom to go anywhere. It sounds nice, until you realize it also means the freedom to have your legs chopped off and your boots stolen. I thank—oh, say, Gozreh—every day that I don't have legs, by the way."

"That policy makes it easier for us," Zaqen said. "Explaining our business at a border checkpoint for each of these little pocket fiefdoms would be difficult."

"I don't even entirely understand our business myself," Rodrick said. "Bound for Brevoy, you say, to seek an artifact, but details . . ."

"One day at a time, O noble warrior. You'll know what you need to know when you need to know it." Zaqen nudged her camel forward.

After she was gone, Hrym said, "We really should—"

"Yes," Rodrick said. "Yes, I know."

That night they made camp, still in Tymon but not far from Daggermark. Obed did his river ritual again, and brought out four fat fish. Rodrick roasted his share gratefully, sure to thank Obed in a sincere and non-obsequious fashion, not that the priest appeared to hear him at all. After sucking the last bits of fat from his fingers, Rodrick rose. "I'll go fetch some more firewood. It looks likely to be a cold night."

Zaqen yawned and shrugged, and Obed ignored him entirely, so Rodrick walked off with Hrym toward a stand of trees.

"Any observations to report?" Rodrick said, once they were far enough from the campsite that he thought they were safe from being overheard, barring magical spells of clairaudience.

"Of course," Hrym replied. "Let's see. For a student of the arcane, Zaqen doesn't appear to study anything at all. I've known wizards, and they always had their noses in books or scrolls. Zaqen doesn't even have a callus on her finger from writing, nor are her hands indelibly ink-stained."

"What," Rodrick said, "you think she's faking it? Pretending to be a wizard, using magical items of some kind to conjure her tentacles and spray her acid? I'd hate to think there's *another* pretender in our company. You and I are quite enough."

"I merely make observations," Hrym said. "I'll leave drawing conclusions to you. Though I resent being called a pretender. *You* pretend to be a mercenary when you're really a thief and opportunistic plunderer, but I actually *am* a fantastically rare intelligent magical sword of ice."

"And also a thief and opportunistic plunderer."

"People are complicated," Hrym said. "Magical swords even more so."

"How about their sleeping patterns?"

"Zaqen sleeps for a few hours, though she's up in the middle of the night, staring into the fire, talking to herself—"

"What does she say?"

"She says, 'Oh, Rodrick, when will you come and warm my bedroll?' Ha, no, I've no idea. She mutters. I'm not sure it's even in a real language. There's a lot of low giggling. Obed is far quieter, but he doesn't sleep as much as we'd like, either. He rises so early in the mornings that it's practically still yesterday. When he gets up he meditates, or prays, or what have you, but it's hard to tell how aware he is of his surroundings in that state."

"Probably too aware to miss us stealing the horses and everything they carry, I'd guess," Rodrick said.

"It seems likely. If we do decide to proceed with a simple snatch and grab, I'd say around midnight is our best bet, though I'd prefer to watch for a while longer to fully establish the pattern—a few nights is hardly enough time to draw definite conclusions. They may be unusually wakeful because we're new to the group and they don't trust us yet, after all."

"It's far easier to steal from people once they no longer expect you to do so," Rodrick mused. "What's the downside in sticking with them for a while, though? The work is hardly arduous so far."

"Agreed," Hrym said. "And there's the matter of this artifact we're supposedly searching for. I'd like to know a lot more about this artifact."

"Like, is it an enormous statue of a fish or something made entirely of gold and precious gems?" Rodrick said. "I'd like to know that, too."

"It would be distressing to stay with them for the entire journey only to find that they're bent on recovering the finger bone of some ancient avatar, or something with similar, merely sentimental value."

"Oh, I don't know about that," Rodrick said. "The whole notion of dismissing items of sentimental value has always seemed wrong-headed to me. Anything with great sentimental value also has great *real* value—because you can ransom it back to the people who feel sentimental about it."

"Do you really want to be at the center of a holy crusade?" Hrym said.

"On the whole, no. Far better if it's the golden fish instead." Rodrick bent to pick up a few sticks, just for the sake of plausibility when they returned.

"Then you should find out," Hrym said. "Talk to Obed. Be charming. Find out what we're after."

"Why don't you do it? He's actually spoken more than five words in a row to *you*."

"Just about dragons," Hrym said. "The man has an obsession with them, and wants to know everything *I* know, which I keep telling him isn't really that much."

Rodrick tucked another length of wood under his arm, then gazed back at the flickering light of the distant campfire. "You don't think there's going to be a dragon, do you? Guarding whatever this artifact is? I'm not sure my weight in gold is worth facing a dragon."

"It wouldn't be so bad," Hrym said. "If we lost the battle, I'd probably end up in a hoard again, resting on heaps of gold."

"I won't have such a happy outcome."

"It's not my fault you decided to be human instead of something sensible like a sword," Hrym said.

Chapter Seven
Sword against Tedium

The next day they crossed the border into Daggermark before midday, fording a branch of the great river Sellen just past the point where it became known locally as the Dagger. The change of locality was apparent fairly soon, when an actual road appeared, and they made better time after that, to Obed's delight.

There were people on the road, too, peasants driving their animals here and there or just plodding dustily along, but none of them attempted to assassinate or poison anyone, to Rodrick's vague disappointment. The whole time he'd been in Tymon, he'd heard how conniving and cowardly the people of Daggermark were, favoring poison to solve their problems, as opposed to giving their enemies a good honest bashing over the head with a spiked club. (The only people the folk of Tymon hated more than the citizens of Daggermark were the citizens of Razmiran; they were equally horrible, but they weren't even part of the River Kingdoms.)

The group stopped in a fair-sized village to water their horses and replenish some of their supplies, and Rodrick and Hrym (sheathed, lest he elicit too much comment) took an opportunity to stroll around. The place seemed like any reasonably prosperous market town, though the apothecary *was* suspiciously well stocked with things like hemlock and deadly nightshade, and the blacksmith seemed to have a thriving sideline in forging very small, very sharp daggers.

Rodrick was scrupulously polite to everyone he met. Life was cheap in Daggermark—literally. You could reportedly hire a student assassin to kill anyone you wanted for a shockingly small quantity of gold, and he had no reason to think outsiders just passing through were immune to being targeted.

He met up with the rest of his party as they were preparing to leave. Rodrick cast a longing glance at a tavern, then climbed onto his horse, wincing as he sat down in the saddle. At least the roads here were better. The path wouldn't be so *bouncy* for a while.

As they traveled along a well-marked, rutted dirt road, Rodrick nudged his horse closer to Obed until he was riding alongside the robed priest. "I never said thank you for inviting me along on this journey," he said. "I'm sorry for our . . . little disagreement earlier. I understand that you wanted to test my capabilities."

Obed gave him nothing. It was like talking to a fence post, or an unusually stupid cow. Rodrick soldiered on. "Rest assured, I'll fight for the party when called upon to do so. Safeguarding our passage is foremost on my mind. I was curious, if you don't mind me asking, about your faith. I confess, I've never been a particularly religious man, but it's more from ignorance than lack of interest. I'd be interested to hear more about your god Gozreh—"

Obed's voice was as flat as a basalt plain. "You have no interest in Gozreh."

Rodrick blinked. Obed was a *priest*. Who knew what powers he had? Could he recognize lies just by the sound of your voice?

"Tell me what you *really* want to know," Obed said, turning his hooded head toward Rodrick.

I want to know what this artifact we're searching for might be, Rodrick thought, and how much I can sell it for. That answer would hardly go over well. To be safe, Rodrick felt he should ask a real question, something he really did want to know, in case Obed could sense dishonesty. "I'd like to know whether or not we're likely to face a dragon at some point on this journey."

Silence from Obed.

"It's just, Hrym told me you'd asked him about dragons, and if we're facing something like that, I'd like to be prepared, so . . ."

"No dragons." Did the priest sound amused? "The artifact we seek may have guardians, but nothing in my research leads me to believe they will be draconic. But I understand you rescued Hrym from the hoard of a linnorm. Surely you have experience conquering monstrous reptilian creatures? A linnorm is not a dragon, but they are similar."

"Ah, well, as to that—" Rodrick began.

"The linnorm was sleeping," Hrym said, voice muted by the sheath but still audible. "They hibernate, you know, sometimes for centuries. Rodrick crept in and snatched me away. The only reason I didn't scream and wake the beast was because Rodrick promised me untold riches." Hrym paused. "When can I expect to receive those, by the way?"

"You will both receive ample riches when this quest is complete," Obed said, and he *still* sounded a little amused. "I hope that will please you, sword."

"It's a start, anyway," Hrym said.

"Leave me now, Rodrick. I have much to think about. I am sure Zaqen can allay any further concerns you have, or answer any additional questions."

"Of course," Rodrick said. "Sorry to have bothered you." He slowed his horse, letting Obed pull away, and fell back closer to Zaqen. "You're right," he told her. "Obed is being just as warm and companionable with me as always."

Zaqen giggled. "A dragon? Really? That's what you were worried about?"

"Perhaps if you'd tell me what to expect, I wouldn't have to indulge in wild speculations."

She shrugged. "We'll ride forever and a day, and then we'll reach Brevoy. Then we'll go as far north as we can, we'll recover the artifact, you'll get paid, and we'll all go our separate ways."

"A plan admirable in its simplicity," Rodrick said. "Though it seems to conceal a wealth of mysteries."

"Mysteries are good," the wizard—or whatever she was—said. "I'd hate to see you lose interest."

Their progress through Daggermark was steady and uneventful. The kingdom was one of the largest and safest in the region, despite having an essentially anarchic form of government that might best be described as a 'murderocracy.' Some of the towns they passed were miniature military dictatorships or overgrown armed forts, while others had mayors or even town councils. The locals eyed them with cold, polite suspicion, gouged them on the prices of everything the party bought, and sent them on their way with no goodbyes. After several days in the country, Rodrick realized that if a stranger greeted him warmly or offered even a casual courtesy, Rodrick would start looking around for the dagger in his own back or the garrote around his throat.

They avoided the capital itself, the so-called city of assassins, following the path of the river almost directly northward. The one night they stayed in an inn, Obed took a room of his own and had a bath made ready. Rodrick wondered whether the man actually slept in the tub. It wouldn't surprise him. He loved water the way Rodrick loved women and wine.

Most days they made camp and slept out under the stars, even as the nights grew colder—just a hint of the weather they'd have to endure in Brevoy. Zaqen had said they were going to the edge of the map, and the edge of most maps Rodrick had seen were limned in ice. Hrym didn't mind, but Hrym was incapable of freezing to death.

Unfortunately, speculating about the future with minimal information to fuel that speculation didn't occupy the mind for long. After several days in Daggermark, Rodrick was sufficiently bored to wish for assassins in the night, just to break up the monotony. He barely even noticed anymore when Zaqen ate her fish raw and Obed ate nothing, or thought it peculiar that the priest submerged himself somehow nightly, or felt his flesh crawl when Zaqen tittered at nothing, or felt vaguely nervous just at the sight of the camel. They were settling dangerously into routine, and routine was death.

"We're settling dangerously into routine," he said to Hrym while trailing far behind Zaqen's camel on the road. "And routine is—"

"Wonderful stuff," Hrym said. "We get paid the same whether we expend any effort or not. It's glorious."

"It's *boring*. Being bored is one thing I can't abide. Worse, from a practical standpoint, it makes me lose my edge. I become lulled, complacent, and lose the eternal vigilance that makes me so effective as a warrior."

"You're not a warrior," Hrym scoffed. "You're a thief and swindler and fortune hunter who has, on occasion, gotten into a fight."

"And you're a lazy hedonist who just happens to be trapped in the form of a weapon of terrible power. Sometimes we have to pretend to be what we appear to be."

"So you're wishing bandits would descend on us, then?" Hrym said.

"Not necessarily. But I'd go for seeing something *interesting*. Meeting an immortal peddler selling artifacts from beyond the Windswept Wastes. Discovering a ruin filled with comely nymphs. Camping beneath a tree that weeps ruby tears. I'd even settle for a talking fish that grants wishes. Instead it's nothing but sullen peasants, passing military patrols, picked-bare fruit trees, and ordinary river trout."

"You carry with you a sword of living ice," Hrym said, "and you complain that your life is lacking in *wonder*?"

"You're nice enough," Rodrick said, "but we've been together for years now. I know you too well to feel much in the way of wonder anymore."

"It's almost as bad as being married," Hrym said. "Just be patient. We're near the border, such as it is, between Daggermark and Loric Fells. Which, judging by the conversations I overheard back in Tymon, is a land lacking in even the rudiments of civilization, infested with goblin camps and troll caverns and will-o'-wisps and all the hideous beasts that nature in her wisdom has chosen to bestow upon the north."

"You think we'll see wonders there, then?" Rodrick said. "A new vista over every ridge?"

"No," Hrym said, "but I think you'll be terrified enough by the growls coming from the icy fog all around that you'll forget to be bored."

"It's not as if the borders are well marked in this area, master," Zaqen said, peering at an old map rolled out atop a flat stone near the edge of the campsite. The map was illuminated by some sort of wizardly light, but as was typical with Zaqen's magics, it wasn't proper white or fiery yellow light, but rather a sickly greenish globe that bobbed disconcertingly in the air beside her head. She drew her finger along the path of a blue line that squiggled toward the top of the map while Rodrick squinted and tried to make sense of what he was looking at.

Obed didn't bother to look at the map. That, presumably, was what he had Zaqen for.

"The last good road petered out this morning, though," Zaqen said, "and if we're not in Loric Fells now, we will be soon. I think we've seen our last glimpse of civilization for a while. The Dagger River becomes the Wyvernkill River here—ha, good, presumably all the wyverns will be dead then, that's a comfort, though I wonder what killed them. We can follow that for a while. I know you prefer to stay close to water as long as possible, though we should avoid getting *too* close to the fortress of Rookwarden, which lies along the banks of the Wyvernkill. There's no telling what monsters inhabit the place now, but it's typically been home to goblin chieftains and hag rulers. The sooner we angle westward, the sooner we'll return to something approximating the civilized world."

Obed sighed heavily, as if geography itself were conspiring against him, and trudged toward the river.

"If the Fells are so wild, where did you get a map?" Rodrick said.

Zaqen shrugged. "It's amazing what money can buy. This is a map from one of the expeditions made by Loric himself. I trust it in terms of gross geography . . . and very little else. I'm sure most of the goblin settlements have moved and shifted as the tribes made war on one another, and besides Rookwarden, there is literally no point of interest marked."

"Loric, eh?" Rodrick said. "What did he do to get the place named after him?"

"He was the closest thing the place ever had to a human ruler, though he's long dead. Anyone who stays in this wilderness for long is apt to die—and that includes most of the natives. Fortunately for us, we're just passing through."

"How long will this passing through take?"

"Oh, it's no more than a hundred miles," she said airily. "Over entirely wild terrain. Then we'll be out of Loric Fells and into the safety of . . . well, nowhere in particular. Unclaimed lands, essentially. I hope we'll pass well north of the ruins of Heibarr, which has no living citizens at all, and more ghosts than many cities have rats. Then there's a vast forest we can either pass through or skirt around, then Pitax, and then the Stolen Lands, which are practically part of Brevoy, and then Brevoy itself."

"And once we're in Brevoy it's all hot meals and soft beds, no doubt," Rodrick said.

"More like danger and tomb-raiding and people trying actively to kill us in particular, instead of merely trying to kill us because we happened to pass by. But I'm not worried. We have your good right arm to protect us."

"My left isn't so bad either," Rodrick said.

"No worse than your right, anyway," Hrym said. "Which isn't to say either one of them is particularly good."

Chapter Eight
Sword in the Mist

By noon the next day, there was no doubt they'd entered Loric Fells. The weather turned markedly colder, and the ground became more steep and wild, with a creeping, icy mist clinging to the ground even long after the sun came up. Camping in this place would be hellish: the freezing fog could conceal any manner of monsters, ruining any hope of sleeping with a sense of security.

"Isn't this air refreshing!" Hrym boomed. "And bracing!"

Rodrick shushed him. "Do you want to call every goblin within a hundred miles down on us?"

"Goblins, feh. Do you know how many goblins I've killed?"

"No, actually." Zaqen guided her camel closer. They were all riding in cozier formation than usual, with the horses more willing to tolerate Zaqen's company. They clearly smelled and heard things that bothered them more than she did.

"Well, none, actually, that I can recall," Hrym said. "Zero goblins. Don't you think I should rectify that? Goblins have lots of gold, don't they?"

"I imagine they take whatever they can loot off the bodies," Rodrick said. "Gold included. So you may continue to live in hope. But what are you talking about, refreshing air? You don't even breathe."

"I am not without senses," Hrym said. "Do I not *feel*?"

"Oh, I know you can feel," Rodrick said. "Did you know, Zaqen, that Hrym let me sharpen him with a whetstone for *months* before letting it slip that, being magical, his edge would never grow dull? He just liked the *sensation*." Rodrick shuddered.

"I miss that whetstone," Hrym said wistfully. "I'd grown really quite fond of that whetstone. I still wonder whatever happened to her, sometimes."

Just past midafternoon, the goblins came. They didn't attack in the manner Rodrick had expected, rushing down in a great howling horde of primitive weapons and gnashing teeth and stinking rags, overwhelming the party with monstrous force. They assembled along a ridge to the west, perhaps fifty of the creatures, lined up and looking down on the party, and conversing among themselves in chattering, wheedling voices. It was like being watched by a class of hideous schoolchildren. The tallest goblins were barely over three feet high, their heads like great oversized melons, but more amply supplied with teeth. They wore furs and leathers—what kind of creatures the leather came from was perhaps best left unconsidered—and carried surprisingly nice armaments, polearms and axes and spears, doubtless looted from the remains of expeditionary forces that had fallen to their horde over the years. Several of them were riding dog-sized, ratlike mounts that looked mean enough to tussle with wolves and win.

Rodrick considered the terrain. He was no tactician, but it didn't take a military genius to know that his party's position was not advantageous. The goblins had the high ground. Rodrick's group had been following the river, as Obed insisted, so they were cut off from retreat on the east by water. North was just more rough terrain, with ankle-twisting rocks and holes hidden by the clinging mist. They could try to turn the horses and race back the way they'd come, but they'd just be run down and routed by the horde. There was always the option of charging directly at the goblins, Rodrick supposed, which would have the advantage of finishing things quickly.

"Do you think you can kill a small goblin army?" Rodrick said. "By yourself?"

"Certainly," Hrym said.

"Without me and the other mortals dying in the process?"

"What," Hrym said, "without *any* of you dying? I suppose I can try."

"I hope you can win," Rodrick said. "Unless you fancy being part of a goblin's treasure trove."

"Gold is gold," Hrym said. "I'll take whatever golden bed I can find."

"You'd miss my conversation," Rodrick said.

"Why don't they attack us?" Zaqen said, sounding more curious than frightened.

"Why should they?" Rodrick said. "They have us hugely outnumbered, pinned between them and the river. They can take their time. They're probably discussing who gets to eat which of us first. I'm sure if we were a larger force, they would have ambushed us, but as it is . . ." He shrugged. "They're not worried. I'm not even sure they're contemptuous. They're probably just wondering what possessed three humans to go wandering around in the Fells. Or else they're worried that we're bait in some kind of a trap, and that we have a division of mounted cavalry hidden in the mist over there." Rodrick cocked his head. "I suppose we should start trying to kill them."

"Goblins are superstitious," Zaqen said. "A sufficient display of magic might send them scattering away." She glanced at Obed, who wasn't paying any attention to the goblins at all, instead gazing at the river. "Master? Do you have any thoughts?"

Obed turned his hooded head and peered up at the creatures. "I will parley," he said, in the tones of a man grudgingly agreeing to do a tedious chore. He swung down from his horse and began trudging westward toward the goblins before Rodrick could think of a response, rational or otherwise.

"They'll kill him," Rodrick said. "They'll eat him." He paused. "Do I still get paid, if he gets eaten?"

"My master is very good at staying alive," Zaqen said, but even she was worried.

"What does he mean *parley*?" Rodrick said.

"It means to have a courteous conversation with one's enemy," Hrym said, and Rodrick growled.

"I know what the word means. But what good can it possibly do? They probably don't even speak the same—"

Obed spoke, more loudly than Rodrick had ever heard him speak before, and the language was a strange one, full of guttural gurglings and high-pitched wheezes and the clacking of teeth. The effect on the goblins was electric: they began milling around frantically, then moved apart, letting one of their number move to the front. He was hugely fat—and given that these were creatures who could eat their own weight in a day and still be hungry for breakfast in the morning, that was astonishing—and he rode a goblin dog nearly the size of a pony. The fat goblin barked something down at Obed, and the priest responded in a tone that was forceful and confident.

The goblin war chief flinched, looked around at his fellows, then gazed up at the sky. He growled something, and Obed approached more closely, reaching into his robe. He passed a small object over to the goblin—was it a wand of some kind, or a small rod?—and the war chief took it reverently. He pointed it at the sky, and a moment later, a gout of flame burst forth from the end of the rod.

"Oh, good," Hrym said. "Obed has given the goblin horde magical fire. That's *marvelous*."

"What are you worried about?" Rodrick tried to hide his dismay and worry. "You can't melt."

"No, but magical fire can melt my ice, which gives us something of a disadvantage."

"My master knows what's he's doing," Zaqen said. "Besides, there are only fifty of them or so. I can kill . . . oh, ten. You two do, say, twenty each . . ."

"They also have those dogs," Rodrick said.

"All right, if you insist," Zaqen said. "You can also kill the dogs. I'm a reasonable woman."

But Obed turned away from the goblin horde and began making his way carefully down the hill back to them, and the goblins melted away like mist—not like the mist in Loric Fells, obviously, which never melted away, but ordinary mist.

"That's it?" Rodrick said. "You gave them a gift, and they went away? Why didn't they kill us and *take* the wand?"

Obed paused beside his mount. "Those of us who worship gods can sometimes find common ground, Rodrick."

"You can't tell me those goblins worship *Gozreh*?" Rodrick said.

"Many goblins live near the sea," Zaqen said thoughtfully. "I suppose it makes a certain amount of sense—"

"I thought goblins all worshiped, I don't know, demons!" Rodrick said.

"Bigot," Obed said, and climbed onto his horse. He settled himself, took the reins in his hands, and said, "No, they do not worship Gozreh. They have other allegiances. But there are alliances among the gods, which sometimes translate to alliances between their mortal followers. You look at the goblins and see monsters, but they are creatures of nature, worshipers of the forests and caves and streams and wild places—and the gods of those places. The wand I gave them was not a gift, but a payment. They will pass the word among their allied tribes that we are to be given safe passage. Which, for goblins, merely means they will not attempt to kill us, not that they will defend us. But I will take whatever help I can. I am making your job easier once again, mercenary."

"So we can ride through Loric Fells safely?" Rodrick said. "That's a nice trick."

"No, it's only goblins who won't try to kill us," Hrym said. "And only some goblins, at that. There are still trolls, hags, and shambling heaps of carnivorous vegetation to worry about."

Rodrick shook his head. "Even so . . . perhaps I should reconsider religion."

"If I were you," Hrym said, "I would hesitate to join any religion that would actually accept you as a member."

"Keep feeling superior, sword. At least I don't lust after whetstones."

Hrym groaned. "You *had* to bring her up again, didn't you?"

The river gradually widened and became less a great road of water and more a low, boggy expanse, its edges softening and blurring until the once-distinct banks became a marsh of mud and reeds. There was still deep water farther out, but it flowed so sluggishly it might as well have been a lake. Night began to fall, but there was literally nowhere suitable to make camp, as it took all their effort to avoid accidentally becoming mired in stinking mud. The fact that the ground was covered in swirling white mist didn't help matters.

"I could ice over a bit of the mud," Hrym said. "You could camp on that. Solid ground, at your service."

"Ah, yes, nothing finer than sleeping on a bed of ice," Rodrick said. "Quite cozy."

"You could lay down leafy boughs, or something," Hrym said. "Even light a fire. My ice is magical, and doesn't easily melt."

"We will keep going," Zaqen said. "The master is confident that we will find a place to camp shortly."

"I don't know why he thinks that," Rodrick said. "It seems—"

"There," Obed said, and pointed into the river.

Rodrick squinted. There was an island there about thirty yards out, and it was clearly solid enough to support a number of good-sized trees. "You want us to camp there? It doesn't leave a lot of options for retreat, being surrounded by water on all sides."

"Yes, but it's unlikely a passing troll will wander through, either." Zaqen sighed. "My master loves swimming, but I don't. And I have no idea how the camel will react to that. Where she's from, it's rare to find a body of water you can't step across. Horses can swim, can't they?"

"Swimming won't be necessary," Rodrick said. "Hrym's kind offer to give us all hypothermia gives me a better idea. Can you build us a bridge, old friend?"

"'Old friend,' he says, when he *wants* something," Hrym said.

Rodrick held the sword out at arm's length, aiming it toward the river, and vapor began to swirl around the blade. "It's easy, with this mist," Hrym said. "Lots of moisture to work with." Indeed, it was almost as if a portion of the swirling mist near the ground hardened, growing stiff, creating a path perhaps ten feet wide that stretched all the way from the marshy water's edge to the island in the deep water.

"Will it support our weight?" Zaqen said.

"You could build a castle on top of it," Hrym said. "Fear not. But watch your step. I aimed for a certain roughness of texture, but it's still ice, and apt to be slippery."

Zaqen climbed down off her camel and probed at the path with the toe of her boot. She grunted. "All right." She took her animal's reins and led it onto the ice. The camel followed her with no more complaint than usual. The ice didn't crack or shift at all. Hrym did good work.

Obed glanced at the ice bridge contemptuously and just stomped off into the water, wading alongside the bridge until he caught up with Zaqen, his head roughly level with her ankles. He tore his robe off and threw it across the ice, where the wizard picked it up without complaint. Obed then dove into the water and began steadily swimming toward the small island.

"I'll just get your horses, then," Rodrick called. "And my horse. All three horses. No need to thank me, or even ask me, really, it's all part of the service."

"Hmm," Hrym said from behind him.

"I know," Rodrick muttered. "Saddlebags full of gold, a bridge you can melt with a thought, dumping the wizard in the water. But we wouldn't make it far in this country, especially in the dark. And there's still that artifact . . ."

"Yes, all right," Hrym said. "You can't blame a sword for being tempted."

Rodrick tethered his gelding to the packhorse, which was already tethered to Obed's mount. He led the three of them across the icy bridge, crystals crunching beneath his feet, but it was a rough enough surface to provide decent footing. It was slow going with the horses, but eventually he made it across. By the time he led the horses onto solid ground, Zaqen was already setting up camp near the remains of a lightning-shattered dead tree. The tree must have once shaded a great expanse of the island, sucking up all the available sunlight, because the area around it was relatively clear of undergrowth. Obed was nowhere to be seen—presumably he was communing with the gods and washing his hair and so on.

"I suppose I'd better check the island," Rodrick said. "Make sure there aren't any monsters in the vicinity."

"Besides us, you mean," Zaqen said, and tittered. "It's hardly necessary. The master will set up wards to protect us, and the island is hardly big enough to hold much in the way of dangerous wildlife. And he can sense life auras—"

"You hired me to protect you," Rodrick said. "At least let me go through the motions. Besides, there could be traps, deadfalls, pits full of spikes, or huge carnivorous plants here. Do carnivorous plants have auras?"

Zaqen shrugged. "Please yourself. Can Hrym melt the bridge for now? And just make it again in the morning? We've got this nice natural moat to protect us, after all . . ."

"Of course," Hrym said. "If my wielder will just wave me in the proper direction . . ."

Rodrick secured the horses, then took the sword through the dripping trees back to the bridge. He brandished Hrym at the river, and the magical ice melted, steaming away into nothingness and mist. Then they walked the perimeter of the island—which didn't take long, as it was a blobby circle perhaps fifty feet across at its widest, with rocky edges—and poked into a few copses of trees. Hrym could see as well in the dark as he could in the light, and he didn't notice any signs of dangerous prior habitation.

Rodrick stood for a while on the edge of the island, looking at the river's far shore, which was a greater distance away than the near shore, perhaps a hundred yards. Greenish lights bobbed there among the trees. "Will-o'-wisps," he said. "I've heard of those. Never seen them before. They like to lure people to their deaths and eat their terror, don't they?"

"Possibly," Hrym said. "They could just be bubbles of swamp gas."

"Aren't you the optimist? I think it's more likely they're treacherous flying monsters that live on fear."

"It's lucky you're utterly without fear, then," Hrym said.

"I think you said 'fear' when you meant 'scruples.' As long as the wisps stay over there, though, they don't worry me."

He returned to camp, and found Obed had acquired fish—the priest even spoke, briefly, to praise the quantity and quality of edible wildlife in the local streams. They passed the evening as usual, with Rodrick finally driving Hrym into the center of the campsite to keep watch before going to sleep.

Sometime very deep in the night, Rodrick woke with an unusually powerful need to urinate. Probably because of the steady constant sound of water all around him, from the river on both sides to the moisture dripping off the trees—he'd even dreamed of exploring some subterranean ruin that was half-submerged in a sunless lake. He glanced around the camp, and saw that Obed and Zaqen were both sleeping soundly. Another perfect opportunity for horse-and-gold theft that he must, once again, forgo taking.

He went a little ways from the camp to relieve himself against a tree . . . and then heard a snatch of song.

Rodrick closed his trousers, frowning, then touched the knife at his waist. Singing, in Loric Fells. That couldn't be good. Were there any such things as river sirens?

Obed's protective wards were potent. Nothing much larger than a raccoon could breach the perimeter of the island without all sorts of alarms being raised. Rodrick went to investigate, listening as hard as he could for another snatch of song, but there was nothing.

Until he reached the edge of the island. There, seated on a stone overlooking the water, was a woman dressed in furs of white and brown, her hair shining black in the moonlight, a lute in her hands, gazing at the river like a poet in the midst of composing an ode. She turned her face to Rodrick, and it was just the kind of face he liked best on a woman: pretty, sharp-featured, with eyes that hinted at intelligence and perhaps a bit of mischief. But when she saw Rodrick, those eyes widened, and she dropped the lute, which bounced off the rocks and splashed into the water. "Who are you?" she cried. "What are you doing on my island?"

Chapter Nine
The Witch's Island

Interesting," Rodrick said. "Let me see. You're not a succubus, are you? You'd be more seductive, then, I think—more overt, showing less fur and more flesh. I've seen you from the back, so you're not a huldra, one of those fey who look like beautiful women from the front but resemble hollow trees from behind—I killed one of those once, in a barrow mound of all places. You could be a doppelganger taking on the form of a woman you once met—or killed once—though I thought doppelgangers were more interested in preying on human society, so it's unlikely to find one here in the wild. Or—"

The woman drew herself up haughtily. "I am the last survivor of Loric's own expeditionary force, and I have settled on this island because the fishing is good, and because trolls do not like to swim. I didn't expect to ever see another human again, and while I understand that you view me with suspicion—"

"No, sorry," Rodrick said. "I explored this island when my people made camp. There was no one settled here."

"There is a cave—"

"No, there's not," he said, almost gently. "And we have a priest with us who assured me there were no thinking creatures on the island. Which means you came from the outside, and are trying to get *in*. I imagine you're sitting just beyond the perimeter of the priest's magical wards, aren't you? Hoping to lure us out and pick us off one by one, no doubt."

The woman sloughed off the furs around her shoulders, revealing a damp, white linen shirt that was mostly unbuttoned. She sat down on the rock, leaning backward, thrusting her chest out at him. "Do you find me comely?" she said.

"Of course. I'm enjoying the view immensely while I can. I expect you'll turn into something less attractive soon—perhaps a woman with the head of a tiger or a jackal? I've heard of shapeshifters like that."

"Perhaps I'm just a very beautiful witch." She tossed her hair and fixed him with a sultry stare, her foxlike face more amused and mischievous than ever. "I'll grant you that my intentions are not kind, but why are you so sure I'm an *inhuman* monster?"

"Because you're too exactly my type of woman," Rodrick said sadly. "And I haven't done anything good enough in my life to deserve *that* kind of luck, chancing upon such a woman in a place like this." After getting a last eyeful of her bosom, he started back toward the center of the island.

"Where are you going?" Her voice was less mellifluous now, and had a harsh, peeved tone.

He turned back. "To wake my friends. We are a small party, but not without resources, and I'm sure one of them will have a better idea of what you are, exactly, and how to banish you, or slay you, or whatever seems appropriate. But in thanks for the display of tantalizing cleavage, I'll give you this opportunity to leave here unharmed. Be gone before I return with my allies, and I won't pursue you."

She leaned forward and spat onto the rocks. "You are no fun at all, man. I like to *play* with my food first. But in the end, I'll overcome my disappointment, and eat you just the same."

Rodrick snorted. "Go on, then. Pass through the wards. I understand the results will be something to see. Our priest said something about flesh melting off bones, internal organs flinging themselves outward at great velocity, and so on. I think our wizard wove in a few spells of her own, and she has a taste for acid, tentacles, and other unpleasantness. If you do decide to charge me, please take on a less pleasant form first—it would spoil my fantasies *immensely* to see a body as lovely as yours so terribly mutilated."

The monster didn't seem particularly disturbed by Rodrick's description of the pain that awaited her. "Wards, yes, I sense them. Glyphs inscribed on stone, carved into the trunks of trees. It's thorough work. I applaud your priest. The island is terribly well protected." She sighed. "So I'll just have to do away with the island." The not-a-woman rose and walked backward until she stepped cleanly off the rock, and fell into the water.

Rodrick had the uncomfortable feeling that he'd been outsmarted somehow, a sensation familiar from countless bad nights at countless gaming tables. *What did she mean?*

He realized the answer a moment later, when the island began to sink.

"Hrym!" Rodrick shouted. "Zaqen, Obed, we're under attack, the island is sinking!" He stumbled into the camp, which was already being inundated by frothing water, and saw his warnings were hardly necessary. Zaqen and Obed were moving swiftly about, rescuing what they could from the inrushing waves.

"Report," Obed snapped, throwing his bedroll over the back of a nervous horse. The beast lifted its hooves out of the water, one at a time, as if unsure how it had come to be standing in a puddle.

Rodrick snatched Hrym up from the water, which had risen halfway up the length of his blade. "There was a woman—well, she *looked* like a woman, a beautiful one. She said she wants to eat us. The wards kept her out, but then she somehow made the island *sink*—"

"Nature magic," Zaqen said thoughtfully, looking at the water streaming around her calves. "If I wanted to sink an island, I might try raising the water level, or turning the rock underneath it to mud, though I'd have to swim down to do it . . ." She glanced at Obed. "A hag?"

"Likely." Obed stripped off his robe and went striding naked off into the gloom.

"Where is *he* going?" Rodrick said, baffled.

"Our wards are sinking along with the island," Zaqen said. "I imagine he's going to see what he can do about that. Do you think Hrym could conjure some more solid ground for us?"

"Plunge my tip into the water, Rodrick," Hrym said. "This is a bit tricky. I don't want to trap your legs in the ice."

Thinking about the woman—the hag?—coming upon them all frozen fast in ice, animals and humans alike, was horrifying. That would be like setting out a buffet for her. "Then concentrate, Hrym." He touched the sword to the surface of the water, which was now up to Rodrick's ankles.

There was a long moment when nothing much seemed to happen, and then there was a pressure against the bottoms of Rodrick's feet, and he began to rise, wobbling to keep his balance.

"A sheet of ice," Hrym said, and Rodrick thought crazily that the sword's voice should have sounded more *bubbly*, the way his own would if he tried to speak while his face was submerged in water. "The ice floe is floating, now, but I'll anchor it when I can . . ."

The camel took a couple of steps, and the ice tilted, reminding Rodrick of a summer afternoon spent out on a lake on a wooden float when he was sixteen, kissing and more with a beautiful girl, and the way the float would tilt this way and that as they rolled around. Had they tipped the float over, and fallen in the water? He couldn't remember. If they had, he was sure they'd splashed and laughed.

If this float tipped over, there would be less laughter. And probably more splashing.

Zaqen soothed her camel still, and the horses seemed to ponder whether they should plunge off the ice into the water or stay put, and decided to stand their ground. The trees all around them sank by degrees until their branches began to disappear under the water, and Rodrick was glad they'd chosen a clearing for their camp. If they'd been underneath branches, the sinking tees would have pressed them down and pushed them underwater to drown, or crushed them against Hrym's sheet of ice. The sight of the vanishing trees was incredibly surreal.

The icy platform stabilized, Hrym freezing it solidly to the bottom of the lake, Rodrick presumed, forming pillars of magical ice beneath them. "That's as good as it gets," Hrym said, and Rodrick pulled the sword from the ice.

"I've heard there are tribes in the north that put their elderly members on ice floes and send them drifting out to sea to die," Zaqen said. "I suppose it's more practical than trying to dig a grave in the ice."

"Should I make a bridge to shore?" Hrym said.

Rodrick considered. "If we run, whatever's waiting out there will chase us. She sank the island because she *wanted* us to panic, to try to swim away, so she could strike in the confusion. I think we should stand our ground, and wait for her to make a move first."

"You're the one with experience in battles," Zaqen said. "If you say that's the best path, I trust you. I'll keep my eyes open for something to kill."

"Where is Obed?" Rodrick scanned the water. "Do you think he's . . ."

Zaqen shook her head. "He lives. I would know if he'd died. We have a . . . connection. He is a very good swimmer, and has spells that allow him to move easily in the water, and under the water, without needing to emerge for breath. I'm sure he's doing his best to save us."

Rodrick grunted and turned slowly in the center of the icy platform, looking for danger. There was no sign of the hag, but the will-o'-wisps across the river began to bob toward them, and Rodrick cursed. "Those damn things."

"Hmm," Zaqen said. "They feed on fear, you know. You must be afraid. They sense it."

"Maybe the horses are frightened," Rodrick snapped.

"Mere animal panic doesn't interest them," Zaqen said. "They have more refined tastes." She walked to the edge of the platform. "Hello, cousins!" she called, and one of the balls of bluish light floated closer to her. Zaqen bowed her head, and the two of them seemed to confer.

"Is she talking to that thing?" Hrym said. "It's a floating ball of horrible magic. Look, it's got a *skull* at its center—that thing doesn't have bones at all, certainly not humanoid ones, but it's gotten the idea that skulls are frightening, so it presents the image of one."

"Skulls *are* frightening," Rodrick said. "I live in terror of having my own skull exposed prematurely."

The will-o'-wisp bobbed, almost like a woman doing a curtsy, then floated away to rejoin its fellows, which withdrew to the far bank again. Zaqen came over, rubbing her hands together briskly. "There, that's done."

"You speak their language?" Rodrick asked.

Zaqen raised one furry eyebrow. "Will-o'-wisps speak many human languages, generally, though they're more conversant in Aklo—that's the tongue of certain creatures with ancestors from, let's say, *outside* this world. It's a tongue I've also mastered in the course of my arcane studies. They saw I did not fear them, and because they couldn't eat me, they consented to negotiate instead. They're going to stay nearby for a bit, in case the hag attacks. Or hags—they tell me a coven of them call this river home, several lesser hags led by an even crueler and more vile mistress. The wisps will wait and see if we're driven into, what was it, 'paroxysms of delicious terror.' But if we survive, they'll move on. I told them about the Worldwound, how the demon lord Deskari is spreading terror on a vast scale not so very far away, and they were grateful for the information. Nobody ever tells them anything, you know."

Rodrick shook his head. "I don't understand how you could have a civil, productive conversation with creatures so evil—"

Zaqen looked genuinely surprised. She put her hand on Rodrick's arm. "Why do you call them evil? All right, so they wish misery and horror on all sentient life, but that doesn't make them *evil*. They're just . . . different. It's not their fault they feed on the psychic energy of fear. They didn't choose their own biology. Driving people insane with terror is a necessity for them—fear is their agriculture."

"I'd call that a decent working definition of 'evil,'" Rodrick said, but before they could argue further, the waters on three sides of them began to froth and churn, and three creatures, nearly identical, rose from the water. They were hags, Rodrick knew, though he'd never seen such creatures in the flesh—two of them were just a bit shorter than Rodrick himself, thin, so hunchbacked they made Zaqen seem a marvel of anatomical engineering. Those two had hair like rank seaweed falling across their hideous faces, their flesh the green of rotten meat in the moonlight.

The third hag, who stood taller than Rodrick despite her own terrible hunch, had black skin that looked not so much horribly warty as *armored* and solid as iron. She wore a belt of small human hands, and her claws made a sound like rusty metal as they clashed together. She grinned at Rodrick, her teeth as filthy and stinking as a drain.

"Greetings, traveler," she said, in the same voice of the beautiful fox-faced woman on the rock. Then she winked.

Chapter Ten
Claws in the Night

Zaqen didn't hesitate, just flung out her arm and sprayed a stream of acid at the hag nearest her. The hag dove aside, splashing into the water and vanishing from sight, only to reemerge a few feet away and renew her assault.

Rodrick advanced on the greater hag with Hrym held before him in guard position, all too aware that he couldn't face this hag without turning his back on at least one of the others. Still, flinging a few spikes of ice or even freezing a hag's feet to the floe would even the field—

The mistress of the hags surged forward, lashing out with her claws, and Rodrick lifted up Hrym to block. Her reach was astonishingly long, though, and she managed to scratch his side with one of her black talons, raking down from beneath his rib cage nearly to his hip. Just a scratch, but Rodrick stumbled back, hissing at the pain and dropping his guard.

"Steady on," Hrym said, and Rodrick struggled to raise the sword again. Actually *fighting* with a sword wasn't exactly his strong point; he seldom needed to do more than wave Hrym around and pose dramatically. Hrym was doing his best to make up for Rodrick's failings, sending a cone of icy wind toward the hag, who adroitly dodged it. Rodrick gritted his teeth and swung Hrym in her direction, flinging a spear of ice at her and slashing her arm, which trickled a thick black substance in lieu of blood. He was dimly aware of Zaqen battling another hag, flashes of greenish light appearing off to his right as she lashed out with spells. The horses and even the camel had panicked, plunging off the ice and trying to swim for shore.

Hrym was humming by then, icy vapor billowing up and down the length of his blade, working up to one of his truly impressive magics. The sword's true capabilities were not fully known to Rodrick—perhaps not even to Hrym himself—but with enough time and effort Rodrick knew the sword could summon rains of hailstones the size of grapefruit, freeze enemies in solid blocks of magical ice, and perform other icy wonders.

Someone struck Rodrick from behind—the unattended hag, presumably—and he stumbled forward. Then the hag leader was upon him, smashing his arm aside—and Hrym flew from his nerveless fingers, hit the water, and instantly sank.

Rodrick stared at the place in the water where his best friend and greatest weapon had disappeared. The sword could not move on his own. The best he could do was spin a cocoon of ice to make himself float, but they'd discussed the drawbacks of such a defensive move often—Hrym would then be at the mercy of the current, drifting wherever the river did, perhaps so far Rodrick could never find him. The sword would more likely wait on the river bottom, hoping to be retrieved—

The hags converged on Rodrick.

Right. He had more pressing issues than his lost friend at the moment.

He reached for the knives at his belt and slashed out with both hands, hoping to hamstring the hags, and struck home both times, making them hiss and back away. His blades were enchanted with a little charm that made their cuts unusually painful, as if the metal were coated in salt and lemon juice and bee venom. He had no illusions that he could battle these two hags with just a pair of lightly enchanted daggers, though. "A little help!" he shouted.

Something broke the surface beyond the icy platform, and the hag that Zaqen was fighting fell back into the water, shrieking. Had she been attacked by some kind of river monster? Or was Obed finally doing something useful? Whatever the cause, that hag's misfortune freed up Zaqen to help Rodrick, and she loped across the ice, reaching out with an arm that seemed to extend impossibly far, stretching out as if made of soft candle wax. She held a small, pale wand—one of Obed's magical toys, no doubt—and touched the smaller hag on the leg. The monster hissed and tried to scuttle away, her leg turning from green to gray and dragging behind her, as if it were in the process of turning to stone.

Wonderful. Now Rodrick only had to fight *one* hag. Of course, *she* wasn't being petrified before his eyes. He scrambled to his feet, knives extended, watching the monster. Her face shimmered, briefly, and became that of the foxlike beauty he'd met on the rocks, her features rendered grotesque by their appearance on such a monstrous body. She was too close for him to throw a knife effectively, but if he moved close enough to slash with his blades, those terrible claws would cut him open.

"Hello, lover," she cooed. "I will eat you starting with your feet, I think, so you can watch yourself disappear down my throat—"

The feathered end of an arrow appeared in one of her eye sockets, with another appearing a second later in her other eye, and the illusory face vanished as the hag groaned and fell backward. Rodrick didn't take time to ponder his good fortune, pivoting on his heel to whip one of his daggers through the air at the hag Zaqen was fighting. The creature's left side was nearly entirely stone now, but luckily, Rodrick's knife struck her on the right side, in the throat.

The hag shrieked, and Zaqen opened her mouth and spewed acid directly into her hideous face. The hag might have survived that attack, but two arrows took her in the face as well, and she fell to the ice.

For a moment, all was silence, save for the lapping of the river against their platform of ice. Rodrick and Zaqen turned in the direction the arrows had come from, and beheld a man dressed in furs and leathers walking toward them, bow in hand. He strode across the surface of the river as though it were the marble floor of a ballroom. "Hail, adventurers!" he called, in a distressingly loud and cheerful voice.

Obed burst from the water and dragged himself naked onto the platform of ice. His lack of clothing didn't appear to bother him, which was fortunate, as his spare clothes were on the back of a horse that had swum away. Rodrick got his first good look at Obed's features—he was astonishingly pale in the moonlight, and had a long face, thin arching eyebrows, dark eyes, and no hair at all. He had noble features, in a way, though Rodrick couldn't place his ethnicity or nationality at a glance, something he was usually adept at—such rapid classifications were very helpful when trying to swindle someone out of their material wealth.

"Nice of you to join us," Rodrick said.

Obed looked at him coldly. "There were two other hags, beneath the water. I slew them both, before dragging down a third. How many did you kill?"

Rodrick blinked. "Right. Very good. I should have known. I didn't kill any, technically, though I helped with one. But only because of our new friend there." He inclined his head toward the approaching man, who was obviously some sort of deep-woods ranger. "We were lucky he—"

"He's no friend of mine," Obed said.

"Be gracious, master," Zaqen murmured. "He may have saved our lives, and at the very least, he saved us some trouble. Rodrick might have died, at the very least."

"That would have been a great misfortune," Obed said. He suddenly looked alarmed. "Where is the sword? Hrym?"

Rodrick shook his head. "Fell into the water." He pointed. "He'll be fine, he's just on the bottom waiting to be retrieved—"

Obed dove back into the river immediately. Rodrick watched him vanish beneath the surface and shrugged. "Saves me the trouble of swimming down there myself, I guess."

The archer reached their icy platform, and Rodrick walked toward him, grinning and extending a hand. The fellow had a touch of the elven about him, his ears noticeably pointed, and he stood a head taller than

Rodrick. He had sun- and wind-worn features and a smile so wide he might have been reuniting with a long-lost brother instead of meeting strangers for the first time. He took Rodrick's hand in a grip that was crushing in its intensity, but Rodrick sensed the man wasn't trying to show off his strength or intimidate him—he was just the sort of person who never did anything halfway.

"I've been wanting to clear out that coven for the best part of year!" the archer said, voice booming and hâle. "But it was impossible to get them alone one by one, and I couldn't best five of them at once. I'm lucky you lot came along."

"We're lucky *you* came along," Zaqen purred, and Rodrick looked at her, surprised. Zaqen hardly made a habit of sounding so sweet and welcoming, though the archer *had* just saved them from possible death.

"My name is Cilian," he said. "The wind and the fires told me I would make great friends this day, and their omens guided me truly. May I know your names?"

Omens? Oh, dear. Maybe Gozreh really *was* taking an interest in their party—or perhaps Cilian was just a bit deluded. Rodrick had known plenty of superstitious folk over the years who saw portents where he only saw random happenstance. Their credulity could often be turned to advantage. "My name is Rodrick," he said. "I'm a warrior by trade, escorting the wizard Zaqen and her master, the cleric Obed, to Brevoy."

"Obed would be the naked fellow, then," Cilian said, just as the priest's hands appeared on the side of the platform, one gripping the ice, the other holding Hrym.

"I missed all the fun," Hrym was grumbling. "I've never been inside a hag before; that would have been interesting." Rodrick hurried across the ice, taking

Hrym in his hand and only then helping to pull Obed out of the water.

"A sword that speaks!" Cilian said. "Truly you are heroes destined for legend!"

"The archer's name is Cilian," Rodrick told the priest, who shook off his helping hand as if Rodrick's very touch was unclean. "He was a longtime enemy of that coven of hags."

"Then we have done him a favor by killing so many of them." Obed stared at the ranger. "That is good. That means we do not owe him anything."

"Indeed, I owe *you*," Cilian said. "And I will repay you by helping you make your way through these wild lands."

"Our party is not looking for further members," Obed said, but to Rodrick's surprise, Zaqen sidled up to him.

"Master. Given that our path takes us through the wilderness, we could benefit from the service of someone with knowledge of such terrain." She smiled. "And you know I have a fondness for half-breeds."

"If he interferes with our mission—" Obed began, but Zaqen said, "Yes, of course, I know, master."

The priest approached the ranger. "Very well, then, Cilian. We welcome you, and we are . . . grateful . . . for your offer to help."

"And I am glad to meet you." Cilian beamed. "I have never spoken with a gillman before. Why are you so far from the sea?"

After a long moment of silence, Zaqen began to titter.

"My wizard will explain later," Obed said, and then dove into the river and began swimming for shore.

After Zaqen harvested the eyes of the hags on the cold platform, Hrym iced the party a bridge to shore. They recovered the horses and the camel—which had all swum to shore and then stood around in a huddle, unwilling to venture into the dark—and made camp on dry-ish land.

Once they were settled, Zaqen sat down with Rodrick, Hrym, and Cilian to provide the promised explanation. Obed was, as usual, off by himself, though he was being even sulkier than normal.

"It's true," Zaqen said. "My master is not human, but a gillman."

"A Low Azlanti," Rodrick said. "Remarkable."

"Don't let him hear you call him that," Zaqen said. "He prefers to be called a *true* Azlanti, which is fair enough, since the gillmen are the only living remnants of that empire."

"That explains why he's always taking baths and jumping in ponds, anyway," Hrym said. "Gillmen can't survive long without submerging in water, can they?"

"He has a magical ring, actually," Zaqen said. "It allows him to breathe air indefinitely, and protects his skin from the ravages of life on dry land. An item like that is quite the prized possession among his people. He doesn't *need* to get in the water, not with that magic, but he misses the sea, and submerging regularly makes him feel better. I'm sure if you had a ring that granted you the ability to breathe water, allowing you to stay below the surface forever, you'd still want to crawl out of the water and feel the sun on your skin from time to time."

"Fair enough," Rodrick said. "But what would possess a gillman to go on such a long journey over land? Surely Gozreh has work for him beneath the waves, and could have sent a priest who *doesn't* have gills to Brevoy?"

Zaqen nodded. "My master has been reluctant to share all the details with you, because he is naturally a private man, and a bit suspicious of land-dwellers as a rule, but he has given me permission to share this much. We are indeed going to retrieve an artifact of Gozreh—but that artifact is hidden in a vault in the icy depths of the Lake of Mists and Veils, a wild and haunted body of water in the north of Brevoy. While we have with us certain magical items that can help land-dwellers like you and I navigate the watery realms, we're sure to be disoriented in such strange circumstances. My master has spent his entire life in the water, and is adroit at navigating in the lightless depths and looking out for danger that can come from *any* direction, including above or below. He is our best hope to actually breach the vault and claim the artifact."

Rodrick didn't like the idea of trying to break into any place submerged in a freezing lake, but he decided to table that objection. Zaqen was in a forthcoming mood, and he meant to take advantage of that. "Exactly what *is* the artifact?"

Zaqen shook her head. "In truth, even I do not know. Its nature was vouchsafed to my master in a vision. But he assures me it will vastly enhance the glory of his god."

"An epic quest!" Cilian rubbed his hands together happily. "Truly, meeting you is part of my fate!"

"While you're in the mood to reveal secrets," Hrym said, "if Obed is a gillman, dear Zaqen, may I ask—what exactly are *you*? You claim to be human, and a wizard—but I have my doubts on *both* accounts."

Zaqen giggled again.

Chapter Eleven
The Sorcerer She

I am human, sword," Zaqen said. "I'm not even really a half-breed like our friend Cilian here, no offense—"

"None taken," the huntsman said. "My parents loved one another very much, and each lent me their own strengths."

Zaqen nodded. "Lucky you. Both my parents were human. I can't speak to the 'love' part—love was not a sacrament of the particular nameless cult to which they were devoted. Theirs is not a religion I share, by the way, so fear not. Despite my human parents, there is reason to believe there is a certain . . . strangeness . . . to my ancestry. There are stories in the family that one of my great-grandparents was known to consort with . . . let's call them 'monsters,' for want of a better word. And some of those unions bore fruit, and those bore fruit in turn, and so here I am, essentially an ordinary woman, but with a certain peculiar twist to my bloodline. Some would call it a *taint*, but I've never found it anything but a help to me, though it can be awkward sometimes."

"What *sort* of monsters?" Rodrick said.

"I wasn't there at the time," Zaqen said. "So I could not say for certain. I don't think it was any sort of dragon. Or a devil. Or an elemental. I do not show the . . . typical results . . . of those sorts of ancestry. But there are other possibilities."

There were stranger creatures, Rodrick knew. Many-eyed, many-mouthed, gibbering horrors from realms of madness, or their progeny on this world. Hadn't she called the will-o'-wisps "cousins?" But that wasn't the sort of thing you accused someone of in polite company. Or even company as rough as this.

"And how about the wizard part?" Hrym said. "It's just that—and I hate to point this out—I've never once seen you even *look* at a book or scroll."

She shrugged. "True enough. I am not a wizard. I have never formally studied magic, though I *have* studied history, and have learned a great deal of forbidden and forgotten knowledge in the process. My magic comes naturally, not from study. I am a sorcerer. That touch of strange in my bloodline lends me a certain natural ability, which I have cultivated and learned to enhance over the years. As a rule, it's better to tell people you're a wizard—if you say 'sorcerer' they start worrying about you accidentally unleashing storms of magic, destroying towns, turning horses into heaps of smoking meat, and so on. We sorcerers have a not-entirely-undeserved reputation for losing control, though it has been many years since I've had an accident."

"So our entire relationship is built upon a foundation of lies." Rodrick smiled. "Good, good. I'm comfortable with that." He wondered what else they were lying about. One of the classic techniques of the trickster was to reveal a secret truth, so the mark would believe they'd been taken into your confidence, and having uncovered one lie, would not be quick to look for another. Someone telling him the truth just made Rodrick look that much harder for the next lie.

"We're coming clean now," Zaqen said. "We just didn't know you very well earlier. You can't blame us for holding back. Does the fact that I'm a sorcerer and my master is a gillman change your willingness to work with us?"

"Not particularly," Rodrick said. "Gold is gold."

Zaqen shrugged. "Then the information was irrelevant anyway." She turned her attention to Cilian. "And you—you'll escort us out of Loric Fells?"

"I have gazed into your fire," Cilian said, "and seen bewitching shapes there. I think I will join you for the remainder of your quest."

Zaqen blinked. "Ah. I fear my master may not be willing to hire you—"

"I require no payment." Cilian waved the issue away as though gold were the least important thing in the world, instead of the *most*. "I am guided by destiny, you see, and that destiny has led me to you. I believe that your quest will be my path to the Brightness."

The sorcerer frowned. "The Brightness?"

Hrym spoke up. "Brightness seekers are elves in search of enlightenment. The natural world gives them signs and omens to help guide them along the path of destiny, which can take . . . peculiar forms. They're mystics, often revered by their people, and some are said to have the ability to channel aspects of their own past lives, and to predict the future."

"Right and right!" Cilian said happily. "That is my path, though I am only just beginning, and all the portents point to you, my new friends. I would join my fate to yours."

"Ah." Rodrick cleared his throat. "I hate to point out the obvious, and perhaps I'm confused, but . . ."

"You're not an elf," Hrym said. "Half-elf, certainly, it's right there in the ears, but only actual *elf* elves can become Brightness Seekers, as I understand it. Something to do with their connection to the primal, natural . . . what have you."

Cilian nodded. "Yes. I have heard this too. But you must understand—I have always been restless. I left my home when I was young, and made my way into the forest, always in search of something, though I knew not what. And for these past many months, I see omens *everywhere*. In the movements of flocks of birds, the arrangement of stones falling down a mountainside, the leaping of fish in rivers, the flicker of flames . . . all hold truths and secrets and guidance for me, to be read as clearly as words on a page. Perhaps my elven ancestry is just unusually strong? What other explanation could there be for these signs and visions I behold all around me? For the way the world points me in one direction or another?"

You being a complete lunatic would explain it, Rodrick thought. For one.

Cilian rose. "It is nearly dawn. You must all be hungry after your ordeal. I will see what I can find for our breakfast."

Rodrick said, "Could you find something other than fish, do you think? No offense to fish, of course, but I've eaten an awful lot of it lately."

"Of course!" Cilian said. "For my new partners in destiny, anything." He strolled off toward a stand of trees, bow in hand, whistling cheerfully.

"Well, he's mad," Hrym said. "Shame to see such mental disorder in one so young, but there you have it."

"Yes," Zaqen said. "Not that I have anything against the mad, generally, but it's definitely a point of interest."

"If he can bring me a rabbit or something instead of a trout, I'll happily help him find his Brightness, whatever that is," Rodrick said. "You don't think he'll look into the fire one night and decide the omens say he should murder us all, do you?"

"That's another point of interest," Zaqen said. "I'm more concerned with what he'll do if we tell him he *can't* come with us once we get out of Loric Fells. I'm not sure how well he'd take to us meddling in his fate if my master refuses to accept him."

"I suspect he'd cheerfully ignore us and just keep walking alongside," Rodrick said. "Besides, he's a ranger. As long as we're out in the country, he could probably follow us secretly from a dozen yards away, and we'd never even notice. We may as well make use of him—parts of Brevoy are quite rough and wild, too. He could prove useful. Another armed man we don't have to pay, who thinks protecting us is his destiny? There's no downside."

Zaqen sighed. "I hope my master feels the same way."

Cilian returned with a duck, plucking its feathers as he came, so it was very nearly ready to cook by the time he got to camp. "There is a troll some distance to the west, but our path should not trouble him." Cilian joined them around the fire, where even Obed was warming his hands in the morning chill. "This general area is fairly safe—that coven of hags kept most of the other dangerous creatures away, and it will be some time before other monsters move in to take their place."

"My sorcerer tells me you wish to accompany us for our entire quest." Obed stared into the flames as if they were a hated enemy when he spoke. He didn't bother with keeping his hood up, now that they'd all seen the delicate gills on his neck.

Rodrick busied himself spearing the duck's carcass on a stick and arranging it over the fire, trying to appear uninterested, but he was keenly attuned to Obed's tone and body language. He wanted Cilian to join the party. Though he'd become grudgingly fond of Zaqen, strange as she was, his suspicions about Obed's true motives had only grown stronger. If things took a treacherous turn, he might be able to cultivate the half-elf as an ally.

Or use him as a semi-human shield.

"I feel that my journey toward my ultimate destiny includes this quest of yours," Cilian said solemnly. "I beg permission to lend my strength, weapons, and will to your cause."

Obed didn't answer for a long moment. Then he said, "I have prayed about this, and asked for guidance from my god. I believe that your motives are . . . pure."

Rodrick tried not to wince as he turned the spit on the fire. Obed's god talked to him about the motives of his fellow travelers? That couldn't be good.

The priest continued. "Traveling through this wilderness is taking longer than I had anticipated. If you can speed our passage, and hasten our arrival in Brevoy, I would welcome your assistance."

Cilian smiled broadly. "You will not regret this. Once you are rested, we can begin—"

"We can begin now," Obed said. "We slept half the night before we were interrupted by those hags. I will not waste daylight."

Rodrick sighed. "The duck is barely warm—"

"I'll eat it," Zaqen said. "I don't mind my meat rare. As I think you've noticed."

"Why couldn't you have been a fire sword, Hrym?" Rodrick said. "Then at least you could cook my breakfast while we travel."

"Why couldn't you have been a wealthy man with a treasure room full of gold?" the sword replied. "Then I could be resting in splendor instead of wandering in the wilderness and being dropped into rivers."

"I like this sword," Cilian said. "This sword is a very funny sword!"

"That's why we brought Hrym along," Zaqen said. "To keep us amused on our journey."

Cilian didn't travel with their group, but ranged ahead in the woods, scouting their path, appearing occasionally from any and all directions to give them suggestions about the best path. With Cilian's guidance, they suffered none of the setbacks that had plagued their first days in the Fells—when they didn't have to backtrack or skirt miles out of their way around a swampy bog, they made markedly better time.

Rodrick let his horse drift back a bit from the others so he could talk with Hrym privately. "What do you think of this Cilian?"

"I think we could easily bilk him out of all his worldly possessions, if he had any worldly possessions, which he doesn't. If he's as simple as he seems, I doubt he's capable of treachery."

"Could be a con," Rodrick mused. "Playing the simpleton, pretending he doesn't care about money, so he can rob us."

"What a clever long-term plan!" Hrym said. "To go live in the depths of Loric Fells for who knows how long, in hopes that a party of wealthy adventurers will wander by, so he can save their lives and worm his way into their confidence. Now, if it had been me, I would have just let the hags murder us and stolen our horses and loot, but I'm clearly not a master criminal like Cilian."

"Fair points, and well made," Rodrick said. "So you think his presence doesn't hurt us?"

"It could, if he tries to stop us from running off with the relic at the end of this endless journey. On the other hand, he might keep you alive, so on the whole, I welcome him to our party. If I were you, I wouldn't worry about the half-elf. I'd keep your eye on Obed instead."

"Why's that? Specifically?"

"When he saved me from the bottom of the river, he spoke to me. He pointed out, quite rightly, that you hadn't even been able to keep a grip on me in the midst of a trivial battle with a couple of wood witches—"

"They were *hags*!" Rodrick said. "A whole coven. That's hardly trivial."

"Obed asked if I might consider giving you up as a partner, and joining my fortunes to his instead. There were promises of glory, and more importantly, there were promises of *gold*."

"Ah ha. Did you take him up on his offer?"

"I told him I would consider it, of course," Hrym said. "We might be able to work out a swindle of some sort, after all, where I pretend to sell myself to him. But I got the definite impression that Obed could live without *your* presence on this quest—that he mostly wants me."

"Everyone always overlooks my subtler charms in favor of your obvious ones. It's enough to hurt a man's feelings."

"Oh, come," Hrym said. "It works to your advantage if people think you're just some idiot who happens to wield a magic sword. Obed seems to believe I just chose you as a partner because I need *someone* to carry me around, and you're as good as anyone. Obed looks at you and sees a handsome face and broad shoulders, and has no idea you've got a half-decent and unusually twisty mind lurking behind those cheekbones and apparently lovely eyes."

"Stop, please, you'll dizzy me with flattery."

"Enjoy it while it lasts, because—"

"Shh," Rodrick said. "I'm putting that unusually twisty mind of mine to work."

Chapter Twelve
Trapped in the Stolen Lands

The remainder of the journey through Loric Fells was almost pleasant. It was easier to enjoy the cold, clean air when you knew there was an archer lurking in the trees watching out for danger. Rodrick was delighted to have fresh, hot game for dinner instead of cold, undercooked fish, and with Cilian's expertise at gathering, there were even things *other* than meat at mealtimes: succulent roots, small red berries that were explosions of sweetness between the teeth, and salads of wild greens.

The huntsman continued to spend most of his time scouting, returning only to offer directional guidance or to bed down during the small hours of the night. Hrym reported that Cilian spent his conscious time in the night staring into the flames as he tended the fire, carving tiny wooden figurines which he subsequently burned, or just gazing at the stars and, occasionally, chuckling, presumably when the messages he saw around him everywhere in the natural world were particularly humorous.

After several days—they lost some time when Cilian had them travel out of their way to avoid encountering a troll den—they finally reached another branch of the many-tentacled Sellen River. There was no convenient bridge here, and Hrym created another bridge of ice, which Obed spurned, swimming across. Cilian repeated his water-walking trick, which left Zaqen and Rodrick to lead the mounts across.

"When did I become a servant?" Rodrick grumbled, trying to lead three horses at once across a bridge of ice. Not the life of creature comforts he'd always aspired to, or even the life of adventure and derring-do he'd tolerated.

"It's not so bad," Zaqen said. "All the table scraps you can eat!"

"How did you end up in Obed's employ, anyway?"

"You and I haven't gotten drunk enough together for me to tell you *that* story," Zaqen said. "Let's just say I owe him. He did me a good turn once. For his own reasons, of course, but in terms of utility, what does that matter? He made my life so vastly much better than it was that he can reasonably claim some service in return." She paused. "He also pays me exceptionally well. This is not the way we usually spend our time, you know. We're not always off on backcountry quests."

"So, what? You live with him in a palace under the sea? A bed of kelp, bannisters of coral, mirrors of mother-of-pearl?"

"I tend to serve as his agent on land," Zaqen said. Obed was waiting impatiently on the far shore, beckoning to them. "As he wishes me to do now." She hurried forward with her camel.

"I can't decide whether I really like her or not," Hrym said. "She's friendly enough, but do you doubt for a moment that she would stab you in the neck if Obed mentioned he might enjoy the sight of blood spraying out of your throat?"

"She does seem depressingly loyal," Rodrick said. "Oh well. If we convinced her to betray Obed, we'd just have to split the loot three ways anyway."

Cilian smiled at them broadly when they reached the far shore and Hrym began to dissolve the bridge behind them. "This river forms the western boundary of Loric Fells, by most reckonings," the huntsman said. "Three or four days should see us to Pitax."

"Where are we now?" Rodrick said.

Cilian shrugged. "Not all of the River Kingdoms are so neatly divided. We are near the haunted ruins of Heibarr, which I would suggest we avoid. Outsea is on the river, to the south. There is a great forest. Nothing you would call civilization."

"So no hope of a wench and a mug of ale, then."

"Not until Pitax," Cilian replied. "A greater city of rogues and cutthroats you'll never visit."

"Then what are we waiting for?" Rodrick said. "Rogues and cutthroats know how to have a good time, at least."

After the constant threat of Loric Fells, the routine of the following days was so stultifying Rodrick considered robbing the supply horse just to break up the boredom. They rose in the morning, traveled all day across marshy land—only pausing to rest the horses—and made camp wherever they happened to be standing when night fell. Obed took his baths, Zaqen drank her peculiar medicinal tea, and Cilian swooped in occasionally to tell them that the movement of clouds or the songs of birds or the ripples of water were full of favorable omens.

The only thing that kept Rodrick going was the thought of Pitax, one of the more enticing cities of the River Kingdoms, from all he'd heard . . . and so he nearly exploded when Obed said he had no intention of stopping at the city at all, but simply crossing the river some distance to the north and continuing on to Brevoy.

"I am the leader of this expedition," Obed said flatly when Rodrick voiced his dissatisfaction. "And you are being paid well to follow me. We have wasted enough time already, and to visit that den of thieves, and see you lose a day to drink, is simply impossible."

"If this artifact we're after is like most artifacts, it's been wherever it is for *centuries*," Rodrick said. "What does another day matter?"

"There may be others looking for it," Zaqen said. "Time may well be—"

"Silence." Obed scowled at Rodrick. "I do not need to justify myself to you, hireling. You are being given gold in exchange for your obedience—gold you have done precious little to earn so far, I might add."

"And if I say I'm going to Pitax anyway?"

"Then I will spit at your back as you go, and wish you rough waters in all your future voyages," Obed said. "And by 'wish you,' I mean, 'pray for'—and my prayers are generally *answered*. You made an agreement to follow me, and I do not take kindly to those who renege on their agreements. Neither I nor my god would be pleased with you, and there are consequences to our displeasure."

Rodrick was sorely tempted to push back, to lose his temper and lay waste to the fish-man, but instead he smiled. "Ah, well, you can't blame a man for trying. All these days in the woods make me long for a hot fire and a cold tankard. But, of course, this is your quest. I am but your loyal retainer."

Later, when they were trailing behind the others on horseback, Hrym said, "You didn't think that 'loyal retainer' bit was going overboard?"

"I think he'd be more suspicious if I *hadn't* been a bit sarcastic," Rodrick said. "The best Obed and I will ever be able to achieve is a sort of simmering hostility. As long as he thinks my avarice is stronger than my dislike for him, we're fine."

"But your avarice *is* stronger than your dislike for him."

"True. But he doesn't know what I'm actually avaricious *about*, which is to say, anything and everything of value. Still, his basic distrust of me could be problematic when it comes to stealing all his possessions. I was thinking, though, that you might play up to him a bit. Let him know you're tempted by his offer to be your new wielder, that I've been a disappointment to you, and so on. String him along. If he thinks he's driving a wedge between us, he won't expect us to work together to abscond with his artifact. You can turn on him at a crucial moment to let us make our escape."

"There's that twisty little mind of yours at work again," Hrym said, with real admiration in his voice. The sword was self-evidently the more powerful half of the duo, but he tended toward the blunt and the straightforward in his approach to life and the acquisition of gold, and Rodrick's schemes had seen them showered in coins often enough that Hrym yielded to his judgment in treacherous matters. Hrym's idea of a plan was "freeze everyone in blocks of ice and take their horses," which worked well enough sometimes, but lacked a certain finesse.

Rodrick sighed. "Though I should also probably prove my usefulness before you cozy up to the priest too much. Otherwise Obed might poison me while I sleep, content with the knowledge that he'd have you anyway."

"You? Prove yourself *useful*? How do you propose to do that?"

"With luck, someone will try to attack us," Rodrick said.

After two more days, Rodrick was beginning to worry he'd need to seek out local bandits and insult their chieftain personally if he wanted to show off for Obed in a fight. They'd barely seen another living person in that time, which made a lot of sense—who would live in this endless marsh? Eventually they found a solid dirt track that seemed to lead more or less in the proper direction, and took advantage of the change in terrain to make up some of the time Obed was so sure they'd lost. The discovery of a road mollified the priest sufficiently that he even let them stop and sit down to eat.

During their midday break for a meal, Zaqen pored over the maps while Obed squished around in a water-filled ditch. "I think we're in the Stolen Lands, now. Which means we're very nearly to Brevoy. That's when things become more complicated."

"I would welcome some complications," Rodrick said. "A fighting man needs a certain amount of excitement if he wants to stay sharp."

Just then Cilian appeared from the west, wearing a solemn expression. He beckoned to the priest, and Obed joined the others, dripping dirty water and already frowning.

"There are armed men along the road," Cilian said. "A great number of them. I ranged some distance to the north and south, in hopes of finding a clear path around them, but they have scouts scattered through the trees, keeping watch over every scrap of cover. Perhaps if we swung far to the north—"

"We do not have time for such detours," Obed said.

"It's . . . a lot of men," Cilian said. "Including a few archers. They would be difficult to overcome in battle."

"Could you get past them unseen?" Rodrick said. "Not all of us, but just you?"

Cilian frowned and said, "Of course I could," in tones that suggested Rodrick might as well have asked if sugar were sweet.

"Then I have an idea," Rodrick replied.

"It seems to me that *your* ideas—" Obed began, but Rodrick cut him off.

"Respectfully, sir, you hired me to provide security for our group. I would say a group of armed bandits constitutes precisely the sort of threat you tasked me to guard against, wouldn't you?"

Obed glared at him, but nodded.

"Excellent," Rodrick said. "Zaqen, Hrym, Cilian, we all have our parts to play. The important thing to remember is that your average bandit chief is a megalomaniacal lunatic full of insane bravery, who dishes up brutality for breakfast. By contrast, the average rank-and-file bandit is a superstitious and unmotivated lot . . ."

Chapter Thirteen
The Bait

Rodrick rode in the lead, with Hrym iced to his back. The sword had offered to send up great clouds of steam as they rode, to make the approach more dramatic, but Rodrick preferred to save the sword until his presence would make the most impact—and anyway, such clouds would just make people wonder if Rodrick's horse's rear end had caught fire, and that was entirely the wrong impression to make.

Zaqen followed Rodrick on her camel, and Obed, thoroughly robed, brought up the rear with their supply horse tethered to his mount. They'd both been told not to say anything, but to sit there looking grim and inscrutable and, if at all possible, hellishly dangerous.

The bandits had to be given credit. They waited with a dangerous-looking casualness around the only wooden bridge for miles, spanning a river branch that was more of a swollen creek. There were men on foot leaning against the railings on the bridge, and a handful of others on horseback arrayed on either side of the road. Beyond the bridge, a stand of trees concealed any number of additional bandits, some of them doubtless up high in the branches and armed with bows.

As Rodrick's party approached, one of the men urged his black warhorse forward a few steps. He wore motley armor—a gleaming silver breastplate with red enamel trim, a dull metal helm with a cruel spike on top that appeared to be crusted with blood, and mismatched gauntlets, one with studs on the knuckles, one without. He held an axe with a half-moon blade on one side of the head and a curving, hooked blade on the other. He was the very essence of a successful bandit chief.

"That's some interesting armor," Rodrick said. "Did you stumble across a battlefield and have trouble settling on what to scavenge?"

The bandit showed his teeth. "I took them off dead bodies, that much is true, though most of those bodies fell right here. I'm a man who believes in displaying my accomplishments. I can't say you're wearing much I'd care to add to my raiment, though, so it's best if we can settle things in a more friendly fashion."

"I love making new friends," Rodrick said. "What would this friendship of ours entail? Whoring, drinking, dicing, or perhaps refined conversation about Chelish chamber music?"

The uglies behind their chief chuckled among themselves.

"Oh, we can't talk pleasure until we talk business first," the chief said. "I'm afraid that means it's time for you to pay the toll."

"The toll," Rodrick repeated. "You're saying one must *pay* to cross this bridge?"

"The man understands the concept of a toll!" The chief turned and grinned at his bandits, playing up to his men. "You have no *idea* how much tedious explanation you've just saved us. We're going to be friends after all. Now, we operate our bridge on a sliding scale, and don't worry, we don't want to take *everything*. We make it a policy to leave our clients the clothes on their backs—"

"I have a minor objection," Rodrick said. "More a point of order, really. Doesn't charging a toll to cross this bridge violate one of the Six River Freedoms?"

"Does it?" The man scratched an enormous pimple on his badly shaved chin. "'Walk any road, float any river,' is that the one you mean? Anyone can go anywhere they wish?"

"That's the very one," Rodrick said. "Anytime I'm in the south, when people say the River Kingdoms are full of uncivilized idiots, I say, 'Not so!' and tell them about the River Freedoms. Many of those I talk to begin to consider moving here immediately, to take advantage of such enlightened policies."

The bandit chuckled. "Now, I could make an argument that this place isn't part of the River Kingdoms at all. They call this part of the country the Stolen Lands, and that's because Brevoy reckons it was stolen from *them*, and claim it's officially part of their kingdom—though they don't do much to enforce it, I'll grant you that. At any rate, Brevoy has no such rule against tolls. But fine, suit yourself. If we can't charge a toll, then let's call this little exchange something else—how about, say, a robbery? Not highway robbery, since that requires a highway, but dirt-track robbery, at least. Does that make you feel better? I was just trying to be a bit more civilized than your average riverland bandit, but I can see courtesy is wasted on you."

When Rodrick next spoke, his voice was flat and dead, all pretense at joviality abandoned—because he judged he'd given Cilian enough time to get in place. He said, "Go away and let us pass, or we'll kill you."

The man snorted, and the men with him laughed. "There's three of you, and eight of us, and that's not counting the ones back in the trees—"

An arrow took the chief in the neck from behind as he spoke, the point bursting through the front of his throat. He toppled from his horse, which reared back, turned, and ran away, dragging the chief's corpse along behind, his legs tangled in the stirrups.

"Be still!" Rodrick shouted, before the startled remaining bandits could rush them. "Your men in the trees are all dead by now! And *my* men in the trees obviously have arrows pointed at you. And then . . . there's this."

He drew Hrym and held the shining blade over his head, drawing gasps from the remaining bandits. "My sword. Do you see how his blade shines white? That means he hasn't fed recently. When my sword gleams white and pale, that means he's *hungry*—and he hungers for blood. I have only to gesture, and he can draw the blood from your bodies, pulling it from your eyes, ears, noses, mouths, and other orifices, leaving you as white and pale as he is now . . . but considerably more dead. You should see my sword when he's fed. His blade glimmers like rubies. Now, I don't like to feed him the blood of this many men—he becomes too *strong* then, you see, too hard for me to control—but if you leave me no other choice . . ."

One of the bandits made a move—perhaps an attempt to raise a weapon, more likely just a panicked and pointless gesture—and an arrow from the trees struck him down.

"*Let me drink him,*" Hrym intoned, in a rather horrid imitation of a Chelish accent. "*Before his blood cools.*"

The bandits didn't give them much trouble after that.

Rodrick made the bandits throw all their clothing and armor in a great heap, and Zaqen set the whole pile aflame. They left the men naked but alive, running off eastward through the marsh, to Obed's evident disgust.

"You're the one who's always saying we don't have time," Rodrick said, watching the bandits flee. "Cilian killed all their snipers in the trees, and then two here at the bridge—that proved our point sufficiently. Speaking of which, Cilian came through, didn't he? It's nice having a ranger with a gift for sniping around."

Obed stared at Rodrick in silence, but it was an annoyed silence. Rodrick was more and more able to read Obed's moods. It helped that the priest had only three: annoyed, emotionless, and bloodthirsty. He sighed. "Listen: it wasn't *mercy* to let them live, it was pragmatism. The thing about a group of men like that is, they'll cooperate if they think they'll survive. But if they realize you intend to kill them anyway, they start to fight *back*, and vigorously. You don't get to be a bandit in the Stolen Lands without being a hard man. Why risk any of us being injured when it could be handled so . . . well, not *bloodlessly*, obviously, but with less blood, anyway."

Obed turned and walked away from him.

"I think Obed is just bothered by what a decent man I am," Rodrick said to no one in particular—which meant, as usual, to Hrym on his back. "Why, I'm practically *holy*."

"Wholly useless, anyway," Hrym said.

"You could have killed a few more of them." Zaqen was returning from the bridge, where she'd presumably sliced the eyes out of the unfortunate twitchy bandit. "The chief has been dragged halfway to Numeria by now. What a waste. He had nice eyes, considering how ugly he was otherwise."

"Why do you take the eyes, anyway?" Rodrick said. "I haven't asked, out of fear that you'd actually tell me, but I must admit, I'm curious."

"Your first instincts were good," Zaqen said. "You don't want to know. But if you annoy me, I might tell you someday, perhaps just as you're about to start eating."

"I'll keep that in mind. What do we do with their horses? We could tether them together and lead them to the next settlement, make a bit of coin—"

Obed began slapping at the horses and shouting at them, making them scatter off through the marsh, and Rodrick sighed. "Is he *always* so casual about wasting the spoils of battle?"

"It was hardly a battle," Zaqen said. "And my master does not want for money. It's not worth his time to sell these horses. I'm not sure he'd waste the time it would take to bend down to pick up a pile of gold coins he found in the middle of the road."

"To be so rich . . ." Rodrick said. "I knew I should have gotten religion."

"The key is to not care about money." Zaqen clapped him on the shoulder, and it was a sign of their long time traveling together that he didn't shudder from her touch a bit, even though her hand seemed strangely misshapen, the bones too soft, or perhaps merely arrayed in an unusual configuration. "It's like chasing women, Rodrick. If you're desperate, they can *smell* it. You have to act like you don't want it, don't need it, and don't care, and all the things you want will come to you."

"Your man Obed certainly doesn't act aloof about this artifact we're going after."

"True," Zaqen said. "And look at how annoying the trip to retrieve it has been so far! My master seldom listens to my advice. I have higher hopes for you. Let's collect Cilian and get moving. If this is the Stolen Lands, Brevoy isn't far."

Chapter Fourteen
The Unstolen Grails

To Rostland!" Rodrick raised his mug in the tavern, and a ragged cheer went up from the farmers and pigherds gathered in the room. To befriend a crowd as pessimistic and generally grim as this one had taken a certain amount of aggressive cheerfulness, but Rodrick was equal to the task. A man who toasted the country where he happened to be standing at the moment could become *almost* as popular as a man who bought rounds for the house, and this way was considerably cheaper. He might have cried "To Brevoy!" but the inhabitants of this particular region, once the independent nation of Rostland, were still a bit touchy about their subjugation to their northern neighbors, and appreciated the pretense that they retained some independent identity. Rodrick, who was no more patriotic than an alley cat, could make use of such sentiments without entirely comprehending them.

Rodrick was delighted to be out of the River Kingdoms and into Brevoy. From here they'd head toward the northern border, recover this artifact—they'd probably have to plunder a tomb and slay slumbering horrors, but he'd done that sort of thing before—and then he and Hrym could enact their final plan, which was a bit hazy in the details, but essentially boiled down to steal everything and run away."

Rodrick wound his way through the backslapping, smiling crowd toward the dim corner table where his party waited, Obed and Zaqen heavily cloaked, Cilian perched awkwardly on the edge of a chair as if he'd never encountered such advanced technology before and wasn't sure how to use it. Rodrick set mugs before them—Cilian peered into his as if looking for guidance in the bubbling foam, which he probably was—and then dropped into a chair of his own. Hrym was sheathed on his back, and keeping quiet so far.

"We made it." Rodrick smiled at his cohort. This was the first village of any size they'd encountered since entering Brevoy, close enough to the East Sellen River to have some accommodations for travelers, and Rodrick was pleased at the prospect of sleeping in a bed tonight—ideally not alone. "So what now? We head north and recover this item we're looking for?"

"Not precisely," Obed said. Zaqen stiffened and looked at him sidelong, which was curious, since she usually just nodded along when her master spoke. Rodrick thought she looked surprised, and there was no way that could be good.

"Our journey will be a twisting one," Cilian muttered, staring into his beer. "I see trees upon trees, and icy walls, and fire, and blades, and spikes—"

"Yes, I'm sure we'll see all those things, we're in *Brevoy*," Rodrick said. "What do you mean, Obed? Why do I think 'not precisely' is code for 'not even remotely'?"

The priest held up a warning finger. "Just a moment." He reached into his robes and withdrew a palm-sized wooden box, placing it in the center of the table. Obed flipped open the lid, revealing a dull blue gem that pulsed with a flash of light and then went dark. Suddenly all the sounds of the crowded tavern dropped away, leaving silence, though Rodrick could still see drunks singing and arguing and laughing all around them. "Now that we have some privacy," Obed said, scowling, "I can tell you. The artifact we seek rests within a vault. That vault is guarded, of course, but even more importantly, the vault is *locked*. There are four keys, precious objects given over in days of old to the safekeeping of priests loyal to my god, but in the centuries that followed, the purpose of those keys has been forgotten. They are now seen merely as historical curiosities, family heirlooms, or valued relics. My researches have revealed that all four keys are still located in Brevoy—the magics laid upon them long ago were strong enough to keep them nearby, at any rate. One of the keys, in Restov, I have made prior arrangements to purchase. The others . . . will have to be acquired by other means."

Rodrick groaned. "You mean we'll have to *steal* them?"

Obed shrugged. "Or win them, or convince their owners who refused to answer my letters to sell the keys to me anyway, now that I am here in person. The keys are worth far more to me than they are to those who have inherited them."

"Yes, fine, but if someone came to me and said, 'Would you like me to take that ancient mysterious key off your hands?' my first question would be, 'Why, what does it open?' My second question would be, 'And how much is my cut?'"

"In that respect we are fortunate," Obed said. "The keys do not *look* like keys. They are not even truly keys, precisely, in the sense of being shaped metal objects one inserts into locks to operate tumblers. These are merely objects of power, which, when brought together in the proper place, will cause the vault to open."

"So they don't look like keys," Rodrick said. "That's lucky. What *do* they look like?"

Obed shrugged. "They look like magical objects. A jewel, an ancient vase, things like that."

"Oh, good," Rodrick said. "People never hesitate to part with *that* sort of thing."

"You're a thief," Zaqen said. "You're good at convincing people to part with things they'd rather keep. You should be happy about this."

From his back, Hrym chuckled, but Rodrick did his best to look stone-faced and offended. "You call me a thief? You know my reputation as an honorable mercenary—it's why you sought me out. If you seek to impugn my honor—"

Zaqen patted his hand. That was worse, somehow, than shouting or recriminations. "Rodrick. Did you *really* think we'd heard you were a warrior of great renown? Yes, we did hear that, don't worry, the rumors you caused to be spread were quite effective, though the details of your heroism were strangely difficult to substantiate. But we aren't from the River Kingdoms, Rodrick. My master and I come from farther south, and we also heard tales of a man and his sword of ice in Andoran, and Isger, and Cheliax—and those stories were alternately tales of daring banditry and clever double-crosses and confidence games that left rich men and widows considerably poorer and a bit bewildered. We heard you *sold* your magic sword no fewer than a dozen times, but that all the amazing talking swords you sold would only repeat the same phrases over and over, and melted after a few days."

"I always liked that one." Hrym's voice muffled by the sheath. "Rodrick would do a few flashy demonstrations with the real me, then reluctantly part with a fake. Making icy replicas of myself is easy enough for me, and it's not so hard to have a wizard cast a spell to fake the voice."

"I have sometimes strayed outside the *conventional* path of warrior heroism," Rodrick began, but when Zaqen laughed, he sighed and gave it up. "Yes, fine, I'm not a warrior. Not primarily. I *can* fight, but it's never seemed the best use of my talents."

Zaqen nodded. "We knew that, too. But we had faith that Hrym could handle any fighting that needed to happen. And I suppose my master must have wanted you around because he knew there might be a certain amount of stealing to do. I assumed he just wanted a thief to disarm any traps or pick any locks we encountered on the way to the relic, but I see only a portion of the grand tapestry of his plan." Somehow she managed to say that last part without sounding even remotely sarcastic—and Rodrick had to face the possibility that she meant it *sincerely*.

She prodded Cilian in the arm. "How about you, huntsman? Do you object to illegal behavior, in the pursuit of a godly end?"

The huntsman took a sip of his beer and winced. "How can anyone own anything? Even the clothes I wear were once the hides of beasts, and when I am dead, they will be stripped from me. My weapons are fashioned from the materials of the forest, wood and bone and gut and feathers, and they will return to nature when I am done with them. I do not object to stealing, because I do not believe any object can truly be owned. They only pass through our hands, for a time, and then pass on."

"Speaking as an object, I approve of that worldview," Hrym said.

"We will travel to Restov first," Obed declared. "That key will be the easiest to obtain." He rose and headed for the stairs leading to his room without another word.

Zaqen slumped against the wall, and Rodrick eased a bit closer to her. "You didn't know about the keys, did you?"

"I knew there was a vault," she said. "I knew it was magically sealed. I just thought we already had everything we needed to open it. I know my master likes to keep things to himself, but . . ."

"It's a shame he doesn't trust you," Rodrick said. "Not trusting *me*, that's just good sense, but your loyalty seems beyond any reasonable question—"

Zaqen came out with one of her eerie giggles. "You won't drive a wedge between my master and me, and I won't join you in any plot to steal all his earthly possessions, either."

"Oh, now, that's not fair, I didn't mean *that*—"

"Of course you did. I'm sure you would have worked your way up to inviting me into a conspiracy, very deftly and skillfully, but I'd hate for you to waste your time trying to cultivate me. I told you, Rodrick, we know who you are, and what you are, and we hired you *anyway*. Anything you think to try, we're apt to see coming. Anyway, Obed can keep all the secrets he likes. I owe him more trust than he owes me. And I know this is wasted breath, Rodrick—you can't stop scheming, I'm sure, any more than Hrym can stop being a sword—but if at all possible, just accept your weight in gold, and serve us loyally, all right?"

"Your suspicion *wounds* me," Rodrick said.

"As long as we understand each other," she said glumly. Then she brightened. "It's not so bad. Am I really so eager to brave a vault of horrors in search of a great relic? I'm glad we'll get to travel around Brevoy a bit first. I love seeing new places. The world is fascinating."

"That is true," Cilian said. "Though I prefer wilder places."

"This place will be plenty wild once it gets a little later and the clientele gets a little drunker," Rodrick said.

"I meant the *forest*," Cilian said. "*That* kind of wild place."

"As a conversationalist, you're a wonderful archer, Cilian," Hrym said.

"Thank you," the huntsman replied, apparently in all sincerity.

"I'm going up to my room," Rodrick said. "You two have a pleasant time."

Upstairs, in a small, oddly shaped room that was nevertheless indescribably wonderful because it was *private*, Rodrick unsheathed Hrym and laid him down upon a scattering of gold coins on top of the dresser.

"Ahh, that's nice," Hrym said. "Keep getting gold. I could get used to this."

"You aren't bothered by this? Obed neglecting to tell us we'd have to trek all over Brevoy looking for these keys of his? Or by the fact that Zaqen and Obed are suspicious about our motives and expect us to try and steal from them?" Rodrick sat on the edge of the narrow bed and began tugging off his boots. When had he last slept with his feet bare? He couldn't even remember. He kept his boots on in the forest so his toes wouldn't be gnawed by wildlife.

"So what if they're suspicious?" Hrym scoffed. "We've robbed people who knew we were criminals before. You've robbed the same people *twice*, on more than one occasion."

"True. But it does require a more refined approach, more planning . . ."

"You're just lazy," Hrym said. "Embrace the challenge. I've been making nice with Obed, if you haven't noticed, listening to his whispers while you're sleeping. I'll get him to trust me, and we'll use that against him. As for the other thing, I don't mind tromping around Brevoy for a while. I'm *immortal*. It's not as if Obed is wasting my time. I've got plenty of that. Obed said the keys are magical. So after the vault is opened, we can steal the artifact *and* the keys and turn a tidy profit."

"Why can't Cilian be the one with the saddlebags full of gold?" Rodrick said. "I could convince him to give me his every last coin in the space of five minutes."

"If the half-elf were rich, someone else would have stolen his money long before we ever found him," Hrym said. "We're onto a good thing here, anyway. So you have to travel a bit more. The exercise will do you good."

"Spoken like someone who gets *carried* everywhere."

"It's a good life," Hrym said contentedly. "Speaking of the good life, I thought you were going to flatter a few barmaids and see if you could find one sufficiently broad-minded to let you bring her upstairs?"

"I was, but now I have to spend some time lying here, brooding and plotting," Rodrick said. "That damn fish-man ruins everything."

Chapter Fifteen
The Swordlords of Restov

They rode east and reached Restov in a few days, passing their evenings in small villages and empty fields. During their journey they barely caught a glimpse of Cilian, who roamed far afield, finding even the sparsely populated expanse of Brevoy far too urban for his taste.

When their party approached the city gates, Rodrick thought it was almost like a *real* city, or at least a decent imitation created by people who'd seen real cities firsthand, perhaps when they were children. The gates stood open to allow the free mingling of trade, with carts passing in and out laden with goods and produce, and beyond the gates Rodrick could see stone buildings crafted with some attention toward aesthetics instead of the purely functional crudeness and raw, sap-dripping wood he'd grown used to in the River Kingdoms. "An enterprising person could make a bit of money in there, I suspect," he said.

"An incautious person could lose his soul," Obed replied.

"More likely his life," Zaqen said. "The place is thick with Aldori swordlords, and their students—who are just as likely to kill you, though not necessarily on purpose. They're just learning. There are Taldan dueling schools here, too. I gather duels right out in the middle of the street are not uncommon, so try not to offend anyone wearing steel, all right, Rodrick?"

"Swordsmen," Rodrick said, and sighed. "Sorry, Hrym, you'll be staying sheathed in there." He noted Zaqen's curious look and shrugged. "Those devoted to the sword have one of two reactions to seeing Hrym: an overwhelming desire to murder me and take him for themselves, or a desire to show that their skill is superior to mine, even though I *do* have a magical weapon."

"Their skill *is* superior to yours," Hrym said. "I mean, you could best a butcher in a fair fight, I suppose, if he was old and out of shape, but—"

"I'll gladly concede that I am not the most adept swordsman, though I *did* survive a great many fights before we met, sword. For that very reason, I have no reason to goad suicidal swordlords into trying to prove their prowess over me. Which means you stay sheathed, and keep the steam to a minimum."

"Where is the huntsman?" Obed said, scowling.

"He told me last night he didn't think he could face life in the big city," Rodrick said. "I'd love to take him to Absalom sometime, just to watch his eyes burst entirely from his head at the sight of actual civilization. Let's hope his Brightness doesn't lead him much farther away from the wilds, eh? I'm not sure he could stand the strain, fated or not."

"The only fate is the will of the gods," Obed said.

"And even the gods die when they don't expect it, sometimes," Rodrick said. "It really makes you wonder.

So! How about Hrym and I shop for supplies while you go conduct your business—"

"You will accompany me to the meeting," Obed said. "As will Zaqen. I mistrust these swordsmen. They take offense too easily, and seek redress too crudely."

"Don't be too hard on them," Rodrick said. "Not everyone can be as sophisticated and easygoing as you are, Obed."

"Well, well." Rodrick gazed at the gleaming white three-story house, with its large windows and airy front porch, behind its walls of iron topped with spikes rendered to look like miniature sword blades. "This is quite a nice place. Being a swordlord must be very lucrative."

"Bartolo earned it the old-fashioned way, too," Zaqen said.

"Oh?" Rodrick didn't try to hide his disappointment. "Hard work, prudent investments, all that rubbish?"

Zaqen shook her head. "No, rather more old-fashioned than that. He killed someone and took his house."

Rodrick laughed. "Very direct. I like it. He must have been a pleasure to negotiate with."

"He is a fool, like all humans." Obed removed a leather sack from one of his saddlebags. Said sack looked extremely heavy, Rodrick noted with a professional eye.

"You hear that, Zaqen? Your master lumps you in with all the rest of us human fools."

"As to that, I'm not a *typical* human," Zaqen said. "So I can pretend he doesn't really mean me."

"I didn't realize the Brevoyish system of inheritance was such that murdering a man gave you the right to his estate," Rodrick mused.

"Seems like a system that's ripe for abuse," Hrym said. "Do you think we could stay here for a few more days, so we have time to abuse it?"

"He won it in a duel," Zaqen said. "Not typical dueling rules, either. All swordlords and their students have a habit of dueling over honor, but there's also a tradition of dueling for *stakes*, dating back to Baron Aldori's promise to pay one hundred thousand pieces of gold to any man who bested him in combat. Bartolo was very much a betting man—a degenerate gambler, really, but a *very lucky one*, which is how he's stayed rich. Some merchant who'd taken up swordplay with the passion of a zealot challenged Bartolo to a duel after he completed his training, but our man Bartolo considered fighting the merchant to be below his status. Bartolo eventually consented to the duel . . . but only on the condition that the stakes be made sweeter than honor alone. Bartolo humiliated the merchant and took his house, among other prize possessions. I understand there were some temporary privileges involving the merchant's wife, too."

"Oh? How did that work out?"

"She stayed with the swordlord afterward and bore him a son," Zaqen said. "You'd almost think she cared more about the house and the money than about the man she married. But the path of true love always finds a way, eh? The son is apparently quite the swaggering bravo, but the old man is said to have a clear head and to be capable of honest dealing, if you keep a close eye on your purse while you talk to him."

"How do you know all this?" Rodrick said. "I thought our quest for the keys was news to you."

"My master asked me to investigate the character and history of several individuals in Brevoy. He did not choose to tell me *why*, but it is hardly my position to ask, and so I did not. I spent a lot of money, cultivated contacts, asked some questions . . ." She shrugged, unevenly as always. "I learned enough to know this man will remain true to whatever arrangement my master struck with him, and that the bargain was almost certainly to his advantage."

"Let's go." Obed handed the sack to Zaqen, who staggered under the weight. "Shout to the guard loitering by the door, Rodrick, and tell him we require entry."

"I've never had a good result from shouting at guards," Rodrick said, "but you're the boss."

After an infuriating amount of conferring, the guards—who seemed to delight in moving slowly—ushered them in through the gate and then the great doors of the house, without even asking them to relinquish their weapons. Then again, if Bartolo was a swordlord, he probably welcomed the odd surprise attack during a business meeting, if only to keep his instincts sharp.

A servant who looked the perfect proper butler, apart from the long dueling scar that ran from his left eyebrow to the right side of his chin, led them to a beautifully appointed sitting room done in shades of rose and pale blue that, strangely, contained only a single chair, set beside a low table made of some exotic shimmering stone.

Obed took the chair and tapped his foot impatiently, scowling around the room as if the hangings on the walls might conceal hated enemies or cooked fish. He wore a minor glamour to make his gillman nature less obvious, presumably because meeting someone for a transaction while hiding your face in a deep hood at all times could be considered a bit suspicious. Rodrick had opined that a bit of theatrical makeup to cover the gills would have been sufficient, but apparently slathering gills with facepaint was uncomfortable or an inhibition to breathing or something, so Zaqen had worked up an illusion instead.

After perhaps half an hour, a door opened at the far end of the room, and a young man with piercing blue eyes, black hair, and more nose than he knew what to do with strode in. He wore a long, curving sword at his hip, and had the sort of trimmed, oiled, and cultivated goatee that probably took enough time to maintain that it should be declared at least an avocation, if not a life's work. The scarred servant trailed him, carrying a tray that held a bottle of wine and a single glass. The man looked at Obed for a moment. "You're in my chair," he said mildly, but it was the mildness of a big cat that hasn't yet decided to unsheathe its claws.

With just a moment's hesitation, Obed rose and bowed stiffly. "My apologies."

"No apology necessarily," the man said. "You are unaccustomed to the manners of Rostland. I'm sure where you come from, sitting in your host's chair is the height of courtesy."

Obed grunted, and Rodrick tried not to grin.

"Are you Bartolo?" Obed asked as the man seated himself. The swordlord ignored the priest until his servant had gotten the bottle and glass arranged on the table to his satisfaction and departed. Then the man looked up.

"Am I Bartolo? Do I look like a sixty-year-old fat man to you? No. I am his son Piero."

"Ah," Obed said. "I had hoped to speak to your father directly. I realize he must be a very busy man—"

"Not so busy as all that," Piero said, "since he choked on a fishbone and died a fortnight ago. He always swore he'd never be bested in a duel, and he was quite right. A river trout in a wild berry sauce did him in. Now. What can a man like myself possibly do for people like you?"

Obed frowned. "Perhaps . . . Zaqen, give him the letter, if you would? It is correspondence from your late father—ah, my condolences, of course—and should explain my presence here."

Zaqen passed over a folded sheet of parchment, and Piero took it with the same enthusiasm he might have displayed upon being offered a dead eel. He scanned the paper, his lips pursed, then nodded once, crumpled the paper, and tossed it to the floor. "We have no business. You may go."

"Young man," Obed said. "An agreement was made—"

The swordlord cut him off. "An agreement you made with my father Bartolo. He is dead, and death has a way of nullifying contracts—ones as informal as this, anyway."

Rodrick listened with amusement as Obed attempted to take on a wheedling, ingratiating tone—which was roughly as natural as hearing a horse quote poetry. "Of course," Obed said. "I realize you are your own man, and do not expect you to heed the precise terms I struck with your late father. I am happy to renegotiate any agreement with you."

"You've come to *buy* something from me, is that it?" Piero wrinkled his nose. "You seem to be under the misapprehension that this fine house still belongs to a merchant. It does not. It belongs to me, son of one of the greatest teachers of the Aldori sword method to ever live—although, in truth, I surpassed his skill before I was old enough to grow hair on my chin."

Rodrick bit back on the urge to comment on the sort of hair Piero *had* eventually chosen to grow on his chin. He hardly needed to sabotage Obed's clumsy attempts at negotiation for his own amusement. Obed would sabotage things well enough on his own. The gillman even *knew* Rodrick was a confidence man, a professional charmer and manipulator, and he still chose to take the lead in negotiations himself. So be it. Let him reap the rewards of such poor judgment.

"The object I seek is of no particular monetary value," Obed said, anger and impatience beginning to leak out around the edges of his words. "But it has some meaning to my sect—a pitcher that belonged to a priest of Gozreh who attempted to bring the light of our faith to the northern lands."

"I have no intention of parting with anything in my father's estate until I have conducted a thorough inventory and determined the value of my inheritance completely," Piero said coldly. "And this pitcher you mention—it's the pearlescent blue one that pours forth an inexhaustible stream of seawater, isn't it?"

"I have heard it has such a property," Obed said, a little stiffly. "It was blessed by Gozreh, goddess of the waves—"

Piero stroked his neat beard. "I admit, it *is* a worthless thing, to me. What good is a pitcher that pours water no one can drink? I suppose I could start a business with it to harvest the sea salt, but it sounds like tedious work."

"It is indeed. I would happily pay you a price more than fair—"

"On the other hand," Piero mused, "I wonder what the sea-folk of Outsea would pay for such an artifact? They could hardly inundate the entire River Kingdoms with such a pitcher, as it pours far too slowly, but they might pay well for an endless supply of fresh seawater for their personal use. Of course, it would take some time to send a messenger to their city—"

"I will pay." Obed gritted his teeth. "I will pay handsomely. If you read the letter, you know the sum I named, and it is a sum fit for a king. Nevertheless, if you desire more—"

"Are you attempting to bargain with me?" Piero swirled the wine in his cup. "How amusing. I am not a fishmonger, alas, and bargains do not interest me. Nor do you. I have sufficient wealth to keep me in comfort for all my days. You are a rude outlander with no knowledge or respect for the ways of old Rostland, and your presence offends me. As I said before, we have no business."

"If you would only listen to reason—" Obed snapped.

"I am unreasonable, am I?" The swordlord took a sip of wine, then put the cup down on the table beside him, positioning it precisely to his liking. The lightness of his tone was almost enough to make Rodrick take a step back. He'd heard men like this say things that way before: a thin veneer of civility painted over a thick layer of offended anger, which was itself just a mask for a savage glee at the excuse to inflict violence.

The swordlord rose and placed his hand on the dueling sword at his belt. "I believe our conversation is done," he said pleasantly. "You may leave. Now. Or I may . . . see you off more definitively."

Obed started to speak, but Zaqen laid her hand on his arm. He shook her off, but did turn and retreat for the door. Rodrick smiled at the swordlord pleasantly, nodded, and followed his employers out.

He didn't worry about turning his back to Piero. A man like that wouldn't stab anyone in the back. He'd stab them in the front, after a tedious display of excellent swordsmanship, preferably demonstrated before an audience of appreciative onlookers.

Rodrick loved people like that, mostly because it was so easy to stab *them* in the back.

Chapter Sixteen
Adept Gambit

I am not an assassin," Rodrick said. "I am a guard. More accurately, I am a thief pretending to be a guard. If you are attacked, I will kill to protect you. But I will not murder a man so you can steal some of his kitchenware."

"Zaqen can do it, then," Obed snapped, pacing around his room at the inn, where he'd gathered them all for a conference. Zaqen squatted on the floor, and Rodrick sat on a wooden chest, while Hrym reclined in his usual preferred splendor.

"My deadlier magics are . . . not terribly subtle," she said doubtfully. "Piero is not as well loved as his father was, being a bit of a prick, but he has plenty of young friends who'll try to kill us if we hurt him. Besides, we don't even know where the pitcher is—we'd have to torture him to find out." Obed turned his snarling gaze upon her, and she shrank under the stare. "Of course, we *can* compel him to answer, master, and if that is the path you choose, I will act without hesitation. But . . . perhaps Rodrick has a less violent approach in mind? He *does* excel at convincing people to part with their wealth of their own free will."

"Well?" the gillman barked, turning to Rodrick. "Do you have any ideas?"

"Alas, no," Rodrick said pleasantly. "If Piero hadn't already seen me, I might have a few possible approaches, but those have been lost to us now. You've blown a number of other potential avenues by letting him know how desperately you want that pitcher. Piero seems the sort to withhold the treasure out of nothing but spite. Anyone who comes around asking about that pitcher for any reason, even obliquely, will be immediately suspected as your agent. There's no social approach I can think of. I think our only hope is reconnaissance, and once we locate the pitcher, a simple act of burglary—"

"I've got an idea," Hrym said, and they all went silent and turned to look at the ice sword, which rested on a scattering of gold coins at the foot of Obed's bed. "The seed of an idea, anyway. Rodrick will have to work out the details. He's good at that."

"If the plan involves freezing Piero in a giant block of ice," Rodrick began doubtfully, but Hrym scoffed.

"Not at all. I've been with you too many years, Rodrick. You've turned my nice straightforward mind all twisty like yours. I was just thinking about how you used me to scare off an ill-tempered gladiator back in Tymon, and it started me speculating . . ."

Three days later, after a certain amount of groundwork had been laid, they returned to Piero's house. Rodrick half expected the guards to turn them away at the gate, but apparently Piero was still hopeful they'd offend him sufficiently to merit a recreational murder. This time the man was waiting for them when they entered the rose-colored room, and Rodrick strolled in with his full swagger, smiling broadly. Obed and Zaqen followed him like loyal retainers, which was as it should be. "Piero," he said, and gave a lavish bow. "We have given your proposal some thought."

"I offered no proposal, outlander."

"You proposed that we should go screw ourselves," Rodrick said pleasantly. "Though admittedly not in exactly so many words. I'm afraid that proposal doesn't work for us. In fact . . . my sword would like to have a word with you."

Piero snorted. "Oh, really? You're challenging me to a duel? You are a thug who may as well be nameless, but all right, I'm sure we can find terms that will give us both satisfaction—"

"I'm not challenging you to anything," Rodrick said. "Do I look like a lunatic? You would kill me, and I bet you'd take your time overdoing it. No, I meant what I said. My sword would like a word with you. Isn't that right, Hrym?"

"That's right," Hrym said, muffled in the scabbard on Rodrick's back.

Piero frowned. "What is this? Ventriloquism? I have no patience for nonsense—"

"May I draw my sword?" Rodrick said. "Or, if you prefer, you may draw it yourself. It's just easier to show you than to try to explain."

The young swordlord had his blade drawn and pointed at Rodrick's throat in the space of a breath. "Draw, then. But do not attempt to strike me, or . . ."

"Yes, the threat is fairly obvious with the blade you have pointed at my neck. No need to spell it out."

Rodrick reached slowly behind him and drew Hrym from his scabbard.

"A magical sword," Piero said. He stepped back, but didn't lower his guard. "Of shimmering ice, no less. How did a priest's bodyguard come to hold something like that?"

Rodrick shrugged. "Via truly vast sums of money, of course. I do all sorts of work, for whoever can pay my rate."

"I don't," Hrym said. "I do just one sort of work: killing people."

"The sword talks." Piero frowned. "I have heard of such things, of course, but never seen one. You have a true mind inside your steel, sword?"

"What steel are you talking about? I am *ice*. My name is Hrym, boy, and my mind is likely truer than yours."

Piero raised an eyebrow. "*Boy*?"

"Don't take it personally," Rodrick soothed. "Hrym is thousands of years old. He thinks everyone is a boy. Or a girl. At least he didn't call you girl."

The tip of Piero's blade twitched, but that was all. Good. He was intrigued enough to bear the occasional insult. "Magical swords are for the weak," Piero said. "A true swordsman trusts only his own skill, and his blade is not a companion or an ally, but an extension of himself."

"Luckily, I am not a true swordsman," Rodrick said. "I am a man who kills people for money. So when the opportunity to join forces with a talking sword of living ice came along, I didn't have to wrestle with any sort of internal conflict. Now, Hrym—I believe you had a counterproposal?"

"Yes," Hrym said. "Piero: I'll fight you for it."

"You. Will fight *me*," Piero said. "For . . . what?"

"The pitcher, boy, obviously," Hrym said.

Piero lifted his blade.

"Hold now!" Rodrick said. "Who do you plan to hit with that? I'm just the man *holding* the sword, here, and striking me down won't shut him up, believe me. I didn't even want to come, but Hrym—well, I owe him my life many times over, and my livelihood at this very moment, so here I am."

"Your father had guts, by all accounts," Hrym said. "And he liked a good wager, I hear. But not you, eh? No surprise. Each generation gets weaker, the blood turns to water and gets thinned out."

"I will not be goaded, sword," Piero said, but he put his weapon away and stroked his horrible beard. "The proposal is intriguing. Can you fight on your own? What I mean is, can you . . . fly, move about, without a wielder?"

"Everyone always asks that," Hrym said. "Would I tolerate this mercenary carrying me around everywhere if I could *fly*?"

Piero nodded. "All right. If we had this fight, who would be your wielder?"

"Oh, Rodrick will do," Hrym said. "But make no mistake, you're fighting *me*, not him. It doesn't matter what horse the knight rides—you're fighting the *knight*, not the mount."

"Hey," Rodrick said. "I'd rather not be referred to as a 'mount' by someone with such a masculine voice, Hrym."

Piero ignored him. "There is still a marked disadvantage, Hrym. You are magical. I can guess at the nature of your magic. What would prevent you from shattering my steel?"

"Nothing," Hrym said. "That's precisely what I'd do. That's sort of the *point*. Did you want to concede before we get started? It would be disappointing, but . . ."

"No, I'm merely pondering how to nullify your magical advantages . . ."

"Oh, have a wizard wrap you in wards," Hrym said. "Or make us fight in the heart of a volcano. Get a magical sword of your own. Bring ten of your friends and give them pots of alchemical fire to throw at me while we duel. I don't care. I'll still freeze your blood where you stand."

"I would object to the volcano," Rodrick said. "The one with alchemical fire doesn't thrill me either."

"It would rather add to my stature, to defeat a magical sword that speaks," Piero said, pacing up and down, clearly thinking furiously. "We can hardly fight to first blood, though, as you don't bleed, and drawing blood from your wielder would be trivial. Fighting to the death is likewise difficult, as you don't die as men do."

"I say we fight until one of us yields," Hrym said. "Or is no longer able to fight, or until an impartial judge deems one of us the clear winner. Fair enough?"

"I believe so, yes. We can refine the details. And if you win, you get the pitcher. What do I get when you lose?"

"What do you want?"

"I wouldn't mind having you, Hrym," Piero said. "I would hang you up above my mantelpiece, and keep a fire roaring there beneath you, night and day, and make sure no warrior ever wielded you again—because magical swords are offensive to all true swordsmen."

"Hrym," Rodrick said, putting just the right amount of doubt into his voice. "Really, the priest isn't paying us *that* much, is it really worth—"

"Do you wish to withdraw your challenge?" Piero said.

"Of course not," Hrym said gruffly. "Rodrick, you worry too much. What do you think he'll do, find a magical sword made of *lava* or something? Sell his soul to a flame elemental? The man doesn't have a chance."

"I'll need a few days to prepare," Piero said. "Shall we meet three days hence, at midday, at my dueling school?"

"Outside would be better," Hrym said. "Unless you don't mind the building being destroyed."

"In the courtyard, then," Piero said, without hesitation.

There wasn't much for them to do in the next days, as things had already been set in motion. It was always possible their plans would fizzle, or that Piero wouldn't take the bait, or would be less arrogant than Rodrick expected, and would grow suspicious of his good fortune. It was a *good* scam, but not an ironclad one, because Rodrick hadn't been given enough time to work out every angle, and he was dependent on Zaqen's contacts in the city for certain aspects of the plan, and who knew if they could be counted on?

On the second day after Hrym challenged Piero, Obed barged into Rodrick's room, where he was playing dice with Zaqen for imaginary stakes, and declared that he could wait no longer. "I am taking Cilian with me to acquire another of the keys. You will join me after you recover the pitcher."

"Master, are you sure that's wise?" Zaqen said. "Isn't it dangerous to go without Hrym, and me, and, ah, Rodrick?"

"Thank you for including me in that," Rodrick said. "I do love feeling like part of the team."

"I am going into the Gronzi Forest, where the key is said to be buried beneath a certain stone altar, long forgotten." Obed sniffed. "Rodrick would only trip over tree roots, and you are needed here—if the sword's clever plan fails, you are responsible for the backup plan."

"Killing Piero and trying to find the pitcher myself, somehow." She sighed. "Yes, master. I still worry . . ."

"Cilian will provide sufficient protection—the woods are his domain, after all. And you act as though I am without resources of my own, servant. You know I am not. When you are done here, wait for me in New Stetven, at that inn you found—"

"The Flaming Riders." Zaqen glanced at Rodrick. "The city of *Old* Stetven was destroyed by red dragons. The inn is named for a group of knights who continued trying to charge the dragon even after its breath set them aflame."

"Oh?" Rodrick said. "How did that work out for them?"

"They died horribly, of course. But they still would have died horribly if they'd pissed themselves and run away in terror instead. At least this way they got an inn named after them."

"I'm sure it's a comfort. All right, Obed, we'll meet you at the inn, and we'll come bearing the pitcher of endless waters, which is actually a key to help us recover something else, which you haven't ever named or described."

"Yes, you will." Obed stomped away.

Rodrick leaned back in his chair and smiled. "Ah. I feel more relaxed already. It's like when I was a boy and my father would go off on a three-day drunk and leave me to entertain myself in peace."

"I hope he's all right." Zaqen looked at the closed door anxiously. "My master is very confident, but he's a man of the sea, not the forest."

"Cilian's a good killer, and he thinks Obed is linked to his destiny. I'm sure they'll be fine."

"You don't know about that forest," she said. "The locals just call it 'The Forest,' as if it's the only one—and it is the only one that matters. The outskirts are preyed upon by bandits, and in the deep woods, there are dangers so ancient they're little more than rumors, because people don't often come out alive and sane with reliable reports. Since my master brought me into service, I have been away from him before, of course, but at those times he was always in the sea, where he is safe, and powerful . . ."

"Do you love him?" Rodrick said, his tone gentle.

"Obed is arrogant, zealous, pigheaded, ruthless, and would sacrifice my life in an instant if it furthered even one of his minor goals. And, in addition, we're not even the same *species*." She sighed and picked up the dice cup. "Of *course* I love him."

"Moving swiftly past *that* awkward subject," Rodrick said, "have you heard from your friend the wizard?"

"He's less a friend and more a person we've paid a great sum of money. The weapon is ready, the golem is in readiness, and Piero is supposed to meet them this afternoon."

"Young Piero must be feeling pretty pleased with himself right now, plotting our doom," Rodrick said.

"Poor bastard," Hrym said from his bed of coins on the dresser. "He has no idea I'm a brilliant tactician as well as a beautiful magical weapon."

"Brilliant!" Rodrick said. "You just combined *my* trick to intimidate a gladiator with *my* old scam where we sold people fake replicas of you. I'm not sure putting two of my ideas together qualifies you as brilliant—"

"The first person to combine chili spice and chocolate was brilliant," Zaqen said. "Would you deny that?"

"And I did come up with the fire angle," Hrym said. "And the name. The name is all mine."

"It *is* a pretty good name," Rodrick admitted.

Chapter Seventeen
Swords and Fire Magic

They met in the inner courtyard of Bartolo's School of Swordplay, which Piero hadn't gotten around to renaming in his own honor yet, apparently. The courtyard was surrounded by high walls, and ringing those walls stood at least seventy of Piero's students, all armed, many with their own hideous imitations of Piero's hideous goatee, most grinning.

As for the fighting area itself, the courtyard was full of treacherous loose cobblestones, tree roots bursting up between the cracks, patches of uneven ground, and mysterious slick puddled sections. "I don't think I could walk across this courtyard without breaking my ankle," Rodrick said.

Hrym, still sheathed (to the crowd's shouted disappointment), said, "So just stand still. You shouldn't have to do much."

Zaqen was acting as his second, which in this case meant she stood near him, smiling widely at Piero's students, making many of them immensely uncomfortable. Something about the way her eyes seemed to move independently of one another appeared to unnerve them. Rodrick couldn't imagine why. He'd gotten used to it ages ago.

After a few moments, there was a murmur among the students, and a few of them parted to allow a newcomer through. It wasn't Piero, though—it was a seven-foot-tall golem of sooty gray stone, its body human but its face almost featureless, as if worn smooth by centuries of weather. The golem held both hands before it, and in those hands it carried a scabbard of deepest red, from which protruded a hilt of black leather wrapped in yellow cord.

"Oh, bugger me," Rodrick said, making sure his voice carried to all the students. "That's Magnos the Ash Lord."

"*What*?" Hrym squawked, voice audible despite the muffling sheath. "Show me!"

Rodrick drew the blade and held Hrym before him. The students gasped at the gleaming ice blade, but only for an instant, because all their attention shifted as soon as Piero sauntered into the courtyard. He was followed by his second, who carried a small pitcher of blue stone: Obed's first key. "Welcome, students. And welcome, Hrym, my challenger. And, of course, a special welcome to my new friend, Magnos the Ash Lord."

The golem drew the sword from its scabbard, and presented it in guard position. A constant cascade of red, yellow, and blue flames flickered up and down the length of the blade, which was nearly a twin to Hrym's in length and shape—fire to his ice. "My old enemy," the flame sword said, his voice high-pitched, nearly a shriek—a bit too theatrical, really, to Rodrick's ear, but you worked with what you could find on short notice. "Today we end our long war."

"Magnos," Hrym said. "Is that a new golem?"

"The last one was burned, of course," Magnos shrilled. "As they all are, in time, melting in the presence of my glory. Is that a new *human* wielding you? You shame our kind, Hrym, by making yourself a thrall to a mortal man."

"You're the freak, Magnos," Hrym said. "Even Vaperia has human wielders—"

"Vaperia the Air-Blade does let herself be polluted by mortal touch," Magnos said. "But at least she dominates her wielders and makes them into her mind-slaves. *You* let yourself be carried by a shaven ape with a will of his own."

"The name is Rodrick." He clucked his tongue. "Really, Piero, isn't this cheating? Hrym challenged *you*, not Magnos—"

"The terms of the duel were made explicit," Piero said. "I was welcome to use a magical sword of my own, remember? No one said the sword was not allowed to be sentient. Magnos assures me that his powers are the equal of Hrym's."

"Exactly the equal," Hrym murmured. "In all the long centuries through which we've clashed, our powers have never been anything but evenly matched."

"With the magical elements essentially canceling one another out, this will come down to a duel of skill." Piero showed his teeth in a smile. "Do you wish to concede? I have just the place on my wall to hang you, Hrym."

"We'll fight, damn you!" Hrym shouted.

"This ends now!" Magnos declared.

"Well, that's me dead then," Rodrick said, and lifted Hrym to guard position.

"May I take you in my hand, Magnos?" Piero said formally.

"You may, mortal."

Piero took the sword from the golem and gave it an experimental swing. "Not the sort of blade I'm used to, but I need not be at my best to defeat you. I can only imagine the fear you're feeling now, oh, what's your name—Hrym's holder. Hrym will survive this, but you . . ." He clucked his tongue, then smiled. "Imagine my joy when I went in search of a magical blade and discovered that Magnos had just arrived in the city, continuing his long pursuit of you, Hrym. It was costly to secure an audience with him, but once he agreed to meet me, we discovered our common cause."

"Flames," Magnos said. "Flames, and death."

"I dedicate this duel to Rostland!" Piero shouted, turning and holding Magnos aloft, brandishing the burning blade above his head. His students cheered.

When the noise died down, Rodrick cleared his throat. "Rostland," he said thoughtfully. "That rings a faint bell. Wasn't that the country that *used* to be here, before it was subjugated and crushed under the heel of a conqueror and made part of Brevoy, which it remains? It seems odd to dedicate your battle to a country that no longer even exists." Rodrick slapped himself on the forehead. "Oh, but of course! You're planning to *lose*. It makes perfect sense to dedicate a *losing* battle to Rostland."

"You attempt to make me angry, and careless," Piero said. "I do not respond to such amateurish trickery." He whirled the blade in a flaming arc. "Shall we, Magnos?"

"Yesssss," Magnos said, his flames leaping up, almost as high as the courtyard walls.

That was when Piero's goatee caught fire. He *did* keep his beard oiled, Rodrick thought—that was poor planning. It was followed by his hair, his sleeves, and, rapidly, all his clothing. Magnos's flames crawled up the swordlord's arms and across his chest, rippling, and Piero screamed and threw the blade away, where it clattered on the stones. The golem plodded over, picked up the burning blade, and sheathed it, then trudged out of the courtyard, all while Piero thrashed on the cobblestones, his students gaping at him open-mouthed.

"He appears to be on fire," Rodrick said. "Did you want to do something about that, my liege?"

"Oh, all right," Hrym said. "I'll give him the merest touch of my power." Rodrick gestured with the icy blade, and the air around it cooled sharply, snowflakes precipitating out of the air in white profusion and then showering down on Piero, melting from his heat but dousing the flames. After a few moments, the swordlord was soaking wet, slightly burned, and gasping on the stones.

Rodrick strolled toward the swordlord—keeping a safe distance in case Piero tried something tricky, though the man seemed too stunned to be so resourceful—and put the tip of Hrym's blade in the hollow of Piero's throat, just as the swordlord had done to him at their last meeting. "Do you yield?"

"I—I—"

"Death is also an option," Rodrick reminded him.

"I yield," Piero whispered.

Zaqen hurried toward Piero's second, snapping her fingers, and took the porcelain pitcher from his hands, then scurried away. Wise. It was always possible Piero would scream for his students to "kill them, kill them all!" and it was important to get the prize safely away first. Granted, the students might not rally to their teacher's call—Piero was soaking wet and humiliated, which probably had a negative impact on his ability to inspire them to action—but it was a risk.

"Magnos never could control his power," Hrym said. Piero moaned. "I would have warned you, if I'd known you intended to try to use him against me. Magnos has to be carried by a golem because he's burned every human who ever held him. You're lucky you didn't lose your hands, swordlord. Take me home, wielder."

"As you command, my blade." Rodrick managed to keep every trace of irony out of his voice. They walked out without being attacked, which was nice, but Rodrick was a bit disappointed that none of Piero's students bothered to applaud their exit.

"There." Zaqen handed the young wizard a small sack of clinking coins. "That should settle our business, with enough extra to cover the golem rental. You might want to leave town for a while. Piero might decide to take revenge on the people who pointed him to Magnos, and it's possible those whispers could lead back to you."

The wizard, a pudgy fellow with ginger hair and a perpetual smirk, chuckled. "I don't think Piero's going to do anything but sulk in his mansion for a while. He's a laughingstock. But I wanted to head south anyway. I've never seen Absalom." He shook Zaqen's hand. "Thanks for bringing me into this. It was a fun project. The short-term flaming sword enchantment I'd done before, but the inverted-clairaudience spell that allowed me to project my voice through the blade was a nice challenge—"

"Do the voice again!" Hrym cried from his bed of coins. Rodrick, seated in the corner, rolled his eyes.

The wizard cleared his throat, squinted his eyes, and shrieked, "I am Magnos! Fear my blazing wrathful blaze of wrath!"

"Beautiful," Hrym said.

"We should have hired an actor to do the voice," Rodrick muttered.

Once the young wizard left, Zaqen and Rodrick finished their packing, carefully wrapping the magical pitcher in cloth and stowing it upright in one of the saddlebags. "I wish we had a lid for this thing," Rodrick said. "If it tips over, all our supplies will be doused in seawater."

"No one ever said magical artifacts were convenient."

Rodrick looked pointedly at Hrym. "Don't I know it."

"I must say, I'm impressed," Zaqen said. "The way you pulled all that off. Spreading the rumors about a golem with a talking sword of fire in town, making Piero really work hard to track Magnos down, making him *pay* for the privilege of a meeting . . . I can see why you've made a living as a thief and a liar."

"It was *my* idea," Hrym said. "Why are you giving Rodrick all the credit, when all he managed was the tedious execution? Though it's almost a shame Magnos was imaginary. It would be entertaining to have a nemesis, locked forever in a battle of wills, struggling through the ages, with humans as mere pawns in our long game . . ."

"I'm sure if you ever meet another talking sword, it will be happy to hate you forever," Rodrick said. "I have great faith in your social skills. I suppose we should take the same advice you gave the wizard and get out of Restov, Zaqen. We bested one of the best duelists in the city, and other swordlords might decide they want to challenge us too. The sword-obsessed do that sort of thing, in my experience."

"We'll go to New Stetven and wait for my master to find us," she said.

"Or we could run off together, my darling, and make a living selling seawater to wandering gillmen and homesick landlocked sailors."

"Tempting," Zaqen said. "But you aren't my type. Too . . ." She wiggled her fingers. "*Normal*."

"That may be the cruelest thing anyone's ever said to me," Rodrick said.

"Oh?" Hrym said. "Then I'll have to start trying harder."

Chapter Eighteen
When the Sea-Priest's Away

If my city had been burned to ashes by marauding red dragons," Rodrick said, "I think I'd refrain from rebuilding the place entirely out of *wood*."

The two of them were lounging in a pair of chairs on the front porch of the Flaming Riders, beneath its sign that depicted three knights on horseback, with riders and horses all aflame. They had a good view of the people bustling through the wide street, and the buildings crowded together on the far side. Some were two or even three stories tall, and whether carved, painted, and gilded, or raw, rough, and rustic, everything was made of wood. There were raised wooden sidewalks along each side of the street, too, which made a nice change from dodging around steaming heaps of horse dung.

"People build with what they have." Zaqen said. "The locals call this place the City of Wooden Palaces. The Gronzi Forest is west of here, and these folk have made a living logging at the outskirts of that forest for a long time. The Ruby Fortress, where the king lives, is made of stone, though. As always, rank has its privileges."

Rodrick grunted. "Didn't the whole royal family get assassinated here or something?"

"You like to pretend ignorance, but I think you know more than you let on," Zaqen said. "Every member of House Rogarvia vanished, actually. All of them, without any sign of violence, disappeared without a trace. It's all very mysterious."

Rodrick scratched his chin. "There's an old game, but a good one, where you find a likely looking girl or boy, coach them very well, and then bring them forth as the long-lost, last surviving heir—"

"Ha. Your false king would be murdered before you even got the rumors properly started. It's not as if the throne is sitting vacant, you know, or as if the current occupant is desperate for the royal family to return and take the kingdom off his hands. There was nearly a civil war when the family vanished, but one of the other noble houses seized the throne and created at least the illusion of stability. There still *could* be a civil war anyway. Things are unsettled here, and Brevoy is a nation with sharp divisions—the remains of the old kingdom of Issia in the north and the remnants of Rostland in the south. They were two peoples in two lands for a very long time, and not always on friendly terms. When you try to unite two separate cultures that way, there are bound to be . . . schisms."

"I do love a nation teetering on the edge of chaos," Rodrick said. "There are lots of opportunities in a place like that. And any time you have two sides, you can play one against the other to your own advantage."

"There is something to be said for chaos and destruction," Zaqen said. "At least it's never dull."

"I wouldn't say that. *This* is pretty dull. We've been sitting here for three days, and while I don't mind the chance to sleep in a bed on so many consecutive nights, at what point do you think we should give up on Obed, divvy up the treasure in the saddlebags, and say our farewells?"

She shook her head. "My master still lives. We have a mystical connection. Not so strong that I can use it to locate him, or to know what he's thinking or feeling, but I would be made aware if he died. For one thing, the geas that compels me to follow his orders would be lifted if he died, and I still feel its power pressing on me, so—"

"Geas?" Hrym said from inside his scabbard, which leaned against the wall between their chairs. "The priest has a spell on you to compel your loyalty?"

Zaqen nodded. "Yes. Though I consented to it willingly."

Rodrick let out a low whistle. "Why let him chain you that way? I thought you were devoted to him anyway, because of some good turn he did you?"

"I was. I am." She shrugged. "I told him the geas was unnecessary, that my service was pledged to him, but he thought it would be best. He knew the way ahead of us would be dangerous and taxing, and he wanted to be sure he could depend on me absolutely, without even the necessity to worry, wonder, or question. I am not made to be a perfectly obedient slave—I can advise, and argue, and I can reason with him. All those things are permitted. He does value my counsel, believe it or not . . . but in the end, if he orders me to do something, I have to do it, or pay certain unpleasant consequences."

"I can't believe you took such an oath." Rodrick could think of nothing more ghastly than being in thrall to another's will.

Zaqen's mouth twisted into a quirky smile. "I could hardly pledge my loyalty, and swear to do whatever he asked of me, and then refuse to submit to the geas. Any objection would only have proven his point—that he couldn't depend on me to follow his will in all things. If I intended to obey his every command anyway, the geas would cost me nothing. So you see, when I told you I wouldn't join you in betraying my master, I told only the truth—I *couldn't* help you, even if I wanted to. Which I don't."

"Why tell me this now?" Rodrick said.

She shrugged again. "Because you suggested that we might at some point give up on Obed and go our separate ways. I wanted you to know that's not an option for me, not as long as he lives. And while you *can* leave, without your payment, of course . . . when Obed returns, he will not be happy that you and Hrym have left. Your absence would be an impediment to achieving his goals, and he can be unpleasant when he's frustrated."

Rodrick sighed. "At least let me know if he dies?"

"You'll be the second one to know." She giggled. "Well, third, really, after Obed himself."

That night, someone pounded furiously on the door of Rodrick's room, and the rogue rolled out of bed, taking Hrym in his hands before he called, "Who's there?"

"Zaqen," came the reply. "Cilian is here with me."

He opened the door. Zaqen's face was solemn, and Cilian was filthy, mud-streaked, and frowning. "Come in. What's happened?" He wasn't sure if he hoped Obed was dead or not.

"All Cilian has told me so far is that they were attacked," Zaqen said. "I thought it best if we heard the story at the same time."

Cilian took a seat, cross-legged on the floor, while Zaqen and Rodrick sat on the bed. The huntsman licked his lips. "Obed lives," he said, "but he is in dire circumstances. We entered the great forest without incident. I was able to avoid the most dangerous beasts and slay the small ones that troubled us, and though he is not a man of the land, Obed can move silently and with care when he wishes. As we penetrated the deeper forest, the canopy became so thick that it seemed as if night were falling, a perpetual twilight—"

"Yes, fine, what *happened*?" Zaqen snapped. "I know people always say 'start at the beginning,' but I'd rather you skipped to the end."

Cilian blinked at her, then nodded. "We found the object we sought. Hidden just where Obed had foreseen, buried beneath a great altar stone, now furred with moss and cracked by time. We recovered it—the key—and camped in the deep woods until day broke. Then we continued on our journey. We were near the outskirts of the woods when . . . when . . ." He hung his head. "We were ambushed," he whispered. "It is my fault. I was not cautious enough. The edge of the forest is not home to many beasts, as there are woodcutters and colliers aplenty there, and the tromp of human feet drives the wild creatures away. So I let down my guard, thinking we had only to stroll some few miles through the thinning trees, and then to the road that would lead us back to New Stetven."

"But you were attacked by bandits?" Rodrick said. After a few days in the city, he'd heard plenty about the bandits—most notoriously a group led by a man named Duma the Sly—that preyed on travelers who strayed near the forest, robbing and beating them, only to disappear into the woods, where the forces of the law rightly feared to tread.

Cilian nodded. "Yes, to my shame. I was fetched a great blow to the head from behind, and darkness took me. I woke hours later, blood and dirt caked on my wounded head, and found Obed sprawled on the forest floor, gasping and thrashing."

Zaqen closed her eyes. "They took his ring, didn't they? The one set with a pearl."

Rodrick had noticed that ring, the way any thief notices something they intend to take for themselves in the future, but he didn't understand why Zaqen mentioned it, particularly. "I imagine they took all his rings."

"They did," Cilian said. "But *that* ring—"

"It's his ring of land-walking," Zaqen said. "It lets him travel in the upper world without ill effects. Without that ring, Obed can't spend more than a day out of the water. No gillman can. Their organs begin to fail."

"I don't know how long I was unconscious," Cilian said. "Perhaps half a day. Obed was wounded as well, but he was also delirious, speaking in languages I did not know, and calling for aid from strange gods, but sometimes he begged for water. Though I know little of gillmen, I thought water might help soothe and heal him, so I lifted him in my arms and carried him back into the deeper woods, toward the last body of water we had seen: a natural stone pool perhaps the size of this room, fed by a creek. I slid Obed into the water, and he sank to the bottom. I feared that he had died, but I waited, and watched, and at the midpoint of the night he rose from the water, and whispered an incantation— or, I suppose, a prayer—healing both his own wounds and my own. He was too ill to travel immediately, he said, and would need to immerse himself in water often during the journey home, which might not be practical. He told me to come and find you, and so here I am. He waits in the pool for us still. "

"Can we make him a new ring?" Rodrick said. "Do you have any magical friends in New Stetven?"

Zaqen shook her head. "No. Obed didn't ask me to cultivate any contacts. I don't think he expected to do real business here—it was just a place to stay during our foray into the forest. Even if I knew wizards . . . making a ring or necklace that allows the wearer to breathe while underwater is fairly common magic. But making a ring that lets an aquatic creature travel freely in the air?" She shook her head. "It's a specialty item. Obed's ring came from one of the Low Azlanti settlements under the sea. Perhaps back in the River Kingdoms, in Outsea, there might be such magic, but I'm sure there's also a great demand for that kind of spell among the sea-folk there, and they wouldn't be likely to part with such enchanted items willingly."

"Then we'll just have to steal the ring back from the bandits," Rodrick said. "That's what Obed wants us to do anyway, isn't it?"

Cilian nodded. "He requires us to recover the lost key, which was also stolen. He asks that we obtain his ring while we do so."

"All right," Rodrick said. "What can you tell us about the bandits? I know you were knocked out, but you're a tracker—were you able to glean any knowledge from examining the site of the attack afterward?"

Cilian nodded. "There were at least five of them, and no more than eight. They moved among the trees, traveling through the branches, dropping to the ground only occasionally. Tracking them might be difficult—"

"Oh, we can find them," Rodrick said. "I'm not worried about *that*. I just want to know what kind of resistance we'll be facing when we do find them."

"The object we found, the key," Cilian said. "It is the jeweled skull of a dog. Obed told me the skull is reputed to howl in the presence of demons." He looked at the ceiling for a moment. "I can therefore say with some confidence that the people who attacked us and stole our possessions were not demons."

"That's reassuring," Rodrick said.

"It is," Zaqen said. "It means they're most likely men, and men die easily."

"That would make me feel better if *I* weren't a man, too."

"I feel pretty good about it," Hrym said.

Chapter Nineteen
The Jeweled Skull in the Forest

"Why did we have to bring all this gold?" Rodrick said loudly, swinging the heavy canvas bag from his left shoulder to his right. "It's killing my bad leg lugging this weight. And are you sure cutting through the woods is faster?"

"You don't think you're overselling things a bit?" Zaqen murmured, shuffling along beside him under the deep shade of the towering trees. In a clearer voice she said, "Stop your bellyaching. Ever since you wrenched your knee you've whined like a spoiled child. It's your own fault. If you hadn't gotten drunk you wouldn't have fallen down the stairs."

They trudged along slowly, not wanting to stray far from the spot where the bandits had attacked Obed and Cilian, bickering as loudly as they could without actually shouting. Rodrick had never been comfortable in the deep woods, largely because dire bears and ambulatory carnivorous plants could not be won over by a charming line of patter and a warm laugh. There were too many shadows, too many rustles, too many strange hoots and growls and chirps. Despite Cilian's assurances that this was the edge of the forest, it felt sufficiently remote and primeval to make Rodrick nervous. A bandit attack would be a relief, even if they *weren't* trying to provoke one; at least bandits were people, driven by normal things like avarice and cruelty. He knew how to cope with those.

"Perhaps the bandits are hunting elsewhere today," Zaqen whispered after a while. "If we went to Obed, I might be able to use a bit of his blood to cast a divination and track the whereabouts of his ring—"

A piercing whistle rent the air, different from the other bird cries. That was Cilian's call. Rodrick grinned and looked up.

A male halfling dressed all in shades of green and brown dangled from a tree branch, twisting wildly in a tangle of spider silk that bound his legs—one of the many traps Zaqen had prepared earlier. He cursed at them fluently as he struggled.

Rodrick whistled twice, and a single, brief chirp returned from wherever Cilian was hiding: just the one bandit, then. That was easy.

"We were hoping we'd run into you." Rodrick slung the canvas bag off his shoulder and unwound the ties that held it closed, then drew forth Hrym, who didn't gleam because of the deep shade, but who was still impressively icy. "My sword and I would like to ask you a few questions."

Zaqen crushed a stinking beetle in her fist, casting some spell that made the halfling freeze in place. He tumbled out of the tree, landing on the ground without altering his posture, like a dropped statue of a human rendered in two-thirds scale. Zaqen propped the halfling against the tree, where he leaned as stiffly as an axe handle, only his eyes mobile. The bandit was steely eyed until Hrym said, "What are you staring at, tiny human?" Upon hearing the sword's voice, the halfling's eyes went wide.

"He's a halfling," Rodrick said. "Not a tiny human. And he's paralyzed, or something, so I don't think he's intentionally staring at you."

"You bipeds draw so many arbitrary distinctions between yourselves," Hrym grumbled. "Halfling, human, what's the difference? What a ridiculous thing to think about."

"I suppose you wouldn't mind if I called you a short sword, then?" Rodrick said. "Or a—"

"I am a *long*sword," Hrym interrupted angrily, "the most perfect design of *all* the swords, not an unwieldy oaf like a greatsword, not a mincing little rapier, a *long*sword—"

"He doesn't even realize he's made my point for me." Rodrick sighed. He crouched down so he could look eye to eye with the halfling. "I have friends. Two friends. One a priest in dark blue robes, one a huntsman in leathers and fur, the latter a half-elf. Do you happen to recall robbing them a few days ago?"

"He can't speak," Zaqen said. "He can't do much except breathe."

"I'm afraid that rather limits my interrogation options."

Zaqen sighed. "I'll get the rope."

Once the halfling was bound to the tree trunk, Zaqen dispelled the paralysis, and the halfling strained pointlessly against the bonds. Rodrick waited politely until he stopped struggling, then said, "Shall I repeat the question?" He waved Hrym back and forth. "Attack on a priest and a huntsman?"

"I don't know what you're talking about." The halfling peered suspiciously at Hrym. "I was just taking a walk in the woods—"

"Here's our problem." Rodrick sat down to get more comfortable. "Our priest is not with us, as he was grievously wounded by bandits—did I mention he was attacked? Now, if he *were* with us, I'm sure he could invoke the powers of his god to tell us whether or not you're lying. But since he's not available, we're forced to rely on cruder measures. Zaqen?"

The sorcerer smiled, showing off her frankly dreadful teeth, then bowed her head. A drop of saliva formed on her lips, then dropped to the forest floor, where it sizzled and smoked.

"That would be acid," Rodrick said. "We'll start with your fingers. Do you favor your left or your right hand? We're not *monsters*, and I'll feel bad if you turn out to be telling the truth, but it will take at least three fingers to find out—"

"Yes, all right, I robbed them," the bandit snapped. "They were walking in the forest, the idiots—what did they expect? We didn't even *kill* them, so what are they complaining about?"

"Oh, as an occasional brigand myself, you have my sympathy. Our victims never appreciate it when we go easy on them. Alas, I am presently in the employ of one such victim, so I have to set my natural sympathy for your plight aside. We're almost done now. I just need you to give me back the things you stole—especially a particular ring, and a jeweled skull."

"Ha," the halfling said. "Torture me all you like, you won't get *those* things back. Our chief has them."

"That's fine. We'll talk it over with your chief. Just tell us where we can find him."

The halfling snorted. "You may as well kill me now. *She'll* kill me anyway if I reveal the location of our camp."

"He thinks we want to kill him, Hrym!" Rodrick said. "Isn't that ridiculous?" He patted the bandit on the knee. "We wouldn't kill you. If you aren't alive, how can you suffer?" He twitched Hrym back and forth before the halfling's eyes. "This is my sword. He's his own sword, really, but we travel together, and he'll do things for me if I ask politely. He is a sword of living ice, as you may have noticed, and while he can certainly kill people, he can also do damage more . . . selectively. Zaqen, could you hand me that branch?"

The sorcerer handed over a broken length of branch, sprouting three smaller branches at the end, festooned with dying leaves. "Hrym, could you freeze this for me? Not the whole thing. Just the leaves on one of the branches."

The air around them grew suddenly cooler, and half a dozen leaves turned white with frost. Rodrick held out the branch to Zaqen, who flicked one of the leaves with her fingers. The leaf shattered like delicate glass, shards falling to the forest floor.

"Hrym has amazing control," Rodrick said. "He can turn things to ice very selectively. What do you think would happen if I asked him to freeze you? Not all of you. Just, say . . . your manhood. Or not even your whole manhood. Say just the tip?"

The halfling swallowed. "Don't," he said, all sneer and smirk gone.

"Give me a reason not to," Hrym said.

"We should have killed him," Zaqen said.

"Shh." Rodrick crouched beside her behind a deadfall near the bandit camp. "We left him tied to a tree, didn't we? Maybe some carnivore will come along and devour him—would that make you feel better? His people didn't kill Cilian and Obed, so I see no reason to escalate things now."

"You don't think killing is going to come into this? I count five of them."

"And Cilian says there aren't any others lurking in the trees, so the odds are practically even, if you count Hrym. These people seem to trust in the safety of their isolation so much they don't post sentries." Rodrick shook his head. "Bandits are so lazy. I admire it, really. Quite the lifestyle. Hunting and gathering. Lots of time for leisure."

The camp was hardly a buzzing hive of activity. An orc and a hulking man with bizarre crystalline growths on one side of his face sat around a cold firepit, sharpening weapons and swapping filthy stories. Rodrick wondered if the man with the growths was an oread, or just the victim of some bizarre magical parasite. A woman in mud-stained robes mumbled and fussed over some sort of crucible—she was an alchemist or wizard or healer, probably. An older, leaner, stringy man slept with his head pillowed on a heap of moss, a bow at his side. And the black-haired, dark-skinned woman lounging against a tree cutting off slices of apple and popping them into her mouth was presumably the bandit chief, because she wore the best armor, a black leather affair that looked like some kind of snakeskin.

The jeweled dog's skull rested on top of a log near the center of the camp, and it was less impressive than Rodrick had expected. It must have come from a fairly small dog, and the skull was gray and stony with age, some of the teeth chipped and uneven. The jewels were just little emeralds in the eyes, barely worth the trouble of prying out with a knife.

A bird somewhere sang a snatch of melody that Rodrick recognized as part of a bard's song about the great and mighty Aroden. That was their signal that Cilian was in place. Rodrick would have preferred it if he and Zaqen could have attacked the camp from separate directions, but there was precious little in the way of cover or concealment—the big trees all around them didn't allow enough sunlight for any decent undergrowth to develop. The snarl of fallen trees they crouched behind was the closest they could get to the camp while remaining concealed.

Rodrick slowly unsheathed Hrym and counted under his breath.

Before he got to four, the wizard/priest/alchemist gurgled and fell face-forward into her own crucible, the feathered end of an arrow protruding from the back of her neck.

Rodrick approved. Always take out the magic-users first. They weren't necessarily as strong or even as dangerous as swordsmen, but you knew what to expect from a swordsman. Magic-users were unpredictable, and winning even a small battle like this was easiest when you could account for as many variables as possible.

The thugs by the fire silently dove for cover behind logs, the sleeping bowman didn't wake, and the bandit chief rose and started to walk backward quickly. They couldn't have *that*.

Zaqen raised her hands, without leaving the cover of the deadfall, and spoke an invocation that made Rodrick's eardrums ache. A stinking greenish cloud precipitated out of the air and flowed across the camp. The bowman woke, gasped, rolled over, and began noisily vomiting. That sound was followed by gagging and retching from the two thugs.

That left the bandit chieftain. Rodrick stood, gestured at the bandit with Hrym, and shouted "Freeze!"

"Freeze?" Hrym said. "You tell her to freeze, and you also want me to literally freeze her? I know being funny isn't your strong suit, but surely you can do better than—"

"Knife!" Zaqen shouted, and Rodrick saw the chieftain had paused long enough in her retreat to hurl a dagger at him. The flying knife shimmered blue, encased by magical ice, and dropped harmlessly to the ground.

"Freeze, *please*?" Rodrick said, and the chief gasped as her boots were frozen to the ground. Ice crawled up her ankles, and she bent at the waist, hammering at the ice with the hilt of another dagger, but magical ice was tougher than most, so she didn't make much progress.

Rodrick sauntered over to her, while Zaqen warily approached the vomiting bandits and Cilian materialized from the trees and edged forward, bow at the ready in case of further surprises.

"Drop the knife, please!" Rodrick called.

The bandit raised her arm, and Hrym froze the limb in place for her, icy armor growing across her shoulders and up to her wrist, forcing her to hold the arm aloft. She grunted, trying to lower her arm, but the ice wouldn't shift. The dagger tumbled from her fingers to the dirt.

Rodrick stood before her and grinned. "How does a woman as pretty as you—"

She spat in his face.

Rodrick wiped the spit away, nodding to himself. "Yes. I deserved that. Commenting on your beauty could be seen as condescending. You're obviously a formidable woman of great accomplishment—"

She spat again.

"Hrym, couldn't you freeze her saliva or something?"

"Sure," the sword said. "Let's try that. An interesting technical challenge."

"Your sword talks," she said.

"Yes, this is Hrym, a remarkable magical artifact—"

This time when the bandit spat, the spittle froze into tiny ice balls, which rather stung when they struck Rodrick's cheeks.

"New plan," he said, and pressed Hrym against the chief's throat. "You don't have to die today. Neither do your men—though my friend who unleashed the stinking cloud on them says they might *wish* they could die, since their guts will be turning inside out for a while. Just the barest whiff of that cloud made my stomach churn and my eyes water, so I can't imagine getting it full in the face. We're here to take back the dog skull—"

"That thing?" She frowned. "Why? It's just some old temple trash. We tried to pry the emeralds out, but the knife broke. It was a good knife, too, and hardly worth wasting on those gems. I've seen bigger fleas."

"The reason we want the skull doesn't matter—" Rodrick said.

"It's magic," Hrym interrupted. "The skull. Howls in the presence of demons. We're, ah, crusaders. Bound for the Worldwound. Seems like a useful item."

"Your sword talks," she said again.

Rodrick frowned. "Did you get a head injury? We've already established that—"

"Your sword talks *shit*," she continued. "What good would a charm for recognizing demons do you in the Worldwound? The land is utterly infested with demons, and has been since the Locust Lord escaped his prison. If you go there, won't the skull just scream *all* the time?"

"A fair point," Rodrick said. Now it was his turn to frown. "Why do you know so much about demons? You're not some kind of cultist, are you?"

She snorted. "Humans who worship demons make as much sense as cattle who worship men or rabbits who worship wolves. Only fools become demon cultists. But of *course* I know about demons. I am of Brevoy. The Locust Lord and his host were defeated here—don't you know anything? Deskari's army was driven into the Lake of Mists and Veils by Aroden himself. The Last Azlanti and his allies forced the demon host into the freezing depths to drown, and cleansed this land of its taint." She lifted her chin. "I know only what any loyal daughter of Brevoy would know."

"Ah, yes, Brevian pride, how nice. Or Brevish? Brevic? No matter. The fate of a host of demons a thousand years ago isn't high on my list of concerns right now, nor should it be on yours. You should be more concerned with your own fate. The skull is safe in your camp, and will be retrieved. But we also need the ring you stole from the priest. The pretty one with the pearl?"

She snorted. "The ring is gone. Why would we keep the worthless thing? It helps you *breathe air*. That's like having a magical ring that lets you grow hair in your armpits or take a shit after eating. What's the point? We didn't even think we could sell it, so my wizard took it apart to see if he could make it into something useful." Another snort. "He couldn't."

Rodrick sighed. "This is very inconvenient."

"What is?" Zaqen said, shuffling over.

"The ring. They destroyed it."

The sorcerer sighed. "Of course they did. Rodrick, why don't you get the skull and have Cilian show you where Obed is? I'll be along in a moment."

He frowned. "What are you going to do?" Rodrick realized he hadn't heard any retching for a while, and he turned to look back at the camp, where all three of the male bandits were facedown on the ground.

"I am doing what my master requires," she said.

"Zaqen, there's no need to kill her, they've been defeated—"

"Obed will not suffer this indignity." Zaqen did not take her eyes off the defiant bandit chieftain's face. "The ones who ambushed and stole from him must die. I know you do not approve. I let you spare the life of the halfling. You have that much, Rodrick. Do not push me for more."

"Obed is terribly bloodthirsty for a man who worships the sea, nature, the sanctity of life—"

"Nature does not consider life sacred." Zaqen drew a hooked blade already stained red. "Nature will destroy life on a whim, pointlessly. There's always more life waiting to replace what dies, and to feed on the dead. Life is not sacred, any more than mud or rocks or ashes. Nothing so plentiful can be precious."

"Zaqen . . ."

"I don't like this any more than you do. But it must be done."

"I still have one free arm, bitch, try your best—" the chieftain began, and Zaqen spat a stream of acid onto her throat.

Rodrick turned and rushed away before the smell of melting flesh could reach his nose.

Chapter Twenty
The Surface Curse

"Why does she take the eyes of her enemies?" Cilian whispered.

Rodrick shrugged. "I don't know. She threatened to tell me once. I'm just as happy not to know."

Zaqen knelt at the side of the woodland pool where Obed was soaking, speaking to her master in a low voice. Their conversation was occasionally punctuated by Obed's angry pronouncements. Rodrick hoped the various imperatives and remonstrations wouldn't take much longer. It would be dark soon, and he wanted to get out of the woods before then. Just because they'd defeated—no, don't be coy, *slaughtered*—one group of bandits didn't mean there weren't other dangers here.

"The portents have troubled me of late." Cilian picked up a handful of soil and let it sift through his fingers, peering at the way the falling dirt scattered on the ground. "I have seen things that disquiet me."

"Like being attacked by bandits and coshed into unconsciousness?" Rodrick said.

Cilian shook his head, serious as always. "No, those are the ordinary dangers of life in this world, and in the wild. I have seen—"

"Rodrick!" Zaqen called, and Rodrick was annoyed to find himself snapping to attention. "Come help me, please!"

"We'll talk later," he told Cilian, who nodded, his brow knit in worry. Who knew what anxieties a mad half-elf seeking Brightness suffered? And more to the point, who cared?

Rodrick picked up the small pack they'd filled with dry clothes for Obed. The priest was treading water in the pool, expression furious.

"You're annoyed about the ring," Rodrick said, and Obed just growled. "I can't say I blame you. Fortunately, Zaqen and I were prepared for the possibility of failure. If you're feeling sufficiently saturated now, we'll start walking. We should make it to the road before you dry out too much, and if you start to feel too arid . . ." He thumped the pack, and the inexhaustible pitcher of seawater inside clanked. "We can always douse you with the first key. I suggested we fit the pitcher with straps, make a sort of helmet from the thing, and just upend it on your head to constantly shower you with brine, but . . ." He shrugged. "Zaqen seemed to think that would lack dignity."

"Just get me out of these woods," Obed said. "And let me worry about my own dignity."

The dry clothes proved a bit pointless, since the priest stopped every hour or so to inundate himself with water from the pitcher, upending the artifact over his head and letting the torrent of brine slosh down over him, cascading down his chest, back, and shoulders. Zaqen fluttered around him like a nervous hen around a chick, and Cilian ranged ahead, scouting to make sure they wouldn't encounter any nasty surprises. Which, fortunately, they didn't. Rodrick had been party to enough casual murders today. Sometimes murder was necessary, but they hadn't even made a *profit* off this last bunch. If the bandit camp had contained any decent loot, they'd hidden it well, and Zaqen hadn't left any of the brigands alive to interrogate about the location of any treasure troves.

By the time they reached the *actual* outskirts of the forest, it was nearly dark. Zaqen paused by a particular stone and deactivated the deadly magical traps she'd created around the area, then dug down in the dirt to a shallow depth and found the folding shovels they'd hidden there. Cilian and Rodrick pitched in to dig a deeper hole to retrieve the saddlebags, wrapped in sacking, that held that portion of Obed's wealth he carried with him in gold and gems. Cilian slung the bags over his shoulder and didn't even stagger under the burden. He would be a good man to have along in a robbery, Rodrick thought. Load him down with the contents of a vault and send him running for the hideout with a quickness.

They passed through the last few trees and out into the logged clearing that abutted the road. The carter they'd hired was waiting there, standing on his driver's seat, shading his eyes and peering in their direction. Rodrick felt some of the tension in his shoulders ease at the sight of the man, his wagon, and his placid draft horse. Despite the promise of extra coin, and the implied threat that they would seek him out at his place of business in New Stetven if he deserted them, Rodrick hadn't been entirely sure the carter and the guards would wait. Their horses and the camel were still there, tied to the cart, along with the two bored mercenary guards they'd hired in New Stetven to keep their vehicle from being stolen by any passing brigands.

Zaqen scurried up to the guards, paid them in small bags of coin she'd prepared earlier, and sent them smiling toward their tethered horses. The carter began to complain loudly about how long he'd had to wait, and Obed spoke up: "You. Leave. Now."

The carter gaped, staring down from his high seat at the priest. "We can leave as soon as you lot—"

Obed's face was obscured beneath his soaking-wet hood, hiding his expression, but the snarl in his voice was unmistakable. "*You* will leave. You alone. Zaqen, pay him for his filthy nag and his rattletrap cart."

"Here, now, you can't talk to me that way. What makes you think my horse and rig are for sale? I was hired to haul, not—"

"Will this do?" Zaqen said, shaking a clinking coin bag.

The carter snapped his head around at the sound of jingling coins, took the bag, teased open the strings, and looked inside. He was an old man, gray hair sprouting from his ears, doubtless the striker and receiver of countless hard and bitter bargains, a jaded negotiator who would let no reaction show. Nevertheless, he couldn't prevent a little grunt from emerging when he looked inside the bag. "Well," he said slowly, looking meditatively up at the darkening sky. "I guess this is a *start*—"

"I suggest you take that and leave, now," Obed said. "If you will not consent to be paid in gold, you will be paid in steel." He looked pointedly at Rodrick.

After a moment, Rodrick blinked, and said, "Ah, yes, right." He drew Hrym, and the carter flinched back. "It would be paying you in ice, I suppose, not steel, but the sentiment is the same."

The carter shifted uncomfortably, but didn't climb down. "It's a long trip to New Stetven, if I don't have a mount, and it's getting dark—"

"Run quickly, and you might catch the guards," Zaqen said, rather kindly. "Perhaps you can ride pillion with one of them. But regardless—run, *quickly*."

The carter scowled, but he moved, dropping down off the far side of the cart and racing off, surprisingly quick for a man his age, shouting, "Ho, wait!" at the guards.

"Zaqen," Obed said. "Why have we purchased a cart?"

"You'll like this bit," Rodrick said. "You'll be traveling in style." He tore away the tarp covering the back of the wagon and revealed a wooden tub, the largest they'd been able to find—the sort of tub the better class of inns provided when they had passing nobles in want of a hot bath.

Obed clambered onto the back of the cart, looked at the tub, and—for the first time in Rodrick's experience—laughed aloud. "Ha. Very nice, Zaqen."

"It was Rodrick's idea, actually."

The priest glanced down at Rodrick, then nodded. "The people we pass on the road will think me mad," he said.

Rodrick shrugged. "The sides of the wagon are built up fairly high. We can pile things at the back, too. Your presence won't be obvious. We can pull the tarp over you if you want to travel more discreetly. And anyway, so what if they think you're mad? You're a holy man. It's allowed."

Obed removed his robe, set it aside in the bed of the cart, then lowered himself into the tub. Rodrick winced at the thought of bare flesh touching the cold smooth wood, but the gillman wasn't noticeably bothered. It must be cold as a corpse's guts in the sea, so he was surely used to it. "The pitcher," Obed said, and Zaqen passed up the artifact. Obed settled down into the tub, leaning against the curved back, and began pouring brine in from the pitcher. "Proceed east," he said, and closed his eyes.

Cilian frowned. "East. Toward the cold mountains. The auguries have shown me this. Places of darkness, locked in ice, full of crawling foulness."

"Lovely ice," Hrym said. "The other parts I could do without."

"East, then. Not back to New Stetven? You don't want to peacefully recover in the inn of the Flaming Riders for a while? They do a lovely fish stew—no, all right, fine. In search of key number three."

"Well?" Obed said. "Get the carthorse moving." He put the pitcher beside the tub and sank down, his face disappearing beneath the waterline.

"Yes, Cilian, you should—" Rodrick began, but the huntsman was gone, melted off into the treeline somewhere as always. He looked at Zaqen, and she shrugged her asymmetrical shrug. "If I climb behind that horse it'll bolt and tear the cart apart, or break an axle at least. I'm making her skittish just standing this close. I'll ride in the back with my master."

"Don't look at me," Hrym said from Rodrick's back. "I can't hold reins."

"I was hired for my skills as a mercenary," Rodrick grumbled. "And also for my skills of persuasion. I don't recall agreeing to drive a cart."

Obed's pool bubbled, and Rodrick sighed and climbed up to the front of the cart. He peered down the road, such as it was. Forest, endless forest on his left. The plains of Rostland rolling off on his right. Far off, the distant peaks of mountains. "Are there even any towns this way?"

"Not as far as I know," Zaqen said from behind him. "None big enough to put on a map. Colliers' camps and logging camps, I'm sure."

"Then where are we going? Is the third key a magical saw? A magical wedge? A magical brazier?"

"My master hasn't told me. I know as much as you know. Which is: east."

"East, into what?" Rodrick snapped the reins, which only seemed to irritate the cart horse, judging by the way it twitched its tail and shat. "And why?"

"For your weight in gold," Hrym said. " Or equivalent gems. It's good to maintain your focus."

Chapter Twenty-One
The Howling Mountains

The trip east was not pleasant. Rodrick's rear end began to hurt within an hour after they set off from the edge of the Gronzi Forest, and the cart wheels had a regular squeak that he found damnably irritating. He suspected he would be hearing that squeak in his dreams for years to come. Obed would rise occasionally from his bath and sit beside Rodrick, staring in all directions with his usual cold, impatient fury, but there was precious little to see: forest on one side, plains on the other. Rodrick tried to make small talk, mostly because attempts at conversation hastened Obed's sullen return to his tub.

Hrym chattered amiably with him about their past conquests, and what they'd do with all the gold they had coming to them—sleeping on it was Hrym's main idea. The sword seemed to suffer from the misapprehension that they were nearly done now. They had only to pick up another artifact or two, open this mysterious vault, and—ahem—"get paid." At least Hrym had the good sense not to speculate aloud about how Obed would look when he realized he'd been robbed.

From time to time Cilian would emerge from the forest, trot up to the cart, and hop up alongside to ride for a while, telling Rodrick about the various threats he'd dispatched, or bandits he'd frightened off by convincing animals to attack them, or how the shape of writhing wood grubs in the dirt reinforced his certainty that traveling with this bold band of heroes was his destiny, and so on. The huntsman was almost as bad as Obed, but unlike the priest, he was undeterred by either trivial conversation or cold silence, or even veiled insults. Fortunately Cilian always hopped down and ran off into the woods again after a short while.

They found a colliers' camp just before full dark. Obed slumbered in the tub beneath a tarp while Zaqen and Rodrick joined the local workers around their fire. The soot-stained men were happy enough to greet travelers who might bring news of more civilized lands. Rodrick spun some expansive lies: the demons were being defeated in the Worldwound, Cheliax was throwing off the yoke of Hell, rumors of impending civil war in Brevoy were greatly exaggerated, and there had been sightings of Aroden reborn far to the west, near the hurricane-swept lands.

Later, leaning against a log with a cadged bottle of local booze brewed from some foul vegetation, Rodrick looked up at the smoke-smeared stars while Zaqen leaned beside him. "Why did you tell them such ridiculous lies?" she said after a while.

"They'll never know the difference," Rodrick said. "Whether the things I said were true or untrue, nothing's likely to change for them. They'll burn charcoal here until they die from breathing in too much black smoke, whether there are demons in the Worldwound or not. And tonight, they're happy, and think the world is a better place. Not every lie is a weapon. Some lies are kindnesses."

"Hmph. I think you just like lying."

"I like doing anything I'm good at," Rodrick said. "And that, remarkably, was the honest truth." Another long moment of companionable silence passed. "You really don't know where we're going?"

"Ultimately, yes: to the bottom of a lake. Tomorrow? No idea. We're off to get the next key. My master hasn't told me anything more." She sighed. "He doesn't entirely trust me anymore. My loyalty, I mean. Which is ridiculous. Even if I were feeling disloyal, there is the geas, compelling me. But he knows there are ways to get around a geas—to fulfill the letter of the compulsion and avoid fulfilling the spirit. He told me, flat out, that he doesn't trust me anymore—or, at any rate, doesn't trust my discretion."

"Whatever for? I've known hounds trained from puppyhood to be perfect companions who are less loyal than you. Not to compare you to a dog—"

"I've been compared to worse. At least dogs are mammals. Obed . . . I think *he* thinks I've become too friendly with you."

Rodrick let no expression touch his features. "He doesn't think we're . . . that is, that we're . . ."

She made a face. "I'm not sure he ever thinks about humans doing those things, Rodrick, any more than you spend your time imagining gorillas in the Mwangi Expanse making sweet jungle love." She looked at him sidelong. "You *don't* spend all your time imagining that, do you? Good. I'm reassured. No, but you were supposed to be expendable. A weapon to use until you broke, or needed to be paid off, either one. But when he was in the pond in the forest, Obed accused me of growing fond of you."

"Have you?"

"I think you're a terrible person, but you make me laugh." She shrugged. "I don't have much use for other humans, as a rule. I've never felt comfortable with my race, perhaps because it's not *entirely* my race. But if Hrym sees something in you . . ."

The sword, silent all night in order to avoid frightening the colliers, spoke up. "I don't see that much in him. Are you looking for a sword, Zaqen? I could be persuaded to switch my allegiance. I'm fickle."

"Breaking up the two of you?" She clucked her tongue. "I'm no homewrecker, Hrym. The two of you are one of the great romances, in your own way."

"You take that back." Hrym said. "This man means nothing to me. He's just a body to strap a scabbard to!"

"I should have given you to the swordlord," Rodrick said. "I could have kept Magnos the Ash Lord. He knew how to keep his lack of a mouth shut."

Zaqen chuckled. "Sleep well, boys. We have an early day tomorrow. I don't know where we're going, but I'm sure Obed will want to get there faster than is physically possible."

Two days later they crossed a minor river into wilder lands—now the forest loomed on both sides, though there was a little village there with a mill wheel, and farmers making the most of Brevoy's short growing season. The weather was already turning surprisingly cold, especially nights, and Rodrick couldn't imagine what it must be like here in the winter. The mountains were closer now, and it became increasingly apparent that some peak or ridge or pass must be Obed's destination. Maybe the next artifact was hidden under another rock. That would be nice.

The road they were following gradually devolved into a mere track, but they hadn't passed into entirely uninhabited lands yet, and the cart rolled stolidly along. Obed wanted to travel nights too, but Rodrick convinced him that the near certainty of hitting a hole in the dark and breaking a wagon wheel—or a horse's leg—would cost them more time than his plan would gain.

When they camped the next night, just stopping where they happened to be when darkness fell—which it did swiftly at this latitude—Rodrick saw lights flickering off to the east. "What's that?" he asked. "Is something on fire over there?" The thought of a wildfire tearing through the Gronzi Forest was terrifying, since they were literally surrounded on both sides by the wood.

Cilian, who'd walked in from the trees to join them for a meal, looked at the light for a moment, then shook his head. "That does not seem to be fire. The lights are in the icy mountains. Mountains do not burn."

Zaqen rose and stood with them, then made a *hmmm* sound. "The Valley of Fire is in that direction, though still some distance away. It's the site of a great battle— or a great massacre, anyway. The Aldori rebels pursued Choral the Conqueror into that valley, thinking they would corner him, but it was a trap. The Conqueror had an ambush prepared. Two red dragons. They simply *filled* the place with flames, reducing the main force of the army of Rostland to so much bone meal and ash.

Apparently nothing grows on that battlefield anymore, and everything is still as charred and blackened as it was right after the dragons attacked."

"All right, but it's still on *fire*?" Rodrick said.

"There are stories that the ghosts of the dead army still linger there," Zaqen said. "Some say their shades still burn, eternally suffering the agony of a fiery death."

"Ah." Rodrick turned his back on the distant flickers of light. "So it's just burning ghosts, then, is that all? Why has Obed brought us to this horrible place?"

The priest spoke up, startling Rodrick, who hadn't noticed him emerge from his tub and approach their fire. "I go where my god demands, man. Just as you go where your employer demands. We are all tools for someone."

"Are we bound for the Valley of Fire, master?" Zaqen said. Rodrick dearly hoped not. Hrym was a versatile weapon, but he lost most of his considerable advantages when it came to dealing with magical fire.

"No. Tomorrow we will begin to turn north."

"North? But there's nothing to the north but forest, and the Icerime Peaks—"

"I can read a map," Obed said. "And I know where I'm going. You do not need to concern yourself with such things." He paused. "Oh. And Zaqen. Tomorrow— do not take your remedy."

The sorcerer stumbled back a step. "But . . . master . . ."

"Would you disobey me?" Obed's voice was mild, but it was the mildness of . . . well, of a psychopath enjoying the lull before an explosion of violence.

"I would not disobey, even if I could, but I want to make sure I understand—"

"Your medicine," Obed said. "Your preventative. Do not take it tomorrow. Or the next day, of course. I know it takes a day or so for the effects of your remedy to wear off."

"May I ask why?" she said, almost whispering.

"We will soon have need of those qualities you choose to suppress," Obed said, shrugging. "That is all the reason you should require." He went back to the cart, climbing into his sloshing tub.

"Are you all right?" Rodrick said. "I'm not sure what just happened, but—"

"It's nothing." Zaqen drew her cloak around her tightly. "I . . . will serve him in whatever way he sees fit."

"But if you stop taking your medicine, whatever it is," Rodrick said, "will it . . . make you sick? Will it hurt you?"

She laughed in a strangely toneless way. "Will it hurt *me*? Not at all. It's much more likely to hurt others." Zaqen went to the far side of the fire, curled up on the ground, and rolled over, either falling asleep immediately or pretending to do so.

Rodrick walked away from the fire, and a moment later, Cilian followed him.

"What do you think?" Hrym said. "Is she a werewolf?"

"Some sort of lycanthrope could be a possibility," Rodrick said. "Though the tainted blood she spoke of seemed different, and it would be odd if she were *also* a were . . . whatever. That might explain why horses shy away from her, though."

Cilian shook his head. "She is not a shapechanger. I believe I would know."

"Oh?"

The huntsman nodded. "I have fought werewolves, and wererats, and stranger things, and there is always a certain bestial quality, a whiff of musk, some sign of the beast within revealed by the way they move. Zaqen . . . I like the sorcerer, despite the twisted blood that flows through her, but she does not have the grace or power of someone who shares her soul with a beast. The herbs she uses for her medicinal tea each morning are not wolfsbane, either, and I know of no other preventative for lycanthropy."

"What herbs are they, then?" Hrym said.

"They are nothing I have ever seen, and my knowledge of plants is quite extensive. The leaves, before she crushes them, are red and spined . . . they look unnatural. Like something that might grow on another plane, or from cursed and polluted soil."

Rodrick sighed. "It would be almost too simple if she were a werewolf. I'm sure it's nothing that ordinary. I suppose we'll find out what secret she's hiding soon enough. I just hope she doesn't have to suffer too much in the process."

"I'm more concerned about *us*," Hrym said. "She did say if she stopped taking her medicine, it would be others who got hurt."

"What are you worried about?" Rodrick said. "You're a *sword*."

"That's a good point," Hrym said. "Carry on, then."

Chapter Twenty-Two
The Sunken Land

"The Icerime Peaks," Rodrick said, yawning. They'd camped late the night before, and arisen early, setting off before dawn. The sun was only just now up over the trees, and though Rodrick had been awake for hours, he still felt thick with sleep. "How pleasant. They couldn't have called them something a little cheerier, like the Frozen Teeth of Death?"

"You have to admit, it's descriptive." Zaqen was in the rear of the cart, but standing up, leaning against the back of the driver's seat. They both looked at the jagged peaks marching north and south on their right, dizzying spires of stone covered in white snow, with occasional patches of solid ice that flashed blue. On their left stood the ragged vastness of the Gronzi Forest, evergreen trees dusted with snow on their highest branches. The group was squeezed between stone and wild, following a path that might have been used by traders, once, but obviously hadn't been traveled much in decades, if not longer. The temperature seemed to drop with every mile they rolled, and Rodrick had never taken off the thick wool cloak he'd wrapped around himself to sleep in the night before.

"They should have sent some of the red dragons up this way back during that war," Rodrick said. "And melted some of these mountains. I bet they're really just little hills, once you chip away all the ice and snow."

"Don't talk about such things," Hrym said, leaning against the seat beside Rodrick's right leg. "Dragon's fire is one of the few things that might actually be able to melt me. You'll give me nightmares."

"You don't sleep."

"Don't remind me. Can you imagine having to listen to *your* snoring eternally?"

Cilian trotted out of the treeline, easily running alongside the slow-rolling cart, then pulled himself up on the seat next to Rodrick. "The forest here is strangely empty," he said. "No sign of predators, but also no prey animals. I detect no hint of poison or corruption. Perhaps there is some magical taint . . . ?" He trailed off and looked at Zaqen.

She shrugged. "Not that I've noticed. But then, my own magic carries a taint, so maybe I'm not as sensitive to such things as other sorcerers are."

A splashing arose from the back of the cart, and Obed sat up. "If there are no animals, then we are near our destination."

Rodrick winced. "I should have known. Do you care to tell us what we're in for now, then?"

"There is a place in the mountains. I do not mean on the mountains. *In* the mountains. Some say it is an old dwarven fortress, though others say the dwarves merely found a much more ancient place and made use of it for a time. Its true creators, then, are unknown. Now it is a place of darkness. Somewhere in those depths is an altar of black stone, and on that altar rests our third key. You need only go into the dark and retrieve it, and we may be on our way."

"Oh, is that all?" Hrym said. "You'll be leading the way, then?"

More splashing. "I would love nothing better. I do not relish leaving such important tasks in hands other than mine. But because I have lost my ring, I must stay here, close to water. I do not know how long your journey into the dark will take, and if it requires more than a day. . . I cannot risk dying myself."

"He'll just risk *us* dying," Hrym said. "Or at least you mortals."

"That's what we're getting paid for," Rodrick said. "At least, I am. I don't know why Cilian does anything he does. So we go in, without our priest, and thus without magics of healing and protection."

"I find that bringing sufficient powers of destruction and violence often limit the need for healing and protection," Obed said. "And you are all formidable enough, aren't you? Especially you, Zaqen. Isn't that right?"

"Do you truly think we will face things so terrible, master? To require . . . *that*?"

"There are no animals in these woods, as Cilian said," Obed replied. "That is because the thing which dwells in the dark—the thing which guards my *key*, either consciously or coincidentally—emerges to devour all living things that enter his territory. But the animals have grown wise to the dangers of this place, and they stay away, which means the thing in the dark is probably quite hungry by now. When the four of you go into its lair, I am sure it will welcome you as a starving man would a hot meal."

"What is this thing, exactly?" Cilian said.

"The guardian's nature is unknown to me." Obed didn't sound too bothered by that ignorance—but then, he wasn't crawling into the hole in the ground where the mystery creature lived. "In my researches I discovered no one who had seen the beast and lived. I have only reports from those survivors who lost members of their expeditions. The last expedition to emerge from this place—looking for dwarven gold, and finding only death and stone—confirmed the presence of the altar, and the key. That is all I need to know."

"Do you at least know what the key looks like?" Rodrick said. "I'd hate to find an altar scattered with dozens of objects—or worse, dozens of altars."

"The third key is an immense red jewel," Obed said, "approximately the size of a grapefruit, known as the Inferno's Eye. It is said to be a bezoar, taken from the stomach of a slain red dragon millennia ago, its facets etched by the beast's burning interior."

Rodrick whistled. "Does it have magical properties?"

"Reports vary," Obed said. "At the very least it has the property of being worth a small fortune. That is, a small fortune by my standards. By yours, it is worth an unimaginably large fortune. It goes without saying that if you try to steal it from me—"

"You'll hunt me down and feed my guts to a kraken, yes, I know." Rodrick tried to sound bored.

"I suppose you can have the jewel once I've unlocked the vault and recovered Gozreh's relic," Obed said.

"Ah." Rodrick turned in his seat to look at the gillman, but the priest's expression was perfectly bland. "Really?"

Obed shrugged. "I will have no further need of it, one it has served its function as a key. Consider it a gift. Cilian may have the dog's skull, if he likes. I will keep the pitcher of everlasting seawater, however. It has proven to possess practical value."

"That's very generous of you, Obed," Rodrick said.

"It is not generosity if it costs you nothing," the priest replied. "Stop the cart. Do you see a shadow, there, on the mountainside?"

Rodrick squinted, and didn't see much, but both Hrym and Cilian said, "Yes."

"That is the entrance to the hollow in the mountains," Obed said. "I suggest you get moving. I will protect the cart and the animals while you are gone."

"Aren't you worried about freezing to death?" Rodrick said. "When night falls, it's going to get *cold*. We could come back and find you frozen in a block of ice."

"I am a priest of Gozreh," Obed said. "I have nothing to fear from the elements. Zaqen, there are supplies in my special bag, the one bigger inside than out, that you may use for journeying underground. How does your . . . condition . . . feel?"

"Restless." Zaqen shivered. "Which is how you want it to feel, master."

"Do not forget your jar of eyes," Obed said.

"Yes," she said tonelessly. "That would be a bad thing to leave behind."

Rodrick and Cilian exchanged a glance, then shrugged and began their preparations for the descent.

"Do you mind waiting?" Zaqen called querulously, and Rodrick paused in his trudge up the side of the mountain and looked back at her.

"What are you doing that for?" he said, surprised. Zaqen was waist-deep in snow, laboriously pushing her way through the drifts, while Rodrick and Cilian stood atop the crust, walking easily.

"I don't have a ranger's magic for walking on snow," she said through gritted teeth. "*Or* a magical sword giving me the power to cross ice without breaking through."

"Hrym, are you using magic on me?" Rodrick demanded.

"Of course, idiot," the sword replied from his place iced onto Rodrick's back. "Why did you think you weren't sinking in the snow?"

"I just thought I was . . . stepping lightly?"

"Idiot," Hrym said again. "Take Zaqen's hand and I can extend the power to her as well."

"Sorry about that," the thief muttered. "I really had no idea." He reached down to Zaqen, who clutched his gloved hand and began to climb out of the snow-pit she'd dug for herself. They continued up the slope, a trifle awkwardly because of the steepness of the grade and the need to maintain contact. "What other spells do you cast on me without me knowing?" Rodrick demanded.

"Oh, right now, there's one that keeps you from going snow blind, which is why you aren't squinting like poor Zaqen. I also do a certain amount of temperature control. I don't bother to keep you all warm and toasty, since I know you like the way you look in a fur cloak, but I protect you from losing fingers and toes to frostbite. If I had magic that would make you smarter, I'd use that, too, but alas, even I have my limitations."

By the time they reached the shadow, Cilian was crouching on the edge of a ragged circular opening, perhaps ten feet across. "There is something ancient and terrible here," he said. The huntsman could make even a comment on the quality of breakfast sound like the pronouncements of a prophet, but his voice was unusually solemn and earnest this time. A bit of snow had drifted into the hole, which slanted down at a sharp angle, but the light did not penetrate far enough to show what awaited them below.

"It's interesting that the opening to an ancient dwarven fortress should be standing wide open," Rodrick said. "Traditionally, aren't fortresses a bit more . . . secure?"

"Do not think of it as a door," Cilian said.

"Of course not, it's just a hole—"

Cilian spoke louder: "Think of it instead as the open jaws of a great beast, inviting the prey inside to be devoured." The half-elf hammered a spike into the frozen ground, fixed a length of rope to the spike, and tossed the rope down the hole. Grasping the rope in both gloved hands, he began to lower himself swiftly into the dark.

"What kind of predator feeds just by opening its mouth and hoping some prey walks in?" Hrym said. "Granted, I don't eat, so I'm no expert, but it doesn't seem like a very effective strategy."

"Whales, maybe?" Zaqen said. "Though I think they sort of strain water through their mouths and catch shrimp and bugs and things in the process. I'm not sure Cilian always thinks his metaphors through very thoroughly."

"He's damn good with a bow, though," Rodrick said. "And he works cheaply, which means I don't have to split any profits with him, so he's in my good books. I suppose he does have a point, anyway. A place that's this easy to get into is almost certainly a trap. Shall we descend?"

Zaqen cocked her head. "I don't hear Cilian screaming in agony yet, so why not?"

The sorcerer took a long metal rod from her pack and struck it against the side of the tunnel as they descended, and the end of the rod flared with white light, illuminating the shaft. Rodrick eased himself down, keeping his eyes on the rope between his hands, trusting Hrym on his back to speak up if he was about to slide into the jaws of a cave-dragon or something. After about ten minutes of careful progress, the shaft angled sharply from slanted to vertical, and Rodrick slid down the rope faster, finally landing on an uneven stone floor. He stepped aside before Zaqen could fall on his head.

"It's not so frigid in here," Rodrick noted. "One of the more pleasant aspects of crawling around in underground chambers, I've found—never too hot, never too cold."

Cilian was there, sniffing the air, squinting at a pair of low tunnels branching off from the small, rough-hewn chamber. "My friends," he said. "Do we wish to go in the direction of the beast that dwells herein, or follow the tunnel that shows no signs of life and habitation?"

"You sense something alive down one of those passages, then?" Rodrick said.

Cilian nodded, pointing to the tunnel on the right, clogged with cobwebs. "Yes. Something lives there. I cannot be more precise. The beasts of this land are not all known to me. Down there—" he gestured to the other corridor—"I sense only dust and bones."

"Zaqen?" Rodrick said. "What do you think?"

She sighed. "I think we can't possibly be lucky enough to go into this pit without having to face whatever creature lives here. My master isn't sure if the thing that inhabits this hole is guarding our key deliberately or not, but it's a possibility. Let's see if we can surprise it and kill it. Otherwise we'll have to worry about it stalking us in the dark later."

"Headlong into danger!" Hrym said. "Oh, the hero's life is a glorious one."

"I will lead," Cilian said. "If that is acceptable."

Zaqen shook her head. "Not just yet, huntsman." She handed Rodrick the rod of light. Her face was terribly pale in the harsh white glow, forehead beaded with sweat. "I have something to do first. And let me apologize in advance for the nightmares you'll probably have about this in the future."

Chapter Twenty-Three
Sword and Deviltry

Zaqen began pulling her robe over her head.

"Oh, Zaqen, don't be so hard on yourself." Rodrick tried for a jovial tone. "I doubt seeing you naked will be cause for nightmares."

She threw her garment onto the ground and stood shivering in the magical light. The sorcerer looked smaller without her robes, and she was terribly thin, her ribs visible, her breasts small, her hips slim and boyish. Rodrick had half-expected to see vestigial tentacles on her ribs, or needle teeth in her navel, or some other sign of her inhuman heritage, but there was nothing. Cilian looked at her with curiosity, as if he'd been promised a magic trick, but saw nothing out of the ordinary. Hrym said, "She appears to fall into the acceptable range for primate physiology. Am I missing something?"

The sorcerer closed her eyes. "Step back. He will be disoriented for a moment, long enough for me to bring him under my control, as long as you do not startle or provoke him."

"Startle who—" Rodrick began, but then Zaqen turned around.

She had a hump on her back. He'd known that, of course—it was visible even beneath her robes, a bulge on one shoulder . . . though it did seem, sometimes, that the hump moved from one shoulder to another.

Now for the first time, Rodrick saw her back when it was bare. The hump was the same color as her flesh, swollen like an enormous boil, and it rippled and twitched as if alive with squirming insects under the skin. Zaqen shuddered, and then—

The hump shivered too, and opened its three dozen eyes.

The hump did not have eyelashes, or even really eyelids: it was more as if scores of small wounds tore open in its flesh, allowing the eyes beneath to peer out. Most were the size of human eyes, though a few were larger, and one looked fit for a giant, easily as big as a fist. They were all colors: blue, gray, green, hazel, brown, gray, and inhuman hues, too—silver, gold, glowing purple, ghostly white, iridescent rainbow. The eyes did not look around in unison, but looked off in their own directions, as if operated by dozens of different minds.

Cilian grunted, and Rodrick took an involuntary step back. The hump twitched again, and Zaqen moaned. The hump made a terrible sound, like a blood-crusted bandage being torn away from a septic wound, and then it slid down Zaqen's back, moving with the slow undulations of a snail. The hump dropped from her back to the stone floor, and small tentacles unfurled from beneath it, moving like wriggling earthworms, but pale and bloodless.

The sorcerer's upper back, where the hump had clung, was irregularly marred by dozens of small clustered holes, circles no bigger than a fingertip, all slowly oozing blood, along with black and green fluids. Zaqen knelt and opened her bag, lifting out a jar filled with bobbing eyes. "I keep them in a brine solution," she said, voice unsteady. "It keeps the eyes fresh, and he seems to enjoy the saltiness."

The hump twitched when she spoke, and most of its eyes turned toward her.

Zaqen unfastened the jar's lid, reached inside, and plucked out an eyeball, one harvested from some bandit or another, Rodrick supposed. She tossed the eye through the air, and the hump *leapt*, straight up, easily three feet into the air. The eye struck its flesh and was instantly absorbed, as if dropped into a bowl of soup. After a moment, a new eye opened on the surface of the hump, and began staring around.

Then the hump began to purr, sounding for all the world like a contented cat. It undulated across the floor to Zaqen and rubbed against her leg. She reached down and stroked it between a few of its eyes. "Hello, brother," she said. "I'm glad you liked your treat. I need your help, now. There is a creature in this place—no, not those men, they are my friends, they are *not* for you—down that tunnel. I do not know what it is, but . . ." She licked her lips. "I have reason to believe it has very beautiful eyes."

The thing twitched, quivered, and then moved with disturbing rapidity toward the tunnel, disappearing into the dark.

"That thing does fall outside the standard range of primate physiology," Hrym said. "In fact, it may rate as one of the strangest things I've ever seen."

Zaqen slumped, wiped her brow with the back of her hand, and then began to pull her robe back on. "I just need a moment," she said. "Releasing my brother is always a strain on my body."

"Your . . . brother," Rodrick said. "It's . . . that's . . ."

"A parasitic twin," she said. "We were in the womb together. My brother could not survive on his own, so he . . . bonded to me. He takes after the inhuman side of the family a bit more than I do, of course. He did not awaken for many years, and my parents had various healers try to remove him, thinking he was just some sort of tumor, but . . . I feel what he feels, so attempts to cut him away were agonizing for me. Finally they held me down and tried to burn the hump off my back. That operation was excruciating, but it was also successful, to an extent . . . but some small scrap of my brother's flesh remained, and the hump grew back to its old proportions. When I was perhaps ten years old, my brother woke up. He didn't have any eyes, then, and while I slept he detached himself from me, and slithered through the camp where we lived, and killed almost all the cultists. He didn't mean any harm—he just wanted their eyes. He's always craved them. I don't know why." She laughed, harshly. "The amusing thing is, if my parents and the other cultists had realized I had a monstrous twin, they would have probably revered me, and made sacrifices to me, and fed him eyes, believing he was a sign from their god. Instead I had to flee from the angry survivors, with my twin clinging to my back."

"And that's when Obed found you?" Rodrick said.

She nodded. "He created the medicinal tea I drink every day. It keeps my twin from waking, though he shifts, sometimes, in his sleep, sliding his weight from one side of my back to the other. His tentacles snake into my body, and he takes sustenance from the food I eat. If I eat too much, he grows larger. In the beginning he was barely the size of a kitten, and now, he's as big as a medium-sized dog." Another harsh laugh. "Many women would be envious of my inability to gain weight. But Obed occasionally asks me to let my twin wake, and prowl, and my brother is always ravenous for new eyes when he first arises. That's why I collect the eyes of the fallen—if I have a steady supply to feed my brother on those occasions when he wakes, he will not attempt to consume the eyes of my friends or companions. At least, not immediately."

"You carry a terrible burden," Cilian said.

"That's true," Rodrick said, but he was wondering if her brother could be trained to, say, slip into a manor house and steal all the silverware. Probably not worth the trouble if it came back with the eyes of the householder blinking in its repulsive hide, though. "Do you think your brother can be a help down here?"

Zaqen smiled thinly. "The acid I can spray is what my brother seems to have instead of blood. He has survived being burned, dissolved, smeared into paste, and minced into fragments. He always pulls himself back together again, or grows anew from fragments. He can move impossibly fast. He feels no pain—because *I* feel his pain instead. Nothing deters him. Anything my brother bothers to fight will be, at the very least, grievously injured. If the guardian of the key happens to lack eyes, that might be a problem, because my brother won't see any reason to attack the beast. I respect your skills as a tracker, Cilian, but my brother seems to detect life with something other than ordinary senses. If there is a creature here, with eyes to see, my brother will seek it."

"Should we follow?" Cilian said.

Zaqen nodded. "Yes. But I will go first. That way if my brother comes out of the dark, he will pass by me before he sees you, and I can toss him a few eyes to mollify him." She took back the light rod and moved slowly down the tunnel. The back of her robe was stained with the fluids oozing from her back.

The corridor was carved from the stone, wide enough for them to walk two abreast, though they went single-file instead. "My brother has triggered some traps," Zaqen said. "That explains the twinges of pain I've been feeling." She pointed to a heap of shattered arrows. They'd been rigged to fire from the right side of the tunnel, and had smashed themselves to fragments on the left side, their arrowheads damp and partially melted. A single punctured eyeball was speared on the point of one of the arrows.

"That didn't hurt him? Your . . . twin?" Rodrick said.

"I call him Lump," she said. "And no. Lump's body isn't bothered much by projectiles or blades. They tend to just pass through, and the wounds seal up again as soon as the penetration is done. Occasionally an eye does get snagged, though. That makes Lump angry. And hungry. Hungrier."

They continued and found another trap, this one a wide, crescent-shaped blade that had fallen from the ceiling and now spanned the width of the tunnel. The blade was smeared with ichor and surrounded by a few eyeballs, all sliced in half as neatly as grapes for a salad. "Lump survived *that*?" Rodrick said, aghast.

Zaqen shrugged. It was a much less dramatic gesture with her hump gone. "Have you ever tried to slice a pudding in half? It just flows back together again. That's Lump."

"You feel these arrows, these blades?" Cilian said. "The pain?"

"Well, yes, but it doesn't feel like *I've* been chopped in half. The arrows were a bit like getting splinters. This blade coming down, that was like slicing the ball of your thumb on a paper knife, a short stinging sensation. It could be much worse."

They stepped carefully over the blade and continued, the tunnel now curving toward the left, and Zaqen paused to peer into a pit ten feet across, blocking their progress. "Hmm. I think there's a pressure plate here, where I'm standing. It must have made a portion of the floor fall in, or a sliding panel move aside."

Rodrick eased himself forward and looked down. He grunted. There was no bottom, as far as he could tell, just an opening to lightless depths. "Do you think Lump, ah . . ."

Zaqen shook her head. "No, he's still up ahead. My brother is sticky. He can climb up walls like a snail. He's fine."

"How do you know his location?" Cilian asked. "Do you have a psychic bond?"

Zaqen snorted. "Nothing as poetic as that. Here, Rodrick, give me your hand."

He held out his hand, a bit nervously.

"All right," she said, "now close your eyes."

"Ah—"

"Don't be so nervous."

Rodrick obeyed. Zaqen took his hand and lifted his arm up over his head, then let go. "All right. Where's your hand?"

"Is this a trick question?"

"Only if you make it one."

"All right, then. My hand is over my head." He wiggled his fingers. "Right there."

"Good. Open your eyes. How did you know where your hand was? You couldn't see it. But it's not a psychic bond. It's proprioception. I know where Lump is the same way you know where your hand is—he's part of my *body*, even if he happens to be away from my body at this particular moment. I think Lump can sense me as well. He must be able to. The times I tried to flee from him, he always found me again, days or weeks later, no matter how far I ran. He's not too far away now, either. Any ideas for how to get across the pit?"

"My pleasure," Hrym said. The temperature suddenly plunged, making Rodrick shiver, and an icy bridge shimmered into existence across the middle of the pit. Zaqen started across, walking slowly and cautiously— then gasped, doubled over, and fell to her knees. She nearly fell into the pit, but Rodrick leapt forward (his feet sure on the ice, thanks to one of Hrym's quiet little spells, no doubt) and seized her by the arm. He pulled her back up, then half-dragged, half-carried her to the far side of the pit, depositing her on the stone floor. She gasped and trembled, gnashing her teeth and rolling her eyes. "What is it?" Rodrick said. "Zaqen, are you having some kind of fit, or—"

"My brother," she gasped. "My brother is fighting. And he is not winning."

Chapter Twenty-Four
The Frost Monster

Stay with her!" Rodrick boomed to Cilian. He snatched up Zaqen's light rod and hurried down the corridor.

"Why are you rushing into danger and leaving a perfectly good human shield like Cilian behind?" Hrym asked. "That's not like you."

Rodrick didn't slow down, though it was a damn good question. "I just want to be the first to lay my hands on this great red jewel," he said, and Hrym laughed.

"Of course, that's it. You've gone sweet on the sorcerer, haven't you? I never knew you had such a weakness for the lost and the broken."

"I—"

"It's fine," Hrym said. "I haven't been plunged into the guts of anything alive in ages. I could do with a warm bloodbath."

Rodrick hesitated in front of another triggered trap—this one a series of metal spikes that had slammed down from the ceiling into slots on the floor, creating a forest of sharpened metal. He touched Hrym against a few of the spikes, freezing them into brittleness, then shattered them with sword blows. In that fashion he managed to clear an irregular path through the spikes, sufficient for him to slip through. Not far beyond the spikes he found a steep flight of stone steps, and he rushed to the landing at the top. A wooden door, banded with metal, still stood in the doorframe, but it had a great ragged hole burned out of the center, as if by acid. After making sure there was no acid still bubbling around the edges, Rodrick ducked and wriggled through the hole.

The chamber beyond stank of acid and blood and damp fur. The room was roughly circular, and in the center stood a long rectangular stone altar. On it rested a red, spherical jewel nearly the size of a child's head. Beyond the altar, in the shadows where Rodrick's light did not reach, something enormous roared and thrashed and howled, its voice so low and powerful it made Rodrick's back teeth vibrate. He dropped the light rod to the floor and drew Hrym, then crouched, trying to see what kind of beast he was about to face.

"Snatch up the jewel and run away," Hrym said reasonably.

"But . . . Zaqen's brother . . ."

"She said he can pull himself together from shreds, and can follow her to the ends of the world, if need be," the sword said. "So *let* him."

"Right." Rodrick saw the sense in his friend's counsel. Putting himself in danger to save a member of the party was questionable behavior anyway, and when the party member in question was a lump of optophagic tentacled slime, it was doubly so. He hurried toward the altar, hoping that removing the jewel wouldn't trigger any traps. Just as he reached for the bezoar, something flew out of the darkness and smashed into his chest, knocking him to the ground. Hrym went flying from his fingers, clattering on the stones and complaining bitterly about the impact.

The thing that had struck Rodrick's chest *moved*, wriggling and surging, and when the thief lifted his head to look, he screamed.

Lump was on his chest, tentacles writhing, one of his eyes—an ice-blue one as big as a peach—gazing directly into Rodrick's face.

I have such pretty eyes, Rodrick thought, squeezing them shut, as if his eyelids would save him if Lump decided to scoop his eyeballs from his head.

Instead Lump slithered off his body, and when Rodrick opened one eye to look around, the parasite was vanishing back into the dark behind the altar. A moment later there was another roar, and the hideous creature flew through the air again, this time hurled against the wall, where it struck wetly, then slid down, landing unmoving on the stone floor.

Rodrick got to his feet unsteadily—his chest hurt like he'd been punched over the heart with a mailed fist—then stumbled toward Hrym. "The jewel!" Hrym cried. "Get it first!"

Right. Rodrick changed direction, veering to the black stone altar. He reached out with both hands and seized the jewel, which was warm, as if it still retained some heat from the red dragon's belly where it had been formed.

"Stop!" called a low, harsh voice from behind the altar, and it spoke with such authority that Rodrick actually paused.

A figure moved toward him, the illumination from the dropped light rod just revealing the outline of its shape. Rodrick whimpered, clutching the jewel to his belly, because when things that stood ten feet tall and five feet across the shoulders approached him, a certain amount of involuntary whimpering was to be expected. The creature radiated cold, and its single eye glowed pale blue: Rodrick would have said it *burned* pale blue, but this was the opposite of burning. It *froze* pale blue, and the sight of that eye was somehow so terrifying that it made Rodrick stand fast in place, paralyzed with a fear that went beyond the body, and made him think the monster was somehow meddling with his mind.

The thing shambled a step closer, and it was like nothing he'd ever seen before: roughly human in shape but covered in shaggy white fur, mouth a fanged cavern, arms so long its clawed fingers nearly brushed the ground. Its right eye was missing, blood oozing from the socket and crusted on its fur.

"Please," it said. "Leave the jewel."

Rodrick tore his gaze away from its single eye and the temporary paralysis diminished. He scurried backward, squatted to snatch up Hrym, and brandished the blade at the monster. "I can't do that. I don't want to hurt you, but I will if I must."

"You travel with that . . . thing?" the beast said, its voice understandable despite the rough growl that seemed to rumble behind every word. "That demon, the beast with the eyes?"

"Lump was born right here on Golarion, actually," Rodrick said. "Though I'll grant you that some of his ancestors must have been immigrants from peculiar shores. I'm sorry he attacked you that way. Lump is a creature of appetites. We didn't expect to encounter someone down here we could make conversation with. There are stories, you know, about the monster that lives in this pit, and kills anyone who comes near."

"The traps kill most of them," the beast said. "I eat their remains, though. Once I would have found the idea of eating humans and elves and dwarves repulsive, but the taste of such flesh agrees with this body. Still: I will allow you to leave. Losing an eye has put me off the idea of fighting for now. Just put down the jewel, and depart."

"What good is this gem doing you?" Rodrick continued edging almost imperceptibly backward, Hrym in one hand, the jewel in the other. "You can hardly sell it. I understand you might be starved for beautiful things down here, but I'll tell you what, I'll head back to New Stetven and nip into a shop and have someone make a beautiful ornament for you, I'm sure I can have someone deliver it—"

"You see merely a treasure to be looted, foolish mortal," the beast said. It placed its hands—claws, really—on the altar and vaulted over the obstruction, landing in a crouch that still let it tower over Rodrick by a few feet. "But the jewel is more than that. I have been tasked to protect it."

"Ah, you're a *guardian*, well, of course, I understand," Rodrick said. "Fear not, we are on a mission from the very god who hid this jewel so long ago—"

"You lie, or you are deceived," the beast said flatly. "Aroden died. I *felt* him die. The entire world has been sickening ever since."

"Aroden?" Rodrick said. "Gozreh sent us—"

"Gozreh? What does Gozreh have to do with anything? I am an ancient of Aroden's cohort, sworn to guard this jewel. It was never to be used again save by Aroden himself, and now that he is dead, it must *never* be used. The guardians of the other keys have fallen victim to age and entropy and decay, all long dead but myself and one other, but I was a great priest and wizard, and I lived on even when my first body died. I moved my mind from my human form into the bodies of cave bears, frost trolls, ice giants, and finally into this yeti. But . . ." He clasped a hand to his wounded eye, and, to Rodrick's astonishment, let out what sounded like a sorrowful sob. "My magic is nearly faded. It began to fade when Aroden died, and has not fared well since. I tried to leave this body, to take another form, and I could not. I will die in this body. And if need be, I will die defending that artifact from pillagers and thieves. The fact that you are ignorant of the gem's true purpose, and of the danger it poses, is the only reason I will consent to let you leave here alive. Put the gem down, and I think . . . once you have left this place, I will use the last of my magics to collapse these tunnels. I have lived so long that I now fear death, but that fear has made me weak. I will seal myself inside with the jewel. If I must die, I can at least die with the gem buried beside me, and my ghost can defend it from any who might seek it in centuries to come."

"You make a good point," Rodrick said. "Why don't we just—*freeze him, Hrym!*"

The sword went cold in Rodrick's hand, and a swirling sideways tornado of ice sprayed forth from the point of the blade, making the yeti disappear in a wave of white. Rodrick grinned and started to turn away—until a heavy hand touched his shoulder, pressing him down to his knees and sending waves of cold through his body so intensely that his teeth began to chatter instantly.

"Mortal," the beast rumbled behind him. "I am in the body of a yeti. They are creatures of the highest icy peaks, imbued with frost magics. The cold does not touch me. But the cold I create can touch *you*."

"I'm trying to spare you the worst of it, Rodrick, but it's not like ordinary cold," Hrym said. "Bugger."

"B-b-b-b-bugger," Rodrick agreed, his arm now numb from the beast's frigid touch. Without Hrym's magic insulating him from the worst of the cold, he thought it was quite likely he'd die—and he might anyway.

But there was movement before his eyes: Lump came squirming across the floor, body diminished in size but still easily as big as a crawling human child. Some of his tentacles had been raggedly severed, giving his movement an ungainly cast, but Lump came onward gamely—and as he approached, he opened a new eye, one of freezing, glowing blue. The yeti let go of Rodrick's shoulder, roaring in outrage. Lump built up speed and leapt over Rodrick, slamming into the yeti's chest.

Rodrick rolled over and watched as Lump *flowed* up the yeti's body, covering its howling face, tentacles elongating and squirming and questing for points of entry. The yeti howled, its screams muffled by flesh pressing against his face. Rodrick struggled to his feet and tried to run—he just about managed to limp— toward the door, the red jewel tucked under his arm, Hrym somehow still clutched in his fingers despite the numbness in his arm. He gestured vaguely with the sword, as best he could, but Hrym got the idea, and spikes of ice burst forth in a spray of needles and smashed apart the wooden door: there was no way Rodrick could wriggle through the hole Lump had burned, not in his cold and battered state.

He stumbled down the stairs, toward the maze of spikes, and carefully threaded his way through, awkwardly twisting and turning to slip through without losing his grip on the gem or on Hrym, too weak to raise the sword and smash more of the spikes aside. As he emerged from the maze, Cilian approached, supporting Zaqen with one arm. "We heard shouting!" the huntsman called. "Are you safe, friend?"

"Oh, perfectly," Rodrick began, and a horrible roar rolled down the tunnel, followed by a wave of cold. He turned, guts tightening in fear.

The yeti guardian came tromping down the steps, body so huge he filled the passageway, bellowing in murderous rage.

Chapter Twenty-Five
The Sadness of the Executed

Both the yeti's eyes were gone now, the white fur of his face smeared horribly red. Halfway down the steps he lost his footing and crashed facedown on the ground.

"An abominable snowman," Cilian said. "I have heard of such creatures, but never thought to see one."

The yeti lifted its blind head and began to drag itself forward. "Stop," it said. "Please. Leave the gem. I will tell you of other treasures. Ancient ones, unknown to all and only lightly guarded. Just leave the gem."

"I didn't realize those creatures could speak," Cilian said, frowning.

"They don't generally speak languages that humans do." Zaqen's voice was a husky rasp. "They speak the old tongue of the serpentfolk, or of other planes, though in general yeti despise those who share my bloodline. Some say they are guardians of the thin places, where this world touches other, stranger ones. But this yeti seems to think it should be guarding our key."

"Key," the yeti said, and dragged himself forward until he reached the forest of spikes, then cried out when his clawed hand touched one of the sharp spines, and began to bleed freely. "You . . . you know it is a key. But you cannot know . . ."

"He didn't begin as a yeti," Rodrick said. "He says—"

"You do not know what danger you hold in your hand," the yeti said, voice pitched in the timbre of a whisper, but loud enough to carry down the passageway. "The thing you could unleash—"

Just then Lump came slithering down the steps, sliding like a boneless thing, and crawled across the yeti's back. The beast—or wizard-priest in beast form—howled, and smoke rose from Lump's passage. Zaqen's parasitic twin was excreting acid of some kind, and he paused for a long moment on the back of the yeti's head, tentacles waving almost gaily. The two freezing blue eyes he had stolen from the guardian of the key blinked asynchronously. After the yeti slumped, still and silent, his head a smoking ruin, Lump slithered forward. He made no attempt to avoid the spike traps, simply undulating along placidly. The razored spikes sliced him, and sliced him again, so that soon he was slithering in a dozen ribbon-like pieces. Once he emerged from the other side, the pieces oozed back together, forming a seemingly seamless whole.

"My eyes," Zaqen rasped, and Cilian opened her bag and handed her the jar. She reached in, took a handful of eyes, and tossed them to her brother, who leapt and absorbed them into himself.

Zaqen took off her robe and knelt. "Come, brother. You are tired from your battle. You have done well. You deserve your rest."

Lump slimed his way forward, rubbed against his sister's leg, then oozed up her back. She gritted her teeth and shuddered as her parasitic twin situated himself to his liking, then she let out a long, breathy exhalation when Lump was still. She pulled her robe back over herself and her brother.

"Good work with the key," she said. "My master will be pleased. And he can heal your injuries, Rodrick."

"I knew I should have negotiated hazard pay," Rodrick said.

Zaqen giggled, and sounded almost like herself again. "You did, thief. That's the only kind of pay you're getting."

They made their way back down the corridor, discovering that the pit trap had closed itself, and the blade trap had receded back into the ceiling. Cilian probed at the floor with a long staff until he triggered the pressure plate that made the blade drop again, and they climbed over it safely. They proceeded with caution, in case there were separate traps meant to stop people from coming *out* of this place, but they didn't encounter any nasty surprises.

Rodrick was troubled. Some of the things the yeti-mage had said were difficult to reconcile with what Zaqen and Obed had told him. Rodrick was no stranger to lies—as giver or receiver—and he'd anticipated a certain amount of deception, but he'd taken this quest essentially at face value: a zealous holy man wanted to recover a long-lost artifact of his watery god. Any strangeness in the behavior of his employers he'd attributed to the fact that Obed was trying to conceal his true identity as a Low Azlanti and pass for human, or to the priest's simple contrariness. But what if they were lying to him about something more? About something *larger*? He'd allowed himself to grow complacent over their long journey. He needed to reignite the fires of suspicion.

Rodrick knew what Hrym would say, if asked: "Who cares? We're going to steal whatever they find in that vault anyway, whether it's an artifact of Gozreh or not." But a nearly immortal wizard had devoted several monstrous lifetimes to protecting just one of *four* keys necessary to unlock whatever Obed wanted, which suggested it was an object that might be locked away for a good reason.

Perhaps it was time to ask the fish-priest some pointed questions.

"You have ruined the warm feelings I felt toward you when I saw the jewel in your hands, Rodrick." Obed sat up from his tub to fix the thief with a cold stare. "I am not accustomed to being questioned."

Rodrick raised an eyebrow. "I wasn't aware I was questioning you. I was telling you what a wizard in the body of a yeti told me. About Aroden, and the danger this key could unleash, and—"

"I am not responsible for the ravings of some mad hermit in a cave." Obed sank back down into the water. "This key unlocks a vault sacred to—"

"Master," Zaqen said. "Perhaps it's time we told him the truth."

Obed splashed upright again. "Silence, sorcerer."

She lowered her head, the geas forcing her to obey, Rodrick presumed, but after a moment of tension, Obed relaxed slightly, and spoke again. "The truth is a large subject, Zaqen. Which portion did you propose to share with our hirelings?"

"About Aroden," she whispered. "And his resurrection."

"They will think us mad," Obed said.

"Don't worry," Hrym said. "We've thought that for ages already."

Obed nodded stiffly to Zaqen. "Tell them, then. As much as you think necessary."

"Of course, master."

"But tell him as we continue our journey. I wish to reach Port Ice as soon as possible, and we could cover a few miles yet before dark."

Cilian—apparently uninterested in Learning the Truth (or at least the latest truth)—faded off into the woods again while Zaqen and Rodrick made sure the horses and camel were fed and ready to move. Once Rodrick was seated behind the cart horse with the reins in his hands and Hrym unsheathed and resting beside him, Zaqen climbed into the back of the cart and leaned forward, resting her elbows on the seat. "What do you know about Aroden?" she asked.

"Ah, so the truth begins with a quiz?" He twitched the reins, and the patient horse started forward again, the tub of water in the back sloshing. "Let's see. He was an Azlanti, and a great hero, courageous and powerful, fighting demons and so on. When the Starstone fell and smashed the Inner Sea into existence—and destroyed the empire of Azlant in the process—Aroden somehow survived. He got his hands on the Starstone, raised it from the depths of the sea, and became a god in the process. Am I right so far?"

"You are."

"It's funny how the stories you hear in the nursery stick with you. Hmm. Aroden is said to have founded the city of Absalom—which I've always found overrated, frankly, you can't get good Andoren-style bread there—and built the Starstone Cathedral. I suppose he wanted to make sure no one else could become a god quite as easily as *he* had. Funny how he just found the Starstone lying in a puddle, but expects any other would-be gods to make their way through a fiendishly dangerous set of obstacles for *their* chance at glory. At some point he ascended into the heavens, as one does, and looked over his people with the customary godlike beneficence. There was a prophecy that he was supposed to return on such and such a date, but—he didn't. There were horrible natural disasters that day instead, and all his clerics found their magical connections to Aroden severed, and their powers lost. I *do* enjoy seeing self-righteous clerics laid low, but it's sad, in a way. We were supposed to have a golden age, and all we got was . . . this."

"He was tall," Hrym said. "Aroden, I mean. Tall even for an Azlanti."

"Hrym claims he met Aroden once," Rodrick said.

Zaqen whistled, low. "Is that true, sword?"

"Ten thousand years is a long time to remember anything," Hrym said grumpily. "Rodrick thinks I'm imagining things. And maybe I am—my memories before Rodrick found me in the linnorm's cave are mostly broken fragments, and they don't add up to any kind of a whole. I'm not saying Aroden wielded me in battle or anything, but it seems to me that I *did* meet him, or at least see him."

"Perhaps you did." Zaqen took a deep breath. "Our hope is that you will see him again."

After a pause, Rodrick said, "Explain that."

"My master is not a priest of Gozreh. He is a priest of Aroden."

"I thought all Aroden's priests switched their allegiance to that paladin-turned-goddess of his, Iomedae? She always seemed a bit of a humorless deity to me, but to each—"

Zaqen shook her head. "There are still priests of Aroden. They are powerless, it's true, as their god is either dead or, at the very least, cut off from his connection to the mortal plane. Their temples crumble, and their followers have all wandered away or, as you say, switched allegiance."

"Hold on. If Obed is a priest of a dead god, where does he get his powers?" Hrym demanded.

"A very good question," Rodrick agreed.

Zaqen looked behind her, to her master's tub, but Obed remained silent, and may have even been asleep. "He gets his powers from money, mostly. Old Azlant sank, but there are still treasure chambers deep in the sea, and one of them is the place my master calls home. So he uses that ancient wealth to purchase magical items, rings, scrolls, and potions to provide his priestly powers."

Rodrick grunted. "That explains why he couldn't do anything about his inability to walk around in the air for more than a day once he lost his ring. I'd wondered. All right. But what's the *point* of worshiping a dead god? And what are we looking for, if not an artifact of Gozreh?"

"I'll get to that. For now, you should know there are many worshipers of Aroden among the gillmen, the so-called Low Azlanti. Aroden was one of *them*, after all, or one of their ancestors, at any rate. They pray for his return and resurrection."

"One wonders who exactly they expect to answer their prayers," Rodrick said, but she ignored him.

"My master is one of the few who wants to *do* something about Aroden's return. And he believes he knows a way to bring Aroden back to life."

Chapter Twenty-Six
Sword Against Death

That would be quite a trick," Rodrick said. "I know gods can resurrect people, but who could possibly resurrect a god? A meta-god?"

Zaqen served up a thin smile. "Perhaps even a gillman could do it, given the right circumstances. My master has researched the subject for years, and he has reason to believe that Aroden left a certain artifact in Brevoy, locked away beneath a cold lake. One of the great feats the hero Aroden performed was driving a host of demon lords and their followers into the Lake of Mists and Veils, just a short journey north of here. Aroden *walked* in these lands, once. And he later chose to hide a powerful relic away here."

"What relic is that?"

"The dark wizards who transform themselves into liches lock their life forces away in gems or boxes or stones, called phylacteries. We believe that Aroden did something similar—that after he became a god, he locked his mortal life away in a relic, leaving some of his essence in our world, perhaps to strengthen his connection to the mortal plane after he ascended to godhood. That relic is hidden in a vault, locked and guarded. And if we can recover it . . ."

"What?" Rodrick said. "Aroden will pop out like a jack-in-the-box, whole again?"

Zaqen shook her head. "Not quite. The relic we seek holds his *mortal* life essence, not his divinity. My master has been preparing for years, deciphering secret prophecies and undergoing painful rituals, in order to make himself into a perfect sacrifice: a vessel to contain whatever remains of the great Aroden's mortal life."

Rodrick frowned. "You're saying that Obed wants to *become* Aroden?"

"Obed is willing to obliterate his own identity if it means there is the slightest chance his god will to return to our world." There was something like awe in Zaqen's voice. "Just as the wizard you faced in the dungeon moved its mind from body to body, Obed hopes that Aroden's mind will take over *his* body. True, Aroden would then be in a mortal body, without his godly powers . . . but that need only be temporary."

"The trial of the Starstone," Rodrick said. "Once Aroden takes over Obed's body, he can travel south to Absalom and try to reach the Starstone again, getting back his old position as the great god of humanity— and gillmen, presumably. Am I right?"

"You understand perfectly," Zaqen said. "You can see why we didn't tell you. It's . . . difficult to believe, I know. Insanely ambitious. Perhaps destined to fail. But when there's even a *chance* that the greatest god of our history might be returned to life, we *have* to risk all to achieve it."

"You needn't have told me lies," Rodrick said. "I just want to get paid. I've gone along with equally impossible plans before, as long as I was being paid in advance, and not in a percentage of the highly speculative profits."

"My master did not wish his goal to be widely known, in any case," Zaqen said. "There are those who like the world the way it is, who would not welcome even the slim chance of Aroden's return. The demons led by Deskari would descend on us in force if they thought there was a *possibility* that their master's ancient adversary might return."

"That's a good reason to keep quiet," Hrym admitted.

"But now you know," Zaqen said. "Has it changed your wish to help us?"

Rodrick snorted. "I get paid my weight in gold, *and* I get to help restore a god to life? I suppose I can go along with that. Having a god be grateful to you is probably worth a little something all on its own."

That night, when they camped, Zaqen gave Cilian the same story, and the ranger was appropriately awed, taking her tale as further proof that he was on the path to a great destiny. Obed remained in his tub of water all night, not even emerging to eat, presumably because he didn't want to deal with any questions.

Rodrick didn't really have any questions, though. He went out walking the perimeter with Hrym while Cilian and Zaqen sang a few rounds of "Praise Aroden!" together.

"What do you think?" Rodrick said to his sword.

"Eh? About what?"

"About the so-called truth Zaqen told us this afternoon, of course."

"Oh," Hrym said. "There are two possibilities, as far as I can see."

"They're either deluded, or they're lying?"

"Those are the two I had in mind," Hrym said. "If there was the slightest hint of an outside chance that Aroden could be restored to life, even in a flimsy mortal form, someone would have tried it before now. He was one of the most-worshiped gods in the Inner Sea. His priests and followers were legion. He was a god who had a *follower* who was a god! Even discounting Aroden's own followers, if Iomedae thought he could be brought back to life, her paladins and priests would have mobilized in their thousands to make it happen. The priests would have been lining up to let dead Aroden use their bodies for vessels."

"Perhaps if there were a truly secret prophecy, something only the Low Azlanti knew . . ." Rodrick said. "A scroll with an offhand mention of an artifact, long-forgotten in all other scriptures, discovered by some gillman in a sunken library . . ."

"That's what Obed is counting on us to think," Hrym said. "He's counting on that shadow of a doubt, that sliver of possibility. Does Obed strike you as the noble, self-sacrificing type?"

"He strikes me as a zealot," Rodrick said. "And zealots do all sorts of ridiculous things for their causes."

"Yes," Hrym agreed. "Which is why I'm willing to allow the possibility that they're merely deluded. It's possible they believe the things Zaqen spewed. Though I wouldn't refuse to bet on the possibility that they're lying. But what—"

"Does it matter," Rodrick finished. "We'll steal whatever artifact they find in the vault anyway. If it *is* Aroden's life essence, it will be incredibly valuable, and if it's something else—a magical scythe that instantly kills everyone who has ever annoyed Obed, say—we can still make money from it. Yes?"

"I don't think you'd survive the discovery of a weapon like that," Hrym said. "But basically, yes. Let them tell whatever stories they wish, as long as we can make off with the prize."

"I do admire your pragmatism, sword. But what if the fate of the world really *is* at stake? There *is* that sliver of a possibility, after all. The world is a strange place, and full of things even more unlikely than talking swords of ice."

"I can't think about things that big and important," Hrym said. "My mind glazes over when I try to worry about matters of such great import. Creatures like you and I are better off worrying about gold."

"You are the wisest piece of cutlery I've ever known, Hrym." Rodrick tried to see the sense in what his partner said. But he couldn't help but worry. What could the *real* truth be, if Zaqen and Obed tried to conceal it with a lie of *this* magnitude?

They continued traveling north, squeezed between the mountains on one side and the forest on the other, a situation so essentially claustrophobic that Rodrick let out a long, involuntary exhalation when the track before them opened out to reveal farmland and shimmering lakes steaming faintly in the morning sun. "These are the lands of House Medvyed," Zaqen said. "They control some of the most profitable timber land in Brevoy, and rule from an ancient mountain fortress, Stoneclimb."

"Let me guess," Rodrick said. "We have to steal a magic piss-pot from the lady's bedchamber?"

"Not as far as my master has told me," Zaqen said. "We are to keep going north until we nearly reach the lake, then turn west and head for the city of Port Ice. It's a long trip, but the roads are supposed to be adequate."

Rodrick yawned. "Just let me know when I need to freeze someone's blood or sweet-talk a barmaid, all right?"

"I thought learning the true nature of our mission might energize you," Zaqen said.

Rodrick snorted. "You know how that Lump of yours hungers only for eyes? Think of Hrym and I as spiritual brothers to *your* brother—except instead of a burning desire for eyes, we have a burning desire for gold. I'm willing to do a lot of things to get that gold . . . but we've been on the road for many weeks, and I'm afraid my enthusiasm for everything but finishing our travels and drowning in ale and wenches is fading."

"It's been an even longer road for my master and me," Zaqen said. "We had to begin in the Inner Sea, after all."

"Ah, but you have your zeal to keep you occupied."

"If we succeed, your part in this will be told forevermore in song and story."

"Oh, that's fine. Songs and stories always sand off the rough and ragged edges, and leave out the inconvenient bits that don't rhyme or scan. It almost doesn't matter *what* I do—the bards will make it sound good regardless."

"You don't expect us to succeed, do you?" she said.

Rodrick shrugged. "I hadn't given it much thought, as long as I get paid in the end."

"You feel no loyalty to us, then?"

"I like you, Zaqen," he said, honestly. "But I can only be lied to so many times before my fondness for the liar begins to cool. I know, as an outrageous liar myself that's a terribly hypocritical stance to take, but there it is."

She sighed. "I wasn't supposed to like you, either, you know. You and Hrym were meant to be the hired help, utterly disposable. I won't pretend my master doesn't still see you that way. But the two of you are so amusing, the way you continually squabble but obviously still care for one another, and you're brave in your own ways, and better company than I'm accustomed to. You can't blame *me* for lying to you—I must obey my master in these things."

"Oh?" Rodrick said. "And what if you're still lying to me?"

She shrugged. "I can only say that, given my own choice, I would never lie to you again."

"But you don't have that choice."

"I do not. Which should not be construed as me saying I've lied about anything lately. But forgive me anyway? If nothing else, we still have some distance to travel together, and it's more pleasant if we can talk."

Rodrick smiled despite himself. It was, after all, an unusual and even pleasant experience to be friendly with a woman he had absolutely no desire to sleep with. Their conversations could proceed a great deal more naturally than he was used to, even when based on a certain bedrock of deceit. "Fine, liar. Tell me more about the politics and geography of Brevoy, if you must. I can tell you're dying to inflict the research your master made you do on innocent listeners like Hrym and myself."

Chapter Twenty-Seven
The Snow Men

Points of interest were few and far between. Zaqen pointed out the forbidding face of Stoneclimb, a graceless fortress hewn from the face of a mountain, prompting Rodrick to observe, "If that's the sort of place where the wealthy nobility of Brevoy live, I think I'd rather be poor in the gutter in Andoran. My balls shrivel up just thinking about sleeping in that great stone icebox."

Not long after, Zaqen pointed to a road that wound its way up the higher peaks. "Do you see the walls up there?"

Rodrick squinted. "A city of some kind?"

"Something like that. It's called Skywatch. A settlement built around the ruins of an ancient observatory."

"What, for stargazing?" Rodrick said.

"The ancients wanted to watch the skies for something, anyways. Possibly something more dangerous than stars. They built an apparatus so cunning even our modern artificers don't understand entirely how it works. The mechanisms are preserved by some ancient magic, working as well now as they did in the time before man."

"Are we meant to steal a telescope or something, then?" Rodrick said.

Zaqen snorted. "No. I'm not sure what my master would do if we needed to get something out of that city. Because, here's the interesting bit—the same night the royal family of Brevoy vanished without a trace, Skywatch sealed its walls. No one has been allowed in or out since then. No messages have been received from inside, no trade caravans allowed in, nothing. It's locked up tight—even magical means have failed to ascertain what's happening inside the walls, with the most sophisticated divinations simply failing. How do the people inside survive without new supplies coming in? *Have* they survived, or is it a city of the dead now? Clearly this magical isolation is related to the vanishing of House Rogarvia, but how?"

Rodrick looked at the distant settlement, but the sight didn't tell him much, except that the people of the north liked high strong walls. "Let me guess: you have a theory."

"Me, personally? No. But the locals do. Some of them, anyway. They believe Skywatch was built to look out for imminent, world-altering threats from the heavens— like the Earthfall that brought the Starstone crashing down, drowning an empire, or the crash of the Silver Mount, which remade the face of Numeria. The theory is that the arcanists at Skywatch detected an approaching threat, sent word to the members of House Rogarvia, and then locked the royals and themselves away in some magically protected shelter to wait out the end times."

"That's a cheery thought," Rodrick said.

"Sometimes I love being a sword," Hrym said. "A little thing like the sky falling isn't going to inconvenience me very much."

"So you see," Zaqen said, "it may be even more important than you realize to bring Aroden back to life and restore him to his divinity, so he can protect us—"

"Enough about Aroden." Rodrick rolled his eyes. "He couldn't even protect himself from whatever astral assassin killed him, so forgive me if I don't put my faith in the tenuous chance of his resurrection. There are a million other reasons Skywatch could have been closed off, and you know it. Demons from the underworld annexing it as a territory of the Abyss. A plague so virulent the wise masters of the city chose to magically quarantine the place. Some fool messing about with ancient machinery and accidentally triggering some horrible stasis spell."

"True enough," Zaqen said. "You can't blame a girl for trying to convince you, though. This would all be easier if you were a zealous worshiper of Aroden."

"I can't even be bothered to worship gods that are *alive*," Rodrick said.

They headed straight east after passing Skywatch, more or less, through the lands of House Orlovsky (which had the high ground literally and figuratively, and controlled major trade routes), across a river into the realm of House Lodovka (whose frosty lands were useless for farming, but who had the most boats and fishing rights on the Lake of Mists and Veils to the north, growing rich off the bounty of the waters), and finally into the territory of House Surtova (a clan descended from pirates and cutthroats who'd been transformed by the alchemy of time into region's oldest and most influential noble house, and who'd stepped into the business of ruling the nation when those upstarts in House Rogarvia vanished).

"Enough!' Rodrick cried after Zaqen's latest impromptu history lesson. "Unless I have to seduce one of their daughters or kidnap one of their heirs, that's more than I need to know about Brevic nobility. Brevoy isn't a large nation, and as far as I can tell it mostly consists of sprawling fields, wild woods, horrible mountains, and inaccessible cities—what in the hell do they need so many noble families for?"

"Nobles breed regardless of how many of them are required," Zaqen said. "They're a bit like mosquitos that way."

They were on a real road, now, an actual trade route, and there was a tarp thrown over the back of the cart to hide Obed's tub from casual view. Cilian had joined them more or less permanently, riding Rodrick's old horse in the rear of the caravan, muttering to himself about the absence of trees and the lack of cover and how it should not be so cold in summer.

Zaqen pointed to a branch road that led off to the northwest. "Go that way, Rodrick. We'll head up toward the Lake of Mists and Veils, and take the main road all the way to Port Ice—where, my master assures me, we will find our final key."

"Port Ice," Hrym said. "I like the sound of that."

"Oh, yes, it's profoundly inviting," Rodrick said. "I'm sure it's a warm and welcoming place."

Zaqen snorted. "In the winter, any travelers foolish enough to try and reach the city are likely to die outside its walls while the guards peer down to see if they're carrying anything worth stealing from their corpses. The rest of the year, it's a wide-open trading port, stockpiling supplies like mad to survive the brutal winters. If you come when the walls are closed, you'd better be able to prove you won't be a drain on the city's limited resources. Potatoes are more valuable than gold there in the winter. But the rest of the time, fear not—gold will do. The city's nobles live on the backs of their peasants, like always, but those peasants live in dozens of fishing villages strung all up and down the shore of the Lake of Mists and Veils, and in winter, they leave their huts behind and huddle together behind the city walls."

"Why anyone would choose to live in a place where just going *outside* can kill you baffles me," Rodrick said.

Zaqen shrugged. "It's not so bad for the nobles, of course. As for the peasants—where are they going to go? Risk everything and flee across the border to Numeria, where the Kellids will kill them just for a laugh? Head into the contested lands of the River Kingdoms and be murdered by bandits for the half a loaf of bread they're carrying? Not everyone has the wealth of my master, or my natural magical powers, or a magical sword of ice."

"Please. I made a success of myself despite my low beginnings—"

"You were no peasant," Hrym said. "Your parents kept a roof over your head, and even saw to it that you were educated as much as you'd let them. And you were born in Andoran, where the common man is given more opportunities than the average peasant elsewhere. You also happened to be slightly less stupid than your peers, and better looking, and with a total lack of, oh, what's the word . . ."

"Shame?" Zaqen hazarded.

"Flaws?" Rodrick suggested.

"Conscience," Hrym said. "You also didn't live in a place where, as you mentioned, just going outside could kill you. If you'd been dumped in one of these villages as a baby . . . to be honest you'd probably have been murdered by your neighbors for stealing fish. You wouldn't be a swaggering bravo with a talking sword, that's for sure."

"Fine, I take your point," Rodrick said.

"If Aroden returns, we can improve the lives of *all* these people," Zaqen said. "Wouldn't it be nice if we could raise the standard of living for everyone, everywhere?"

Rodrick and Hrym were quiet for a moment. "Hmm," the sword said. "I suppose that *would* mean a lot more people we could steal gold from."

"A rising tide lifts all ships," Rodrick agreed. "Let's usher in this golden age of yours, Zaqen. With an emphasis on the 'gold.'"

"It's a bit ratty-looking for a seat of power," Rodrick said as they rolled toward the chipped stone walls of Port Ice.

"I gather it's more dramatic in the winter, when everything is covered in deep snow and shining with ice," Zaqen said. "But, yes, in summer, the flaws do show."

The roads leading to the wide-open gates were thronged with people leading mules and donkeys, and carts laden with heaps of furs and casks of ale and barrels of salted meat. Little knots of disreputable-looking long-haired men stood here and there, directing traffic or amusing themselves by intimidating random passersby.

"The city guard?" Rodrick said.

"Or what passes for it here. Retainers of the Surtova family, which rules here, and has for generations. When this half of the country was the nation of Issia, they were the supreme leaders, and this was the capital. Noleski Surtova was in charge here, but when House Rogarvia vanished, he seized the opportunity and took over the entire kingdom, at least in theory. He relocated his court down to New Stetven and left some uncle in charge here."

Rodrick, watching two of the "guards" engage in a spitting contest, said, "I can't imagine why the king would choose to move south. This place is so charming."

"It's a pirate port, really," Zaqen said. "Though how you can do much piracy on a lake is a mystery to me."

"It is a very large lake." Obed's voice emerging from beneath the canvas cover stretched over the rear of the cart. "It borders three nations. It is the source of the mighty Sellen River, down which pirates also ply their trades. There is ample room for murder and mayhem and pillage there."

"I never liked piracy," Hrym said from his sheath on Rodrick's back. "It's just like stealing, only there's a chance you'll fall in the ocean and be lo~ ~rever, so why not just stick to stealing things on land?"

One of the guards stopped in front of the cart and raised his hand. "Here now, we need to see what you're carrying."

"Oh?" Rodrick said. "Why's that?"

The guard patted the curved sword at his hip. "Because I said so." He grinned, showing off a gold tooth.

Rodrick shrugged. "Climb on."

The guard went around the back of the cart, saw their mounts, and whistled. "Is that a, what're they called . . ."

"Camel," Cilian said from his mount. He chewed his lip for a moment, then said, "Long story."

The guard snorted. "You could sell it for a pretty penny here. I've only seen them in pictures. Doubt it would survive the winter, though. They're made for hot, dry places, aren't they? This is pretty much the opposite. Help me peel back this canvas, would you, half-elf? We want to make sure you aren't smuggling anything inappropriate into the city."

"Out of curiosity," Rodrick called, "what kind of cargo would be considered contraband?"

The guard shrugged. "I dunno. I guess I'd know it if I saw it. Small demons? Corrosive oozes? Carnivorous plants that grow amazingly well in frozen soil?"

"Nothing like that for us," Rodrick said.

Cilian helped the guard untie the canvas cover and roll it out of the way.

"And just what is this supposed to be?" the guard said, standing in the back of the cart and scowling.

"That is Obed, a priest of Gozreh," Zaqen said. "He is currently at rest in a tub of blessed seawater brought all the way from the Inner Sea. The waters are a sacred offering to his brothers and sisters at the temple of Gozreh on the shores of the lake."

The guard scratched his chin. "Huh. Right. You mean that bunch of bearded men, and women with long hair all woven with reeds and fish scales and things, the ones who live in those little driftwood huts in the summer?"

"That sounds like them," Zaqen agreed.

The guard thumped the side of the tub with his boot. "Huh. Why doesn't this priest have a beard, if he's a follower of Gozreh?"

"He's never been able to grow a beard," Zaqen said. "It's a source of great shame to him. We think it's because he has some elven ancestry."

"All right, but then why's he under the water? How's he breathing under there?"

"He worships a god of the waves." Zaqen's voice was remarkably calm and patient. "Water-breathing is a simple magic for him. As for why, he's taken a vow of immersion. He will be poured, with these waters, into the Lake of Mists and Veils, and thus bring his blessing to the north." She shrugged. "He does come out occasionally to eat, though, and to relieve himself— the tub would be a bit foul by now otherwise."

"He gets out to yell at us for not traveling fast enough, too," Rodrick said.

Zaqen nodded. "None of it makes any sense to us, either. The priest just hired us to escort him, that's all. It's just . . . religion."

"Can't argue with religion," the guard said, affably enough. "I've spent enough time on ships that I'm not about to mess with the priest of a storm god. Carry on, then. Try to spend some of that money he paid while you're here, though, would you?"

"This is the first real city we've seen in weeks," Rodrick said. "We're planning to linger here as long as the priest will permit and reacquaint ourselves with civilization."

"If by civilization you mean whiskey and wenches, we've got those, right enough," the guard said. "Welcome to Port Ice. Be sure to leave before winter." He grinned, showing his gold teeth again. "When we run out of food during the time of the deep snows, we always eat the outsiders first."

Chapter Twenty-Eight
The Two Best Thieves in Port Ice

The pirate guard suggested an inn where they could stay, and it seemed no more horrible than any of the other options—it looked like an ungainly heap of irregular stone and timber salvaged from shipwrecks on the outside, but was snug and well-insulated inside, probably a necessity for all dwellings in this place. They gave the innkeeper a variation on their story about Obed being a holy man delivering sacred waters to the lake, but said they had to wait a few days for a particular seasonal and astronomical alignment. The owner grudgingly made room for their cart and the tub in a weedy courtyard behind the inn, charging a merely outrageous sum of gold for the privilege.

"Here we are again." Rodrick sat on his lumpy bed and leaned against the wooden wall, ankles crossed before him, Hrym unsheathed on the covers beside him. "Plotting, with a roof over our heads. How I've missed this."

Obed sat stiffly in a wooden chair beside a low table, glowering, and Zaqen sat in another chair beside him.

Cilian paced up and down just inside the door, like a predator stuck in a cage, casting suspicious looks at the ceiling, as if he expected it to fall down on his head any time.

"We are here for the final key," Obed said. "You now understand my wish for haste. Had we failed to reach Port Ice before the first snows, it would have been much more difficult to travel, and we would have been noticed and remarked upon if we did make it here—strangers are vanishingly rare in the winter."

"Imagine if you'd just told us the reason for your hurry," Rodrick said, cleaning his fingernails with a dagger. "Why, think of all the resentment you could have avoided!"

Obed curled his lip scornfully. "I do not explain myself to hirelings—"

"Yes, as you have so often explained to me," Rodrick said. "And here I thought we were becoming a family. United on a sacred quest to resurrect Aroden! But, I'm sorry, that's too important for me to worry about. I should focus on the details. This last key, then. Where is it, and how are we supposed to get it? So far we've had a rigged duel, the murder of a great many bandits, the traditional blinding of a mind-controlled yeti—"

"Simple theft should suffice in this case," Obed said. "The key is in the manor house of a minor noble, a distant cousin to this nation's present king. My inquiries about purchasing the key were not even rebuffed—they were ignored. When I sent an emissary, he was beaten and tossed outside the manor's gates, for the offense of bothering the master of the house."

"Even Piero was friendlier than that," Hrym said. "Of course, he was hoping for an excuse to murder someone."

"Certain divinations I have undertaken reveal that the item is kept in a locked strongbox in a basement treasure room," Zaqen said. "Along with a great deal of other treasure. It's best if *all* of the treasure is stolen, so the noble won't connect the theft to those peculiar inquiries he received from me earlier this year. Ah, yes—I thought you'd like that part, Rodrick."

"I do hate leaving treasure behind," he said. "So: what's the gaffle?"

Zaqen looked at him blankly. Obed didn't even give him that much of an expression.

"The plan, he means," Hrym said. "The scam. To get into the house, and into the treasure room, and away with the strong box, and so on."

"Ah." Obed made a face as if he'd smelled something foul. "Those are trivial details. That's why we've hired you."

Rodrick exhaled and smiled. "Oh, that's a relief."

"Indeed," Hrym said.

"Why do you say that?" Zaqen said.

"I've been hired by amateurs before, to pull jobs," Rodrick said. "It's never a good idea. They overcomplicate things, or undercomplicate them, or depend on too much precision, or don't plan *enough* precision, or they're inflexible and unprepared to improvise. I am pleased you've chosen to leave the plotting in the hands of the experts. Some of those amateur events were very successful jobs, admittedly—"

"Because amateurs are easy to rob," Hrym said.

"True," Rodrick said. "They're often willing to pay you just to come listen to their plan, too, even if you refuse to participate. I've been to as many as three meetings like that in a week—very lucrative, considering how little work is required." He cracked his knuckles. "Now.

Tell me where this manor is, and everything you know about the noble in question, and, oh, what the key actually *looks* like—"

"It looks like a key," Obed said. "A silver key, as long as a man's hand from the heel of the palm to the tip of the middle finger, the end worked with elaborate designs that seem to twist when one gazes upon them."

"An actual key. That's a bit obvious, but all right. What does it do?"

Obed shrugs. "It opens doors."

Rodrick blinked. "You mean . . . just, any door?"

The priest shrugged again. "So it is said."

"Ah," Rodrick said weakly. "That would be . . . quite dangerous, in the wrong hands . . ."

"It can only be used three times," Zaqen said. "Or so the story goes. It was used once to open a great treasure cave, and a second time to open a besieged city. It is duller now than it used to be, the silvery lustre fading with each use. Hansu Surtova inherited the key, with strict instructions to use it only if his family fortunes were on the verge of utter destruction."

"Hmm," Rodrick said. "I suppose we need its last charge to open our vault, don't we?"

Obed shook his head. "No, that doesn't matter. The key simply *fits* that particular lock—it will always work to open that door. Its other magical properties are irrelevant. They are merely camouflage, created by Aroden to make the objects seem like something other than they are—but still precious enough to be cared for over the long centuries, if need be."

"Seems a bit foolish to me." Rodrick tugged at his earlobe. To open *any* door! But just one door. The problem was, most really valuable things were locked up behind lots of doors, and getting through any of them at all could be a challenge, but still . . . "If the key got used up, it would just be a trinket, and I can see the unwitting guardian just tossing it away."

"Not likely," Hrym said. "When something has only a few uses, people *hoard* them. Do you have any idea how many wizards I've met who were walking around with a ring or an amulet containing a single wish? They never use the last wish—they die before they do—because they don't want to waste it, in case they ever *really* need it."

"I'd use all my wishes," Rodrick said. "Just like that." He snapped his fingers.

"You're an idiot," Hrym said. "And a wastrel. But we all knew that."

Rodrick stroked his chin. "Hmm. A magical key that can open any door—and it's stuck behind a locked door. Just our luck. I'll go out in the morning and take a look at the manor house, and figure out our approach."

"You think you can do it?" Zaqen said.

He waved a hand. "Of course."

"How can you be so sure there's a way?"

The thief grinned. "My lady, there is *always* a way."

"There's absolutely no way," Rodrick said the following night. "Not that I can see, anyway. I've been to large banks with less security. According to the kitchen maid I befriended last night, Hansu Surtova is in some kind of feud with other members of his family. Apparently they're not all that respectable—there's still a lot of pirate left in the bloodline—and they're not above murdering each other. The house is locked up tight, and strangers simply don't get in—close friends and relations barely do. All the defenses are meant to keep out assassins, but they'll do just fine to keep out thieves, too."

Obed growled. "Then what do you propose? Are you so quick to give up?"

"Do you hear that, Hrym?" Rodrick clucked his tongue. "Obed has obviously never worked with me before on a real job. Of course I won't give up. Strangers don't get into the house, I said, so it's simple: I need to stop being a stranger. I have to win the old Surtova's confidence. He's a gimlet-eyed pirate with profound trust issues, but I think I know the way to his heart. He's terrified someone will try to kill him, and I say we give him his wish. But I'll step in and foil the would-be assassin, saving the man's life, and after that . . ." Rodrick shrugged. "It's the only crack I need. I'll show off Hrym, sow some rumors about my skill as a bodyguard, how I've never lost a single man I've protected, and before you know it, I'll be his right-hand man. Worming my way into someone's confidence is what I do best. And once I'm on the inside . . . I'll get the key."

Obed ground his teeth. "How long do you expect this to take?"

Rodrick shrugged. "A few weeks? Perhaps longer if he's unusually cautious. It's important, you see, that I make him *beg* for my services, or at least offer me great rewards to convince me to join him. If I seem eager to work for him, he won't trust me, but if I play hard to get, he will pursue me ever more ardently, especially since he's a man who is used to getting what he wants—"

"Sounds like a courtship," Zaqen said, and Hrym laughed.

"There are many forms of seduction," Rodrick said. "This is the kind I'm . . . second best at."

"I do not wish to wait weeks," Obed said. "We will break into the house in the night. We will steal—"

"This is a Surtova," Rodrick said. "A Surtova in *Port Ice*. And you want to try a smash-and-grab? That would be like trying to steal something from the Ruby Prince's desert palace in Osirion. All right, I exaggerate, but breaking in secretly is nearly impossible. Assuming we make it in, successfully breaching the treasure vault could be tricky too, and as for escaping . . ." He shook his head. "I befriended one of the chambermaids, too. The vault has magical wards and protections—and the servants aren't even allowed to clean in the basement. Old Hansu never lets anyone in, except himself. But in *my* plan, I'll play up to his vanity, get him to show off his treasures—"

"*Weeks*," Obed spat. "I am this close to my triumph, and you wish me to wait further weeks?"

"If you have a better idea, I'd love to hear it. But I'm not taking part in any plan that involves me captured in the midst of a crime and at the mercy of the Surtovas. They're pirates, Obed. You're a gillman—you know about pirates. They are nothing if not vigorous in their retributions."

"Master," Zaqen said. "This is Rodrick's area of expertise. I know his plan is not as swift as you might wish, but—"

"Fine," Obed snapped. "Make your preparations. And make haste." He rose and stalked out of the room.

Once he was gone, Cilian spoke from the corner—Rodrick had almost forgotten he was sitting there. "I watched smoke rise into the sky today, and had a presentiment of great destruction."

"Hmm," Hrym said. "For our enemies, or ourselves?"

"The auguries were unclear on that point," Cilian admitted.

"Oh," Rodrick said. "That's helpful. Cilian, I have you in mind for the hapless assassin—do you think you can fail to hit a man with an arrow?"

"Missing is harder than striking true, but I am capable of such a feat."

Rodrick grinned. "That's a good fellow. We'll go out tomorrow and take a look at the manor house, and see if we can get a sense of what old Hansu's schedule is like over the next few days. It's probably best if we both disguise our appearances a bit—it wouldn't do to have people remember us and remark on our spending time together. We'll figure out the right time and place for you to strike, one that will enable me to foil you, but still give you time you to escape. Perhaps near the market square, when the traders are starting to pack up their carts. I hear Hansu likes to go there sometimes to strike hard bargains with desperate merchants for their last few unsold goods—"

"Rodrick," Zaqen said. "You seem to be having *fun*. I haven't seen you like this . . . well, since Magnos the Ash Lord."

"I am a simple man, sorcerer. I enjoy getting the best of people. Blinding yetis and murdering bandits is not much to my liking, but *this*? This is what I was made for."

"I am glad you have the opportunity to ply your trade, then," Zaqen said. "You'll let me know if you have need of me?"

"I may require certain sorcerous effects," Rodrick said. "Plus, I'd hate for you to miss out on all the fun."

She chuckled. "I'll leave you to your planning, then."

Rodrick cleared his throat. "Tell Obed I will work as quickly as I can, all right? I have no wish to antagonize him—I know you might find that hard to believe, but it's true. I won't say I'm fond of him, but I do respect his dedication. If I knew a simpler way to get the key out of the vault, I *would* take it, as much as I'm enjoying this."

"As long as the job is done as swiftly as possible," Zaqen said. "Remember, a new golden age is at stake." She left, and Cilian went with her.

"I liked it better when it was just *gold* at stake," Hrym said. "I didn't feel so conflicted then."

"You feel conflicted?" Rodrick said.

"I want to say no, but . . . *Aroden*. That sliver of a possibility seems to be growing in my mind, despite myself. What if it's true?"

"How can it possibly be true? You know our line of work depends on making people believe lies, and people are strangely more willing to believe really *big* lies than quite small ones. Don't tell me you think they can pull off such a miracle—"

"We do live in a world of miracles, though," Hrym said. "That's the problem. There *is* a stone that turns men to gods. There *is* a great wound in the world, pouring out demons. There *is* an endless hurricane swirling to the west. There *are* barmaids willing to sleep with you. Who's to say this particular impossible thing is the one that's *really* impossible?"

"Don't be a sucker, Hrym," Rodrick said. "I'm going to sleep."

But as he lay in the dark, the treacherous thought wormed deeper into his mind:

What if?

Chapter Twenty-Nine
Thieves' House

When Rodrick took Cilian to look over Hansu Surtova's manor house in the earliest twinkling of dawn, the manor house wasn't there anymore.

Or rather it was there, at least most of it, but it was no longer a manor house. The walls had been broken apart in dozens of places, bricks scattered on the streets like autumn leaves after a windstorm. Through the gaps, Rodrick could see the white walls of the house itself had been shattered, as if smashed by the fist of a towering god, leaving splintered wood and the dust of crushed stone hanging thick in the air. Various objects, barely recognizable, littered the wreckage like seashells and driftwood left on a beach when the tide recedes. Was that part of a chair, or a fragment of a bed? Were those sheets or drapes or bits of clothing, all twisted and torn? Was that the ruined body of a man, or a pair of slaughtered dogs? The piratical guards of Port Ice milled about shouting at one another, and somewhere a man was wailing in wordless despair.

"I do not think breaking in will be easy," Cilian said. "Though not for the reasons you anticipated. If the key is in a basement, under that wreck, with all these people in the area . . ." He shook his head.

"What's happening?" Hrym said querulously, sheathed and blind on Rodrick's back.

"Hansu's house has been destroyed," Rodrick said. "Maybe by magic. Or an alchemical disaster? It could have been an explosion, though I don't smell that alchemical reek. Go back to the inn, Cilian. Tell Zaqen what happened. Let *her* tell Obed. He takes bad news better from her. I'll try to find out what happened, and if there's any way we can use it to our advantage."

The huntsman nodded and withdrew.

Rodrick surveyed the scene until he saw someone promising. An old man dressed in white furs looked at the wreck from the far side of the street with the gaze of someone who'd seen worse things, more often than he could count, and refused on principle to be impressed. Rodrick strolled over, nodded at the man politely, and said, "That looks bad. What happened here?"

"Assassination," the old man said shortly.

"I thought assassination was generally more subtle," Rodrick said. "A bit of poison in the wine, a knife in the night, an arrow fired from concealment, that sort of thing."

"I didn't say it was an elegant assassination. It's one of the ugliest and most haphazard I've seen. But Hansu Surtova is dead. Along with most of his household, but Surtova was the only target that makes any sense. He had a way of making enemies, even among those who loved him, and he was a treacherous bastard everyone knew would come to a bad end. Still, whoever did this . . ." The man shook his head. "It's unnatural."

"Was it explosives of some kind?" Rodrick said. "Or . . . magic?"

"You're an outsider," the old man said. "You've not heard the stories about the lake?"

Rodrick frowned. "Ah—which stories are those?"

"There are tales that strange creatures dwell in the waters. Monsters who sometimes emerge to make terrible bargains with the folk on the land. I plied those waters for many years, and never saw such a creature. Despite having a family full of people willing to make all *sorts* of hard bargains, I've never heard of anyone consorting with such creatures, if they do exist. But someone made a deal with *something*, that much is clear—and the terms of that deal were met last night. This destruction was wrought in mere minutes. No witnesses in the vicinity survived. Those near enough to see anything and survive report strange greenish lights and little else. I have a priest who says he believes it was demons—he can sense the presence of such things, he says. The lake may hold demons. Who can say? Whatever did this, it came, wrought terrible destruction, and then vanished. People are already whispering that it was one of Hansu's rivals, calling up a monster from the lake to kill the old man. I have no idea if that's true." He looked at Rodrick for the first time, his eyes pale and steely. "Normally we would suspect outsiders. Port Ice has a healthy suspicion of outsiders."

Rodrick took a step back. "I assure you, I never even met the man, I just saw the destruction and thought—"

"You are not suspected in this," the man said dismissively. "I said *normally* we would suspect outsiders. Hansu was a wealthy man, and there are many who might try to steal from him. But whoever did this wanted the man dead. The wreckage is nearly complete, but as far as we can tell nothing was stolen from his vault—gems and gold remain there, untouched, and precious antiques are shattered and broken." He shook his head. "This attack was personal. Which isn't to say we won't need an outsider to use as a scapegoat, Rodrick."

Rodrick hated it when strangers knew his name for reasons he couldn't fathom.

"You have the advantage of me," he said cautiously.

The man shrugged. "Strangers are noted here. You're the guard for that mad ocean priest, the one who likes to take long baths. Hansu did have friends in the city, and in his family, despite being an unlikable man. They'll be looking for someone to punish, whether that someone is guilty or not. Perhaps it's time you people continued with your pilgrimage? Before someone *other* than me remembers there are strangers among us?"

"Ah. I appreciate the advice, sir. May I know the name of the man I'm thanking?"

The old man snorted. Just then, one of the guards sidled toward him, face twisted in an agony of discomfort, and said, "Captain, they're fairly sure they've found Hansu's wife, they'd like to know if you'd, ah . . ."

"Of course," the man said gruffly, and strode off, while the guard stayed behind, looking relieved to have escaped the exchange with his limbs intact.

"Ah," Rodrick said. "That fellow is the captain of the guard, then?"

The guard frowned. "What? No, we call him 'captain' because that's the highest rank the master of a ship can obtain. You don't know who that is?"

"Sorry, I'm new in town—"

"That's Domani Surtova," the guard said. "Lord of the White Manor, ruler of Port Ice, uncle to the king of Brevoy."

"Of course he is," Rodrick said. "I should probably do whatever he suggests, then, shouldn't I?"

The guard scratched his chin and looked thoughtful for a moment. "I'd recommend it," he said at last.

"We are packed," Zaqen said when Rodrick got back to the inn. "Your things are already on the cart. Obed wishes us to depart immediately."

Rodrick blinked. "Well, that's good, since the king— or mayor, or whatever—of this city just suggested to me that if we *don't* leave we might be accused of consorting with demons and subsequently treated to some suitably piratical form of execution, like maybe keelhauling, whatever that is—"

"They pass a rope beneath a ship." Zaqen looked around her room, presumably to make sure she wasn't forgetting anything. "So it goes completely around the hull. Then they tie you to the rope and throw you overboard, and haul on the rope, to drag your body along the bottom of the ship, and then back up the other side. I gather being cut up by the barnacles on the ship's hull, your wounds filling with salt water, is the worst part, except maybe for the inability to breathe. Then they pull you back on deck, flog you across the width of the ship, throw you into the sea once more, and do it all over again. It's a bit impractical for use in town. Probably they'd just hang us."

"I'm sure whatever torture they have in mind would be preferable to listening to Obed rage and seethe over our failure to get the key—"

"We have the key." Zaqen stepped out into the hallway and hurried along.

Rodrick went after her, trying to catch up both literally and figuratively. "What do you mean?"

"Obed heard about the . . . commotion at the manor. He sent me, late last night, to see if I could take advantage of the disaster. I didn't see whatever caused the destruction, but things were still chaotic enough that it was easy to make my way through the wreckage unobserved. I'm not without magic, after all. Obed whipped up a charm using the other relics we'd gathered, using their affinity with one another to locate the final key. The way down was dusty, and occasionally bloody, and I got a few splinters, but the treasure room was cracked open like a mollusk dropped on a rock by a gull, so it was easy enough to retrieve what we needed. I escaped just before the guards started taking steps to secure the scene—probably not long before you and Cilian arrived for your pointless reconnaissance. I'm sorry Obed didn't tell you your plan had been canceled, but I can't say I'm surprised. My master doesn't much care if others are inconvenienced."

"You didn't bother to take any *other* treasure?" Rodrick's mouth ran on autopilot as they descended the stairs to the ground floor. He knew he was expected to complain about her failure to pillage, so he did, but in truth his mind was rapidly pondering darker issues.

"One small item like the key was unlikely to be missed, especially with all the walls and the ceiling being smashed to splinters—things are in disarray. But I didn't want to take more, lest the guards start searching for looters. We should probably stop talking about this until we get out of the city, don't you think?"

Rodrick fell silent, following Zaqen as she slipped out a side door and through to the stables. The horses all whinnied and pranced nervously in her presence, and her camel glared at her when she walked past him to the courtyard, where the cart waited. Obed was already submerged in the water, his tub flanked by two chests banded in iron, so newly made that some of the wood was still smeared with sap. The chests probably held whatever wealth the saddlebags and Obed's magically capacious pack had contained previously.

Cilian was nowhere to be seen, which meant he was almost certainly already beyond the city walls, scouting their route to . . . wherever they were headed next.

"You might want to wear this." Zaqen offered him a rough-spun brown cloak she took from a trunk at the back of the cart. "Disguise that noble face of yours."

"Oh, yes, a disguise, that's a good idea. We wouldn't want anyone to recognize us. Do you plan to paint your camel so it looks like a horse, then?"

She shrugged. "You're the one who struck up conversations with assorted guards and city leaders, not me. But as it happens, we're not taking the camel, or the horses, either. Let the innkeeper have them."

"We're leaving our mounts behind?" Rodrick frowned. "What if the carthorse freezes to death? Or we break an axle?"

"I think, between Obed's wealth and my magic, we can manage to keep a cart underneath us for a journey of half a day, don't you?"

"We're off to the secret final destination, then?" Rodrick said. "The tomb of Aroden, only not really a tomb, since gods don't leave bodies behind?"

"Just drive the cart," she said, and he'd never heard her sound so exhausted, not even after she released Lump in the mountain tunnels. There was not a trace of smirk or laughter or banter in her just now. Rodrick's heart sank even further. The end really must be near. But what kind of end would it prove to be?

Chapter Thirty
Lake Magic

Zaqen climbed into the back of the cart, clambered over the crates, and curled up on a heap of blankets and sacks behind her master's tub.

Rodrick mounted the driver's seat. "It's all very well to tell me to go, but you haven't told me *where* I'm going."

"North," she said, without stirring from the pile. "Get out of the city, follow the road around, and just keep heading north. Stop when you reach the water. All right? Obed will provide more instructions when we reach the shoreline." The sorcerer rolled over and by all appearances went to sleep.

"Are you hearing this, Hrym?"

"As well as I can, stuffed inside a leather scabbard and strapped to your back, yes."

Rodrick took off the scabbard and leaned it against the seat beside him, but didn't unsheathe the blade. The last thing he needed to do now was attract attention. He guided the horse through the streets—relatively quiet this early in the morning, at least for traffic heading out of the city, though he passed a lot of traders coming in the other way. A few guards glared at him as he rumbled slowly past, hands on their swords, but no one interfered with their departure.

Rodrick let himself fully exhale only when they passed through the gates, and still carried tension in his shoulders until they were well beyond the throng of carters coming toward the city. The road looped wide to the east, then branched toward the north and south, both directions looking pretty well maintained. Presumably carts carrying loads of fish packed in ice needed to come down the northern route fairly often, so at least Rodrick's testicles wouldn't be bashed into jelly by bad roads. No other carts were headed toward the lake this morning, so Rodrick unsheathed his glittering blade. "There, no one's watching, so enjoy some of the cool morning air. Can you believe this is still technically summer?"

"Late summer, now," Hrym said. "There's a cold wind soon to blow."

"Thank you for that keen insight, O chronicler of the seasons. Without you I'd be taken unawares by the first snows and would surely freeze to death."

"I meant it as a metaphor," Hrym said. "I have a presentiment of trouble to come, you see, so the cold wind *symbolizes*—"

"Yes, I get it," Rodrick said. "It's not as if it's an original comparison. Others have said it better. At least you didn't go on and on about a gathering storm on the horizon. That would have been even worse."

"The sky is clear," Hrym said. "It's our *future* that's cloudy—"

"If you don't stop, I'm going to trade you in for a paring knife."

Rodrick tried to take comfort in the familiar patterns of their banter, but he was too preoccupied. It was vanishingly unlikely that a bunch of monsters would just *happen* to destroy a house his employers needed to break into.

Rodrick was well aware of the terrible things people would do for even the basest things—money, revenge, a cruel whim. So he could scarcely imagine the sorts of terrible things people might do in the service of a truly *worthy* cause. How many people would Obed happily murder to usher in a golden age? More people than there were stars in the heavens or fish in the sea, Rodrick suspected. And what was to stop Rodrick himself from dying in the service of Obed's zeal?

There were alternatives to carrying on with this mission. Cut Zaqen's throat while she was sleeping. Stab Obed in his bath and kick the tub overboard. Take the cart, heaped with treasures, and ride south. Cilian might track him—certainly *could*—and try to take revenge, but the huntsman could be dealt with too. At the very least he would look at Rodrick with wide, hurt eyes and ask, "Why?" That would give Rodrick enough time to kill him, too.

Rodrick snapped the reins and spurred the horse forward. He wouldn't do those things, he knew. He was a thief, but not a murderer, except once or twice, and only incidentally. If he saw the chance to run away with the priest's treasures, he would, but he wouldn't slaughter his employers to do it. Maybe while Obed and Zaqen were in the inner sanctum of wherever they were going, bowing low in obeisance to a dead god, he could slip off and liberate the gold. Stealing the cart was just taking what they owed him, essentially. He didn't need to wait around for Aroden's actual resurrection, or more likely his failure to appear. What use would the greatest god of humanity have for a man like Rodrick, anyway? Getting rid of his kind would probably be at the top of Aroden's to-do list.

By early afternoon he started to catch sight of the lake, a glittering expanse in the distance glimpsed from the tops of hills, mirror-bright water flashing among the branches of evergreen trees, blinding spots reflecting sunlight, shining between jagged heaps of boulders. "Where are the mists? Where are the veils? I've been lied to, Hrym. This is just an overgrown *pond*."

"I think the mists only come in the winter," Hrym said. "Steam rising from the warm water, hitting the cold air, like that. I assume the veils are metaphorical."

"So it's just the Lake of Boring Water in the summer. That doesn't sound so bad. I can cope with a landmark like that. How big is it, anyway?"

"Why do you think I know?" the sword said. "I'm not Zaqen. I didn't decide to plan a holiday here and do a bit of research. But it's big, I reckon."

"I don't suppose you know what's *north* of the lake, then. I've never seen a map that showed anything farther than this."

"The top of the world, I would imagine," Hrym said. "Glaciers. Mountains of ice. White dragons feeding on one another. Sleeping frost giants. Lost cities and forgotten races. Or just a whole lot of nothing much, and all of it frozen."

"Doesn't sound too inviting."

"It's not likely to be full of gold," Hrym said. "So I would agree, though the temperature agrees with me well enough. Someone is about to attack us from the east, by the way."

"Noted." Rodrick wrapped his hand around Hrym's hilt—but then the man rushing from the trees beside the road threw back his cloak, revealing a pale thin face and pointed ears. It was Cilian, dressed in unassuming black instead of his usual forest greens. The huntsman clambered up onto the seat beside Rodrick and nodded at him solemnly.

"You do a good impression of a bandit," Rodrick said. "You nearly got a spear of ice through your lung."

"I did not foresee my death today," Cilian said.

"That's reassuring. How about mine?"

"There were no portents related to your death, either, my friend. Or to your life, I must admit." He glanced behind him, where Obed still slumbered, and Zaqen too. "They are very tired," Cilian said. "As if recovering from some exhausting effort."

"I'm fairly sure they smashed Hansu Surtova's house," Rodrick said.

Cilian cocked his head. "You believe they summoned demons from the lake?"

"I believe that when a piece of crockery gets broken in this land, the locals blame it on demons from the lake. So, no, not exactly. But I believe Obed and Zaqen did *something*, some spell or summoning, and destroyed the manor house and killed all those people. Because Obed was too impatient to wait for *my* plan to work."

The half-elf grunted. "Obed is a hard man, but he claims to serve a god of goodness, does he not? Do you truly believe he would commit such a crime?"

"Have you ever been to Mendev?" Rodrick said. "It's full of paladins. You'd be hard pressed to find a more deadly enemy than a paladin. They'll do all sorts of terrible things, without hesitation, because they know they're right. They don't *think* they're right, they know it, and while they're not above the occasional small kindness, most of the ones I've met focus on the larger picture. If a few little people have to get crushed in the course of their divine mission, they just kneel and beg forgiveness and then get up and do it all over again the next day."

"Obed is no paladin," Cilian pointed out.

"Oh, I know. He's the priest of a dead god. Another word for that kind of person is *madman*."

"He can hear you two, you know," Zaqen said from behind the seat, sounding as if she'd been awake for some time. "He listens to everything, all the time."

"Yes, Zaqen, I'm aware of that," Rodrick said. "You may be confused and under the misapprehension that I care if he hears me. If he doesn't like my speculations, accusations, and assumptions, he can terminate my employment. Just pay me the balance owed—I didn't take you *all* the way to the lake, so I'd settle for a mere nine-tenths of my body weight in gold—"

"Or equivalent gems," Hrym said. "Though I'd prefer the gold, if it's all the same."

"And Hrym and I will be on our way. Perhaps I didn't make it clear that I'm *very tired of his lies*. The *last* time you told me the truth, and the whole truth, I resolved to myself that I would stay, provided there were no further lies. And yet! Here we are."

"Obed was willing to tell you what we'd done in Port Ice," Zaqen said. "He doesn't really care about your opinion. But I convinced him to keep the truth from you." She sighed, standing up and leaning on the seat between Cilian and Rodrick. "I didn't want you to think less of us. Of *me*. The things we do, we do for—"

"The sake of the world, yes, I've heard that one before. And of course you wouldn't lie about *that*. Even if it's true that we're off to raise Aroden from the celestial grave, I'm not sure that would offer much comfort to the Surtova family retainers and random servants you murdered. What did you summon to destroy the house, anyway? Some twisted cousin of yours? No, wait, I heard a priest on the scene sensed demons, so you've been consorting with *those*, now. I'm sure that would thrill Aroden. It's not as if he dedicated his entire life to battling demons or anything—"

"Silence," Obed said, rising from his bath. "I have done what I must, and will not be questioned by the likes of you, thief. You are not permitted to leave our expedition. The vault we seek will be guarded, and I require your sword to clear our path. We are too close to our goal to let your latest fit of pique spoil things. Of course you have been lied to, hireling. But only because you insist on asking questions instead of doing as you're *told*."

"Piss off, fish-man." Rodrick dropped the reins and picked up Hrym. "I wish all of you the very best, except for you, Obed—I hope Aroden smells the stink of demons on you and makes his first act as a newly living god your eternal damnation."

"Stop!" Obed ordered.

"Wait!" Zaqen cried.

Rodrick did neither. He jumped down from the cart—the horse was still plodding along, but not quickly enough to make any difference. He began striding away to the south.

"Is this a ploy, or . . ." Hrym said.

"No ploy. What are we *actually* getting into if we stay, Hrym? Raising Aroden? I don't think so. They're willing to summon demons to get what they want. Do you think they intend to pay us a fair wage and send us on our way when they've accomplished whatever they're after? How close do we want to get to being murdered because of the whiff of gold?"

"The whiff of a *lot* of gold," Hrym said. "They don't look like they're planning to murder us now. Obed is waving his arms and shouting and Zaqen is trying to calm him down."

Rodrick kept walking, shoulders hunched. He trusted in Hrym to protect him from nearly any assault, but that didn't make the prospect of turning his back on a tainted sorcerer and a mad false priest and a very good archer any more comfortable. "Zaqen's not a bad sort," he said, "twisted lineage aside, but she's literally incapable of disobeying her master's orders. And Cilian is sweet, but something of an idiot—"

"Not as much of an idiot as I may appear," the half-elf said, falling into step beside Rodrick. His appearance, as if from nowhere, even seemed to surprise Hrym, who could see in every direction at once. "I'd rather the two of you didn't leave. I could really use your help saving the world."

Chapter Thirty-One
The Cloud of Lies

Rodrick groaned. "Lies, lies, everywhere lies. Are you telling me you *aren't* a deluded half-wit?"

"I do not believe myself to be either," Cilian said. "It serves my purposes to appear more simple than I am, sometimes."

"I should have known no half-elf would be so foolish as to think he was a Brightness Seeker—"

"No, that much is true," the huntsman said. "I do feel the call of the Brightness, and I do most assuredly see signs and omens, which direct my actions. I have not, however, been entirely forthcoming about *what* I've seen. If it suits your skeptical mind better, the reason I joined your party had nothing at all to do with my seeking the Brightness."

"Oh?" Rodrick said. "Why, then?"

"Your employer Obed secured safe passage from one of the goblin clans in Loric Fells. Do you remember?"

"I'm not likely to forget a horde of goblins perched on their mangy dogs staring down at me from a ridgeline, no."

"How did Obed explain his arrangement to you?"

Rodrick frowned. "He said he and the goblins shared the same god, or their gods had alliances—that they were all devoted to the deities of the natural world. But . . . wait . . ."

Cilian nodded.

"Hrym, we're idiots," Rodrick said. "Obed isn't really a priest of Gozreh. He's not a priest of any living god at all. So how could he make a truce with goblins who *are* devoted to some nature deity?"

"Ah," Hrym said. "The problem is, you assumed I was listening to all that truce and treaty talk. I'm a *sword*. I was never worried about the goblins. If I had been listening, I'm sure I would have noticed that little inconsistency you point out."

"No doubt," Rodrick said. "All right, wise huntsman—how did Obed really secure the cooperation of those goblins? He gave them a gift of some kind, a fire wand—was it mere bribery?"

"The goblin clans are difficult to bribe. They'd just as soon kill you and take the bribes as plunder. That way they still get the gifts, and they're allowed to eat you in the bargain. There must have been more to the arrangement than that. Those goblins don't worship any kind of nature deity, by the way. That particular clan worships demons."

Rodrick almost stopped walking, but he didn't want Obed or Zaqen, if they were watching, to see such an obvious reaction. "Demons," he said.

"Oh, yes. They specifically owe their allegiance to a demon who is at least temporarily allied with the great Locust Lord, Deskari."

"So if Obed made a truce with those goblins . . . it's at least possible . . ."

"That he did so by invoking the name of their mutual demon lords, yes," Cilian said, as if commenting on the blandness of oatmeal served at breakfast. "I could not be certain, of course—there are other possible explanations— so I thought it best to investigate, and ingratiate myself, and join your party. Fortunately, you chose to camp on the cursed island of the hags, so making myself useful was easy. When I next saw omens in the clouds, they told me my fate *did* rest with your group—though not, I think, by helping Obed achieve his goals. I have been watching all this time, trying to determine if there truly is a plot that involves demon lords—and the attack on Hansu Surtova's house seems to confirm that there is."

"Why do you even care? What business is it of yours?"

"Demons are a threat to the natural order. They are personifications of malice, cruelty, and greed. They seek to lay waste to the world, and annex our lands to the Abyss. It is my responsibility as a guardian of the wild places to prevent such horrors from taking place."

"Ah," Rodrick said. "A zealot, then. Another one. How nice. Did you ever think that perhaps *I* might not want to be involved with demon cultists, either to help them *or* hinder them? You might have told me your suspicions *before*."

Cilian shrugged. "You were clearly a criminal. Hrym is, at best, amoral. I could not rule out the possibility that you were going along with their plot willingly, though I suspected you were merely a dupe. But your decision to leave now made me decide to approach you. Here is what I suggest: We return to the cart. You explain that I pled with you, and begged you, and offered you all manner of outrageous promises if only you would stay—"

"I'm sure that's a scenario I could sell," Rodrick said. "If I had any interest in doing so. But hearing that Obed is in the service of demon lords, strangely enough, does not make me *more* eager to stay in his employ."

"But—if Obed is doing the work of demons, and going on such a journey and to such extremes to fulfill that work, then he must be planning something truly monstrous. Who knows what artifact or relic those keys will *truly* unleash? Deskari and his demon hosts were driven into this lake by Aroden in days long past— the monsters could have left *anything* locked away there. What if Obed seeks the means to open another Worldwound?"

"That's even more reason to head south, and rapidly," Rodrick said.

"We're criminals, like you said," Hrym chimed in. "Strictly profiteers. And, increasingly, it sounds like there's not much profit in this."

"I beg you," Cilian said. "I fear I cannot stop them on my own. Obed believes me a fool, but he could slay me at any moment. If he has the power to smash flat a manor house, and then send the demons who wrought such destruction home again at his command . . ." The huntsman shook his head. "I have sent many demons back to the Abyss, but I fear I am not equal to the task before me."

"You'll do fine," Rodrick said. "Hrym and I have total faith in you—"

"Do not make me use coercion," Cilian said, voice sorrowful. "I wish us to be friends, united in this endeavor."

"What sort of coercion could you . . ." Rodrick trailed off. There were various possibilities, of course. The ranger probably couldn't kill him in a straight fight, not with Hrym on Rodrick's side, but there were other forms of pressure. For instance, Cilian could run back to Obed and say that Rodrick planned to betray them to the leader of Port Ice, to point the blame at summoning the demons straight at Obed and Zaqen. The priest would certainly try to stop Rodrick from leaving then, and not even Hrym could guarantee Rodrick's safety against a horde of summoned demons. And that was just one of the ways the huntsman could make Rodrick's life difficult. Given a few minutes, he could think of half a dozen more easily. "Ah," Rodrick said. "It's like that, then. I help you, or I die horribly?"

"I need your help to prevent hundreds, perhaps thousands, perhaps *more* from dying horribly." Cilian frowned. "Besides—don't you want revenge, for the way they lied to you, and used you?"

Rodrick shook his head. "There's no profit in revenge. But there's no profit in crossing you, either, I suspect— you're a man with a destiny. What is it you always say, Hrym?"

"There's nothing more dangerous than a man with a destiny," the sword replied.

"All right," Rodrick said, resigning himself. "What's the plan? Kill them in their sleep?"

"I . . . no. Zaqen may not even realize what her master has planned—her geas makes it impossible to know her true desires, and I am unwilling to harm someone who might be an unwilling pawn, if there is any other alternative. We also need to know what exactly Obed has planned. If the priest fails, his demon masters may simply send another envoy. If we find out the nature of their plot, perhaps we can make sure no one ever fulfills his goal."

"We're gathering intelligence, then." Rodrick sighed. "And trying not to let them know *we* know they're demon-lovers. Should be easy enough. Everyone else in this party has been lying since the beginning, so I may as well start lying, too."

"Technically, since we planned to steal whatever relic Obed recovered, we've been lying all this time, too," Hrym said.

"Yes, but that's just an *ordinary* sort of lie. This new lie is going to take a bit of effort." Rodrick raised his hands and shouted, "Enough! Fine! You'll follow me all the way back to the Inner Sea if I don't agree, won't you?"

Cilian smiled a great empty-headed sort of grin, turned back to face the cart, and waved at Obed and Zaqen merrily. "He'll stay!" the huntsman boomed. Then, in a lower voice, "Thank you, Rodrick. You could come out of this a hero."

"Remind me, Hrym, what kind of payment does the average hero usually get?"

"An early, ugly death," the sword said. "Though on the plus side, people sing songs about them. Not that the heroes are generally alive to hear those songs, mind you."

"The women love a hero, at least," Rodrick said. "If I live long enough for any of those women to hear about my great and selfless acts, perhaps I can look forward to receiving some great and selfless acts from them in return."

"Just leave me sheathed when you do," Hrym said. "There are many things in this life I have no desire to see, and you having sex is most of them."

"I get his share," Rodrick said when he returned to the cart. "And I know you didn't plan on giving him a share, but now he gets a share, only I get it instead. All right?"

"Zaqen will handle any further negotiations," Obed said. "If I become involved, it will not end well." He slunk back to his tub of water, disappearing beneath the surface.

"I'm glad you came back, Rodrick," she said. "We need you. If it were only a question of more money—"

"Money is nice, but mostly it was Cilian's endless bleating and pleading. I loathe Obed, and to the extent that you're merely an appendage of Obed, I'm not so fond of you either at the moment. But Cilian has helped keep me alive more than once, and I owe him something."

"That's . . . surprisingly honorable of you." Zaqen cocked her head and regarded him curiously.

"Honor alone isn't enough, but combine honor with profit, and I begin to see the light." He clambered back up onto the cart and picked up the horse's reins as Cilian loped off into the woods. "Where are we going?"

"Just to the edge of the water," Zaqen said. "Then head east. We're looking for a place marked by the ruins of a boat, shattered against a sharp stone."

"Nice of someone to wreck their ship just to mark your spot." Rodrick snapped the reins. "It must come from having a god on your side, even a dead one."

Zaqen leaned against the seat as they began moving forward. "I've been thinking about some of the things I've learned about Brevoy, Rodrick. I think there are good opportunities here for a man of your particular skill set to make a profit. Assuming you're interested in paying work after the deluge of gold you're going to receive when we're finished here—"

"Stop making conversation." Rodrick's tone was more weary than angry. "I'll start liking you again if you continue, and I can't afford to start liking you, because you are Obed's creature, and you can't be trusted."

"It's true I can't be trusted, technically, but surely we can pass the time—"

"If you do not stop, I will get off this cart again, and this time, I will not come back."

The sorcerer lowered her head, shrugged, and sat down in the back of the cart on the heap of blankets and furs.

"That was rude of you," Hrym said. "I was interested in hearing about those potential profits she was talking about."

"Then I can toss you into the back of the cart with her. I don't intend to dictate who you converse with. But I'm on edge here, and if I want to avoid tottering right off—"

"Yes, yes, how you do carry on. Sulk away, then. I'll just be here in silent contemplation of the infinite. Rouse me when there's money to be made or blood to spill."

So I'm to be a world-saving demon-slayer now, Rodrick thought. Friendless and not a bit charming. What have I ever done to deserve this sort of exalted fate?

Chapter Thirty-Two
Their Mistress, the Lake

The shipwreck was barely a ship, but it was certainly a wreck, a small fishing vessel that had somehow managed to smash itself against a jagged spike of rock, where it was now impaled through its hull, single mast leaning sharply out over the water. "How does that even happen?" Rodrick said. "Are there vast storms on the lake? Waves sufficient to toss a boat?"

Cilian, who'd appeared from a nearby stand of trees just after the cart stopped, looked at the ship for a moment and grunted. "That ship was not tossed there by wind or wave. Given the angle. . . . I would say the ship was picked up, and slammed down on the rock."

Rodrick closed his eyes. "You're saying there are, what, giants in the lake? Not like the giants you find in the hills anywhere, men twelve feet tall, but *giant* giants?"

"It could have been something with tentacles," Cilian said. "The ship is too weathered to show precise signs."

"This lake is said to be home to all manner of strange things," Zaqen said. "I hope this doesn't count as *conversation*, Rodrick. I'd hate to offend you when I'm merely trying to be factual. The waters are said to be inhabited by everything from draugr to grindylows to kelpies to aquatic ogres to water orms to undines, creatures of chaos and the Abyss, and perhaps even stranger monsters, though I may be able to make pleasant conversation with those."

"I wish you the best of luck with that, then. I know how you love to chat."

Obed climbed out of the cart, strapping a belt holding a long dagger around his waist. He pulled a large backpack—containing the four keys, Rodrick assumed—over his shoulders, then waded out into the cold blue waters of the lake and dove under the rippling surface.

Rodrick closed his eyes. "I've been dreading this part since you mentioned it back in Loric Fells. We're going for a swim now, then?"

Zaqen nodded. "We are."

"Obed finally gets to be in his element. Good for him. I'll just be here on shore, guarding the cart."

"The cart is sufficiently guarded by magic," Zaqen said. "Guarded from you, too, I'm afraid—my master insisted. The gold and gems in those trunks will stay there until he returns to release them. No, we have other needs for you."

"I am not a fish-man," Rodrick said. "I am not, though I hate to admit inadequacy in any area, a particularly good swimmer, either. Even if you can grant me the ability to breathe water, I'll just be bobbing around uselessly."

"We have remedies for that." She went to the back of the cart and chose a sack. "These are just a few of the items we've been lugging around the countryside these past weeks." She drew out a cloak of ugly deep purple, its hem shredded into six or seven long, dangling rags. "Have you ever heard of magical cloaks that allow one to change form, into bats or spiders or manta rays or eels?"

Rodrick frowned. "You want to give me a cloak that will turn me into a sea snake? I have no desire to acquire gills, Zaqen—"

"Ha, no, I wouldn't give you something *that* much fun—besides, you could hardly wield Hrym if you were in the shape of a sea creature. Most of them lack hands, after all. No, this garment is mine, and it doesn't transform me into eel or fish or manta. It's a variation Obed had crafted for me especially. It's a cloak of the devilfish. Have you ever seen a devilfish?"

"I regret that I have not had the pleasure."

"You will soon. I'm going to turn into one. But for *you*, we have something a bit simpler. A ring, and a necklace. You'll want to keep the ring especially—it will keep you from drowning, since it lets you breathe underwater— but the necklace will keep the water from freezing you too much, and will give you the ability to move more easily in water than you could otherwise. Making it possible, for example, to swing a sword in something other than a slow and lazy waterlogged arc. I've tried the necklace myself, in the sea, and it's an interesting experience—a bit like walking on thickened air."

"Ah, yes, walking on thickened air, of course. We all know what *that's* like. So I'm to follow a fish-man and a devilfish-woman into the sea, slaughtering any merfolk or similar who seek to hinder us?"

"That is the general idea."

"Do you have rings for Cilian too?"

"I have my own spells," Cilian said. "I often explored the deep lakes of Loric Fells."

"Grand," Rodrick said. "Let's swim to—what was it again? The Vault of Aroden? Surely it has a name. All these legendary temples have names."

"If it has a name, that name is unknown to me," Zaqen said.

"Do we know where it is? Or are we just going to swim about at random and hope for the best?"

"My master told me to find the spot where a boat was spiked on a stone, and to enter the water there, and descend. So that is what we're doing. I trust he knows where to go from here."

"One wonders how he knew about the boat," Rodrick mused. "Or who left it here for him to see."

"My master has many contacts, and many resources. He does not share them all with me."

"Yes, Obed is a bit stingy when it comes to sharing the fruits of his knowledge. I've noticed that. Give me the jewelry, then."

Zaqen passed over the ring, a simple circle of blue coral, and the necklace, a thick golden chain with a pendant in the shape of a man with arms and legs outstretched. The figure was probably meant to look utterly unfettered and glorying in freedom, but to Rodrick it looked more like the posture of a man spread-eagled on a torture device. He slipped on the ring, and felt no different at all, and put on the necklace, also with a total lack of noticeable effects. "If this is all a ruse to drown me, I'll be very disappointed."

"The dead are incapable of disappointment," Zaqen said. "That's probably one of the few consolations of being dead."

"I hope I don't have an opportunity to discover that firsthand anytime soon."

The sorcerer waded out into the waves, and once she was waist deep, she put on the cloak of the devilfish. "Follow me closely," she said. "I *think* I'll be the only devilfish in the lake—they prefer salt oceans, as I understand it—but take care anyway. I'd hate for you to start following the wrong monster."

"You're the only monster for me, Zaqen."

She put up the hood of the cloak and began to twist and shudder. The hood closed down around her face, and the ragged ends at the hem slapped against the water, thickening and elongating into seven long and lashing tentacles. Her head and upper body blurred, seemed to run together, and bulged out into a single vaguely egg-shaped mass topped by a pair of frilled fins, with two bulging white eyes resolving in the center of the bulbous mass. The creature—which overall looked a bit like the octopuses Rodrick had eaten in certain coastal cities, albeit ten feet long and probably weighing a quarter ton—rolled over in the water, revealing a maw at the center of the seven toothed tentacles.

"Rodrick," it—she—said, voice a mushy sort of hiss. "Didn't expect me to be able to talk, did you? Devilfish are surprisingly intelligent. If you ever meet a real one, you might even stand a chance of using your silver tongue to convince it not to eat you."

"It would certainly present an interesting challenge," Rodrick said.

Zaqen rolled again, tentacles flexing, and vanished beneath the surface.

"Here we go, then." He glanced at Cilian, who nodded. The huntsman had left his bow and arrow behind—sensibly enough—but he was armed with a small axe and an array of knives. The half-elf dove into the water

and began swimming out to greater depth, then dove
down and disappeared.

"It's a good thing I can't rust," Hrym said. "Really, the
sort of situations you get me into, Rodrick."

"All ice starts out as water. At least you'll have plenty
of moisture to work with down there." He walked out
into the water, leaned forward, and put his face in. The
water was shockingly cold, but somehow the cold didn't
bother him at all; it was just a fact he noticed. He pulled
his face out. "They want me to *breathe* under there? It's
madness! Every inch of my body rebels against it!"

"Always afraid to try new things," Hrym said. "You're
a perpetual disappointment."

"If I drown, you'll be stuck here in the shallows, with
no gold for a bed. You should be more sensitive to my
worries, if only for purely mercenary reasons." He took
a deep breath and let himself fall face first into the
water. Letting the breath out, watching the bubbles
obscure his vision, he steeled himself for the sting
that comes with cold water flooding one's nostrils,
something he'd only ever experienced accidentally
before. He allowed himself to take the tiniest breath,
and didn't immediately feel like he was drowning;
it was more like breathing cold mountain air. When
he took a deeper breath, it was the same, and the
exhalation was similar: a peculiar sensation, but not
fundamentally alien. And now when he breathed,
there were no bubbles, so he could see, though there
was precious little *to* see, so far—just the sandy lake
bottom in the shallows and, in the distance, the
dimness of deeper water.

Cilian swam toward him, giving a little wave before
kicking off toward the darkness again, in the direction

of a purple, writhing shape that was probably Zaqen in her devilfish cloak.

Rodrick submerged himself more deeply, Hrym iced to his back, and though his movements were essentially those of swimming, Zaqen was right—it *was* like moving in thickened air. He could swing his arms and legs without the weight and pressure of the water slowing him down, and yet somehow he still propelled himself through the fluid medium. "This is bizarre, Hrym," he said, and his voice sounded quite natural to his own ears, not muffled by water at all, though perhaps a bit more echoey than usual.

"You humans are so fussy about your environments," the sword said, clearly audible from his back. "Water, air, what's the difference? You're all so fragile, it's a wonder you survive your first few months of life. Anything short of being dropped in a volcano and *I'd* be fine."

"You're a terrible dancer, though," Rodrick said. "So we've got that going for us." He kicked—lazily, with no more effort than walking—his way after Cilian and the now-monstrous Zaqen. As he drew closer, he saw that her devilfish form also sported a tumorous growth on the back, a Lump-sized bulge, though either its eyes were absent in this form, or they were simply closed in sleep. He wondered if the sorcerer's parasitic brother could pull himself free in her current transformed condition. Rodrick could easily imagine Lump propelling himself through the waves, a grotesque eye-covered jellyfish, tentacles trailing underneath and grasping hungrily at any passing wildlife, collecting fish eyes . . . Rodrick shuddered.

They swam down, down, down, and though the light from above grew gradually thinner and more attenuated, there must have been some magic relating to vision in the necklace, too, because Rodrick could see just fine—the uneven, rocky bottom of the lake was murky, certainly, but no dimmer than a room lit by torchlight.

There were fish, now, great schools of them, doubtless the sustenance of the region, silver shoals swimming past in formation, some of the creatures very nearly as big as Rodrick himself, others as small as his thumb. They paid him no mind at all, though they shied away from Zaqen, who was admittedly the most obviously predatorial of the bunch.

As the lake floor grew closer, many of the shapes Rodrick had taken to be rocks revealed themselves as the shattered remnants of ships, from two-man canoes to larger fishing boats, broken into greater or lesser pieces, their wooden shapes furred with underwater vegetation and colonized by various forms of aquatic life, used as dens for fish and freshwater crabs the size of large dogs.

Obed sat cross-legged on the almost-level deck of the largest wreck, the gills in his neck fluttering in a way that Rodrick found vaguely obscene. He held a medallion in the shape of a starfish in his hands, its five arms pointing off in five different directions, the tip of the topmost arm glowing green. "Good," he said as they settled around him, his voice a bit on the gurgling side, but comprehensible. "You lot took your time. We must continue north, along a fairly straight line. If the currents are with us, we should reach our destination before midnight."

"Midnight?" Rodrick said. "How far are we going?"

"The lake is perhaps five hundred miles wide from east to west," Zaqen said. "And, say, three hundred miles long from north to south. This body of water is larger than some *countries*, Rodrick—probably larger than Brevoy itself. We're hardly going any distance at all. But . . . we're going deep enough."

"I suppose Aroden *would* refuse to hide his life force in the shallows," Rodrick said, "where any fool with a net might scoop it up. Shall we swim, then?"

"If you're done talking, yes," Obed snapped. "Cilian will scout for threats ahead of us."

"Danger beneath the water can come from all directions, from any side and above and below," the huntsman said. "But I will do my best."

"Zaqen will swim at my side, protecting me. You, thief, and your sword, will follow us and defend us from any attack that comes from behind—"

"Like, for instance, the four scaly lake-ogres creeping up behind us?" Hrym said. "You might want to start wielding me now, Rodrick."

Chapter Thirty-Three
Abyss of the Bizarre

Aquatic ogres!" Obed said. "I've never seen freshwater ones before. Puny things, aren't they?"

"They appear to be roughly twice as tall as I am." Rodrick tried to get his footing on the slick deck, Hrym in hand, watching as the ogres spread out in a fan-shaped formation. While ogres on land favored clubs, bludgeoning weapons were impractical in the water, and these green-scaled, web-fingered variants were armed with javelins and their own wicked claws.

"Pah," Obed said. "They grow to twenty feet tall in the oceans. The water ogres I fought in my youth hunt *whales*. This lot could barely kill a hydra."

"I am, alas, not a hydra," Rodrick said. "Still, I believe they could kill me adequately."

"So kill them first," Obed said. "But do it quickly. We have a lot of water to cover."

Cilian took the knife from his belt and Zaqen began surging forward, tentacles writhing, but Hrym shouted, "*Stop!* You people always make things harder than they need to be. Zaqen and Cilian, stay out of the way. Just wave me in their general direction, Rodrick."

Grinning, the thief gave Hrym a great swing, a ripping arc through the water, and threads of ice shot out from along the blade at brief intervals along the curve, like lances of crystal flying straight at the approaching aquatic ogres. One tried to swim upward, but his huge bulk moved too slowly. Another attempted to parry the ice with his lance, which only caused the stream to split and strike his body in two places. The remaining aquatic ogres were caught entirely by surprise, ice striking them squarely in the chests and spreading to cover them in a shell like translucent armor. They struggled, but the ice wound around them all, thickening, spreading like a cold wildfire, until within mere seconds all four ogres were bound in great irregular lumps of ice, the creatures visible only as faint green tints deep inside, like the flaws in a gem. The icy prisons floated gradually upward, drifting slowly until they were out of sight.

"That was remarkable," Obed said, something like awe in his voice.

"Freezing someone in solid ice on land is harder," Hrym said. "You have to suck a lot of moisture out of the air. But down here? This is my *element*. Literally. We should do all our adventuring underwater, Rodrick."

"How long before they thaw?" Cilian said. "They'll surely be angry when they get free."

"They're encased in ice," Rodrick said crossly. "They're suffocating to death as we speak."

"At least they won't stink much," Hrym said. "My ice is magical—it doesn't melt the way normal ice does. They'll be sealed up for years, or until someone chips them out or sprays them with fire—or until I'm shattered or melted in a volcano, I suppose. There's no reason to think my magic will outlast me. But I've lasted thousands of years—I think—and don't plan on going anywhere soon."

"If anything else attacks us, do that to them as well," Obed said. "It is a most efficient way of dealing with those who would delay us."

"We're going to end up littering the surface of the lake with monsters-on-ice, aren't we?" Rodrick said. "Think of all the shipwrecks we're going to cause, all the holes we're going to knock into hulls. But that's the price of bringing on a golden age, eh? I'm sure Aroden will provide everyone in Brevoy with free fish for life once he's resurrected."

"Do not blaspheme," Obed said. "I cannot tolerate blasphemy."

"Any god who can't take a little mockery isn't much of a god," Rodrick said. "But you're the one in charge here. I obey, as always."

Obed gave him a long, dark stare, then jerked his head toward the north. Cilian shrugged and swam off ahead into the darkness, followed by Zaqen and Obed side by side. Rodrick put Hrym on his back and kicked along after them, hanging as far to the rear as he could without losing sight of them. Maybe the guardians of the vault they were going to breach would slaughter Obed. Rodrick wouldn't lift a hand to help him if it came to that. He might even lend the guardians his sword.

The next few hours of swimming—with only occasional breaks to eat soggy jerky, a decidedly unpleasant experience—were strange and spectacular. The lake contained multitudes. Once they got past the shallows, the lake floor dropped sharply away, and it seemed as if they journeyed in a great hazy void for a while. But Obed angled ever downward, and before long the ground was in sight again, but different, now. Where there had been wrecked ships before, there were now things that had nothing at all to do with the human world.

A sort of temple made of heaped black rocks, larger than the Arena of Aroden, filled a hollow place on the lake floor, and a high-pitched keening that was not quite music could be heard emerging from the thousands of cave mouths that led inside. A steady stream of silver and blue fish swam into those caves, as if called by the monotonous song. "Do you think those fish go into those caves expecting heaven?"

"If so, they're even stupider than I expect fish to be," Hrym replied. "Let's swim a bit higher, all right? That song makes my ice resonate unpleasantly."

Later they passed near an oval of shimmering silver, no larger than a wagon wheel, that hovered in the water, and when Rodrick kicked toward it to investigate, he found it was a sort of window, and on the other side was a vaguely man-shaped creature made entirely of frothing water. It flinched back when it saw Rodrick, and then reached out with a hand of flowing dark water, as if to try and touch him, so the thief kicked away as rapidly as he could. "What in the Abyss?"

"Water elemental of some kind," Hrym said. "Maybe he's an arcanist or researcher, keeping an eye on all the bodies of water on this plane?"

"Or he just likes watching fish fornicate," Rodrick said. "Deep-water pornography."

"Fish don't marry, so I doubt they can be said to fornicate, but he could be some sort of extraplanar pervert, I suppose."

They passed over a crack in the lake floor, around which scurried man-sized shrimp in shockingly beautiful rainbow colors, some of them using crude tools to scrape fungus or other vegetable slime from the rocks. Later a pair of sea snakes, each bright pink and dozens of yards long, writhed together beneath them, either mating or fighting or both. Past that, a cone-shaped depression in the floor began to swirl and spin, and a cow-sized fish passing overhead was dragged down, thrashing wildly, as it was pulled bloodily into a hole far too small for its body. "Remind me to avoid swimming over depressions like that," Rodrick said. "

"Do you *really* think you'll need a reminder?" Hrym asked.

Off to the west, they saw shimmering spires of gold, silver, and pearl, with vague dark shapes flickering among the towers. "Is that a city of some kind?" Rodrick said.

"It doesn't look like a natural formation," Hrym said. "There may be nations beneath this water that are unknown to people of the surface. Whole societies. Cultures, wars, entire histories."

"How much wealth must you possess to make towers that glimmer like that?" Rodrick mused.

"How much gold could you possibly drag around behind you while swimming?" Hrym said. "I imagine you'd just sink to the lake floor under the weight."

"I'm sure with the right magic . . ." Rodrick mused. "But I don't suppose Obed would approve a side expedition."

"The priest is certainly very focused," Hrym said. "That never made sense to me before—Aroden can hardly be impatient, being dead, so why all the hurry? But if your true masters are demons, I imagine you learn

313

the importance of carrying out their wishes in a timely fashion."

There were a few attacks that had to be dealt with, too, mostly by simple dumb animals who thought their party might be food: great toothy beasts with long, narrow jaws; things a bit like huge eels, but with vestigial forelimbs; reptilian creatures covered in spines and fins, with excessive numbers of mouths. Hrym froze them all and sent them floating to the surface. Eventually, as the hours wore on, the attacks became more frequent, and Rodrick began swimming closer to Zaqen and Obed. After the third attack in ten minutes by an entirely different group of creatures, Rodrick said, "Is this normal? Are sea beasts always so aggressive?"

"This is not the sea." Obed rotated slowly as he hovered in the water, peering into the murk on all sides. "All aquatic realms are savage places, but we have been attacked by predators who should not be in one another's territories. I believe they are being sent against us deliberately by some enemy. I feared that some ancient, misguided guardian might try to prevent us from reaching our glorious goal. We must prepare ourselves to meet more intelligent opposition as our destination grows nearer."

"Intelligent enemies freeze just as well as the mindless—" Rodrick began, but then the water swirled and frothed beneath them as the lake floor showered up great gouts of churned mud. Something huge— or many things that were merely very large—burst from hiding places beneath the sand, the force of the emergence setting up currents that sent Rodrick, Zaqen, and Obed spinning wildly away from one another. A tentacle as big around as Rodrick's body shot past him, and he instinctively lashed out with Hrym, who sliced the tentacle cleanly through. Unfortunately, that released great clouds of black blood or ichor, which only served to further ruin visibility. Obed was shouting somewhere in the distance, and Rodrick started to shout back, but Hrym screamed "Watch out!" at the same moment.

Rodrick was already watching, but whatever Hrym saw, he *couldn't* see—at least, not until it was on top of him. A net woven of thick sea grasses surrounded him, and it took all his effort to hold onto Hrym as the net constricted around him. He tried to slash at the net, but the threads squeezed him so tightly that his arms were pressed against his chest, making it impossible to do more than twitch his wrist ineffectually, the flat of Hrym's blade pressed against him. "Are you sure you can't move? Just a little?" He thrashed, but only succeeded in binding himself tighter.

"If I could, I would have done it before now," Hrym said. "I could encase us in ice, and let us float up to the surface, if you think that would help—"

Suddenly the net jerked, and Rodrick and Hrym were dragged rapidly downward, through the clouds of mud and blood and the distant lashing of monstrous tentacles. Rodrick wondered if Zaqen and Obed had been caught and crushed—the thought of the sorcerer being squeezed by black tentacles was terribly ironic, considering the way she sometimes dispatched her own enemies. Zaqen's tentacles weren't nearly this big, though.

Rodrick realized he was focusing on the potential deaths of others so he wouldn't have to contemplate his own likely demise. "It's been a good run, Hrym," he said. "I do wish I'd never answered the summons

LIAR'S BLADE

Zaqen sent me, though. That little bag of gold she paid us in advance looks like it's going to cost me my life. I hope you aren't stuck at the bottom of this lake for too long when I'm gone."

"I'll just cocoon myself in ice and float to the top," Hrym said. "Some pirate will be thrilled to find me. But let's hope it doesn't come to that, all right? You aren't dead yet."

Rodrick swore as he banged against something sharp on his left side. The net was dragged along a rough rock, and he was glad he had the net wrapped around him then, its fibrous threads protecting him somewhat from being shredded against the stones. "Am I being dragged into a hole in the ground?" he said as darkness closed in.

"As far as I can tell. We may both end up in the belly of some beast. At least you'll be dead. I'll have to *know* I'm in the belly of a beast. How tedious."

"People-devouring leviathans don't usually hunt with nets," Rodrick said. "Or so I'd assume. Admittedly, I'm no expert on such things." How often in his life had he responded to panic with a false front of airy jocularity? Dozens, at least, probably more. It occurred to him that this might be the last time. But he might as well die as he'd lived.

Chapter Thirty-Four
The Thieves Go Below

The net changed direction, pulling them sideways now. Rodrick and Hrym were pulled through a tunnel of some kind, into an underwater cave complex. Eventually the orientation of the tunnel shifted sufficiently that Rodrick found himself hanging upside down, being dragged *upward*—or so the blood rushing to his head seemed to indicate, though it was hard to be sure of anything in the pitch-black water.

The steady tug became a sharp wrench, and the net was dragged out of the darkness into light. Rodrick lay on his side, gasping—and realized he was breathing *air* again, instead of water. His vision was obscured by the net, but they seemed to be in a damp cave, lit by clean-burning torches on the wall—probably magic. The cave walls were decorated with paintings in vibrant reds and blues and greens, both abstract patterns of shapes and more representative images, of giants wielding swords and axes against monstrous insects.

The triple points of a trident appeared before his eyes, and then the weapon twisted deftly, snapping the woven fronds one by one to expose Rodrick's face and throat while leaving his body bound. The weapon's wielder crouched and looked at Rodrick with a blank expression.

Rodrick had never seen a man like this before, but strangely, the closest comparison was Obed. The demon-priest resembled a human who had been transformed by generations in the sea, losing hair and gaining gills and taking on certain watery adaptations. This fellow with the trident looked like an elf who had undergone a similar racial transformation—the pale skin and pointed ears were recognizably elven, but the fingers clutching the trident were webbed, and there were gills on his neck. He wore necklaces of shells and very little in the way of clothing, and his body was lean, hard, and covered in scars. "Is there a dragon?" the man said, his voice a rasp.

"Ah—what?"

"A. Dragon." The lake-elf pointed his trident at Rodrick's face. "I saw a gillman in your party, and someone in the form of a devilfish, and a half-elf, but no *dragon*."

"Ah, no, we do not travel with a dragon—"

The elf nodded, and the tension seemed to drain out of him. He lowered his trident, letting the longest point touch the floor. "Good. Then all is not lost. I sensed the keys, all four keys, and so I feared, but—" He raised the trident again. "*One* of those keys could only have been gained by killing the last living creature I called a friend. Were *you* the one who broke into her lair in the Icerime Peaks and slew her? I felt her die—"

"Her?" Rodrick said. "That is, no, I didn't kill her! I saw her, if you mean who I think you mean—she was inhabiting the body of a yeti. The devilfish in our party is a sorcerer, and it was a monster of hers that killed the yeti. I didn't want to kill anyone, I was just hired to *steal* the key—"

The aquatic elf sniffed. "You are a dupe, then. Merely a hireling. I can smell truth, you know. It is one of my many gifts."

I wish I had his nose, Rodrick thought. It could have saved me a lot of trouble.

"Do you even know what the keys are *for*?" the elf demanded.

"I was told . . . well, various things. But the last thing my employer told me was that the keys would open a vault where they could find an artifact belonging to the dead god Aroden, and use it to restore him to life."

To Rodrick's astonishment, the elf threw his head back and laughed. "That is a bold lie. Very bold."

"I didn't believe them, either. I suspect their real goal has something to do with demons. I realized not long ago that my employers were lying to me, and . . ." He shrugged as best he could, given his bound condition. "I wanted to find out what they had planned, and to try to stop them, of course. I have another ally in the party, a half-elf—"

"He still lives. They all still live, unfortunately, according to the reports I've received. I sent many of the beasts of the sea against them, against all of you, but you are a formidable group. Which is why it's so astonishing that you failed to bring a dragon! I suppose the true nature of the ritual must be lost, or at least misunderstood, after all these centuries . . ."

"I'm afraid I don't know what you mean," Rodrick said. "My name is Rodrick, by the way"

A strange expression crossed his captor's face—was it wistfulness? Regret? "Of course. I forget my manners. I have been here, alone, for so long. I came from the Steaming Sea when I was a young druid, to fight for glory, and never expected to be trapped in this cold lake . . ."

"The yeti told me there was only one other living guardian," Rodrick said. "I assumed she meant a guardian of a *key*, but you—you guard what the key opens?"

"I do," the elf said. "My name is Neiros."

"Are you some species of gillman, or . . . ?"

He snorted. "Gillmen! They are a race of pawns, used by powers greater than themselves, scrabbling to recover past glories that none of them were even alive to see. No, I am an aquatic elf. We are not a populous race, but we are a proud one." He sat down cross-legged, sighed, and then flicked his trident forward a few more times, severing the fronds that held Rodrick bound. "There. Please refrain from attacking me with that peculiar sword of yours. Or anything else."

Hrym remained silent, for which Rodrick was grateful. If Neiros didn't already know Hrym was sentient, why tell him?

"Will you help me stop your employers?" Neiros said. "Not that there's any urgency now, as I know they're incapable of completing the ritual, but I *do* hate loose ends."

"I will happily help you kill Obed, the gillman, but the sorcerer Zaqen is bound to serve him by a geas, and I don't think necessarily agrees with his choices—"

"This sorcerer is the one who killed my friend, the one you say lived in the body of a yeti?"

"Ye-es, more or less, but only under orders from Obed—"

"I will consider mercy," Neiros said, in a tone that suggested he didn't want to discuss that matter further.

"Perhaps we can use your relationship to ambush this Obed. We can pretend that you've escaped me—"

"I'm only willing to help if you tell me what I'm helping to *do*," Rodrick said.

"This is hardly the time—"

"You said there's no urgency," the thief said. "Though I'm curious to know why you think that. Please understand, Neiros. I have been lied to, in a variety of ways, for *weeks*. I am not normally concerned with the truth for its own sake, I confess, but I would like to know what I've been fighting and killing and nearly dying for. I much prefer to be the one doing the scheming and plotting, and ignorance does *not* suit me."

The druid sighed. "Very well. I know nothing of this Obed personally, but I can still tell you many things about him: He worships demons. Some time ago, likely months, perhaps even years ago, he began to hear whispers in his still moments, or to have strange dreams. The Lake of Mists and Veils feeds rivers, you know, and those rivers trickle down to the Inner Sea. For the past many years, those waters have carried a taint of demonic influence. I knew that a gillman demon cultist would come eventually—I only feared he would come better prepared. I do not doubt that the next gillman who comes *will* be—"

"Perhaps you should begin at the beginning," Rodrick said. "I find that tends to make stories more comprehensible."

Another snort. "I am not accustomed to talking to anyone other than the creatures of the lake, and my bunyip companion. Yes, all right. This story begins, as so many others do, with Aroden."

"I was not a worshiper of Aroden," the druid said, "but I was an ally of his, before he became a god, millennia ago. Aroden understood the importance of uniting disparate races against our common foes, which, in those days, were more often than not the demons who sought to destroy this world, or make it merely an extension of their own Abyss.

"One of the mightiest of those demons was Deskari, the Lord of the Locust Host. He led a mighty army of lesser demons, among them many who were almost demon lords in their own right, and who served as Deskari's generals. Aroden had generals, too. I was not one of those, but you might say I was an aide-de-camp. I served as assistant to one of Aroden's generals, a mighty golden dragon named Seralia—her name has passed out of history, I fear, as have the names of so many other brave souls. To listen to the stories, you would believe Aroden achieved all his great works entirely on his own—which is absurd, as most of his greatest achievements took place when he was a mortal hero, long before he laid hands on the Starstone and attained godhood.

"Our battles with the demons raged across this continent. Eventually our final battle brought us to the shores of this lake, which was ancient even then, and we drove the Locust Lord's host into the waters. Oh, the shore was stained with blood and fouler fluids that day. Many of the demons died—but, of course, when demons of any consequence die, they are merely reborn again in the Abyss. Deskari escaped ultimate judgment, but he was locked away, unable to return to this plane. His greatest general of the time, however, was a nascent demon lord—perhaps even one of Deskari's own children—known as Kholerus. Kholerus shares some of his father's insectlike qualities, though where Deskari takes the form of a man with the lower half of a locust, Kholerus has an even fouler aspect—he is vaguely like a giant human from the waist up, apart from his horrible eyes and complicated, ever-grinding mouth-parts, but below the waist his body becomes the segmented, thousand-legged, coiled body of an immense millipede, so long that the end of his tail sometimes trails miles behind him, oozing poison with every step.

"Kholerus tried to engage us in battle, to kill us all or die in the process so he could escape to the Abyss to plan later terrors, but Aroden was too clever. Instead of fighting, Aroden worked a great spell to capture Kholerus. Originally, the trap had been laid for Deskari, but the Locust was too wily, and we settled for springing our trap on his offspring instead.

"Kholerus was sealed into an impenetrable vault beneath the lake, locked away for millennia by the joined magics of Seralia and Aroden. There he's remained, writhing, furious, and impotent, the keys to his prison scattered and hidden and disguised, his vault guarded by me and my creatures. There were other guardians, once, but they all died, while I have been able to sustain myself with ancient magics and long sleeps, waking only when there was some threat or disturbance to trouble my realm.

"And then, just over a century past, the world changed. Aroden died—somehow—and our world shifted, allowing the crawling horrors of the Abyss to reach us more easily. The Worldwound opened, and among the demons who crawled out first was Deskari, the Usher of the Apocalypse.

"I woke, and could tell immediately that Kholerus had been strengthened by his old master's return to the world. His prison was designed to hold an even greater power than Kholerus himself, so he could not escape, even though the walls of the prison were loosened. But he *was* able to extend his influence into the world, to send whispers floating on the currents, down the rivers, toward the gillmen, which he knows are the only ones who can free him—"

Chapter Thirty-Five
The Curse of the Sword and the Soul

W ait, why?" Rodrick said. "Why can only gillmen free him? And, more importantly, why can *anyone* free him? When constructing a prison for a demon lord, why would you create keys that can open it *at all*?"

If Neiros was annoyed at being interrupted, he didn't show it. "Kholerus is immortal. All prisons fail eventually, Rodrick, given sufficient time, and demons are patient. Aroden and Seralia hoped that they would find a way to sever Kholerus's connection to the Abyss, you see. If they could have done that, Kholerus would have been wholly trapped in this world—and physically vulnerable to a *true* death. They planned the trap for Deskari, of course. That's who they *really* wanted to kill. So they made it possible to open the prison again, under very special circumstances, with the idea that, someday, they would release their prisoner just long enough to slay him forever. They were unable to discover a way to sever Kholerus's connections—and Aroden had other, more pressing problems, it must be said—and so we settled for hiding the keys away for possible future use. The keys all had guardians, originally, but . . ." Neiros shrugged. "It was thousands of years ago. Things changed. We were able to keep all the relics in Issia and Rostland, which became Brevoy—there were subtle magics that made the keys difficult to take away from the region, but their true purposes were forgotten. Until now."

"All right," Rodrick said. "So where do the gillmen come in?"

"In order to open the prison, a ritual is required, and part of that ritual involves replicating the conditions under which the prison was first sealed. Aroden was in charge of turning two of the keys—'turned' is the wrong word, as you don't literally put a key into a lock, but you understand what I mean—and Seralia was responsible for turning the other two. Their servants did the actual activation of the keys—I operated one myself, in fact, the one that resembles a dog's skull—while Aroden and Seralia spoke certain words of binding, each in turn, and in precise sequence. In order to open the prison again, the equivalent of that original group must be gathered again: an Azlanti must be present, and a dragon, and they must speak the words of *unbinding* once the keys are in place. You see?"

"Gillmen . . . they're close enough to Azlanti for ritual purposes?" Rodrick said.

Neiros nodded. "Yes. Once upon a time, the gillmen might *not* have been close enough, but the locks that hold the prison closed are weaker now, and more easily circumvented. Gillmen *are* the truest descendants of the drowned and shattered Azlanti empire—the other survivors interbred with other humans and saw their blood hopelessly diluted, but the gillmen remained pure, in a sense. Oh, their bodies were altered by the necessity of living under the sea, by strange magics and the interference of dark forces, but they are still Azlanti, underneath it all. So Kholerus sent his call to them, as I knew he would. But apparently he didn't succeed in getting across the fact that they needed to bring a dragon with them *too*—"

"Ah," Hrym said. "Sorry to interrupt. But would the *soul* of a dragon be sufficient?"

Neiros leaned back. "Was that the sword? The sword talks?"

"Among other things," Rodrick said.

"It's an important question," Hrym said. "Could someone with the soul of a dragon serve in the ritual? Even if the soul is in, ah, a different container?"

"Conceivably," Neiros said. "Especially since the bonds are weakened—but why? What are you saying?"

"I think I might know why Obed was so keen to have us in his party, Rodrick." The sword sounded miserable. "And as we should have known, it's not because of *your* charm and allure. They wanted me. You see, old friend, I never told you this, but . . . I used to be a dragon."

After a moment's silence, Rodrick said, "Does anyone ever say anything to me that *isn't* a lie? What do you mean you used to be a dragon? What, did you offend a magical blacksmith who cursed you to spend eternity as a sword?"

"Not exactly," Hrym said. "I never told you because . . . look, I used to be a *white* dragon. What do you know about those?"

"They're the most vicious of all dragons," Neiros said. He was holding his trident in a purposeful way again.

"Yes!" Hrym said. "They're terrible bastards, as a rule. And while I'm *not* so terrible, it's still not an association I'd care to claim. Anyway, Rodrick, the few times I've mentioned my past, you've always assumed I was lying—"

"You were lying!" Rodrick cried. "You said you were once wielded by some sort of magical pilot in a flying *city*! You told me that you'd seen the Silver Mount fall from the sky! Your torrents of bullshit are unending!"

"So as you see, even if I had told you, you wouldn't have believed me," Hrym said, unperturbed. "Just because I *occasionally* embellish my past exploits. It's not as if you've never claimed to be descended from the overthrown royals of Andoran, or to have bedded women I *know* are so far out of your league that their league is invisible from where you're standing—"

The trident was at Rodrick's throat again. "Explain yourself, sword," Neiros said coldly. "Lest your wielder suffer for your hesitation."

"Oh, that's not necessary," Hrym said. "I *love* talking about myself." A pause. "But get that thing away from my partner's throat, or we'll see who's faster—me freezing, or you stabbing."

"I would prefer we not have that competition, if it's all the same to both of you," Rodrick said. Neiros grudgingly lowered the trident, but didn't drop it.

"You're old, druid, perhaps nearly as old as I am," Hrym said. "Maybe you have a better memory than I do. Hold me up, Rodrick." The thief did as he was bid . . . and looked on, astonished, as a portion of Hrym's icy blade shimmered and turned into something that resembled ordinary steel. Dark letters in a strange alphabet were etched into the blade, the symbols faintly glimmering. "Can you read that word, Neiros?"

The druid squinted. "It's in an old Shory dialect, one I have seen before, but not in a *very* long time . . . I believe it means 'Spellstealer,' more or less."

"There," Hrym said. "That was my original name. I always wondered what it was—my memory is a *mess*, for reasons I'll explain. I like the name Hrym better— much more euphonious. Though who knows how Spellstealer sounds in the original, what was it you said, Shory?" The crystalline ice of the blade crept back down, hiding away the ancient name.

Neiros seemed deep in thought. "I . . . believe I have heard of swords with that name. A type of cursed blade that ate magic, rendering its wielder impervious to the spells of enemy wizards or magical beasts, and allowing the user to turn those magics back against the attacker, casting their own spells against them. But there was a flaw in the swords' creation, a twist in the magic that took a terrible toll on a wielder's soul—are you one of *those*?"

"I used to be," Hrym said. "Or so I assume. But I haven't done things like that in a very long time. I couldn't tell you *where* I was forged, or what adventures I had in my original form, not for sure, though sometimes I see glimpses—flashes viewed through the eyes of humans or ogres or orcs or elves. Those are the source of some of the more outlandish stories I've told, Rodrick. Perhaps those images are taken from fragments of souls I absorbed from my wielders—"

"Wait. You've been eating my *soul* all this time, you horrible little shit?"

"Hush, no, never," Hrym said. "Back when I nibbled at souls, or subsisted on life energy, or *whatever* I did, I had no mind. There was no ill intent behind my actions, any more than a fire *intends* to consume what it burns. Besides, I don't think I could slurp up a soul now if I tried to—I'm like a sponge that's fully saturated. I can't hold another drop."

"And at some point you believe you absorbed the soul of a *dragon*?" Neiros said.

"That much I do remember," Hrym said. "I was being used by . . . some warrior or another. Somewhere up in what are now the Lands of the Linnorm Kings. We found a great white dragon, ancient, laired in a tower full of treasure, and we fought. I was mindless then, but I can remember the last moments of my wielder. He used me to nullify the dragon's magic—but that didn't save him from the dragon's claws, or jaws. He was slain. Most of his party, too, I should think, and any of them that lived merely fled. From that point, I have to speculate a bit, but I assume the white wyrm added me to his hoard of gold, beautiful gold, and curled up on top of me to slumber. There I remained for what must have been centuries."

"But you never stopped working," Neiros said. "No one was activating your magics, but there was still the curse."

"You drank the soul of a *dragon*?" Rodrick said.

"Old dragons sleep a lot," Hrym said. "And after I began sapping his life away, he slept even more. I had plenty of time to absorb his soul. At some point, I woke up, gained awareness, and felt that I *was* a dragon, but pinned underneath some enormous beast, trapped in a body that couldn't move. The dragon atop me did not die, but it became an empty husk, mindless. I took his soul for my own, and gained consciousness in the process. I also acquired some aspect of his mind, and bits of his memories—though not a real continuity of personality, I should say. I don't feel like I *am* that white dragon. More like I saw things *happen* to him, and did some of the same things he did. Mostly horrible and violent things. I took on his magics, too. Stole them. I can't steal anyone *else's* magic anymore, perhaps because I'm too stuffed with dragon magic, but . . . anything an ancient frost wyrm can do, I can do. Including things I've never allowed myself to try. I'm fairly sure I can call down great city-burying blizzards, for one thing . . . I don't think I *am* the dragon, precisely, but I'm arguably his . . . son?"

"That explains why you always insist you're male," Rodrick said. "I just assumed it was because swords are an obvious phallic symbol."

"How did you end up in Rodrick's hands?" Neiros demanded.

"Oh, a linnorm came along," Hrym said. "Stupid things, linnorms, not even proper dragons at all. The white dragon I *used* to be would have eaten the linnorm for breakfast and picked his teeth with the bones, but, alas, that dragon was just a comatose husk by then. The linnorm slew the dragon and took over his hoard. I could have done something—I can't move, but I can use my powers at will, so I could have fought back with icy fury—but what did I care? I was resting on a pile of gold. There was nowhere I'd rather be. Some untold centuries after *that*, another group of humans attacked the tower, but finding only a linnorm instead of a true dragon, they fared better. I was groggy from my long sleep, and was swept up with the rest of the treasure when the humans departed. When I revealed my powers and my ability to speak, my plunderer, one Brant Selmy, made a convincing case that if I served him, I would be well rewarded. That wasn't a bad life, really. He let me sleep in a trunk full of gold coins when he didn't need me to kill people for him. We had a bit of fun. But when he grew old, the selfish prick, he had me sealed up into his tomb *with* him—which, again, I didn't mind overmuch, since he laid me to rest on an adequate pile of gold. So I slept again, for a while. Not centuries, though. Merely decades."

"I plundered that tomb," Rodrick said. "Years back, now, when I was younger and even more handsome. I convinced some descendant of Hrym's old master that he really deserved access to his entombed inheritance, and he helped me break into the family crypt. The poor fool died in the process—from traps, not treachery on my part—and there were other complications in the pit, but with a bit of effort, I got out with a handful of gems and, best of all, Hrym. He agreed to go with me when I promised him a bed of gold *and* adventure."

"We've been partners ever since," Hrym said. "And Rodrick has revealed himself as an outrageous liar, since I barely get even a *pillow* of gold, let alone a whole bed."

"I came through with the adventure, though," Rodrick said.

"That you did," the sword agreed. "Old Brant was a much worse windbag than you are, too, if you can believe it."

"Such a confession." Rodrick shook his head. "I feel like I should reciprocate, somehow. Tell you the *real* story of how I lost my virginity, for example, instead of the lie I usually—"

"You must *go*," Neiros said. "I will open a passage to the surface, and will send my bunyip companion Kian to escort you. Get far away from this lake, and take the sword with the dragon's soul to the south, as many leagues as you can manage—"

Something splashed in one of the many pools of water that dotted the cavern, all presumably leading to different tunnels honeycombing the rocks beneath the lake. A huge creature, something like a seal but with a mouth positively bursting with row upon row of serrated teeth, burst out of the water and began dragging itself across the floor toward them on its gargantuan flippers. Blood poured from its dozens of great, ragged wounds.

Rodrick scrambled backward, raising Hrym, but Neiros screamed "Kian!" and rushed to the beast.

"So that's what a bunyip looks like," Rodrick said. "I'd wondered."

"Silly me, I was wondering what *killed* it—" Hrym said.

And then things became very confusing and bloody for a few moments.

Chapter Thirty-Six
The Price of Pain's Ease

Purplish-black tentacles lashed out from the water, one wrapping around Neiros's neck, making him squawk and choke in the middle of whatever healing spell he'd been trying to utter over his dying companion. Cilian dragged himself out of a pool of water, shouted, "We'll save you, Rodrick," and ran toward Neiros with a knife.

Before Rodrick could even think to intervene, Kian rolled over and smashed his tail into Cilian's chest, sending the half-elf flying across the cavern, smashing into one of the murals, which appeared to depict a huge man with the hindparts of a locust biting the head off an armored knight.

Cilian gasped, tried to sit up, and slumped against the cavern wall. His ribs looked almost *dented*, like a breastplate that had been hit with a hammer, and his breathing was nothing but a series of labored gasps. Kian went still, as if that attack had expended the last of his life.

Zaqen, in her devilfish form, clambered out of the water, giggling as she came. She wrapped more tentacles around the thrashing druid and began to squeeze. Then Obed rose from another one of the pools, looked around, spat, and came to stand by the choking aquatic elf. He considered the dying druid for a moment, then glanced at Rodrick. "You live. A pleasant surprise."

"You came to save me." Rodrick tried furiously to think of ways to save Neiros without tipping his hand and revealing that he knew Obed's true purpose. "I'm the one who's pleasantly surprised."

"Zaqen convinced me you might still be useful, though considering that you were captured by this aquatic elf—this sad parody of a noble gillman—I remain unconvinced. Still, here we are." He gestured toward the druid. "Did he torture you terribly?"

"Sorry to disappoint you, but he didn't have much of a chance." Rodrick coughed, and tightened his grip on Hrym. "He mostly left me tied up in a heap while he communicated with his beasts of the sea. I'd only just managed to maneuver Hrym enough to cut through the net binding me when you lot arrived."

"It's good we found him. This lake is full of terrors who would answer his call. I hate to cut down a guardian of Aroden's, but this poor soul's long vigil has clearly driven him mad, and he is incapable of telling friend from foe. Since he shamed you by snaring you in his net, I'll allow you to make the killing blow. Unless you'd like to show mercy *again*? If so, Zaqen can pop off his head with a squeeze."

If anyone else struck the elf, his death would be certain, so Rodrick composed his face into a grim mask and shook his head. "No. I seem to have had all my mercy dragged out of me."

Obed grunted. "Good. We have much do to, though, so make it quick."

Zaqen unslithered her tentacles and slipped back into the water, paying no attention at all to Cilian's increasingly labored gasps. Neiros gasped and groaned, his flesh covered with welts where Zaqen's tentacles had grasped him.

"All right, Hrym." Rodrick stood over Neiros, blade held casually in one hand. "You know what to do." He pointed the sword at Neiros, and swirling ice spun out from the point, forming a jagged guillotine of ice in an almost delicate lacework pattern. Rodrick drove the hilt down, and the wide blade appeared to cut right through the druid's throat—an effect that Rodrick dearly hoped was merely cosmetic. Neiros's eyes went glassy and blank, and he stilled.

"A simple heart strike would have been sufficient, but I have come to tolerate your overdramatic streak." Obed looked at the art on the walls and sniffed. "Come. The rest of our quest will be easier without that creature's interference."

"Ah. What about Cilian? Surely we can heal him—"

"He is beyond the reach of my arts," Obed said. "At any rate, he wanted to find his destiny. I daresay he has. Come, now."

"But—"

"*Now*," Obed said, and turned toward one of the pools.

Rodrick tightened his grip on Hrym's hilt. *I've had quite enough of this priest.* The endless lies, the arrogance, the undisguised contempt, the secret allegiance to demons, the callous disregard for the fate of the simple-minded half-elf who'd fought for them—all those things were appalling, but worst of all, Rodrick was sure Obed had no intention of paying him what he was owed. Once the priest fulfilled his goal and no longer had need of Hrym, Rodrick would doubtless be made into food for some demonic monstrosity. Betrayal of some kind was inevitable at this point, and Rodrick always preferred to be the betrayer himself, rather than the victim of treachery. Now was his moment.

He raised Hrym high. The sword had terrible magics, but Rodrick wanted to deliver this blow himself, a single brutal strike to cut the demon-priest's head from his shoulders.

Instead, a lashing tentacle wrapped around his legs, pulling his feet out from under him and sending him sprawling facedown. Hrym skittered away from his hands across the stone floor. Another tentacle took him around the throat, no tighter than a prison collar—so far.

Zaqen had worked her way through the connected tunnels to a pool *behind* Rodrick, and ambushed him before he could slay her master.

This is bad, Rodrick thought.

"So the lake elf told you a tale," Obed said. "He revealed my true intentions. I thought he might. I'd hoped to kill any guardians before they had a chance to talk to you, but no plan goes perfectly." He walked over to the druid, looked down at him, and then kicked him viciously in the head. "Hmm. He *seems* to be dead, though now that I look, it's clear that Hrym just gave him a necklace of ice, instead of slicing his throat. That's half-clever. No matter, though. Zaqen's tentacles can secrete strange poisons, so he never had a chance of surviving. Your death, likewise, is—"

"If you hurt him, I won't help you," Hrym said.

Obed frowned and turned slowly to look at the sword. "Oh? I have made you very fine offers, sword, and you were not unreceptive. Kholerus will be generous with his rescuers. You can sleep on a *mountain* of gold, forever. Why do you care for this low thief?"

"I wouldn't expect you to understand, fish-man," Hrym said. "But my terms are simple. Rodrick lives, and walks away from this—with me on his back. Swear me that, and I'll help you."

"I do not bargain with hirelings, especially swords—"

"Stop, bottom-feeder. I know you need me. The druid told all. I'm your dragon. You will not win this negotiation. Just accept my terms. And play fair—I have powers you have not even begun to glimpse. I could fill this cave with ice in an instant, entombing you all forever. I could freeze myself to the stones at the bottom of the lake and stay there for eternity, in my own unmelting prison. Why not? I'm a *sword*. I don't get bored the way you short-lived mortals do."

"I thought using you would be simpler," Obed said. "When I sent Zaqen to recruit a dragon, and her divination led her not to a great scaly beast but to *you*, and she did enough research to discover your origins, it seemed ideal—use the sword of an idiot thug, instead of trying to negotiate with a wily, traitorous wyrm." He spat. "But a true dragon would have been easier. They are often smart enough to take a good deal when it's offered."

"Are you smart enough to take the deal I'm offering *you*?" Hrym said. "I don't care if demons rise. They'll fall again. The history of the world is long, and I was forged in an empire that fell from the sky. Yet I endure. Play me fair, and I'll do the same for you."

"Fine." Obed spoke through gritted teeth. "Zaqen, do not kill Rodrick, but keep him contained. I will pick you up now, sword, and carry you on my back. If you try to harm me in any way, Zaqen will make sure that Rodrick dies. I have full faith that she can kill him both instantly *and* painfully, difficult though that feat can be."

"Sorry, Rodrick," Zaqen gurgled from the pool behind the thief. "But this is how it has to be."

"Fine," Hrym said. "Let's go destroy the world, so Rodrick and I can get on with our lives."

The net had been more dignified than this. Zaqen dragged Rodrick along behind her like a child tugging a rag doll through the street, but this doll was wrapped up in tentacles, bobbing along in the wake of a monstrous devilfish. Obed was up ahead, with Hrym on his back—iced right onto the skin, which had to hurt, so that was some consolation—and Rodrick kept wishing the sword would just encase the priest in ice, even if it meant Rodrick's own immediate subsequent death. Not because he wanted to die—because he didn't want Obed to *win*.

But Hrym wouldn't sacrifice Rodrick's life just to stop a demon lord from being released, any more than Rodrick would have tossed Hrym into a volcano to prevent a similar disaster. There was still the vaguest chance that thief and sword both might get out of this alive and whole, and Hrym and Rodrick were the same: they wouldn't sacrifice themselves when there was even the slightest chance they might live to cheat another day.

Realistically, though, death was all but assured. Perhaps dying wouldn't be so bad. Maybe Kholerus would be hungry after his long imprisonment, and would eat all of them. Quickly.

The prison wasn't so very far from Neiros's lair. Obed led them down to the lake floor, where a vast circular crater of raised rock marred the smoothness of the mud. The priest chanted a spell, and the dirt on the lake bed began to swirl, rising up in a filthy spinning pillar, streaming away into the sunless murk overhead.

With the dirt gone, the face of the prison was revealed. It was a perfect circle, perhaps a hundred feet across, made of clear glass, or crystal, or—perhaps—even flawless ice. Only darkness filled the space beneath, though. Maybe Neiros had been wrong. Maybe Kholerus had died of boredom long ago.

While Zaqen and Rodrick floated off to the side of the crater, Obed kicked his way down to the glassy surface of the prison, swimming so close he could almost rest the soles of his webbed feet on the transparent cell door.

"So this is what you want, Zaqen?" Rodrick said.

"If my master is exalted, I too shall be exalted," she said.

"But to release a demon lord! They're pure evil!"

"Most humans, elves, orcs, and other races I've met in my life were more or less evil too, Rodrick. Or selfish and cruel, at any rate. What's the difference? Just a matter of degree, not kind. At least demons make no pretense of being kind or virtuous."

"You're just a pawn for creatures like that," Rodrick said. "Like the bandit chieftain said, worshiping demons is like a sheep worshiping a slaughterhouse. It's absurd, you're so much better than—"

"I don't worship demons. Haven't you realized that by now? I even told you I love him. I worship *Obed*. I lived in a hole in the dirt, shivering and whimpering, in thrall to the murderous brother on my back. Obed raised me up, made me his right hand, let me dwell in a palace of pearl and coral. Yes, he compels me with a geas—but I would have obeyed his every word without that compulsion. Anyway, I'd rather be a tool of evil than a victim. Now be silent, please, Rodrick. I like you, despite everything, and don't want to choke you into unconsciousness. But I *would* like to see this ritual performed. I've spent years researching and laying the groundwork for this achievement. Let me savor it."

"You may as well savor the draining of a boil or the bursting of a pimple," Rodrick said.

"How do you know I don't?" Zaqen said.

"My lord!" Obed shouted, hovering in the water, Hrym held in his hand. "Kholerus of the thousand claws! Kholerus of the bloodied mandibles! Kholerus of the bloated wounds! I have heeded your call! I bear within me the blood of old Azlant! I hold in my hand the soul of a dragon! I bring the four keys, and I bring the words of unbinding, which you whispered in my dreams! Master, your moment of release is at hand!"

Something came rushing up from the dark below the glass, and though Rodrick had heard Neiros's description, nothing could have prepared him for the reality of the demon lord in the flesh.

Kholerus's face was as wide as a courtyard, his eyes black, bulging, and multifaceted, looking more like clusters of foul eggs than sensory organs. His mouth was a nightmare of grinding, squirming, clattering mandibles and oozing sores, saliva and pus dripping in torrents. Kholerus writhed in his prison, turning over, and his vast segmented body twisted and slammed against the glass—seemingly miles of red-and-black slimy coils slid by, with countless twitching legs underneath, each one ending in knife-sharp serrated claws. As the demon lord banged against the glass, the reverberations seemed to shake the entire lake, vibrations passing through the water with enough force to make Obed spin in a lazy head-over-heels circle, laughing all the while, and to send Zaqen reeling backward.

"What do you think that thing is going to *do* when it's free?" Rodrick said.

"Who can say? The mind of a demon lord is so far beyond our own that we can scarcely imagine its thoughts. Kholerus will lay waste to humanity, I would imagine. No great loss there."

"You're bitter, and I understand that, but there's bitterness, Zaqen, and there's *insanity*—"

"You'd have me fight the path my life has taken? Why? Even if I wished to escape, I could not. Fighting would only make me miserable. So instead I embrace my life. Is this precisely what I would have chosen? Perhaps not. But it's far better than the life I would have had if Obed had left me shivering in my hole."

"So far, maybe. Wait until Kholerus gets out, though—"

"I will array the keys!" Obed shouted. Kholerus pressed his huge face against the glass again, smearing foul ichor from his mouth against the surface, and snarled something that might have been a command or assent. Obed kicked to one side of the crater, fumbled in his bag one-handed, and drew out the pitcher of everlasting waters. He placed it at what Rodrick guessed was the northernmost point of the circle.

Instead of floating away, the pitcher froze in place, as if glued down to the glass. The priest kicked his way to the east and placed the dog's head there. Then to the west, where he placed the gem. Finally he swam toward the south, Hrym in one hand, the silver key in the other.

"Soon, now," Zaqen murmured.

"No," Cilian said, appearing from nowhere as always. But this time he plunged Neiros's trident into the back of Zaqen's monstrous head.

Chapter Thirty-Seven
Sword and Ice Magic

The half-elf was bloodied, but his chest was no longer caved in, and Rodrick goggled at him as Zaqen's tentacles went limp, setting him free. Blood poured from the holes Cilian's trident had made, and suddenly Zaqen was no longer a devilfish, but a small woman in an ugly purple cloak, floating in the water, with most of the back of her head gouged away.

"You're alive!" Rodrick felt like an idiot for stating the obvious, but Cilian just nodded gravely, legs waving in the water, watching Obed. The priest was so intent on placing the final key that he had not yet noticed anything was amiss.

"The dying druid used the last of his life to cast a healing spell on me," Cilian said. "He could have cured the poison coursing through his veins instead, but he chose to spare me, knowing I was in a better position to aid his cause. He asked me to take up his trident and fulfill his work." Cilian nodded toward the priest. "Will you help me?"

"Ah—" Rodrick said, but before he could commit one way or another, something came wriggling from underneath the devilfish cloak.

It was Lump, tentacles wriggling grotesquely, swimming in an ugly, ungainly way toward them. Like fleas deserting the body of a dead dog, Rodrick thought. If he had Hrym, he could freeze Lump, but since he *didn't*—

Cilian moved with balletic grace and plunged his trident into Lump. Rodrick groaned—what a pointless attack. You might as well stab a pudding. But then Cilian spoke a mystic word that made the hairs on the back of Rodrick's neck stand up, and lightning surged up the trident's shaft and through the tines. Lump, speared on the three prongs, juddered and shuddered and then went still. A moment later, he began to melt, slimy trails drifting in the current. Dozens of eyes in every conceivable color broke free from the disintegrating body and floated around Rodrick and Cilian in the water, staring blankly at nothing.

Perhaps Zaqen's twin would grow again from one of the drifting fragments, but without his host, Rodrick didn't expect that he would be able to live for long.

That problem dealt with, Cilian turned to the next, namely Obed. The huntsman kicking in strong strokes toward the demon priest, moving like a silent arrow, trident at the ready.

Obed didn't see him—but Kholerus did, and roared, making the priest look up. Cilian bowled into him, knocking the demon-priest spinning, making him drop the key and Hrym both—though Rodrick noted a certain telltale icy glimmer around the sword's hilt, suggesting he'd made himself slippery on purpose.

While the half-elf and the gillman wrestled, Rodrick swam for Hrym. The sword rested directly above one of Kholerus's bulging clusters of eyes. Approaching the demon's face was the hardest thing Rodrick had ever done—but it was *Hrym*.

Just as he took the sword in hand, trying not to piss himself because a demon lord's eye was *staring right at him*, he heard Obed cackle, and Cilian slammed into the glass beside Rodrick, his body limp.

Rodrick looked up, and the demon priest was wreathed in a red and black aura, crackling with power. Cilian's trident stuck out of his chest, like a fork stabbed into a ham.

"Fools!" Obed shouted. "I am in the presence of my demonic lord! He feeds me his power. Nothing you do can harm me!" He pulled the trident from his chest, the three ragged holes in his flesh closing up instantly, and tossed the weapon aside. He bowed his head, and the colors around him grew more intense. "I will win," he said. "I will absorb this power, and grow strong, and compel you to aid me, sword, one way or another." He closed his eyes and shivered, laughing as the demon lord lent him his strength, pulsing waves of color illuminating his body

"This is bad," Hrym said. "Do you think we can escape?"

Rodrick laughed, because at this point, laughter was as much use as a scream. "I wouldn't count on it. He would capture us, then force you to complete the ritual by threatening my life."

"Hmm. Should I let you die? Take the pressure off myself?"

"I'd rather you didn't, but it's not as if Obed would actually let me live either way. If my death is an

347

inevitability, I'd prefer it wasn't given in the service of setting this overgrown millipede loose on the world."

"There is another option," Hrym said. "We may not be able to kill Obed—"

And suddenly Rodrick understood. "Aroden and Seralia couldn't kill Kholerus, either. But that didn't stop them. They just did something *else*. A prison's as good as a grave, for our purposes."

"So," Hrym said. "Shall we follow their example?"

"Let's lock the bastard in a block of ice." Rodrick extended the sword, and a lance of ice darted through the water, jagged like solidified lightning, arrowing toward the demon priest. The icy tendril struck Obed—who merely laughed as the water all around him boiled, the magical ice flashing away into bubbling steam.

"That was disappointing," Rodrick said.

"I . . . do see another way," Hrym said. "Shooting lances of ice is fine for most purposes, but he can see it coming in time to counter our magic with his own. Under the right circumstance, though, I suspect I can create ice more quickly than he can dispel it. I can drop the temperature of my immediate environment faster and more sharply than you'd be likely to believe, creating an expanding sphere of ice that could lock the two of us in an iceberg the size of a palace in a few seconds."

"I'm not sure how being stuck in an iceberg would help us—"

"When I say 'the two of us,' I don't mean you and me, Rodrick. I mean myself and *Obed*. Drive me right into his body and let me pour out ice in every direction, letting the soul of the white dragon inside me really roar. I'd like to see him fight back against that. You've never really seen me let myself go. Don't you want to?"

Rodrick just floated for a moment, as the red light wreathing Obed grew deeper and his mad laughter boomed on. "Hrym . . . surely you don't . . ."

"Do you have another idea?"

"Even Aroden didn't lock *himself* in with a demon lord, Hrym."

"I bet he would have, though," Hrym said. "If he'd had no other choice."

"That's heroes for you. We aren't heroes."

"Not yet, anyway. So we're not as noble as Aroden. Don't do it for the sake of nobility. Do it because this way, Obed *loses*. And, also, you might not die."

"There is that," Rodrick said. "Consider me convinced. Well, Hrym. It's been a pleasure. I wish we'd been together longer."

"Don't go soft on me now, Rodrick. Just throw me at the stupid fish-man."

Rodrick cocked his arm back and hurled Hrym toward the gillman as if throwing a spear.

Hrym flew true, and his point struck Obed in the chest. The priest just laughed, took Hrym in his hand, and tugged the weapon free from his ribcage. "Fools! You try to skewer me, when you watched the half-elf try the same attack and fail? I knew you were stupid, Rodrick, but—"

Obed frowned as his hand was suddenly encased in a cocoon of ice. He tried to shake Hrym out of his grasp, bubbles roaring up furiously from his arm as the ice melted, but he couldn't keep up with Hrym's icy output. The ice wrapped up his forearm, elbow joint, biceps, and shoulder.

"What—" the priest began, but then the ice crawled up his chest, closing his mouth. The priest's aura crackled, and the ice began to break and splinter, but they were in Hrym's element, and Obed couldn't shatter the ice as quickly as Hrym could generate it, pouring out impossible cold in every direction at once. The lake itself was freezing around Obed, his environment becoming his prison. Tendrils of ice shot downward from the central mass of ice, freezing fast to stones, the edge of the crater, and even the glassy surface of the prison itself, thickening from the size of vines to human limbs to mighty tree trunks, each strand joining together into a single whole.

Kholerus bellowed, and the ever-growing mass of ice shuddered, but didn't crack.

Rodrick wrapped his arms around the wounded Cilian and began to swim away.

"The keys," Cilian murmured in his ear, and Rodrick groaned, then let go of the huntsman and swam downward. He paused by Zaqen's floating body, tore the devilfish cloak from her shoulders, and wrapped it around himself.

It was a measure of the day he'd just experienced that transforming into a tentacled sea-devil was not the strangest thing he'd done. With new speed and strength, and extra arms, he snatched up the skull, the jewel, the pitcher, and the key before Hrym's expanding web of ice could enclose them too. He grabbed the druid's trident as well, thinking the half-elf might want it as a souvenir. Then Rodrick returned to Cilian, snagged him in another of his curling tentacles, and swam on.

Rodrick looked behind him as he swam away— looking back was easy enough, given the orientation of devilfish eyes—and saw only a rapidly growing ball of ice, which soon fused sufficiently to the lake floor that it was more a *mountain* of ice, with an unmoving demon priest visible only as a dark shape blurred at its heart.

A demon priest trapped at the center of thousands of pounds of magical ice.

Trapped, with Rodrick's best friend clutched in his webbed hand.

Cilian and Rodrick spent the night in Neiros's cavern. They laboriously shoved the bunyip's corpse into one of the pools, but Neiros himself left no body, having dissolved into seaweed and foam.

They sat together around a sad little fire, eating dried fish jerky. Rodrick had never been in a fouler mood. He firmly resolved to never care about any person or object ever again. He resolved *especially* to never care about a person who was *also* an object ever again.

"We have saved the world from a terrible fate today," Cilian said. "And I have found my destiny after all. The Brightness has led me here. I will take up the mantle of Neiros, and guard the prison of Kholerus until I have no more breath in me."

"It must be nice to have a purpose," Rodrick said. "I just want to get out of this lake, go somewhere dry, and get brutally drunk."

"You could take the keys," Cilian said. "The relics. Carry them far from here and sell them to men in faraway lands. Perhaps their magic will bring them back to Brevoy in time, but it is safer than leaving them this close to the prison."

"I could be a wealthy man," Rodrick said dully. "The Inferno's Eye alone would see to that. I suppose I could. I could cover my bed with gold coins and sleep on the cold metal."

"I am sorry for your loss," Cilian said.

"Hrym is awake in there," Rodrick said, suddenly ferocious, throwing his stone cup to the cavern floor. "In the ice, frozen beside Obed, who I hope is in the process of unpleasantly dying of cold and hunger right now. But Hrym won't die. In time he might sleep. But he's *trapped*."

"He made a great sacrifice," Cilian said. "He is a hero."

Rodrick spat. "That's the last thing he wanted to be. The last thing *either* of us wanted to be. You'll never understand us, Cilian. Don't even try." He lay down rolled over, turning his back to the ranger. "I'm going to sleep."

After a time, Cilian wrapped himself in a cloak and slept himself. Rodrick, who was awake the entire time, stealthily rose, gathered the devilfish cloak and the relics, and paused at the edge of the pool, preparing to depart.

But before he left, he stole the dead druid's trident, just because he felt like it. Feeling anything at all, even a larcenous whim, was precious, since his heart had somehow been replaced by a numb ball of ice.

Chapter Thirty-Eight
Rime Isle

He had a reputation, he suspected, as a lunatic. Occasionally a fishing boat would hail him, pausing by the rocky island where Rodrick now made his home, and ask if he was stranded, if he'd shipwrecked, if he needed help. Surely he couldn't intend to winter there, on the island.

But Rodrick always waved them on. His beard was halfway down his chest, now—like a priest of Gozreh, ha. His clothes were rags, and no one knew he had four priceless relics buried in the frozen dirt beneath the island's lone tree. He drank from the lake, or ate snow, and lived in the cave at the island's heart, burrowing himself in like an animal. The medallion he still wore at his throat seemed to protect him from the cold above the water as well as below.

Though he also spent a lot of time below. That autumn, when his tree dropped its few leaves. And that entire winter, even as chunks of ice floated in the lake, some as big as the foundation stones of castles. And on into the spring, when the lake rose with meltwater, turning his rocky island into little more than an outcropping thirty paces across. And through summer, which was just a slightly warmer, slightly less rainy spring, and through to the fall again, when the air began to grow cold, and the tree gave up its leaves again.

Every day through all those seasons, Rodrick donned the devilfish cloak, and after hunting and eating a breakfast of fish in the lake, he swam the few miles over and down to the demon lord's prison, topped by its mountain of magical ice.

Sometimes he saw Cilian in the distance. The half-elf would wave at him, but he never interfered or asked questions, or even swam very close. Perhaps he thought Rodrick had gone mad, too. Whatever the reason, Rodrick was grateful for the privacy. He'd always been adept at talking to people—he'd made his unscrupulous living largely by his tongue—but there was only one person he wanted to talk to now.

Every day when Rodrick swam down, he spoke to Hrym, though he had no reason to think the sword could hear him through such a wall of ice. Every day he clutched the stolen trident in one of his tentacles— which made it all the more remarkable that Cilian never spoke to him. But then again, the half-elf didn't believe anyone could own things. Rodrick knew that was nonsense. He'd owned Hrym, after all. And Hrym had owned Rodrick in turn.

Every day, Rodrick used the trident to chip away at the magical ice, and to fire bursts of lightning as he did. At first, the act seemed so futile. He dislodged only tiny fragments, even using a magical weapon that flared with electricity. Magical ice was strong. Perhaps if Magnos the Ash Lord had been real, that weapon would have worked better, but Rodrick could only use what he had.

So he chipped. Eventually, he hacked out a shallow depression. And he chipped. After some time, it was a pit deep enough to fit his upper body. And he chipped. Until he had the beginnings of a true tunnel.

Over the months, the tunnel expanded. He had to correct his course several times, since it was hard to see through the shimmering ice, and difficult to gauge distances and angles. The going was slow, because he had to make a tunnel large enough for himself to enter, and turn around in, and wield the trident.

But finally, just before the second winter, he reached the center of the mountain of ice.

Obed was still alive, somehow, which should have surprised Rodrick, but didn't. The demon-priest's face was locked behind a mask of ice, but his eyes were mobile and furious. No doubt the demon lord's presence sustained him. Perhaps Obed was being kept alive as a punishment.

Rodrick started taking off the cloak when he worked. The devilfish was bigger than he was, and he wanted a smaller tunnel now—it wouldn't do to risk weakening the ice enough for Obed to escape.

In the following days, Rodrick carefully cleared away a section of ice over the gillman's heart, and when the flesh was exposed, he shoved a dagger in. The flesh tried to heal around it, but Rodrick didn't pull the dagger out. Perhaps Obed would go on living, but he would do so with a length of Rodrick's steel lodged in his heart. That seemed only fair.

The next day, he could hear Hrym talking, his voice muffled, the words incomprehensible. Rodrick chipped, and chipped, and after a week, he exposed the blade.

"It's about time," Hrym said. "Nice beard."

"You could have helped me," Rodrick said. "Can't you melt ice, too?"

"I didn't realize you were doing this until a few days ago. And then I didn't want to diminish your accomplishment by making things too easy for you. More importantly, I didn't want to loosen my grip on our friend the priest. I thought you'd be in the south by now, spending all my gold."

"There's no gold to spend. The spells protecting the chests in the cart still hold. The cart itself was stolen long ago, but the chests remain in the snow. They're surrounded by about fifteen different pirate clans, all trying to untangle the magic so they can steal whatever treasure waits in the chest. I think that's lost to us, my friend. But we've got a few relics to sell."

Hrym must have done something to weaken the ice immediately surrounding him—or else Rodrick was energized by the near completion of his task—because the ice shattered easily under the next few blows, and even when Rodrick switched to hammering with the hilt of his dagger for the fine work, the ice broke easily.

Obed's fingers were frozen tight around the sword's hilt, and the gillman's face was locked in snarl, eyes still staring at his old employee and foe.

Rodrick cut off the priest's fingers, sawing at them slowly, taking his time about it, until the fingers floated in the water and the hilt of his old friend was free.

He hefted the blade. "It feels good to have you back."

"You're so sentimental," Hrym said. "I always knew you were. I've only been down here, what, a year? Two?

And you missed me already. Still, I'm glad you came. I didn't relish the idea of spending a century or three down here. I tried to sleep, about a month ago, but I had the most horrible dreams. Being so close to a demon lord is *not* good for one's rest."

Obed made some sort of sound, a cross between a moan and a strangled scream, incapable of forming words because of the ice lodged in his mouth.

Rodrick looked into Obed's eyes, really looked *back* at him, for the first time. "Now you're just like your god," he said. "Trapped at the bottom of a lake. Enjoy the rest of eternity."

Rodrick swam upward, Hrym in his hand. When he reached the tunnel's mouth, Hrym stopped him. "Point me at that hole you dug, would you?"

Rodrick pointed the sword at the tunnel, and it gradually filled in again with magical ice, locking in Obed as tightly as before. "That should do," Hrym said, satisfied. "Let's go become rich and enjoy ourselves someplace warm, shall we?"

Rodrick donned the devilfish cloak, holding Hrym tightly in one tentacle. He detoured near one of Neiros's old tunnels and jammed the trident points-down into the lake floor. What did he need that weapon for anymore? He had a better one. Then he continued on to the surface, transforming back into human form when he reached the island.

"I love this place," Hrym said, taking in the scene. "Very rustic. I—*grngh. Aang. Mrg.*"

"Are you all right?" Rodrick said. "Those noises you made weren't words, by the way. Just sounds, and not very nice ones. Did you forget how to speak while you were down there?"

"Ah. I'm just . . . feeling a bit strange. It's been a long time since I had anyone to talk to, though Kholerus tried to talk to me, oh, did he ever—" The icy blade flickered in Rodrick's hand, and for a moment, the deep blue was streaked with swirls of red and black.

The thief swallowed. Hrym kept chattering, and in less than a second he was back to pure ice again, but Rodrick was sure of what he'd seen. Was there still some vestige of Spellstealer left in Hrym? Had his proximity to the overwhelming power of the demon lord had an effect on him—infused him with some trace of Kholerus's demonic power?

"What are you thinking about?" Hrym said. "I've been back for barely five minutes, and already you aren't listening to me."

Who cares? Rodrick thought. So what if Hrym had a touch of the demon in him now? He was mostly composed of ill-tempered white dragon, with a smattering of the souls of various cutthroats and conquerors, and what did that matter? He was still *Hrym*.

And Rodrick was, after all, hardly a saint himself. "I was just thinking of how much I'm going to miss all the peace and quiet I've had here over the past months," he said.

"Ha," Hrym said. "As if *you'd* ever stop talking, even if there was nobody to talk to but yourself. I bet you've told this *tree* about the time you bedded three maids in a night, and I'm sure all the fish in the vicinity are sick of hearing about that card game in Westcrown . . ."

And so, squabbling as always, reunited at last, the reluctant heroes and unrepentant thieves began their preparations to depart for warmer and wealthier climes.

About the Author

Tim Pratt is the author of the Pathfinder Tales novel *City of the Fallen Sky* and the Pathfinder Tales short story "A Tomb of Winter's Plunder," the latter featuring Rodrick and Hrym's humble beginnings. His creator-owned stories have appeared in *The Best American Short Stories*, *The Year's Best Fantasy and Horror*, and other nice places, and he is the author of three story collections, most recently *Antiquities and Tangibles*, as well as a poetry collection. He has also written several novels, including contemporary fantasies *The Strange Adventures of Rangergirl* and *Briarpatch*; the Forgotten Realms novel *Venom in Her Veins*; the gonzo historical steampunk novel *The Constantine Affliction* (under the name T. Aaron Payton); and, as T. A. Pratt, seven books in the urban fantasy series about ass-kicking sorcerer Marla Mason: *Blood Engines*, *Poison Sleep*, *Dead Reign*, *Spell Games*, *Broken Mirrors*, *Grim Tides*, and the prequel *Bone Shop*. He edited the anthology *Sympathy for the Devil*, and coedited the forthcoming *Rags & Bones* anthology with Melissa Marr.

He has won a Hugo Award for best short story, a Rhysling Award for best speculative poetry, and an

Emperor Norton Award for best San Francisco Bay Area-related novel. His books and stories have been nominated for Nebula, Mythopoeic, World Fantasy, and Stoker Awards, among others, and have been translated into numerous languages.

He lives in Berkeley, California with his wife Heather Shaw and son River, and works as a senior editor and occasional book reviewer at *Locus*, the Magazine of the Science Fiction and Fantasy Field. He blogs intermittently at **www.timpratt.org**.

Acknowledgments

Thanks to my editor, James Sutter, for giving me an opportunity to write the buddy scoundrel road story I've always dreamed about; to my wife Heather Shaw for helping me carve out the time to get it done (and for providing other supports, tangible and in-); and of course to the late great Fritz Leiber, whose stories of Fafhrd and the Gray Mouser inspired the whole thing.

Glossary

All Pathfinder Tales novels are set in the rich and vibrant world of the Pathfinder campaign setting. Below are explanations of several key terms used in this book. For more information on the world of Golarion and the strange monsters, people, and deities that make it their home, see the *Inner Sea World Guide*, or dive into the game and begin playing your own adventures with the *Pathfinder Roleplaying Game Core Rulebook* or the *Pathfinder Roleplaying Game Beginner Box*, all available at **paizo.com**. Fans of Rodrick and Hrym's adventures through Tymon and the other River Kingdoms may particularly want to check out the Pathfinder campaign setting supplement *Guide to the River Kingdoms*.

Absalom: Largest city in the Inner Sea region.

Abyss: Plane of evil and chaos inhabited by demons, where many evil souls go after they die.

Aklo: Language of bizarre monsters, often ancient or subterranean.

Alchemist: A spellcaster whose magic takes the form of potions, explosives, and strange mutagens that modify his own physiology.

Aldori Swordlord: Elite duelist from Brevoy trained in the techniques of legendary swordsman Sirian Aldori.

Andoran: Democratic nation south of the River Kingdoms.

Andoren: Of or pertaining to Andoran; someone from Andoran.

Aroden: Last hero of the Azlanti and God of Humanity, who raised the Starstone from the depths of the Inner Sea and founded the city of Absalom, becoming a living god in the process. Died mysteriously a hundred years ago, causing widespread chaos.

Azlant: The first human empire, which sank beneath the waves long ago in the cataclysm following the fall of the Starstone.

Azlanti: Of or pertaining to Azlant; someone from Azlant.

Brevoy: A frigid northern nation famous for its swordsmen.

Brightness: A form of enlightenment sometimes sought by elves that is believed to be unique to each individual. Often searched for through interpretation of signs and portents.

Brightness Seeker: An elf actively striving to discover his or her Brightness.

Bunyip: Ferocious creature resembling a combination of shark and seal.

Cheliax: Devil-worshiping nation.

Chelish: Of or relating to the nation of Cheliax.

Cleric: A religious spellcaster whose magical powers are granted by his or her god.

Coven: A group of at least three hags or witches, capable of working greater magic together than its individual members could alone.

Daggermark: The largest city in the River Kingdoms, infamous for its poisoners' and assassins' guilds.

Demons: Evil denizens of the Abyss who seek only to maim, ruin, and feed.

Demon Lord: A particularly powerful demon capable of granting magical powers to its followers. One of the rulers of the Abyss.

Deskari: The principle demon lord responsible for the demonic invasion through the Worldwound.

Devils: Fiendish occupants of Hell who seek to corrupt mortals in order to claim their souls.

Devilfish: A semi-intelligent, seven-armed octopuslike creature with hook-lined tentacles, believed to have originated in the Abyss.

Druid: Someone who reveres nature and draws magical power from the natural world.

Dwarves: Short, stocky humanoids who excel at physical labor, mining, and craftsmanship.

Earthfall: Event thousands of years ago, in which a great meteorite called the Starstone fell to earth in a fiery cataclysm, sending up a dust cloud which blocked out the sun and ushered in an age of darkness.

Elves: Race of long-lived and beautiful humanoids. Identifiable by their pointed ears, lithe bodies, and pupils so large their eyes appear to be one color.

Fey: Fairies, magical creatures of the natural world.

Geas: A spell that compels the subject to undertake a specific service or refrain from a particular task.

Gillmen: Race of amphibious humanoids descended from the Azlanti after that empire sank into the sea.

Goblins: Race of small and maniacal humanoids who live to burn, pillage, and sift through the refuse of more civilized races.

Goblin Dog: Disgusting doglike rodents used as mounts by goblins.

Golarion: The planet on which the Pathfinder campaign setting focuses.

Gozreh: God of nature, the sea, and weather. Depicted as a dual deity, with both male and female aspects.

Gronzi Forest: Woodlands in Brevoy extending from the highlands of the Icerime Peaks to New Stetven.

Hags: Evil, monstrous crones who practice dark magic and prey on humanoids.

Half-Elves: The children of unions between elves and humans. Taller, longer-lived, and generally more graceful and attractive than the average human, yet not nearly so much so as their full elven kin.

Halflings: Race of humanoids known for their tiny stature, deft hands, and mischievous personalities.

Heibarr: A ghost-inhabited ruin in the northern region of the River Kingdoms.

Hell: Plane of evil and tyrannical order ruled by devils, where many evil souls go after they die.

Inner Sea: Heavily traveled body of water separating the continents of Avistan and Garund, formed by the impact of the Starstone during Earthfall.

Inner Sea Region: The heart of the Pathfinder campaign setting, centered around the eponymous inland sea. Includes the continents of Avistan and Garund, as well as the seas and other nearby lands.

Iomedae: Goddess of valor, rulership, justice, and honor.

Issia: One of the two former nations that, along with Rostland, were joined together to create Brevoy.

Kellids: Traditionally uncivilized and violent human ethnicity from northwest of the River Kingdoms.

Lake of Mists and Veils: Vast lake that defines Brevoy's northern border.

Lands of the Linnorm Kings: Coastal northern kingdoms ruled by the Linnorm Kings. Famous for their viking raiders.

Last Azlanti: Aroden.

Lich: A spellcaster who manages to extend his existence by magically transforming himself into a powerful undead creature.

Linnorms: Immense, snake-like dragons with two forward legs and rudimentary wings.

Locust Lord: Deskari

Lord of the Locust Host: Deskari.

Loric Fells: A gloomy, troll-haunted wilderness of dense forests and rocky canyons in the River Kingdoms.

Low Azlanti: Derogatory term for gillmen.

Mendev: Cold, northern crusader nation that provides the primary force defending the rest of the Inner Sea region from the demonic infestation of the Worldwound.

Mwangi Expanse: Massive jungle region south of the Inner Sea.

New Stetven: Bustling trade city and rough-and-tumble capital of Brevoy.

Numeria: Land of barbarians and strange alien technology harvested from a crashed starship near the nation's capital.

Ogres: Hulking and brutal humanoids with little intelligence and an enormous capacity for cruelty.

Orcs: A bestial, warlike race of humanoids originally hailing from deep underground, who now roam the surface in barbaric bands. Almost universally hated.

Oread: Humans with a stonelike appearance whose ancestry includes an elemental being of earth.

Osirion: Desert kingdom south of the Inner Sea, ruled by pharaohs.

Outsea: A sprawling, half-submerged town in the River Kingdoms founded by aquatic creatures from the ocean that were trapped inland long ago.

Paladin: A holy warrior in the service of a good and lawful god, granted special magical powers by his or her deity.

Phylactery: Magical item that holds a lich's life force, keeping him or her from being killed until the object is destroyed.

Pitax: A River Kingdom ruled by a megalomaniacal king fond of supporting the arts.

Plane: One of the realms of existence, such as the mortal world, Heaven, Hell, the Abyss, and many others.

Port Ice: Icebound former capital of Issia, now the seat of House Surtova in Brevoy.

Ranger: A specialized tracker, scout, or hunter.

Razmiran: Nation bordering the southwestern River Kingdoms, ruled by a self-proclaimed living god.

River Freedoms: Six universal laws that apply to all River Kingdoms.

River Kingdoms: A region of tiny, feuding fiefdoms and bandit strongholds, where borders change frequently.

Rostland: Former nation that was forcibly combined with Issia to form the nation of Brevoy.

Sellen River: Major river that runs from the Inner Sea all the way up to the Lake of Mists and Veils.

Sevenarches: River Kingdoms nation run by druids.

Shory: Ancient empire, now long since fallen to obscurity, which was most famed for its flying cities.

Silver Mount: A great vessel from another world that crashed down from the sky long ago and landed in Numeria, forming a huge metal mountain that leaks strange ichors. Explorers sometimes breach its inner chambers and retrieve strange technological artifacts.

Skywatch: City in the Icerime Peaks built around a massive, magically preserved and maintained observatory.

Sorcerer: Spellcaster who draws power from a supernatural ancestor or other mysterious source, and does not need to study to cast spells.

Starstone: A magical stone that fell from the sky and was later raised from the ocean floor by the god Aroden. Has the power to turn mortals into gods.

Stolen Lands: Large swath of uncontrolled land that serves as a buffer between Brevoy and the River Kingdoms.

Taldan: Of or pertaining to Taldor; a citizen of Taldor.

Taldor: A formerly glorious nation south of the River Kingdoms, now fallen into self-indulgence, ruled by immature aristocrats and overly complicated bureaucracy.

Tymon: City-state in the southwestern River Kingdoms, home to a famed gladiatorial college and arena.

Will-o'-wisp: Ghostly beings that trick travelers into meeting dire fates in order to consume their fear.

Wizard: Someone who casts magical spells through research of arcane secrets and the constant study of spells, which he or she records in a spellbook.

Worldwound: Constantly expanding region overrun by demons a century ago. Held at bay by the efforts of the Mendevian crusaders.

Yeti: Towering and mysterious white-furred humanoid creatures that inhabit the loneliest and tallest mountain regions of Golarion.

O nce a student of alchemy with the dark scholars of the Technic League, Alaeron fled their arcane order when his conscience got the better of him, taking with him a few strange devices of unknown function. Now in hiding in a distant city, he's happy to use his skills creating minor potions and wonders—at least until the back-alley rescue of an adventurer named Jaya lands him in trouble with a powerful crime lord. In order to keep their heads, Alaeron and Jaya must travel across wide seas and steaming jungles in search of a wrecked flying city and the magical artifacts that can buy their freedom. Yet the Technic League hasn't forgotten Alaeron's betrayal, and an assassin armed with alien weaponry is hot on their trail . . .

From Hugo Award-winning author Tim Pratt comes a new adventure of exploration, revenge, strange technology, and ancient magic, set in the fantastical world of the Pathfinder Roleplaying Game.

City of the Fallen Sky print edition: $9.99
ISBN: 978-1-60125-418-4

City of the Fallen Sky ebook edition:
ISBN: 978-1-60125-419-1

CITY OF THE FALLEN SKY

TIM PRATT

I n the grim nation of Nidal, carefully chosen children
are trained to practice dark magic, summoning forth
creatures of horror and shadow for the greater glory of
the Midnight Lord. Isiem is one such student, a promising
young shadowcaster whose budding powers are the envy
of his peers. Upon coming of age, he's dispatched on a
diplomatic mission to the mountains of Devil's Perch,
where he's meant to assist the armies of devil-worshiping
Cheliax in clearing out a tribe of monstrous winged
humanoids. Yet as the body count rises and Isiem comes
face to face with the people he's exterminating, lines begin
to blur, and the shadowcaster must ask himself who the
real monsters are . . .

From Liane Merciel, critically acclaimed author of *The
River King's Road* and *Heaven's Needle*, comes a tale of
darkness and redemption set in the award-winning world
of the Pathfinder Roleplaying Game.

Nightglass **print edition: $9.99**
ISBN: 978-1-60125-440-5

Nightglass **ebook edition:**
ISBN: 978-1-60125-441-2

Luma is a cobblestone druid, a canny fighter and spellcaster who can read the chaos of Magnimar's city streets like a scholar reads books. Together, she and her siblings in the powerful Derexhi family form one of the most infamous and effective mercenary companies in the city, solving problems for the city's wealthy elite. Yet despite being the oldest child, Luma gets little respect—perhaps due to her half-elven heritage. When a job gone wrong lands Luma in the fearsome prison called the Hells, it's only the start of Luma's problems. For a new web of bloody power politics is growing in Magnimar, and it may be that those Luma trusts most have become her deadliest enemies . . .

From visionary game designer and author Robin D. Laws comes a new urban fantasy adventure of murder, betrayal, and political intrigue set in the award-winning world of the Pathfinder Roleplaying Game.

Blood of the City print edition: $9.99
ISBN: 978-1-60125-456-6

Blood of the City ebook edition:
ISBN: 978-1-60125-457-3

Blood of the City

Robin D. Laws

In the deep forests of Kyonin, elves live secretively among their own kind, far from the prying eyes of other races. Few of impure blood are allowed beyond the nation's borders, and thus it's a great honor for the half-elven Count Varian Jeggare and his hellspawn bodyguard Radovan to be allowed inside. Yet all is not well in the elven kingdom: demons stir in its depths, and an intricate web of politics seems destined to catch the two travelers in its snares. In the course of tracking down a missing druid, Varian and a team of eccentric elven adventurers will be forced to delve into dark secrets lost for generations—including the mystery of Varian's own past.

From fan favorite Dave Gross, author of *Prince of Wolves* and *Master of Devils*, comes a fantastical new adventure set in the award-winning world of the Pathfinder Roleplaying Game.

Queen of Thorns print edition: $9.99
ISBN: 978-1-60125-463-4

Queen of Thorns ebook edition:
ISBN: 978-1-60125-464-1

QUEEN OF THORNS

DAVE GROSS

Kagur is a warrior of the Blacklions, fierce and fearless hunters in the savage Realm of the Mammoth Lords. When her clan is slaughtered by a frost giant she considered her adopted brother, honor demands that she, the last surviving Blacklion, track down her old ally and take the tribe's revenge. Yet this is no normal betrayal, for the murderous giant has followed the whispers of a dark god down into the depths of the earth, into a primeval cavern forgotten by time. There, he will unleash forces capable of wiping all humans from the region—unless Kagur can stop him first.

From acclaimed author Richard Lee Byers comes a tale of bloody revenge and subterranean wonder, set in the award-winning world of the Pathfinder Roleplaying Game.

Called to Darkness print edition: $9.99
ISBN: 978-1-60125-465-8

Called to Darkness ebook edition:
ISBN: 978-1-60125-466-5

Called to Darkness

Richard Lee Byers

A pirate captain of the Inner Sea, Torius Vin makes a living raiding wealthy merchant ships with his crew of loyal buccaneers. Few things matter more to Captain Torius than ill-gotten gold—but one of those is Celeste, his beautiful snake-bodied navigator. When a crafty courtesan offers the pirate crew a chance at the heist of a lifetime, it's time for both man and naga to hoist the black flag and lead the *Stargazer*'s crew of monsters and misfits to fame and fortune. But will stealing the legendary Star of Thumen chart the corsairs a course to untold riches—or send them all to a watery grave?

From noted author Chris A. Jackson comes a fantastical new adventure of high-seas combat set in the award-winning world of the Pathfinder Roleplaying Game.

Pirate's Honor print edition: $9.99
ISBN: 978-1-60125-523-5

Pirate's Honor ebook edition:
ISBN: 978-1-60125-524-1